Grace Ingram

GILDED SPURS

STEIN AND DAY/*Publishers*/New York

by the same author

Red Adam's Lady

First published in the United States of America in 1978
Copyright © 1978 by Grace Ingram
All rights reserved
Printed in the United States of America
Stein and Day/*Publishers*/Scarborough House,
Briarcliff Manor, N.Y. 10510

Library of Congress Cataloging in Publication Data

Ingram, Grace.
  Gilded spurs.

  I. Title.
PZ4.I542Gi 1978   [PR6059.N54]   823'.9'14   77-17104
ISBN 0-8128-2335-4

Dedicated to my first fan
and dear friend Peggy Arnett
who shares my addictions to
ruins, secondhand bookshops
and needlework

Chapter 1

The dawn woods were unnaturally hushed. The big young man on the dun gelding, who had been starting up screeching jays and clattering pigeons since first light, was too much a townsman to appreciate their silence's significance until a horse whinnied close at hand. Steel glittered between the leaves alongside the track. He hauled fiercely on the packhorse's leadrope, dug in his spurs and hurtled through the ambush, ducking his head as a bolt hummed past his ear. Yelling faces streaked back. Then his horse's legs were snatched from under him. He kicked his feet from the stirrups, catapulting over its head to land on his shoulders. He rolled with the impact, snatching at his dagger, but as he jarred flat a point pricked his throat. Rigid, he stared the length of the sword-blade, past the brown hand gripping it to the amused face regarding him.

'Very foolish,' the ambusher observed. He lowered his hand a trifle, and his victim felt a warm trickle start from the pain and course round his neck. His belly dissolved, but he tightened his lips and waited. Other men were gathering; a half-dozen iron-framed faces looked without feeling from him to their leader. The packhorse peered over one's shoulder while another briskly disembowelled the panniers.

'Armour, cap'n,' he reported. 'A good hauberk, a pair o' mail chausses, and two helmets – one new, one mended.'

'Happily encountered,' said the swordsman. The prisoner snarled. His captor glanced aside at his sprawled feet. The spurs at his heels were of plain steel, unlike his own gilded ones that proclaimed him knight. 'You've no right to bear arms, churl,' he pointed out reasonably, in a marked Welsh accent. 'We'll confiscate them.'

'I'm delivering them to Lord Henry of Trevaine after repair –'

'Lord Reynald of Warby will make better use of them.'

'Warby! You're near ten miles outside Warby boundaries!' He had indeed ridden half the night to achieve that distance.

The swordsman smiled pityingly. 'You've brought us ten miles out of our way. Warby boundaries reach as far as its sword's point.' He prodded shrewdly to emphasize his words.

'Thieving routiers!'

'Here's heat!' The swordsman withdrew his point, considering him with singularly pale eyes, clear grey with a sharp dark ring about the iris. 'And for goods not yours.'

'They're entrusted to me,' the young man declared fiercely, thrusting up on one elbow. 'But what's honour to a brigand?' He rolled over and pushed to his knees, and the point lifted level with his eyes.

'Disrespectful,' murmured the Warby captain. 'We'll mend your manners with a rope.'

The young man struck the sword up and over his shoulder, launching himself under it at his captor's legs. His dagger skidded and screeched on the knight's hauberk-rings as they sprawled into the brambles. Before he could find the chink he aimed for, hands grappled him, wrenched agonizingly and hauled him off. Deft kicks behind his knees forced him down on them. Held so, he watched the knight scramble erect and scowled malevolently up, anger and terror churning within his bowels.

The captain had lost his helmet. He thrust back his mail coif from the face of a Lucifer, a damned angel, and plucked a thorn from his hand with his teeth as he contemplated the captive. 'Reckless,' he sighed, and the fair lad crouching at his feet chilled to his vitals. 'If you'd been meek we'd have dealt gently.'

A square-set ruffian gathered up the fallen dagger and grinned as he tried its edge with his thumb. 'His eyes first, Captain, or his privates?'

'Cut out his insolent tongue,' suggested another.

'It's no great matter,' said Lucifer gently, 'but we'll leave

8

his tongue until last, so that he may beg to be hanged.'

'Wasteful of you,' the prisoner retorted.

Lucifer's eyebrows lifted. 'Wasteful?'

'I'm a skilled armourer – of whom your hauberk stands in need.' He nodded to a gap beside the knight's armpit, where a ring was missing.

Lucifer poked a finger into the hole. The garment was too big for his slim body, probably battlefield loot. 'Satan guards his own,' he commented. 'And as I'm a just man, in return for the warning I'll merely hang you.'

The young man swallowed. 'Take me before Lord Reynald,' he commanded.

'You're cracked in the wits. Lord Reynald's devisings make ours seem children's amusements.'

'You'll not deny me – or him.'

'Why, no,' the knight conceded instantly. 'So bold a cockerel should provide rare entertainment.'

He nodded to the troopers, who trussed the captive's elbows and wrists at his back with savage thongs. One suggested tethering him to a saddle-bow to be dragged afoot to Warby, but the captain decided to save time and their prisoner's vigour. They led up his own mount, still trembling from the fall. He inspected its grazed knees resentfully. They boosted him up, tied his ankles beneath the beast's belly, looped the rope that had felled it around his neck and made it fast to Lucifer's saddle.

'So if you regain your wits before we reach Warby you may choose to break your neck,' the knight suggested.

The young man shook his head, and his blue eyes regarded Lucifer with a contempt that pricked him, for he half lifted a hand to strike and then checked. He stared more keenly, and asserted, 'We've met before! I know your face.'

'No.'

Lucifer opened his mouth to dispute it, and then shrugged. 'Am I to take account of every craftsman I've set eyes on?'

The prisoner's mouth twisted in a grim smile. 'Your choice.'

Lucifer shrugged again and signalled to his men. They got to horse and started back the way the young man had come,

9

through russet woods under the climbing sun. They baited him with descriptions of Lord Reynald's ingenuity in devising entertainment upon his captives, which had the ring of grisly truth. He remained unresponsive. The thongs ate into his bound arms, that cramped into torment and then grew numb. Riding along the rough track without their use strained every muscle of his body. His face grew gradually whiter with pain and fatigue. He tightened his jaw, his blond head erect. Some measure of respect at last stilled his escort's tongues, or his silence defeated them. At length they let him be to endure his discomfort, the plaguing flies and the dust that mingled with sweat on his skin to an itching plaster. The sergeant who had acquired his dagger wrangled with a subordinate over the prospective ownership of the captive's good blue tunic and chausses.

Lucifer pushed briskly along the upland road and scarcely turned his head. The rope hung slack. They climbed Thorgastone Waste, a league of rocks, thickets and rough grazing that the young man had prudently skirted under last night's moon, and from its ridge he sighted Warby keep across the valley, its new stone shining pale grey against the dark woods. His weary horse stumbled, and the rope clutched harshly at his throat. Lucifer jerked at it irritably and he lurched in the saddle, strangling until his mount caught up again. The troopers jeered as he gasped and coughed, but the knight moderated his pace.

All life emptied from the village street before they trampled through it. A woman's voice called urgently to a scurrying urchin, a lame crone hobbled to an open door that slammed behind her heel, and a gaunt cur yelped and fled as they passed. Faces peered dimly round half-doors and shutters, lean pigs and squawking hens scattered from the hooves, and fear hung in the air like the stinks from the steaming middens.

The horses slowed for the climb to the castle on the ridge above the river. A horn bellowed, and the gate in its squat tower swung open. They passed under a portcullis's menacing teeth, into a sunny bailey, and dismounted. The gate thumped shut. The troopers hauled the captive from his saddle, and

10

one cut the thongs from his arms, which fell uselessly at his sides. He made no attempt to struggle, but met Lucifer's malicious smile with composure. The knight twitched the rope and led him like a dog across the bailey to the keep, apparently unaware of the hoots and yells, the sympathetic mutters and the stares that followed him.

He mounted a flight of stairs and entered stone-grey gloom. Men casting dice on an upturned shield scrambled to their feet. Lucifer flipped his end of the rope into the nearest pair of hands.

'He's Lord Reynald's meat.'

The fellow grinned, and then made a startling discovery. 'He's not afeared, Captain!'

'I believe you expect Lord Reynald to spare you!' Lucifer exclaimed.

'Yes.'

They hooted. 'As long as it takes him to think o' some new sport!' mocked the fellow with the rope. 'Last man he spitted alive and roasted over the hall fire!'

'And the one afore that he had took apart joint by joint,' added another with relish.

'So I have already been informed.'

'He's cracked in the wits,' a third man declared.

'All the better sport!'

'I'll wager a month's pay –' began the rope-holder, and then checked. 'God's Blood, all your gear's ours, so what have you to bet with?'

'I wager my life,' the young man replied, with a small grim smile. His neatly-clipped fair beard did not conceal his mouth; the left corner tilted up and the right down. The trooper flinched, backed a pace, and stared uneasily. All were suddenly silent.

'Your name and home?' Lucifer demanded.

'Guy Armourer of Bristol.'

He turned and made for a curtained corner. His footsteps pattered up a stair. Guy Armourer, very white in the face, moved to a bench against the wall. Life was returning to his numbed arms in a red-hot throbbing of thwarted pulses. He endured in silence, watching his blue and swollen hands gradually turn crimson. The men had returned to their game, and showed a tendency to regard him white-eyed over their shoulders. He perfectly understood the reason for their uneasiness, which was more than they did themselves, but his face betrayed nothing.

The throbbing diminished, and the swelling lessened as the colour of his hands faded to pink. They had not died of the constriction, and his body relaxed against the wall behind him. He gently rubbed his arms. Though grimed from the forge, his hair was so fair that it shone against the stone, and his eyes were sparks of blue light in the gloom.

Other feet descended the stair, deliberate steps accompanied by the tapping of a stick. The curtain lifted, and the men-at-arms flinched like balky horses. One surreptitiously jerked up his hand with the first and last fingers extended, the sign to ward off the Evil Eye. An old woman stalked over the rushes, and they scuttled from her way. The last man yelped as her staff cracked across his rump. She ignored him.

Maybe she had seen three-score years; the wisps of hair escaping from her black kerchief were white, and her pale eyes showed the white rim of age round the iris. Yet there was force in her arm, and the staff was not needed to support her. The prisoner looked up into her face and felt the hairs prickle erect on his spine.

A bony talon gripped his arm, probing the muscles that knotted against her clutch. She gave a harsh chuckle, and her claws dug deeper.

'Now here's a fine angry cockerel to please Lord Reynald!' she proclaimed. 'An upstanding lad with a blacksmith's thews, and look at the bold eye of him!' She slapped his shoulder as though he were flesh on a butcher's block, then cracked him across the shins with her staff. 'Up on your feet, cockerel! Where's reverence for white hairs? Where's courtesy?'

He did not move. 'Where it's due,' he retorted.

She laughed. 'And what sport's to be had out of a craven that squeals at the first tickle? We'll tame you, bold whelp!

You'll cry and crawl and beg – if you've a tongue left to beg with !'

'Hell will be home to you, when you reach it,' he answered.

Fury flared in her wizened face; her lips lifted from half a dozen snags of yellow teeth. 'Crow now, cockerel !' she spat. 'I'll remember it when you're singing another song !' She jabbed him in the belly, and swung away. Every man-at-arms flattened himself against the wall, wooden-faced and wary, but she stalked across the guardroom and tapped up the stair. Every man released his breath, and as one they moved forward to stand over the captive.

'You're mad !' declared one. 'That was Wulfrune, Lord Reynald's old nurse, and she rules him yet.'

'She's mistress here more surely than his wife.'

'She's a witch !' said the man who had made the sign to avert the Evil Eye.

'She's as crafty as he is in devising torments,' said the first, 'and takes as much delight in it !'

Guy Armourer said nothing, very eloquently.

They glared at him, obscurely angered by his imperviousness to fear, and returned to their game, but after a few throws one pouched the dice, another set the shield in a rack with a dozen others, and they hunched on the rushes, muttering together.

Soft boots ran down the stair, and Lucifer put his head round the curtain. 'Lord Reynald's eager for a relish to his dinner. Fetch him up !'

Guy Armourer rose and moved to the stair. Lucifer lifted his slanted black brows, his pale eyes widening, and led the way. The men-at-arms tramped up behind, but the prisoner did not even glance over his shoulder at them. His only move was to unfasten and loosen the throat-lacing of his tunic. He was nine-tenths certain of being granted his life; whatever qualms the one-tenth doubt induced his face betrayed none of them.

The stairhead opened into the hall, opposite a shallow dais. Just before it a man was adjusting the ends of a rope that had been tossed over a great hook set in a ceiling-beam, and

13

at one side a brazier glowed red, with irons and pincers thrust among the coals. The fellow dropped his rope-ends and skipped aside, and Guy Armourer stared straight into the blue eyes of Reynald de Warby.

He sat in the high chair, a small slight man something past forty, with hair so fair it showed no grey, uncommonly good-looking but for his peevish little mouth. Old Wulfrune leaned on the back of his chair, and on a cushion by his feet sat a lovely girl who was surely his daughter.

The troopers gripped Guy's arms from behind and thrust him forward, between men and women crowding expectantly. He halted at the dais foot, the rope brushing his shoulder, the brazier's heat tingling at his other side. Lord Reynald leaned forward, his elbows on the chair arms and his folded hands propping his pointed chin. A small grim smile tilted the left corner of his mouth up and the right down. 'You resisted my men when they would have taken my rightful toll?' he asked softly.

'I fought your thieves.'

'And you insulted Mistress Wulfrune?'

'That would not be possible.'

She squawked. 'This cockerel crows too loud! Make a capon of him!'

'Does the hen rule this midden?' the captive enquired.

'First tear out his ugly tongue,' suggested the girl, gazing eagerly at the red irons in the brazier.

But Lord Reynald was frowning at the prisoner more in puzzlement than in wrath. 'Where have I seen your face before?'

'In your mirror.'

For a moment surprise stilled them all in mid-breath; then folk began to push and crane and murmur, staring from one blond head to the other. Lord Reynald stiffened, sharply scrutinizing the young man. His beard partly disguised the likeness, but once remarked it was sure enough.

'You claim to be my bastard?'

'With regret, yes.'

14

'Guard your tongue! Beside your face, what proof can you show?'

'Four-and-twenty years ago,' Guy Armourer said harshly, 'a merchant was riding from Gloucester to Bristol with his daughter and four serving-men, when you and a dozen men-at-arms attacked them. You butchered the men and ravished the daughter. Before you rode away with all their goods you told her your name and tossed her this.' He shrugged off the slackened grasp on his arms, and from under his tunic drew a silver disc suspended from a thong. 'Maybe you've forgotten, among so many murders and rapes. Let it remind you!' It streaked in a glittering arc to Lord Reynald's hand, that lifted automatically to catch it.

He tilted it to the light, a coin about twice the diameter of a silver penny, its centre pierced and surrounded by scrawled yet decorative symbols. 'It's Saracen. I won it at dice the night before from a returned Crusader.'

'Warby luck, you called it.'

'Warby luck indeed!' His face lighted with triumph. 'So I begot me a son!' He tossed the coin carelessly, appraising the young man, and then anger flared. 'I told the wench if she whelped to bring me the brat when it was weaned!'

'Nothing would have brought her to do so.'

'By the Horns, the bitch withheld my own son from me?'

'In law,' Guy Armourer responded without heat, 'a bastard is his mother's.' Only the faintest tremor in his deep voice betrayed his own anger; a bastard received harsh training in self-control.

'Law? You're mine! And your name – Guy – how dared she not give you a true Warby name?'

'Why should she?'

'I've a mind to ride to Bristol and seek her out! My son – my own son denied me by a – '

'By his mother.'

Lord Reynald laughed harshly. 'And how did she breed up her bastard? Whoredom?'

'She married an honest man.'

15

'Honest, to cheat me of my son?' He checked himself, realizing that his words did nothing to commend him to that son. 'You *are* mine!'

'If that induces you to forgo your entertainment,' Guy said, glancing distastefully at the brazier, 'bid your routiers restore my property and I'll be on my way.'

Lord Reynald snapped to his feet, almost oversetting the girl. 'What's this? Go? You're my son – yourself you declared it!'

'To purchase my life. You can be nothing to me, my lord, nor I to you.'

Lord Reynald advanced impetuously to the dais's edge. 'You're mine! I'll not let you go!'

'Will you chain me to your wall?'

He reached to clutch the young man's shoulders. Guy jerked back in revulsion. 'But I'm your father! You cannot leave me!'

'You raped my mother and murdered her father.'

'I was nineteen, and drunk. You'll not hold a boy's error against me forever?'

'You've progressed since that beginning,' Guy answered, glancing at the brazier.

'Take those things away! It's a father's right and duty to provide for his son. I'll acknowledge you formally – grant you lands and power – wed you to an heiress – knight you – ' He broke off with a sudden crow of hard laughter. 'Ah, that touches you! Knighthood – that's what you aspire to?'

Guy drew a long breath. 'Yes.'

'Yours, yours, if that's your price! And all the rest too, if you stay by me!'

Guy's eyebrows twitched together. Mention of price had a flavour of bribery to it. Hands gripped his arms, seizing and demanding. He looked up into the handsome face that had nothing in it of kindness nor love. 'I must consider.'

'What is there to consider? You are mine!'

'What's one forgotten bastard out of the crop you've doubtless sired?'

The horrid hush stilling the hall informed him that he had

16

spoken shockingly amiss. Fury flared in Lord Reynald's face, and his hands closed to print bruises. The pretty girl on the cushion snickered all too audibly, and as he looked at her she eyed him with bright malice and hugged her knees.

'No other!' Lord Reynald said thickly. 'You're mine!'

Guy stood pondering a long moment, his face showing none of the emotions churning behind it. Then he shrugged free. 'I'll complete my errand,' he stated, adding, to forestall objection, 'That's a matter of honour. And then I must return to Bristol —'

'If you're not here within seven days I'll ride myself to Bristol, and slay those who withheld my son from me and every living thing in their household!'

'If you do the least hurt to my mother and her husband I'll disown you forever,' Guy promised without heat.

Chapter 2

On Thorgastone Waste the bracken fronds were browning, and the scrubby thickets were jewelled with berries. A kestrel hovered above a space of tussocky grass and suddenly stooped. Not far away a hart bellowed challenge, startling Guy so that he jerked on the reins and his mount tossed his head and snorted. He leaned to pat his neck in reassurance. The hawk, with an indignant shriek, lifted from the grass and flapped away, a fieldmouse dangling from its talons. He watched it go, a smile momentarily banishing the trouble from his face. Then, as the bird disappeared, worry knotted his brows again.

As far back as he could remember knighthood had been a crazy dream, stirring the warrior blood in his body; for as many years his monster-father had shadowed his life with shame and bitterness. If the price of knighthood were subjection to Lord Reynald's rule in that fear-ridden hold, it would be dearly bought but within his grasp at last. Misgivings remained, but he smothered them. 'And what future have I as my father's bastard if I refuse?' he asked aloud, and had nothing but the backward twitch of his horse's ears for answer.

There was no track, no more than the vaguest hint of a path that threaded between thickets, rocks and bracken patches. He mounted the ridge, letting his tired horses pick the way at their own pace. Yet, though Warby and Trevaine had no commerce with each other, even his townsman's eyes could discern that other horses had trodden this way. Rain had blurred the prints, but only hooves shod with iron could have so scarred the turf. Scattered droppings, weathered and crumbled, added proof. He rode warily, his eyes searching the rough waste, and drew rein on a small rise as an odd structure loomed out of the thickets on his left.

A giant child had built a table of stone slabs, two set on edge and a third balanced atop. Beyond it a score or so more slabs had been erected in a circle. Guy regarded it in puzzlement, and then started his horse forward. A few yards further, and the hoofprints angled towards the stones. Curiosity turned him aside also, and he followed the tracks. A tangle of brambles barred his way, and his horse shied and whinnied as a trailer clawed at his legs. Undeterred, he moved along the barrier seeking an opening. His mount snorted and laid his ears back, and he had to touch spurs to his ribs to urge him on. Crooked blackthorns hung with scarlet-fruited briars, bryony and the delicate whorls of old-man's-beard rose out of the brambles, hiding all but the tops of the stones, and he had to follow half-way round the circle before he came to an opening.

His horse snorted and jibbed, ears flattened and eyes showing white-rimmed. 'Come up, Dusty!' Guy admonished him, and used the spurs more sharply. The brute reared up with a sudden squeal, almost unseating him. He backed, snorted and tossed his head, fighting the bit, dug in his hooves and refused to budge. He was sweating and trembling with terror. Guy tried to soothe him, frowning in perplexity. This was a gelding of mature years, no skittish colt, and he had never behaved so before. The stolid packhorse had also caught the infection and was kicking and sidling. In mercy Guy retreated a few yards and tethered them to the stoutest branches he could find. Then he returned.

A few steps inside the gap he halted. Two arms of brambles had been drawn across it waist-high and tied together with a scrap of black cloth. Knotted into the cloth were a few draggled black feathers and a small thin bone. He frowned at it, half-guessing at a warning, but curiosity and stubbornness moved him to duck under the barrier and walk into the circle.

Here was a thirty-yard space of grass, level and trim as though it had been scythed. The stones towered above his head, weather-worn and lichened. One or two leaned like lurching topers, but most stood erect, deep-sunk in the ground, and he wondered at the labour that had set them in their places. They were old, ages old; older than the legends of the English who had come over the sea when Rome fell, older than Rome, older than the Lord Christ and His sojourn on this earth. Awe's finger touched him. This was a place of worship. Men had set up these stones as a temple to forgotten gods, and bowed down in ignorance and fear.

Almost in the circle's centre another huge slab lay flat in the grass, and near it a broad patch had been burned black. He crossed to it, and looked down on a litter of charcoal, half-burned fragments and grey ash beaten into the earth by rain. A great fire it had been, enough to roast a side of beef or signal alarm across a county, but why any should light it in this wild secret place was beyond his guessing. A smaller fire had burned on the flat stone, and there leaped unbidden into his mind the story of Abraham, who would have sacrificed his son as a burnt offering had not God's angel stayed his hand. There were burned bones among the charred sticks, and he shuddered and crossed himself. Then he almost laughed aloud, stooped, and picked up a fragment from a fowl's wing still holding a few scorched and shrivelled feathers.

He cast it from him in sudden loathing and rubbed his grimed fingers in the grass. A burned wing made no culinary sense; one plucked a fowl clean before the cooking. A sacrifice, the thought persisted, burned on this altar-stone as offerings had been burned to some unappeasable god in the ages before Christ was born; a denial of Christian faith. He crossed himself and whispered an *Ave Maria*. Sweat chilled on his skin. Evil was strong in this place, and all at once he was urgent to get out of it.

Dusty whinnied. The horses, brutes not beglamoured by reason, had sensed this evil before him. Guy plunged across the smooth grass. He missed the way out, and made two false casts before he found the right pair of uprights and the gap in the thicket. He found himself scuttling, his heart thumping as though he had been running as irrational fear mounted in him. He scrambled under the barrier, and swore under his breath as his hair snagged. The gelding whickered as he strode towards the horses, and the pack-animal tugged at his tether. He reached for the bridle and then checked, all his pulses jolting in alarm as a large body moved behind the blackthorns. A girl on a bay mare emerged.

Surprise had him gaping for a moment, and then relief set him grinning far too appreciatively. 'God save you, fair mistress!' he greeted her, without thinking, in English.

'Save you,' she acknowledged curtly in the same tongue, and looked him over without favour. 'Who are you, and what are you doing here?' She moved into the open, a tall lass in a dark-green riding-dress. With her horse-furniture and fine palfrey it proclaimed her of knightly breeding, but not so certainly as her peremptory manner. It did not commend her to Guy. His smile vanished.

'My name is Guy Armourer. I went up yonder from curiosity.' He jerked his head at the looming stones.

'What's your business in these parts?'

'It does not concern chance-met strangers.'

Her head lifted, her brows twitched together in affront, as though no man had ever so rebuffed her; certainly some knight's daughter. 'You're insolent!'

A man thrust from the bushes after her, middle-aged and scrawny, unmistakeably an escorting groom. 'Shall I mend the oaf's manners, Lady Helvie?' he demanded, lifting his riding-whip.

Her glance measured Guy's imposing inches, and her mouth twitched a little as she shook her head. 'You're over-matched. Let be.'

The groom thrust belligerently between Guy and his mistress, but an imperative gesture brought his whip-hand down and sent him to heel. Guy gathered the reins, set his foot in the stirrup and swung astride. It offended his pride that she should look down on him.

'You're a Warby man!' she challenged. 'None else would venture within that unholy place.'

'You are here yourself.'

'We heard your horses – '

'Is not curiosity common to us both?'

21

She scowled at him. He regarded her with acute dislike, and she flushed, jerked on the reins to whirl her mare about and was gone. The groom loosed an oath at Guy and pounded behind. Branches crashed, the drumming of hooves diminished, and Guy shrugged. He pulled on the leadrope, clicked his tongue to the packhorse, and followed more soberly.

He wondered rancorously who permitted the arrogant wench to roam loose about the waste accosting travellers, instead of keeping her fittingly to stitchery or spinning. The groom had called her Lady Helvie, and her ways proclaimed her of noble blood, yet she had conversed in English, showing greater mastery of that tongue than most gentlefolk achieved. Also she was at least sixteen, maybe seventeen; by that age she should have been three years wedded and tending a household, with a brat in the cradle and another in her belly.

Guy passed close by the stone table, and gazed up at the vast slab balanced across the other two, higher than his head as he sat his saddle. He marvelled afresh, wondering how ever men could have hoisted that enormous weight and set it in place, and what ages had passed since their strength and ingenuity dwindled to dry bones. Then he pushed his horse harder. Speculation was one thing, but an errand to complete was another, and a sensible man timed his arrival at a castle for the dinner-hour.

From the ridge Trevaine's tower beckoned across a couple of miles of valley. The girl and her groom had vanished, and he thought no more of her. He came cautiously down the broken slope that presently flattened into rough pasture, where herdboys watched cattle and sheep. He came upon a track and followed it between stubble-fields where three plough-teams striped the faded gold with brown. He passed through a hamlet where women cooking over outdoor fires looked curiously at him and a smith came to his forge door to watch him pass, and plunged into coloured woods. Another mile, and they opened before him on wider fields, a larger village, and the castle above it on a low rise. And Trevaine was not Warby; a ploughman shouted a greeting, and the urchin leading the ox-team waved to him.

Trevaine was in no way like Warby. Women greeted him from doorways, children and dogs skirmished about his horses, and hens took off in squawking flurries from under their hooves. The cottages were trimmer, fresh with whitewash, the garden-patches prosperous with onions and cabbages, the hives humming content, the very dunghills steaming complacently. Behind a barn door someone was whistling, and a couple of girls gossiping by a well giggled at Guy's salutation.

Small qualms assailed him when he clattered over a drawbridge and under a portcullis for the second time that day. The gate-guard sergeant was civil; he called up a groom to tend the weary horses, and appointed a trooper to lead him to Lord Henry, 'Try the hall first, Piers. Drill's been over this half-hour, and the dinner-horn will be sounding any time. And main glad he'll be to have his good hauberk mended fit to wear.'

Guy met his bland gaze and smothered a grin as he shouldered the weighty packs. He knew, and the sergeant knew, that the hauberk had not been repaired, but let out to accommodate Lord Henry's expanded paunch, but neither would say so.

Lord Henry was indeed in the hall, where the servants were laying the tables for dinner. He stood by the edge of the dais, a large tawny man in the early fifties who had given up the struggle against encroaching weight, talking to a tall woman who presented a trim back in dark crimson and a tawny bare head. Guy spared her shape an appreciative glance as he tramped up the hall.

'Ha, the armourer from Bristol! You're well come!' Lord Henry boomed. His voice was designed by nature for encouraging a hunt or commanding a cavalry charge, disconcerting within doors.

'God save you, my lord.' Guy bent his knee to the rushes, shrugged off his burden at the dais steps, and looked past Lord Henry into the startled hazel eyes of the girl from the waste.

'God's Grace!' she blurted. 'Here's the lout himself!'

Lord Henry looked from her to Guy, menace kindling.

'You're the fellow who showed my daughter discourtesy?'

Guy looked up into his purpling face. 'I returned what I was offered, my lord,' he answered coolly. 'And the lady did not tell me her name or station.'

'Offered?'

'Would you tell your affairs on a chance-met wench's demand?'

The girl flushed scarlet. Lord Henry spluttered. 'God's Throat, you've an insolent tongue in your head!'

'He was in the Devil's Ring! He'd come from Warby!' the girl exclaimed.

'Since the fords lie westward that's the road a man must take, unless he'd travel five leagues out of his way.' Guy stooped to swing the packs on to the dais, and his sleeves pulled up his arms.

'He *has* come from Warby! Look at his wrists!' she cried.

The welts left by Lucifer's thongs had scarcely faded. Lord Henry stared, his anger suddenly sharpened by suspicion. 'If you were taken by Warby, how did you come alive out of it?'

'Lord Reynald freed me.'

'He never spares any!' the girl declared.

Guy shrugged. 'I'm here.'

'Why should that devil loose you? For what service?'

'It was his whim. There was some talk of Warby luck.' Guy was sticking fast to the truth, if only part of it; a knight did not stoop to lie. The trooper who had escorted him was poised to use his spear at a nod from his lord, and half a dozen servants had moved up behind him. His palms were sweating as he remembered Lord Reynald's parting words. 'If he learns you're a son of mine, he'll hang you from his gate-tower.'

'He's no armourer! He's a spy, or a witch sent to overlook us! He was in the Devil's Ring!'

'You spoke with me in my stepfather's forge,' Guy reminded Lord Henry, his glance dwelling briefly on the belt-line round which his own hands had run the measure.

'That's so. You were the one who was to do the repair. But to come alive and whole out of Warby – no man's ever done that before.'

24

'And if you'd seen fit to warn me of that, I'd have gone round by Etherby and never set foot in Warby,' Guy replied with a faint edge to his voice.

'Warn you?' The notion that he owed a warning to the man who must deliver his armour had obviously never occurred to him, and Guy let slip his hold on prudence.

'It might have cost you your good hauberk.'

'God's Head, so it might!'

The girl, keener-witted than her sire, felt his point's barb and flushed with chagrin and fury. Then her gaze went past him, and her face hardened. Skirts swished in the rushes behind Guy, and another girl came to the dais foot, attended by two waiting-women; a smaller, younger girl in a fine blue gown, with the chatelaine's keys chiming at her girdle. She swept up the steps and laid a hand on Lord Henry's arm, smiling up at him. No glance, not even an eyelid's flicker, acknowledged that Helvie existed. She turned her smile on Guy, oblivious of the tension between them.

'The armourer from Bristol with my lord's gear? You are well come; he has been fretting for it long enough. And what news do you bring from Bristol?'

Guy bowed. 'Very little, my lady, since the Duke of Normandy is still abroad.'

'And new-married to King Louis's divorced Queen,' she said with relish. 'Have you ever seen the Duke?'

'Yes, my lady.'

'Close to, I mean?'

'I have spoken with him, when I repaired his mail, my lady.'

'Is it true what they say, that he dresses like a woodcutter?' she asked eagerly.

'More like a huntsman, my lady, for he is always in the saddle.'

'And they say he has a taste for low women, even tavern-wenches –' She checked on a giggle.

'As to that, my lady, I have no knowledge,' Guy answered austerely, hoping that he had not betrayed his surprise and amusement that a great lady could be as silly as any gossiping housewife.

25

Lord Henry scowled at her like any husband whose wife makes a fool of herself in public. 'So you've encountered the Angevin cub. What do folk think of him in Bristol?'

'Why, that he will be a greater King than his grandsire.'

'King? They reckon he'll take the crown, then?'

'Who's to prevent him,' the girl asked une..pectedly, 'when he has all the wealth of Aquitaine behind him?'

'He'll not need it. He is of the breed of Kings,' Guy answered, remembering the demon's energy that had flared in the armourer's shop.

'When Robert of Gloucester died,' Lord Henry growled, 'men of sense hoped the war would die also. Now this devil's whelp from Anjou will fight it again.' He shook his head heavily, but Guy's pulse quickened. Warfare gave the landless knight his chance to distinguish himself.

'You smile at that?' the girl challenged. 'Reckoning how your trade will prosper from slaughter?'

Guy flushed, opened his mouth to refute the accusation and then realized that it had been just. His anger burned hotter.

'There's no profit in war,' Lord Henry stated. 'A man can ride three days through the debated land and see never a house standing nor a field tilled, and peasants' bones picked clean in the waste. Where's the profit to their lords? Eh, wife?'

'I thank the Saints I was bred up to know that when men discuss matters of state, a woman should hold her tongue.'

Since that was Guy's own belief he should have been gratified by this endorsement. He looked up into the tall girl's face, and sympathy sprang perversely in him. Gratification came when Lord Henry turned on his wife; the spiteful fool had over-reached herself.

'God's Head, you should have an opinion, since the war's cost me a good half of your dower!'

A horn blasted outside, announcing dinner. The wife flounced to her high seat on the dais, tears of mortification glittering in her eyes, and Guy watched her thoughtfully. She was surely a fool. Difficult it might be for a new-wedded wife to be burdened with a stepdaughter older than herself, but her display of malice would not endear her to her husband. If Lady Helvie were his heiress she was crazed to antagonize her so before supplanting her with a son.

Guy was not enlightened about Helvie's status until the first course was being cleared. He had been placed, as a guest of less than gentle blood, at the top of one of the tables below the dais, presided over by Lord Henry's huntsman. There had been no further word of his sojourn in Warby. A stridency in the talk at the high table, though words did not reach them, turned his neighbours' heads.

'Two women in one house,' commented the huntsman.

'He'll have no peace in bed or at board while Mistress Helvie remains,' said a sergeant of the garrison lower down the table.

'He should have married off his daughter before ever he brought home Lady Alice,' declared a sour cleric in a threadbare gown.

'It's none so easy to find a good husband for a bastard, and he's fond o' the lass,' the huntsman objected.

'It's an insult to his wife and no kindness to his daughter,' said the cleric primly.

Guy looked across at the high table and inwardly agreed with him, but marvelled that Lord Henry had not enforced some semblance of amity with his belt. As for the girl, he might have known more fellow-feeling for her if he had liked her better. He caught her eye, and she scowled at him; if Lord Henry's suspicions had been distracted hers had not. He shrugged and turned his attention to a trencher piled with boiled salt beef. Castle folk might reckon it a matter of course to eat flesh twice a day, but a townsman was lucky to taste it twice a week.

Either Lord Henry was all bluster and no action, or as easily diverted as a weather-cock, for he still made no further mention of Warby. He tried his hauberk and commended the alterations, paid the charges without quibbling and even suggested genially that a skilled armourer might do well in private service. In normal circumstances Guy would have remained overnight, but he was in haste to be outside Lord

27

Henry's reach before news of his identity should fly to Trevaine. Shortly after midday he passed under the portcullis again, with an odd mingling of relief and disappointment that he did so without encountering the girl Helvie.

His horses, well-fed but barely rested, were disinclined to travel far, and once inside the woods Guy found an open space well away from the track, unsaddled and tethered them. Rolled in his cloak on a heap of bracken, he slept uneasily, used to the stuffy loft over the forge and the snores of his half-brother and the journeyman, not to the scent of crushed fern and the sound of the horses tearing at the grass. He was on his way as soon as the waning moon gave him light enough, for he was anxious to cross the fords beyond Warby before sunrise. So he saddled up, fingers and leather equally awkward in the dawn chill, huddled his cloak about his ears against the dew spattered by the trees, and growled curses at his balky horses.

Early as he was, others had been earlier. He heard the owl-hoots before and behind, but thought nothing of them. Mist smoked from the river and filtered between the trees, and as he slackened speed a half-dozen tattered wraiths put on substance all about him. Guy looked at two spear-heads poised to thrust him through the belly, and beyond them at three arrow-points glinting above tense knuckles. A middle-sized brown man, empty-handed, caught his bridle close to the bit as he halted.

'You're the fellow crossed before dawn yesterday,' he stated. 'It doesn't work twice. Dismount!'

'Don't spoil his tunic!' besought the larger spearman. 'I'm claiming his clothes! Knock his head in!'

Guy looked down sourly on the fellow at his bridle and spoke the password Lord Reynald had provided for just this contingency. 'The Horns protect me.'

The leader's jaw dropped, and the horse snorted and threw up his head at the tug on his bit. 'God's Head, how – ?'

'Lord Reynald's own word,' Guy answered grimly. 'Stand away!'

The robber jerked his head, and three arrow-points stooped

earthward as the bows unbent. One spear-butt grounded. The big ruffian who claimed Guy's clothes protested.

'Fattest spoil this half-year gone! Good gear, horses, an' that's money he's gotten!' He jabbed at the bulge above Guy's belt, where the leather bag of silver pennies nagged his ribs. 'An' his clothes'd do me!' His need was extreme; a couple of untanned deerskins cobbled with thongs over filthy tatters comprised his attire.

'He has Lord Reynald's word.'

'We're letting him go on Warby madman's say-so?'

'We only live by his leave, and hang without it,' the leader answered, his voice sharpening dangerously. He loosed Guy's bridle and started round the horse's head.

'Hell burn you, I'm taking tunic afore frosts start!'

The eyes glinting through tangled hair narrowed, muscles knotted in bony arms, and the spear lunged at Guy's throat. He struck it up and over his shoulder, and as the fellow, with nothing to resist his thrust, stumbled closer, he kicked with all his force. His boot crunched into nose and mouth. The spear clattered. The robber sprawled on his back three yards away, and then lurched groaning to his knees, groping for his spear-shaft and spitting teeth.

'Drop it!' barked the leader.

He grabbed up his weapon and lifted his broken face, his defiant snarl bubbling through blood. He heaved to one knee, and Guy tightened his thighs on the gelding's barrel to urge him forward. The brown man moved up behind his follower. 'Who commands here?' he demanded, jerked his head back by the hair and cut his throat.

He dropped the dead man in the gush of blood. As it steamed in his nostrils the gelding shrieked and reared up, striking at the empty sky. Guy, half-prepared, clung with all the strength of his legs, hauled on the reins and struck him between the ears with his clubbed fist to bring him down. The instant his forehooves touched the earth he spun about and bolted back the way he had come, dragging the pack-horse after him.

They fled the best part of a mile before Guy could check

them, and then stood trembling and snorting, their hides lathered and their eyes rolling white-rimmed. He waited a while, soothing them with hands and voice, while the morning lightened and the grey woods gathered colour from the dawn. He was shivering himself, his belly churning. A robber captain, he supposed, could tolerate insubordination even less than other commanders.

'Why should it surprise me that Lord Reynald is abetting outlaws for a share in their plunder?' he asked the silent trees, and stroked Dusty's nose. The leaf-patterned sky overhead was blue now, the mists almost swallowed by the risen sun. He swung back into the saddle. 'I gave my word,' he said aloud, as though refuting an accusation, 'and how else can I reach knighthood?' He tightened the reins and forced the beast back towards the ford.

The body was gone. The blood was jellied black on the fallen leaves, blue flies buzzing and crawling, and a trail of drying splashes led to the ford. He grimaced, wondering to whom the river would bear it, and fought his frightened horses down to the water, on the way home to Bristol.

Chapter 3

The person Guy had expected to make least turmoil about his decision made the most. When the enormity he proposed reached her wits, his mother leaned forward on her stool and demanded incredulously, 'You'll go to *him*? The devil who murdered my father and raped me – you'll go to *him*?'

'I gave my word.'

'What's that worth, a promise forced from you by threats? Any priest will absolve you, whatever you swore by!'

'I'm not seeking absolution. He will provide for me.'

'God's Body, isn't the craft in your hands enough to live by, that you must turn to that monster?'

'I'd always expected,' complained Guy's half-brother William, 'that when – when the time came you'd set up with me.'

'With you as master and me as servant.'

'Has the lawful son no rights before the bastard?' Emma blazed. 'A very proper provision –'

'For the elder and the better craftsman? No.' He regarded his half-brother without liking, now his intentions had been spoken. 'I'd have set up among strangers first. Lord Reynald has promised to knight me.'

His mother's distaff and spindle clattered against the hearthstone. 'Yes, that's what you've always wanted! To prance abroad on a tall horse like the mailed thief that begot you, robbing and killing and ravishing, instead of earning an honest living by a decent craft!'

'Wife,' said Kenric temperately, 'remember the blood that was born in him.'

'The foulest blood in England. D'you think I've not seen it, not watched him grow liker and liker every year? Yes, it was born in him to turn from us and his honest rearing!'

'Wife –'

'If he'd had any sense of decency, any regard for what was right and fitting, he'd have stayed at school – all those fees you paid for nothing – and taken the cowl in atonement for the sin.'

'The sin was not mine,' Guy answered calmly, though his heart flinched inside him, 'and God set no vocation in me.'

'Obedience was your duty!'

Kenric suspended his smoothing of the stake he was making for shaping helmets, and levelled his knife at her for emphasis. 'Now, wife, Guy was in no way at fault.'

Her face convulsed in the flickering firelight, and tear-tracks glimmered down her cheeks, round and comely yet. 'He turns to the devil that spawned him and betrayed me!' She sprang up, the stool tumbling backward on the rushes, and cried at him, 'Have you no feeling for me who bore you, no heart to remember the love that bred you up all these years, that you would forsake your home and parents for that devil?'

Guy got to his feet, the fire's glow colouring his pallor. If she had started with that appeal she might have prevailed, but she did not love him. She had never loved him. In childhood she had done a mother's duty by him, but all her devotion was for her first lawful son. Since he reached years of understanding he had not held it against her. His resemblance to the raptor who had begotten him continually fretted the old hurt, and his differences with William increased the friction. 'Mother –'

'In Mary's name, why did you ever claim kinship with him?'

'To save my life,' he reminded her, and added, between anger and amusement, 'And who insisted I hang that token about my neck, against that very need?'

'The day will come,' she prophesied bitterly, 'when all of us, and you yourself, will wish you had hanged instead!'

Guy looked at her a long moment, that plump housewife standing by her own hearth. Firelight and rising smoke wavered about her, and she was a Sibyl of ancient times foretelling doom. He turned from her without a word, strode across the floor and into the forge, shoving the door shut behind him.

There was no light but the dim glow of the charcoal fire, banked for the night. His nostrils filled with the faint, acrid odour, mingled with those of hot metal, oil, soot and scorched leather, familiar as the breath he drew. He needed no light here, where he spent his working days, and moved surely between ordered obstacles to the chest in which Kenric locked completed work. He sat down, his chin propped on his hands, and stared at the forge's red eye, contemplating the wreckage he had wrought.

He had been a complacent fool. His mother did not love him; but he owed her a son's grateful duty, and had turned from her to the monster who had begotten him in rape. No man could ever comprehend what that meant to a woman, but dimly he perceived that it must outrage the very source of maternal feeling. Yet, understanding, he must abide by his treachery. He could not continue in this household, subject to her carping, forever subservient to William, scratching together his journeyman's wages until, years hence, he might have enough to set up for himself.

The door opened on the sound of gusty sobbing, and Kenric's stocky bulk was briefly outlined against the firelight before he closed it behind him and advanced as surely as Guy had done into the darkness. Guy got to his feet and waited on his word. He had no quarrel with his stepfather.

Kenric perched his rump on the largest anvil-block. Guy could just distinguish his shape in the forge's glow. 'Sit, lad,' he bade him, and Guy sank back on the chest in silence. 'Must you go, son?'

'I promised.'

'His threats can't touch you.'

'He threatened all in this household.'

'Worthless. He daren't show his face in Bristol, since all men know he robbed and murdered Aymer the wine-merchant last year.'

'I know he is a villain,' said Guy slowly, 'but he claimed a father's right. And he will knight me.'

'Which has been your heart's desire since you were a little lad, climbing into the Alderman's orchard to ride his palfrey rather than pilfer his apples. Aye, and persuading drunken Gamel of the gate-guard to teach you sword-play.'

'You knew?'

Kenric chuckled. 'I've been a lad myself. What puzzled me was how you managed to bribe Gamel.'

'No bribe. I'd noticed where he hid his wine when he was on duty.'

'Conscienceless whelp! But I feared once, when you came home from the monastery, that you'd run off to be a common soldier.'

'I thought of it often enough,' Guy admitted. 'But common soldiers are dirt beneath the knights' feet. A good armourer commands more respect. Bristol's been the head of the Angevin strength in this war as long as I can remember; I've known soldiers all my life. There's no rising to knighthood that way. So – I shut my ears and learned my craft.'

'Your mother should not complain at your lack of a vocation. No one could have squealed louder when her cousin tried to force her into a nunnery.'

'She feels I have betrayed her. But – but – is it not justice to her and to you also, that the man who begot me should provide for me?' His voice wavered for all he tried to hold it steady.

'He has no right, unless you give it,' Kenric answered gently.

'But he owes it to me, does he not?'

'A bastard has no claim beyond what his father chooses to give.'

'Forgive me, Father, but what provision is there for me elsewhere?'

'In law, my eldest son's, since you were born in wedlock.'

'Almighty God!' Guy exclaimed, in appalled amusement. For a moment his misery lifted. 'Oh, to tell William so and see his face! But it's not possible. He is your lawful son, and

I another man's bastard. I'll never dispute his right as your heir, but neither will I own him my master.'

'It would be possible if he'd been born with the grace of generosity,' growled William's father.

'He's jealous.'

'He's a fool. You're already as good a weapon-smith as I am, and the best hand at this finicky ring-mail I've known. Given three more years I could set you up for yourself, but four daughters to dower decently took what little portion your mother brought and more, and I'm still in debt for Aldith. But if you'd wait, lad – ?'

'You're generosity's self!' Guy exclaimed, his love for his stepfather closing his throat so that he had to swallow twice before he could command his voice. 'But do you think I could lay such a charge on you? A poor requital for all the years you've been my father.'

Kenric sighed. For a long moment the only sound in the forge was the faint purr of the banked fire. Then he asked, 'Have you never wondered why I married your mother?'

'Often,' Guy admitted candidly. 'You were barely acquainted with her father, her cousin had made off with most of her dowry, and she was pregnant with another man's bastard.'

'You know I'd been married before? My first wife, God rest her, was a widow who'd borne two children, but in over ten years with me she never quickened. So I reckoned, as any man must, that the fault was in my seed. I wedded Emma for the child to comfort my old age, a son to train in my craft if God granted that.'

'And got six of your own,' Guy murmured.

'You have been that son. You've never disappointed me.'

Guy dropped to his knees and gripped Kenric's hands. 'You – you are my true father!' he jerked out. 'In love and honour – believe me –'

'Be easy. You shouldered one yoke and made a craftsman. Knighthood you'll achieve, for it's in your blood.'

'In blood and brain and heart. I must. Not that I expect

to enjoy its apprenticeship,' he added, contemplating existence in Lord Reynald's hold. His resolution wavered. It was on his tongue's tip to renounce it, hold by his familiar, well-ordered life, and by diligence, thrift and prudent alliance rise to be a master armourer and maybe end as Alderman. He owed it to Kenric, who depended on his stepson more and more as age encroached on his strength; he was sixteen years older than Emma. Then he remembered William, and that he had given his word. He had as much pride as any knight. 'Give me your blessing, Father,' he requested steadily, 'for I think I shall need it.'

Kenric laid his hands lightly on Guy's hair. 'God bless and guide and keep you safe, my son, now and always.' He was silent for a space, and then said briskly, 'I'll give you Dusty.'

'But –'

'Who's to ride with the deliveries when you're gone? William sits a saddle like a sack of grain, so his backside's blistered inside a mile, and I'm past it. So you'll take him.'

'Very gratefully.'

'I've as much pride as Lord Reynald. No son of mine tramps into Warby afoot like a beggar. Dusty's not much – I dare say Lord Reynald would reckon him only fit for hounds' meat.'

'He'll carry me.'

'And what will you do with the Slut?'

'Take her.'

'Lord Reynald will not fancy her.'

'With two or three score hounds about that hold, he cannot complain of mine. What else can I do? She'll take food from no other's hand; she'd pine to death. And she's *mine*.'

'Her paw is healed now.'

'If some fool hadn't cast broken crockery into the mire she'd have been with me – as I'd reason to wish more than once. She'd have winded that ambush, I'd have escaped it, and never come nose to nose with Lord Reynald.'

'All things are in God's hands,' said Kenric, and heaved himself up. 'Get to bed, lad. Leave your mother to me.'

Guy obeyed, but it was long before he slept, and on the other side of the partition between loft and bedroom the two voices murmured on far into the night.

He was packing his gear next day, after spending half the forenoon making the rounds of Bristol to bid farewell to his half-sisters, their husbands and children, when Kenric climbed into the loft with a bundle under his arm. Guy glanced up, and dropped the shirt he was folding; only one article in an armourer's shop was a yard long, narrow and rigid, even swaddled in oiled woollen cloth. His fists clenched and his breath came sharply as he looked from it to his stepfather's face.

'You need a sword, and it's a father's right to arm his son.'

'I wish,' said Guy, his throat thick with feeling, 'that you *were* my father!'

Head bent, he unwrapped the sword. He did not need to look at the crumbling leather that covered the scabbard to see that this was very old. No swordsmith in living memory had made such a hilt, with its three-lobed pommel and short guard curving towards the blade, nor inlaid the bronze with interlaced silver lines. It answered smoothly to his hand, and he tilted the blade in the light; its razor-keen edges were worn with use and many sharpenings. It was a little longer, more finely tapered than swords were made now, and it came to life in his grip. He cut and thrust, and its reflection jumped about the loft in brilliant flashes. He turned to Kenric.

'Whose — ?'

'An English earl left it with my grandsire's father for repair — a broken rivet in the hilt — as he went to join King Harold for the great battle. He never returned for it.'

'Near ninety years — '

'It's lain on the forge rafters,' Kenric told him, chuckling. 'Four generations we ha' cleaned and polished and greased it.'

'It was old then,' said Guy in awe.

'My guess is it came to England at a Dane's belt, maybe as long ago as King Alfred. Many a sword I've handled in my time, but never a better blade. No man has a claim to it.

37

Take it, and never draw it in an unjust quarrel.'

'You have my word.'

Emma was not in the house or the garden-toft behind it. Guy waited for a time and then, troubled, set to saddling Dusty, while his bitch sat by the stable door, ears pricked and tail twitching with anticipation. Her view of Heaven was an expedition with her master, and they came rarely, tied to his work as he was from week's end to week's end. The Slut was half-mastiff, half-wolf, and bigger than either, a guard-dog respected by all Bristol. Guy had never dared tell even Kenric that she had once killed her man lest her execution be demanded, as it had been when he rescued her from the river as a new-born whelp. She was six years old now, a stately matron whose parentage was no longer held against her and whose pups were spoken for before she bore them.

Guy strapped his bundle behind the saddle and made the wrapped sword fast to it. The Slut uttered a faint, warning whine in her throat, and he swung round. Emma, who detested the bitch and would not permit her within doors, drew the skirts of her gown close about her as she passed.

'Mother?'

She held out her hand. Silver glinted on the palm, a round medallion stamped with a crude image of the Virgin and Child, strung to a plaited leather cord. 'Lord Reynald, as all men know, harbours and leads a vile brood of witches,' she said abruptly, her high colour coming and going. 'This has lain on the altar through three Masses and been blessed with special prayers, to make it a sure protection against all evil enchantments. Wear it always.'

For the first time since early childhood he embraced and kissed her spontaneously. She stiffened in his hold, and then pecked him awkwardly on the brow. He put the loop over his head and dropped the trinket inside his shirt, its impact chilly against his skin. 'Always, be sure of that,' he said gravely. 'And I will remember always that it was your gift.'

She followed him to the street, and waited as he made his final farewells, bridle on arm and hound at heel. As he mounted she came to his stirrup and looked up for the last word.

'God guard you. And I trust you'll find knighthood worth the price.'

'What price?'

'That we'll not know until you're called upon to pay it.'

Chapter 4

Rain hunted Guy through woods whose October colours were all drowned to sodden brown, so that when he first sighted Warby keep on its ridge his misgivings and apprehension were smothered by relief. His cloak was long since soaked through, and his hood clung flat to his head with the weight of water that streamed over his face. Dusty plodded dismally under the dripping trees, his head drooping, and the Slut slouched alongside, her belly-fur clogged with mud. Then they came to the woods' fringe, and flinched from the wind that lashed their backs. The fields were empty. They squelched up the track that was running like a muddy stream, between cottages whose thatch and whitewash were blackened with wet. The street was deserted, but Guy was aware of eyes watching under eaves and behind doors as he leaned to the last climb up the ridge.

Guards saluted him at the gate and passed him through without challenge. He swung stiffly out of the saddle, stretching cramped legs with a thankful grunt, and at once two grooms came running from the stables. One seized Dusty's bridle to lead him away. The other unstrapped his baggage from the saddle, and when Guy extended his hand for it, shook his head with an expression of horror. Guy had never in his life been waited on, but the thought that Lord Reynald's son should carry his own bundle so plainly shocked the groom that he flushed and dropped his hand, resolving to accept all proffered service.

Lord Reynald was in the hall, playing chess with a thick-chested brown man whom Guy had glimpsed in the crowd that had witnessed his first confrontation with his sire. At sight of his son he sprang up, oversetting the board and scattering the pieces. As he advanced to the dais steps his opponent grimaced in relief and stooped to collect them.

'At last! I wondered whether you had failed me!'

Guy put back his hood and bent his knee in greeting. 'God save you, my lord.' The Slut, halting beside him, shook herself. The groom jumped aside. A bucket of water over his head could not have made Guy wetter. He patted her lightly as she thrust her muzzle against his thigh, and felt the hairs lift on her crest, the vibration of the almost soundless growl that filled her throat.

'That's your bitch?'

'I trust you'll grant her house-room, my lord?'

'Who gave her to you?'

His brows lifted in surprise. 'No one, my lord. I took her from the river as a half-drowned pup.'

'Oh. If you ask it, I'll keep her.' The Slut wrinkled her nose at the scent of him and the sound of his voice, and her lips lifted from teeth that had once torn a man's throat out. 'She's an ugly brute, and savage too!'

'Like me, she is misbegotten and half wolf.'

He took it for a compliment and laughed harshly. As Guy reached the dais and again formally went on one knee at the step, he caught him by the shoulders in a half-embrace and shook him slightly. The Slut snarled, and he let go. 'Pah, you stink like a wet dog! A bath and dry clothes for you, at once.' He snapped his fingers at the groom still in attendance. 'That's your servant. My own man has instructed him in his duties. Take a whip to him when he forgets them.'

'Why, my lord –'

'Make yourself fit to eat at my table, and quickly!'

Guy silently followed his servant out of the keep to a building between it and the outer wall. It was a laundry. Water simmered in a cauldron over a low fire; wooden tubs were ranged against one wall, buckets against another, and two benches were littered with dippers, ladles, bowls and paddles. The groom dragged a tub up to the fire and began dipping water from the cauldron. Guy unstrapped his baggage-roll of waxed leather and shook out his best tunic and hose, creased but dry. The groom tipped a couple of

41

bucketfuls of cold water into the tub, tried it with a finger and ladled more from the cauldron until satisfied. The Slut watched with deep interest, and he regarded her uneasily.

Guy wrestled out of his garments and dubiously eyed the steaming tub. Since his unremembered infancy he had never immersed his whole person in hot water, and though he knew the gentry were addicted to it, the procedure to him seemed unnecessary and perilous. He was not dirty. A respectable craftsman engaged in a grimy occupation, he washed all exposed parts daily, and otherwise acted on the artisan's excellent principle that one good sweat washes off another.

He glanced at the groom, a slight brown man of about his own age. No one should spread it through Warby that Lord Reynald's bastard flinched from a washtub. He tested it with a toe, stepped into it, summoned his resolution and sat down. The hot water lipped against his belly, and he loosed his breath. The sensation was entirely pleasurable. The chill and stiffness soaked from his muscles. He grunted in satisfaction, and relaxed.

The groom floated a wooden dish of soft greenish soap beside him, handed him a wash-clout and with another began to scrub Guy's back and shoulders. His ministrations stirred an obscure uneasiness in Guy, but he supposed that it was customary for a body-servant to do such service for his master and accepted it, until the fellow began to hiss between his teeth as he worked.

'I'm not a horse,' he protested, and the groom dropped the cloth and started back as though he expected a blow. For an instant Guy glimpsed fear and resentment in his face, before the stolid mask covered all feeling. 'What's your name?'

'Oswin, Master Guy.'

'I don't kick or bite, either.' He soaped his cloth and started on his feet, which after a little friction became disconcertingly white. Oswin silently took up his task. Guy, his tentative jest fallen flatter than the flagstones, wondered whether he had violated the conventions by trying it. Then he realized that to jest with a servant who could not answer back required long familiarity and complete understanding, and flushed at his thoughtlessness.

To cover his embarrassment he scooped a palmful of soap
and lathered his hair and beard. Oswin poured dipperfuls
of water over his head, sluicing away the forge-grime in dark
rivulets and drowning out the lice. Working folk took vermin
for granted, but the gentry who practised strict cleanliness
were less tolerant. He lathered again, noting how the water
in the tub had discoloured, and worked with particular care
at the dirt engrained round his nails and in his hands. Now
Oswin was proffering towels. Guy surged up, water flying
abroad, shivered as the draught from unshuttered windows
found his wet skin and rubbed with energy.

He fastened his belt, settled his wallet and dagger, and
carefully combed his hair. There was no mirror, but he peered
at his dim reflection in a bucket of water, braced his shoulders
in an unconscious betrayal of unease and hurried through
the rain to the keep. The sentinels brought their spears to the
salute, lounging guards jerked to attention, and a servant
held aside the leather curtain at the stairhead, flinching from
the Slut who sniffed at him as she passed.

The tables had been set up, and servants were laying
trenchers and horns at the lower tables, metal cups and dishes
and thick slices of bread at the high table that stood, draped
with a white cloth, on the dais. Their curious eyes followed
him up the hall. A slim man with light-brown hair was
supervising the work; the white wand in his hand declared
him the seneschal. In the cavernous wall-hearth blazing logs
challenged the draughts that swooped from unshuttered windows and curtained stairs, and Lord Reynald was warming
his back before it, talking to the thickset chess-player and
Lucifer. He beckoned Guy, and studied him from flax-pale
hair, waving as it dried, to sturdy shoes. The Slut's hackles
lifted, and Guy laid a hand on her head.

'You look like a journeyman,' Lord Reynald observed
sourly. 'Tomorrow you'll have that beard off in knightly
style.'

'As you wish, my lord.' An apprentice delighted in the first
quilling of his beard as a token of manhood, but other fashions

prevailed among gentlefolk.

'And that tunic – you might be a peasant, with it up to your knee.'

It was an excellent tunic, of dark-green English broadcloth, and had cost him far more than he should have afforded. He had had it made by a tailor, after listening to his mother's carping about stitching day and night for too many men. He had of course erred in that too, exposing her to neighbours' criticism for neglecting her duty as a mother. Guy flushed slightly; he did not care to be censured before the chess-player and Lucifer.

'That shall be amended too. Now meet my marshal, Sir Gerard FitzGilbert.' The stocky man acknowledged him with a curt nod. 'Sir Conan de Guinec you have already encountered.'

'But not socially,' Guy replied. His guess had been wrong; the mercenary was not Welsh but Breton, by his given name. Bristol was near enough to the Welsh Marches for its citizens to cherish a cordial dislike for the Welsh, and he supposed that there was nothing much to choose between one breed of Celt and another.

'And that's my seneschal, Sir James of Malbury,' Lord Reynald concluded. The slim man nodded amiably, and Guy was cheered a little by the first friendly gesture he had received in that hold. No one smiled; the scuttling servants ventured neither jest nor horseplay, and even the knights were tense, warily watching their lord. Guy's misgivings crowded thicker, and he retreated behind the mask he had used for so many years to conceal hurt or fear.

A servant jumped to pull back the curtain at the stairhead for a woman in a plain dark-blue gown, leading a small boy by the hand. She was slight and fair, so unremarkable that Guy did not realize her status until he saw that she was attended by a pretty woman wearing the kerchief of marriage, and behind her two bare-headed girls. Then, as she moved up the hall, he recognized that her dignity needed no trappings. The child, a white-headed creature with Lord Rey-

44

nald's face, looked fragile as spider silk, and clung close to her skirts.

'Ah, my lady!' He looked with aversion at the boy, set a hand on Guy's shoulder and thrust him forward. 'See what I got out of a peasant wench!'

The Slut growled. Guy flushed hot and then chilled; he had never imagined this. The woman glanced at him, brows lifting slightly, and nodded.

'When you were young and vigorous,' she said sedately, and Guy inwardly applauded her. Lord Reynald's look paralysed every tongue, and in the grisly hush Guy became aware of a thin rhythmic sound like a kitten's mewing. The boy's face was tight with strain, his neck-muscles taut cords as his breath creaked in his chest. Pity stabbed Guy. He had known an elderly neighbour who wheezed so whenever the weather turned damp, and this child with the old man's affliction could not be more than eight years old.

His mother drew him closer to her skirts as though to cover him from Lord Reynald's gaze, and looked up to consider Guy with lovely grey-green eyes. Here was one person who did not shrink from the tyrant, and Guy took a step forward and bent his knee in respect. 'God save you, my lady.'

'God be with you, young man.'

'His name's Guy,' Lord Reynald broke in. 'And that puling misery who can't even breathe if the wind blows damp is my only lawful get, Roger. Be off to your bed, whelp! No, my lady Mabel, you don't go to coddle him! Even if you can't bear me a son worth having, like this tall lad here, you'll take your place at table as a wife should.'

Guy felt the blood scorch to his brow. The child uttered a half-choked whimper, turned and scuttled like a scared rabbit, his breathing noisier for his distress. His mother's hands clenched against the blue gown, but when Guy ventured a glance, her face was expressionless. She moved away from her husband to the other side of the hearth, and the woman in the kerchief slipped towards the stair. The two girls arranged themselves behind their mistress, a decorative contrast, one slender and dark, the other buxom and fair. Guy recovered sufficiently to regard them appreciatively.

The tables were ready. The seneschal descended from the dais, exchanged glances with the lady, and made some sort of signal. Moments later a horn bellowed in the bailey, and men and women began to seek their places. Lord Reynald moved towards his high chair, his lady beside him, though for all the attention he paid her she might have been invisible. When almost all places were filled, a stick thumped on the threshold, and Wulfrune stalked in with Lord Reynald's daughter. Guy caught her glance of malice at her father's wife; the two had delayed to show contempt for her rule.

'Your half-sister Rohese,' came the final introduction. 'She'll be your partner at table, and teach you to eat in seemly fashion, instead of putting your feet in the trough.'

Guy flushed again, and Rohese giggled. 'That's a lifetime's task!'

Guy's sense of humour, which had been bludgeoned almost insensible, suddenly revived. 'Do you expect so short a life? Take heart, sister viper. Only the virtuous die young.'

She gaped at him as though no one had ever dared retaliate before. Lord Reynald gave his mirthless bark of laughter, Lucifer chuckled, and Wulfrune jerked up her staff in menace and then thumped it back, scowling. Guy followed to the high table, reflecting that an unpleasant tongue must be part of the Warby heritage; he had one himself at need. He took his stool at the end of the high table and waited. The Slut lay down at his feet and rested her head upon them.

There was no priest present to ask a blessing on their meat. The seneschal spoke a layman's curt grace, and Guy noted that neither Lord Reynald nor his daughter made the sign of the cross. The food was borne in with ceremony; lavish enough but little more elaborate than that served at a prosperous craftsman's table, and the flavourings and sauces were compounded of the same herbs that grew in his mother's garden. Then he realized that the spices, almonds, dried fruits and exotic delicacies he had expected were no longer available. The years of civil war had closed fairs and markets, and

46

driven foreign merchants from the land.

Guy's table-manners had been refined in the monastery but he had not learned the conventions of sharing cup and platter with a lady. His stepmother's married attendant sat at his other side with Sir Gerard, so he concluded they were man and wife; beyond Lord Reynald the other two knights partnered the girls. He watched his neighbours to copy their ways. A page of about ten and a small lame man who seemed to be Lord Reynald's personal servant came round with ewer of water, basin and towels. Since they were served in order of rank, he saw he should hold his hands above the basin while water was poured over his fingers, and a gentleman assisted a lady with the towel. Rohese had long hands with prominent knuckles that had never scoured a pot nor soused in a washtub. It was for her to choose their dish, and she selected pigeons from the spit, glancing at him under her lashes with malicious amusement; no one else had taken them. The servant slipped two on to the trencher between them.

Guy hesitated, and then drew his knife, keen as an oilstone could make it, to split the squab down the breast. The flesh fell from its bones. A surreptitious glance along the table showed him what next to do, and he cut the meat into neat portions so that Rohese could eat without soiling more than her finger-tips.

'Fairly imitated,' she mocked him, 'but you carve like a butcher. A gentleman lays no more than two fingers and a thumb on his meat.'

'I shall learn,' he said, dealing with the second pigeon as she had recommended. 'And if you practised courtesy you might even be mistaken for a gentlewoman.'

Lord Reynald laughed. 'Try again, my girl, but I think you're over-matched.'

Guy marvelled at the man who set his children at each other's throats for his entertainment. His own practice fell far short of courtesy. He was eating a dispiriting mess of boiled fowl in frumenty, new wheat cooked in milk, and left his lady to fend for herself. The page, a snub-nosed boy with a strong likeness to Sir Gerard, filled the cups with wine. It was harsh to the palate after the ale Guy was accustomed to drinking, and he used it with a caution shared by no other man at the board, nor by Rohese.

The dishes were cleared, and Guy presented his gravy-soaked trencher to the Slut, who disposed of it in three gulps and then laid her muzzle back upon his foot. Ewer and basin came round again, and then the second course. This time Rohese chose chopped meat so highly seasoned that he could not be sure what beast provided it, in a coffin of savoury pastry. She ate more of it than he did; she must have the digestion of a winter wolf to fill herself so with rich meats at the day's end and sleep untroubled. Sweetmeats and fruit finished the meal. Guy took one little honey-cake knobbed with nuts, and then contented himself with an apple, but Rohese gobbled one sticky delight after another.

'Only peasants fancy raw fruit,' she jibed as he bit into his apple.

'And guzzling wenches end their lives as toothless lard-bladders.'

She jerked back the hand that reached to the dish. 'You – you *dare*?' she spat. 'Remember who I am!'

'My lord's bastard, as I am. You shall have as much courtesy as you give.'

'My lord!' she appealed to their sire.

'The brew's of your own stirring, and he's the son and the elder,' he denied her. The blow struck the colour from her pretty face, before hate and fury transfigured it. Lord Reynald turned to his lady.

'Wife, tomorrow you'll see to new clothes for this son of mine. Set all your wenches stitching, and no country weave, but scarlet or purple to match his standing.'

Guy's tongue knotted so that no word would come. The lady's lips curved faintly as she looked on him, and she answered indifferently, 'I am at your command, my lord, in all things.' She reached to the dish for an apple and gave it all her attention.

Hands were washed again, the dishes carried out, the cloth

removed. Lord Reynald called to the page for more wine, and sat glooming into his cup. There was no entertainment, not even a recorder or viol such as any craftsman's household, or for that matter a peasant's, could muster to supply music at the day's end. With a sweep of skirts Lady Mabel rose from her chair, her move bringing her attendants to their feet. Guy eyed them appreciatively. Though no longer young, the marshal's wife was sweet-faced and graceful, and the girls were comely. The fair one glanced at him sidelong from her eye-corners, the dark one lowered her lashes. He smiled at both.

'Which d'you fancy?' demanded Lord Reynald.

He started. 'My lord?'

'Which will you have for a bed-mate?'

Taken aback, he stammered like a fool. 'M-my lord, I had – had no such –'

'Don't pretend any finicky scruples. They're both whores. Gertrude –' he jerked his head at the fair girl – 'or Agnes. Which?'

Gertrude smiled expectantly. Agnes stiffened and scowled. But Guy, big and blond himself, had always cherished a fancy for little dark girls, and his look betrayed him. Lord Reynald grinned. 'Agnes, I see. She's yours.'

Agnes had recoiled, and Guy, recovering his composure, said firmly, 'Only if she be willing.'

'Willing? What's a whore to pick and choose? She'll reckon herself favoured if my son condescends to bed her. If she doesn't please you, thrash her.'

'But, my lord –'

'Enough!' His hand slapped the table so that the cups jumped, and the Slut heaved up her forequarters, ears pricked and muzzle wrinkling. Guy laid a reassuring hand on her head and subsided, his face afire, conscious of the girl's resentment, Lady Mabel's contempt and the company's amusement. He was glad when Agnes's gown vanished behind the door curtain. Rohese, who had not withdrawn with the other women, giggled beside him. Wulfrune came to her, glee in her face.

'What, our cockerel's a capon for all his bold crowing?'

'He's a virgin, Grandmother. A timid virgin who has never dared venture – '

'No more a virgin than you are!' Guy blazed.

She blanched with fury. He had made no error; she was unchaste as any other wench in this hold, and she its lord's daughter and unwed. The Slut was on her feet at the angry voices, her lips wrinkling from her teeth and a growl rasping in her throat. Rohese shrank back. Lord Reynald was starting up, and she scuttled for the door, pausing with her hand on the curtain for the last word. 'Agnes will instruct you, novice!'

Wooden-faced, the page refilled Guy's cup. The women had all retired, and the men were watching him as though he were a fool performing for their entertainment. He took a deep gulp of the wine. Though it set his teeth on edge, it had more authority than any but the most potent ale, and by the time he reached the bottom of the cup his resentment had dissolved into a comfortable haze. He retained sense enough to shake his head as the boy approached again, and when the company rose he was no more than mildly cheerful.

Lord Reynald thrust reality upon him. 'Tomorrow you'll start your schooling in knightly exercises.' Guy kindled to the thought, his face lighting, and his sire grinned. 'Sir Conan will teach you.'

'That's your marshal's duty!' Lucifer expostulated, and indeed Sir Gerard's face of protest matched his and Guy's.

'Will you contest who is the better man-at-arms, or do my bidding as I hired you?'

Marshal and mercenary measured each other and then Lucifer shrugged. 'God's Head, it's a harder penance than any priest would set for my sins,' he declared, and stalked out.

The company dispersed. Guy, left standing angry and bewildered among servants taking down tables and stacking benches, found Oswin at his elbow to lead him to a chamber recessed in the wall's thickness, with a heavy leather curtain across its arched doorway to provide a semblance of privacy. There was just space for a chest, a rod above it for hanging clothes, and a bed. The window-slit was shuttered against the rainy night, but Oswin darted out and returned with a candle, which he set on a pricket by the door. The walls were plastered and whitewashed, reflecting its light, and Guy looked about him with pleasure and never thought to wonder who had been dispossessed to make room for him.

The Slut, never permitted within doors in the Bristol house, sniffed the room over and then dropped on the wolfskin by the bed, her tail thumping. Guy began to undress, and Oswin came forward to help. As he hauled his tunic over his head and the candle flared, Guy surprised such a look of misery and hatred on the man's face that he checked, his arms still inside the garment. 'What's amiss? If you dislike serving me, go back to the stables.'

Oswin flinched back. 'No, no!' He caught his breath and went on desperately. 'Me lord's bid me serve you! In God's Name, don't you say naught to me lord, please, Master Guy, or he'll ha' the hide off o' me!'

Guy frowned at him. The fellow reached to take his tunic, ingratiating as a whipped cur, and he relinquished it absently. There was more honour and greater ease in serving the lord's son than in grooming his horses, and for the life of him he could not see what cause the man had for resentment when they had barely met. This household was a tangle of enmities. He would unravel them in time.

He submitted to being assisted out of his clothes. Gentlefolk, with ample bedcovers, got within them naked. He dismissed Oswin, glad to see him go, and knelt to say his prayers. In this hold he would have great need of Heaven's protection. He patted the Slut for good night, blew out the candle and slid between the sheets. Since leaving the cradle he had slept on a straw pallet. This was a real bed, with a feather mattress over the straw base, linen sheets and pillow-covers, woollen blankets and an embroidered coverlid. He sank into its embrace, more comfortable and more uneasy than he had ever lain in his life.

The hall settled to quiet beyond his doorway, lights extinguished and the fire covered with ashes so that only a dull glow crept round the edges of the curtain. The servants had ceased bustling about. The Slut stood up, poking her cold nose at him for reassurance, and he fondled her ears and muzzle. She turned round and round on the wolfskin and at last curled up. Guy thought of the morning and Sir Conan, and his mind jumped to understanding. Whatever malice had prompted Lord Reynald to appoint Lucifer as his teacher, reason was there too. Each would strive his uttermost, to be the sooner quit of the association.

Guy grinned wryly and rolled on to his side. He was just sliding into sleep when the curtain rings rattled faintly on the rod, and the Slut was up, growling challenge. He lifted on his elbow.

'Who is it?'

'Call off your dog!' a girl's voice said breathlessly, and he reached out to quiet the Slut. Someone slipped round the curtain, and a flicker of firelight touched dark hair floating over the folds of a heavy cloak.

'Agnes?'

'Who else did you expect?'

She was at the bedside, the Slut backing from her with a low growl. The cloak's weight fell across Guy's feet, the bed-covers lifted, and a cool smooth body joined his. Serving-wenches and an occasionally-afforded harlot had shown him what delight a man could take in a woman, but they were clumsy fumblings beside those he learned in Agnes's arms. He did not wonder who had taught her until he woke in the dawning and found her gone.

Chapter 5

Lucifer lowered the blunt practice sword and wiped his brow, surveying his pupil. 'Whoever taught you sword-play made a passable job of it,' he conceded, 'considering the stuff he had to work on.'

Guy's lop-sided smile was tight with resentment, but he chose to take his words as commendation. He was woefully out of practice, Gamel having died shrieking at unseen horrors two winters ago, and his shoulders and chest must be bruised purple even through the padded leather tunic he wore for protection.

'We'll see now how you shape on a horse, and since Lord Reynald is lending his own destrier, use him carefully.' Lord Reynald had been constrained to that generosity because only he owned two destriers. Naturally he provided the worse, an elderly bay who looked to have scarcely a charge left in him. 'God's Bones, you don't climb him like a tree,' Lucifer jibed, and as Guy started to swing his right leg over, he poked the stallion with his sword so that he snorted and pranced sideways. Guy half-sprawled over the saddle, the pommel driving into his belly, righted himself and settled firmly, held by the high pommel and cantle.

'Legs well forward, toes down, and your rump hard against the cantle. Off and try again. You must be able to mount a plunging horse during any alarm, by day or night. Again. You're still climbing him. Up with you as soon as your toe's in the stirrup. Saint Gildas, you ride like a faggot of sticks on a woodcutter's donkey! Try again.'

Guy mounted over and over, spurred by the jibes and instructions Sir Conan kept up, under the critical gaze of troopers, grooms and urchins, until the old destrier had had enough and plunged in protest. He tightened the reins, and the stallion squealed and reared as the ferocious curb bit savaged his mouth. Perspiring, Guy held him with thighs and knees until he ceased bucking and stood, stamping and tossing his head.

A soldier handed up a shield, and told him how to sling it over his shoulder by the carrying strap or guige and put his left forearm through the straps. He had to hold the reins breast-high to keep the long shield up to cover his face and chest.

'Let them hang loose. If you jerk on that bit he'll rear and maybe fall on you. You ride with your legs, and stand in your stirrups to fight. Draw your sword and try a swing or two. Walk him forward. Keep your shield up. Legs forward and weight on your stirrups. No more than a touch on the reins; turn him with your legs. And back again.'

Sweating and determined, Guy walked the old destrier up and down the bailey, trying to obey the orders that accompanied him. For a craftsman, he rode well enough; as an aspirant to knighthood, very ill. A gently-born boy began his training at seven years, and was schooled daily in horsemanship and arms.

Lucifer halted the lesson when the bay was tired, and the grooms led him away to be rubbed down. Guy eased his legs, strained by the unfamiliar seat, and Sir Conan called for his own charger and demonstrated all that Guy had tried to learn with a careless grace he knew he could never master. He came to it too late. Then one of the grooms brought out a fresh horse wearing the shabby saddle allotted to his use, and Lucifer pulled up beside him.

'We'll try you with the lance now. Fetch one, Alan. See, you grip it under your right arm, hard to your side, and it slants across your horse's neck to the left. Keep the point up; you aim for the shield. The helmet's for experts, not cow-fisted smiths. In the tourney you pass your man on the near side, lance to lance, so the horse must lead with his right. You have it? Face me and show. Higher – remember I'll have my shield up. Yes. We'll let you try at the quintain.'

Covert grins appeared and were banished from the faces

54

of troopers and grooms. They drifted towards the quintain, set to one side of the stable dunghill moistly shining in the sun. It was an upright post, and pivoted on top of it was a horizontal bar, a shield depending from one arm and a bag of sand from the other. Guy's own mouth twitched. He had often watched young knights tilting in the fields outside Bristol, and he knew the trick of the quintain. It was designed to overcome a man's instinctive checking before an impact; unless he kept up his impetus after striking the shield the sandbag, whirling round, would beat him from his saddle to squelch into the dunghill. All waited eagerly to see Lord Reynald's son meet that disaster.

Guy set his teeth, and without waiting for Sir Conan to utter a word of instruction clamped the lance under his arm and jabbed spurs into his stallion's flanks. Turf flew as he thundered across the sodden grass, the shield leaped to his lance-point and slammed against it a hand's breadth off centre. He flinched involuntarily at the impact, but kept the reins slack and his legs tight, and was past the dunghill when the sandbag hurtled round. He reined in and cantered back, surveying disappointed faces, his own blank.

Over the spectators' heads he saw Lord Reynald descend the keep steps and advance across the grass, shaking out the lash of his riding-whip. A man squalled as it cracked across his shoulders. 'Idling wastrels!' he snarled, slashing indiscriminately, and they scattered like panicked fowls. One urchin slipped in the wet mud and sprawled headlong. The lash caught him twice before he could scramble shrieking out of reach. Guy frowned.

Only Sir Conan's men stood fast, stiffened to attention. Guy, prompted by a memory of some knightly encounter, dipped his lance-point in salute and brought it upright. Lord Reynald, coiling his whip, nodded acknowledgement.

'He knows enough to charge full-tilt at least,' he observed, and Guy wondered how long he had been watching.

'It seems there's more to him than bullock-beef,' Sir Conan conceded.

'How does he shape?'

'His sword-play won't discredit you, but he rides like a ploughman.'

'We'll work on that. You'll ride out after dinner each day with Sir Conan, boy.'

'My lord, I'll oversee his exercises here, as a favour to you, but I've my own troop to drill and lead abroad.'

Lord Reynald's hands tightened on the whip. 'You refuse?'

'My lord, I'm a mercenary captain, not a nursemaid to take your whelp on a leading-rein.'

Guy looked at him, his resentment qualified by respect. 'And I'm no whelp to need a nursemaid.'

Lord Reynald's grim smile twisted his mouth. 'No? Come with me, boy.' He led back to the keep, and the Slut heaved up from her station by the steps as they passed and padded after.

Next to the guardroom was the armoury, with racked spears, hauberks on rods and helmets on posts, sheaves of arrows and chests for more valuable weapons. Lord Reynald flung one lid back.

'It's a father's right to arm his son,' he said, echoing Kenric, and like Kenric he laid a sheathed sword in Guy's hands.

Already Guy had learned enough of him to make no mention of another man's gift. 'My lord,' he said formally, summoning what enthusiasm he might to his voice and face, 'I thank you, and trust to make good use of it in your service.' He drew the blade and held it to the light so that it shimmered all its length; a blade of the kind turned out by every competent swordsmith throughout England. It did not leap to life of its own like the Danish sword that had perhaps known the days of King Alfred. He swung and thrust to feel its balance, and Lord Reynald nodded.

'Yes, you've used a sword before. Now we'll see if there's a hauberk to cover your blacksmith's carcase.'

Only one was large enough to fit, and it might have been left over from the Conqueror's time, of age-blackened leather disintegrating at the edges, with sleeves that only reached his elbows, sewn over with iron rings. Guy drew breath carefully

56

and shifted his shoulders against the weight, feeling its seams creak protest.

'It will have to serve, you overgrown hulk,' Lord Reynald told him, as though his size were blameworthy.

Guy wrestled out of it unassisted, and laid it across a chest. 'If your armourer has the tools I can make one.'

'*Make* one? Have you no shame? Aren't you disgrace enough, a son who's worked with his hands for pay, without your proposing to do it now you're training for knighthood? You dishonour *me*, your father!'

Guy stood fast under the tirade, a frown gathering his brows. 'As you will, my lord,' he said.

'That's your peasant dam in you that I honoured with noble seed! Remember only that I got you, and don't shame me again!'

He stormed out. Guy stood a moment, listening to his footsteps crossing the guardroom and diminishing down the stair, and then put away the hauberk, took the sheathed sword under his arm and trod up to lay it in his own chamber off the hall. Knightly honour to his thinking had oddities. It would be disgrace to employ the skill of his own hands to provide good mail, yet he knew that if he had proposed to ride forth and waylay some traveller on the highway for it, that would be applauded as a very proper project for a young man of spirit. The great bitch, sensing his disquiet, nudged his thigh; he fondled her head absently, swinging the sword in his other hand. Then he hung it by the belt from the perch, and checked that the Danish blade was safe. He must hide it before Lord Reynald learned that he had it. The chest had no lock to it, and he had enemies enough already who might think it profitable to pry and make mischief.

Two sucking-pigs and an array of poultry were roasting before the hall fire. A grey-muzzled hound stretched beside its warmth lifted his head and gently thumped his tail. Guy stooped to pat him and fondle his ears, and the Slut pushed her nose between them for the caress she reckoned her exclusive right. He straightened and idly watched the scullion in charge halt the spit to baste the meat, dipping up the fat from the dripping-trough with an iron ladle. He glanced nervously over his shoulder at Guy, jerked a bow and jumped back to the handle. Guy nodded acknowledgement, noting that every servant he encountered seemed to expect a boot in his backside for greeting, and estimated that the roasts had the better part of an hour to go yet.

'I trust your pork will taste as good as it smells,' he said, and started down to the bailey.

He strolled the length of it, curious to learn all he could. He peered into dim stables, but they were empty; the horses would be out at grass as long as it would serve them, for not even a lord could be prodigal with hay. The hawks were out in the sun, leashed to their perches, and the falconer was moving about inside the mews. The dog-boy plodded to the kennels with a couple of buckets of offal from the kitchens, and the hounds' clamour followed Guy as he moved on, past forage-sheds, a barn where workers were threshing corn, lean-to huts under the wall where married servants made their homes, and a carpenter's workshop echoing to active hammers. He checked outside the open-fronted forge. A hairy lout who looked as though he bedded down in his charcoal-bin was idly scraping at a rusty hinge-strap with a file.

No sensible person intruded on a kitchen so near a meal; it was a confusion of glare and scurry. Bakehouse, brewhouse, dairy and laundry, close under the keep, were deserted. Behind them a quickthorn hedge closed off a space of grass, trees and garden-beds. Guy moved towards a wicket-gate, and as he laid hand on it a child's voice squeaked distressfully.

'Please, Philip, give it back! Oh don't!'

'There it goes!' exulted a boy's voice. A small white ball flew up beyond the hedge. High overhead it opened, turning into a scrap of cloth that caught on a tree's topmost twigs, and loosing a stone that clattered through the branches. The child wailed protest.

'Philip, get it back, *please*! I'll be whipped —'

'You got *me* whipped,' the boy answered with satisfaction.

'You know I never meant to! Roger –'

'He daren't try. He knows what I'd do to him if he did, don't you, wheezy?'

'When I'm lord – of Warby,' Roger jerked out with venom, 'I'll know – what to do – with you!'

'God's Death, d'you reckon when I'm a man I'll ever serve a misery whose chest plays a tune whenever it drizzles?'

'Sit,' said Guy to the Slut, and opened the gate.

The three children did not notice his advance over the grass behind them. Last night's page menaced with hands on hips and legs straddled; Warby's heir stood whey-faced, breathing with effort, and a girl younger than either stared up at the bit of cloth fluttering high in a pear-tree, tears brimming. They spilled down her cheeks, and she gulped a sob.

'It wasn't my fault! Please, Philip, get it back, or I'll be whipped!'

'You got me whipped,' he repeated, and she began to cry.

'For what?' Guy asked, and they jerked about, gaping like unfed nestlings. 'For what?' he repeated peremptorily, as none seemed inclined to answer, and looked to his half-brother, who gulped and obeyed, stammering a little.

'Philip w-went ferreting with the r-rat-catcher, when his father t-told him not to, and – and Sir Gerard asked Matilda where he was.'

'I didn't know he had forbidden him!' Matilda protested.

Guy regarded Philip with lifted brows, and the urchin kicked at the grass and nodded sulkily. 'Then it was for disobedience you were whipped, and rightly. Who's to blame but yourself?'

'If she hadn't told –'

'So you try to hurt a little maid? What knightly conduct is that, you nasty whelp?'

'What do you know of knightly conduct?' he flared. 'You're nothing but a craftsman, and my father says it's an insult to true knights –'

He checked, and the colour drained from his face. For a long moment they stared with breath suspended; even the little girl understood. Guy contemplated him, stubborn and arrogant and stupid, the type of a true knight indeed, a

59

mocking thought insisted.

'We will repeat that neither to Lord Reynald nor to Sir Gerard, or it would be matter for more than whipping a foolish brat,' he said flatly, and Roger and Matilda nodded scared agreement as he met their eyes in turn. 'Go, and learn to guard your own tongue.'

He ran head-down, and they heard him stifle a sob as he clashed through the gate.

The other children gazed up at him with anxious hope, and Matilda put out a hand to catch at his tunic. 'Oh please –'

He gazed at the fluttering rag. He was far too heavy to entrust his limbs to the pear-tree's, but a gardener had left a rake leaning against the keep wall. With its handle he reached down the scrap of linen, smiling at the first stitches lurching across its blood-spotted breadth. Matilda squeaked with relief to find the needle still dangling, and thrust it securely into the cloth. He nodded; in his mother's household also a beating had been mandatory for any daughter who lost so precious a possession.

'Oh thank you, thank you!' She dipped him an unsteady curtsey, bobbed up and flung her arms about his middle, jabbing the needle into his short ribs. 'You are so kind –'

He knew what was required of him, and stooped for a moist kiss, his heart reaching out to this plain little maid with her smudged face and brown hair tangled over her shoulders. Roger, more wary, was still withholding judgement.

'Run to your mother to have your face washed, demoiselle,' Guy advised.

'My mother died when I was a baby,' she told him. 'Roger's mother washes my face for me, or Philip's. They smack me too, if I'm very dirty.' She grinned up. Her front teeth had fallen and their replacements were but half-grown, making her smile the more endearing. 'Am I?'

'Not smacking-dirty,' Roger assured her, a sudden smile transfiguring his face. They trotted hand in hand after Guy to the gate. The Slut heaved up and nudged her master's thigh, her eyes reproaching him for having deserted her.

Roger and Matilda stared awe-stricken, but put out their hands when bidden. The Slut sniffed at each grimy fist and wiped a warm tongue across it, and then pushed under Guy's hand again for his approval. She was entirely safe with children, but not enthusiastic.

'She knows us now? She's our friend?' Matilda asked.

'She knows her friends,' Guy agreed, fondling the bitch's head as she pressed against him, but none the less they preferred to walk on his other side until they reached the keep steps and ran ahead.

Lord Reynald stood on the dais amid the bustle of setting up the tables for dinner, and summoned Guy with a peremptory jerk of his head. His scowl, and the smiles of Wulfrune and Rohese behind him, were warning of trouble. The Slut stiffened, her hackles rising under his hand.

'What's this I'm told?' he demanded without greeting. 'You attended Mass this morning in the village church?'

'What else should I do, my lord?'

'You'll not go again!'

Guy stared at him. This was lunacy. The worst of men paid that respect to the Faith. 'In that, my lord, I must not obey you,' he declared.

'Must not? You dare say that to me?'

'You have no right to command it.' He laid his hand on the Slut's head as she bristled and her lips curled from her teeth.

'By the Horns, no son of mine shall kneel to a crucified felon!'

Guy crossed himself, and had to swallow twice before his voice would answer that blasphemy. 'My lord, I kneel to my Saviour – and yours.'

'Have you forgotten what you are, and what you were?'

'If the price of knighthood be my immortal soul, I'll not pay it.'

'You're my son. You'll obey me.'

'I am a bastard, and of full age. You have no lawful hold on me. Press this, and you give me no option but to quit your household.'

61

'I'll not allow – '

'Unless you hold me prisoner, I have but to ride out and keep riding.'

'You'll crawl back to Bristol and beg another man to provide for you?'

'I've a craft in my hands will provide for me.'

'If you go, you'll leave your right hand here!'

Shock struck cold to Guy's vitals, and he knew his face had blanched. The threat had been hurled in overmastering fury by a man who could not abide the slightest thwarting of his will, but while his rage boiled he meant it.

'Do that!' grated Wulfrune, grinning satisfaction. 'Lop his hand and cast him forth. He'll do us no good.'

Her intrusion was an error; it broke the tension like a snapped thread, and distracted Lord Reynald. 'What's that you say?'

'Have his hand off and be done with him.'

'He's my son!'

She snorted. 'Ha! What's a son but proof you've a man's parts? Aye, and a proper man 'ud ha' gotten hisself a dozen, sons and to spare.'

His face turned greenish-white. 'By the Horns, you – you forget – '

'Whenever you've gone against my advice you've rued it. It was an unlucky day when you found this whelp, and since you never knowed you'd got him, what loss? He'll bring you worse luck until you're rid o' him.' She thumped her staff once for emphasis, and when he made no answer for strangling wrath, stared round the watchers. All averted their eyes rather than meet hers. Only Guy looked fairly into them, and regretted it; automatically his hand lifted to press the silver talisman over his heart. She thumped her staff again. 'Gran'daughter!' Rohese scurried to her side. She stalked down the long room and out. Serving-men who had stood like carved images came to life and scrambled to set up the furniture.

Lord Reynald stood scowling and breathing hard for a moment, and then turned to Guy. 'How should you under-

stand what you miss, ignorant whelp? And if that bitch of
yours shows her teeth at me again I'll have her knocked on
the head!'

Guy patted the Slut's head, and she subsided, still bristling.
He judged this no time for further defiance, and retreated
to his chamber to change his tunic. He found his heart was
hammering, his shirt sticking to his shoulders. He sat on the
chest, staring out of the window with eyes that saw nothing,
and then thrust to his feet and fairly wrenched himself out
of his old work-tunic. Wulfrune might not be alone in reckoning it an unlucky day when he entered Warby.

The more he saw of Lord Reynald the less Guy liked him,
but he had not yet come to hate him, and until this encounter
he had not feared him. The horn's note urged him to haste,
and he was sitting on his bed winding his cross-garters when
Oswin ducked round the curtain, mumbled some apology for
his lateness and knelt to finish the task. Guy's mouth twitched.
He had a body-servant of sorts to wait on him and do his
bidding, and was lodged and fed as a baron's son. He had
that day engaged in knightly exercises, the first fulfilment of
his ambition, and neither Lucifer's goading nor Lord Reynald's jeers could spoil the satisfaction he had found. Even so,
he had to brace himself to lift the curtain, and hoped that
Oswin did not notice.

Lord Reynald's manner had declined from menace to mere
peevishness. 'That workman's garb again? Wife, what start
have you made on his new clothes?'

'We have looked out what suitable cloths we have, my
lord.'

'You've done nothing? Did I not bid you – '

'I have been engaged all morning practising arms and
horsemanship,' Guy hastened to the lady's defence, seeing the
reasonless rage gather in Lord Reynald's face again, and
fearing for her.

She gave him a faint, composed smile, and he reddened,
realizing that she had not needed his defence. 'Come to the
bower after dinner to choose your stuff and be measured.'

'See to it at once; he's an affront to my sight in that,' Lord

Reynald ordered, and moved abruptly to his high chair, exchanging scowls with Wulfrune as he went. Guy followed, more perturbed by his change of mood than he would have been by resolved wrath.

Unless expressly commanded there by the lady herself, men were forbidden a bower, and Guy looked about the upper room with an interest reciprocated by nearly a score of women. Needles suspended, they appraised him frankly, except for Agnes, whose head bent assiduously over her sewing. Matilda jumped up from beside Sir Gerard's wife and capered to him, thrusting a familiar rag under his nose.

'See, I've done it! I've done it right!' she crowed.

He was inspecting the lame stitches when the marshal's wife retrieved her pupil, dealing her a smart slap and scolding her under her breath for forwardness all the way back to her seat. One did not interfere with another household's discipline, so Guy kept his mouth shut and exchanged grins with Matilda behind the woman's back.

'You've won two partisans today,' said Lady Mabel beside him. 'I've been hearing of a sampler in a pear-tree.'

'What else could I do?'

'There's not another man in this hold, except her father, who'd have lifted a hand. "Let the brat learn young that man is the master," they'd have said, and let justice go hang. You've a softness for children.'

He chuckled. 'The eldest of seven needs to have, my lady, for he serves a long apprenticeship in child-tending.'

She glanced up. 'Then your mother married?'

'A master-armourer, and the best of men.'

'That eased the bitterness of your begetting?'

'In some measure, my lady.' His mouth tightened.

'Yes, there are always oafs to cry "Bastard" – as though you chose that condition.' While they talked she watched the women at work. Late-comers, reproved with a look, caught up their sewing. A little group about Agnes teased her, whispering and giggling as she steadfastly kept her face averted. Guy had not thought her capable of embarrassment, and felt vaguely sorry for her as she blushed. Then Lady

64

Mabel said briskly, 'Time we saw about clothes to match your standing.'

'My – my lady, I – I am ashamed that you were offered such affront – '

'Clothes you must have, and whose duty is it to provide them?' She looked up again, and he knew the jab had been deliberate; for some purpose of her own she was trying him. She led him behind a wooden partition that screened off a corner of the bower, giving a measure of privacy to the lord and his wife. She pulled aside the curtain over the doorway and left it so. Bolts of cloth lay on the great bed. 'Whatever you expected, there's no purple and scarlet here,' she informed him with gentle malice. 'They must be bought with silver, and if my lord had coin to spend on them, the cloth fairs are closed and merchants dare not venture on the roads. We've nothing but country weaves.'

'I'm no peacock,' Guy answered agreeably, aware that he was still being tested, 'and by the Mass, there's too much of me to go decked in scarlet.' He considered the sound coarse woollens of the sort he had worn all his life, dyed with berries and leaves and barks to colours pleasant and mellow but lacking the brilliance of imported dyes. 'This, if it pleases you.' He indicated the purplish-blue of blackberry.

'You'll need another.' She opened a copper-brown end to the daylight from the window. 'Also a winter cloak lined with fur.'

'Fur, my lady?' That was luxury he had not expected.

'Have you forgotten your standing? And we've coney-skins to swaddle half the household.' Whatever the test, he had passed it; she was smiling.

He grinned. 'I put myself into your hands, Lady Mabel.'

'And that green is too good to give a servant. There's an end of crimson, if the moths have spared it, enough to put on a border.'

'And make it acceptable in my lord's sight?'

'Only his own provision can be that.'

'He is generous.'

'Don't delude yourself he has any love for you.'

65

'I don't.'

She nodded grimly, and hesitated as though reluctant to go further yet having more to say to him. She produced a length of cord, and stood for the space of half a dozen breaths drawing an end through her fingers. He watched and waited. She moved closer, and her voice dropped to a murmur. 'I don't believe he *can* love. Wulfrune's doing; whatever he is, she made him. His father died before he was born, his mother in bearing him, and he was given over to that witch with his first breath. He sucked in hate and fear and malice from her breast, until there was no room for aught else in him.'

'He hates her.'

'Of course. It galls him to fury, but he cannot throw off her rule. She has made a witch of him, and they are bound together and to the Devil.'

'Why do you tell me so much?' Guy asked bluntly. These were not fit confidences for his father's son; for all she knew of him he might go tattling to Lord Reynald.

'To win you for my ally,' she murmured with the same alarming candour. 'I'd thought merely to use you, but you're an honest lad with a softness for children.'

'Roger?'

'They are seeking to destroy my son. He's past seven now, too old for the bower.' She came close, signed to him to raise his arms, and passed the string about his chest. As she knotted it to mark the measurement, she went on in that desperate murmur. 'I want to place him in my brother's household, but my lord won't hear of it. He's frail, and fright and carping make his sickness worse. Time's short. Already they work against his faith. A year or two, and they'll make a witch of him.'

Whatever means she used to save her child's soul and body, Guy reckoned her justified. She took the cord across his shoulders, down one arm, from shoulder to waist and waist to calf, knotting her marks in turn. 'I hoped, with an upstanding bastard to fill his thoughts, I might get Roger beyond his reach.'

'I'm your man for that, my lady.'

She looked up, her eyes filling, blinked fiercely and sleeved them. 'Then in Mary's name don't defy him to his face!'

'For my soul I must.'

'Keep a still tongue and go your own way. What use will you be to me dead or maimed?'

'But surely –'

' "Surely" nothing! With Wulfrune to goad him he'd do it in a fit of rage, and if he wished it undone a moment after, what use? Remember she rules him and hates you, and remember too that he has no love for you, only pride.'

Guy grinned wryly. 'He's shown none.'

'Not in you, in himself, that he's proved he can beget a worthy son!'

He was beginning to understand. 'Then Wulfrune spoke the truth?'

'It's common knowledge,' she said, half-defensively. 'I'm betraying no secret of our marriage-bed. Wulfrune taunts him with it in open hall. He can only perform the man's part when spurred by strong excitement. He finds that in cruelty.'

Guy nodded, recognizing his unease in his sire's company as normal humanity's shrinking from the monstrous.

'Moreover there's small virtue in his seed, since only thrice in his lifetime that we know of has he quickened a woman.'

'I thought that witchcraft offered remedies for such a state?'

'I don't doubt he's tried them all. Too many of Wulfrune's brews would unman any.' She moved to the bales of cloth on the bed. 'Yes, and disorder his belly so that it's always at war with his meat. Have you not noticed?' She began to unroll the blackberry-blue stuff. 'Mary Mother, you'll have paid a high price for knighthood if you win to it here!'

'I've begun to think so too.'

'It's your right –'

The rushes scuffled softly in the doorway, and Rohese's head appeared round the curtain. She seemed disappointed to see Guy near the partition, Lady Mabel spreading and folding the cloth with the string to guide her. She glanced up. 'What is it?'

Rohese stood just before the curtain. Her very attitude,

hands on hips and feet straddled, betrayed her origin; she looked like any peasant harridan initiating a brawl. 'Someone with my father's welfare at heart should see what you're about, alone with a young man in your bedchamber.'

'You see what I'm about. Out!'

'Surely I should stay, to guard your virtue.'

Guy took one long stride that brought him to her, and she jerked back from the wrath and loathing in his face. 'Your mind reeks like a garderobe-pit, sister viper,' he told her, and as she glared at him, 'Yes, and your face begins to grow as foul.'

'When my father learns –'

'He knows already you're a lewd liar, so will you prove you're a fool also? Out, as you were bidden!'

'*You*'ll learn,' she spat, 'to bear yourself courteously –'

'You'll get from me just as much courtesy as you give. What you need is a strong-armed husband to beat some decency into you, but where's the fool who'd take you?'

'I've powers, as you'll know before the day's out –'

'Use them to sweeten your disposition, or you'll die an unwedded hag with nothing else to boast of.'

Her fingers clawed as though she would tear his eyes out, and then she whirled and ran. Lady Mabel was clutching the bedpost in an agony of stifled laughter. He began to grin himself.

'I'm sorry,' he began.

'Don't be. I've heard nothing that gave me such pleasure since my marriage-day.' She wiped her eyes and collected herself. 'You've gone now beyond all warnings. She and Wulfrune will seek to destroy you by witchcraft or any other means. In God's Name guard yourself.' She joined him at the curtain. Needles were suspended, heads close and tongues clacking. At their appearance a dozen pairs of eyes swivelled towards them, and the tongues halted in mid-sentence; then all heads bent over work. Matilda, too young to appreciate the scandal, waved her bit of linen at Guy and grinned.

'I look at Matilda, and wish I had a daughter,' Lady

Mabel observed. 'Then I see Rohese, and thank God I have none.'

Guy made for the stair, ignoring the glances that followed him. Rohese had vanished. He reckoned that the gift of prophecy had been vouchsafed him for her future. As he ran down the spiral there came to his mind unbidden a memory of another man's bastard daughter who would find marriage hard to achieve, the masterful girl who also needed a man to humble her.

The Slut, on guard beside his bed, thumped her tail and bounced from the wolfskin. She pranced up to him, laid something at his feet, and grinned up, lolling half a foot of broad tongue from her jaws. He stooped and picked up a chunk of raw meat.

Alarm clamoured through his brain, and a memory of Rohese's face as she threatened to prove her powers before the day was out. He pushed aside the Slut's muzzle, thankful that he had trained her to take food from no other hand but his. Neither eye nor nose could discern anything amiss with the meat, but it was a piece of fresh beef, good butcher's meat, not the offal fed to dogs. Again he pushed her persistent head aside.

'It's not food you need but exercise,' he admonished her, and picked up his cloak. The old hound sprawled by the hall fire lazily cocked an ear and opened an eye, and Guy tossed him the meat. A snap and a gulp, and it was gone. He lifted his grey muzzle for more, and the Slut pushed between them, bristling resentment. Feeling like Judas, Guy watched him subside and lay his muzzle on his paws, dozing his last days away in the warmth. Nothing happened. Poison might take some time to do its work; it was that or witchcraft. No one threw kitchen meat to another's dog with honest intent. He waited a little while, and then shrugged and ran down to the bailey.

Roger was loitering disconsolately near the stables, a bruise swelling under one eye and dirty smears across his cheeks. Leaving boys to resolve their own differences in rough and tumble was very well in theory, but not when in practice the two were so unequally matched. His half-brother's face lighted at the sight of him, hope glinting through his misery, and he checked, smiling. He had made a promise.

'Why not have your pony saddled,' he suggested on impulse, 'and show me Warby?'

'Truly? Oh yes!'

The bored gate guards saluted carelessly and passed them through, and they trotted down the track to the village. The pony was frisky, and made it plain he did not care for the Slut's company, but Roger handled him easily, better indeed than Guy managed his equally restive stallion. No knight would bestride a common gelding like Dusty, and Guy enforced his will on the brute more by strength than skill, suspecting that he had been allotted the least amenable mount in the stables.

When he could spare attention for anything else but the horse between his thighs they were half-way down the track. A cottage sat alone on the slope a quarter-mile off, more solidly built than most on stone footings, trimly thatched and fresh with whitewash. A dense hedge of quickthorn surrounded the garden, but because of the slope Guy could see a woman at work with a hoe. Peasants huddled close in their villages for neighbourly association, and he wondered who she was that they would not have among them.

'That's Rohese's mother,' Roger confirmed his suspicion. 'She's my father's milk-sister; they were born the same week. She's a witch; she grows poisons and brews spells.' He crossed himself, and Guy imitated him. As though she had sensed their action, the woman straightened herself and turned to watch them, leaning on her hoe. She carried herself with the same arrogance as her mother and her daughter, holding the hoe like a spear. There was no wonder the village excluded her from their fellowship; fornication with a milk-brother the peasants would reckon a kind of incest, and incest, like parricide, blackened Heaven's face against the whole community, bringing blight on crops and murrain on beasts.

70

'My mother blames Wulfrune for making my father what he is.'

'I don't doubt she's right.'

'If I succeed to Warby, and Wulfrune's still living, I'll see she hangs.'

Jolted, Guy stared at the implacable seven-year-old face; this was not a child's resentment, but a judgement more resolute than Lord Reynald's fury. 'It will be not only your right but your duty,' he agreed. 'But that intention is best not uttered aloud.' The track was empty, the waste about them unpeopled; the nearest ears were in the village below, yet he felt unease between his shoulders, and turned in the saddle to see the witch busy again in her garden. 'And why should you not succeed to Warby?'

'Lady Cecily – Philip's mother – thinks I'm too sickly to be reared. I heard her say so.'

'She's wrong,' Guy declared with conviction.

The small boy with the old man's affliction looked searchingly into his face, and began to smile. 'You're sure?'

'You've too much obstinacy to die young. And count me your man when the time comes, brother.'

'Wulfrune says,' Roger remarked dispassionately, 'that the bastard always hates the true-born son and seeks to harm him.'

'That sounds like Wulfrune. Do you believe her?'

'No.'

'You've judgement of your own.'

'I'm glad you've come.' His wary face suddenly smiled. Guy noted also that Roger's breathing was quite normal.

They cantered along the village street. Animosity apparently exempted none of Lord Reynald's breeding; peasants going about their affairs found them within doors, brats and beasts retreated, and the salutes they did receive mocked at courtesy. Roger looked straight before him, acknowledging them with stiff nods, and turned from the track running between the fields to follow another way beside the osier-fringed river. In the meadows alongside sheep were grazing the aftermath in charge of a boy and a dog.

The path dived between thickets of willow, alder and thorn, water roared ahead of them, and they came out into a clear space beside the mill. An ox-cart stood with shafts upraised, the ox grazed on the verge, and a mat-headed serf was arguing with the meal-whitened miller beside the mill-race. Peasants always argued with a miller, suspecting that he took more than his lawful share of the grain as the price for grinding. The mill was owned by the lord, whose forebears had built it, and who also took his share of the profits. Miller and serf suspended their dispute to gape, ducking their heads in surly greeting.

As they passed the building a raucous bleat and a rank stink startled the stallion into plunging; a long-bearded he-goat with majestic horns backed to the end of his tether amid the bushes. A dozen goats were pegged out along the side of the mill-garden, the largest flock Guy had seen. A few folk kept goats; being browsers, they would thrive where a cow would starve, and there was a vague belief that their milk was more healthful for sickly infants, but they were too destructive to be popular. Something about this flock seemed wrong to Guy. Then another waft of rankness brought comprehension; at least half the flock comprised mature he-goats. That was ridiculous; one was enough to quicken a dozen females, and common-sense insisted that male kids should be slaughtered while young and tender enough to be acceptable at table.

The mill-race was still roaring in their ears when the Slut barked once for warning. A boy of about Roger's age leaped whooping into the middle of the track, causing both horses to squeal and shy. He snatched up a stone, and then checked with his arm drawn back to throw, taking in Guy's size and frown and the Slut's menace. She bayed and bounded forward at the threat to her master. He dropped the stone and retreated to cover, lifting a wolf-whelp's face, and then plunged back into the woods.

'That brat needs his backside belting,' Guy commented.

'He's Wulfrune's granddaughter's bastard,' Roger told him. He waited until they were well past the mill and climbing through the woods before he went on, 'The miller's wife is Wulfrune's other daughter.'

'And another witch?'

'With all her family.'

'Roger, will you tell me about Wulfrune?'

'You know she was our father's nurse? She married a man from Trevaine – a smith, he was – and brought him to Warby.' His brow creased as he dredged his brain of facts. 'They were free, not bond. I think there was a son too. She brought the girls with her when she came to suckle our father, but the boy stayed with her husband. Then her husband died, so she never went back to the village.'

'And the son?'

'His kinsmen in Trevaine took him.'

'And Wulfrune was mistress of Warby until Lord Reynald married.'

'She treats my mother horribly, she and Rohese. They daren't do her any real harm, because my uncles have sworn to kill my father when she dies, but you've seen. They've made Warby into a den of monsters.' He spoke vehemently, obviously quoting some adult. 'There's only Sir James who's kind, and Matilda who's too little to understand. And you now. And I don't suppose they'll let me ride with you again, once Wulfrune's got at my father with her lies.'

'We'll enjoy what we have, then,' Guy offered bleak consolation.

After a fashion, they did enjoy the excursion along the woodland paths, where the leaves twirled down and rustled under the horses' hooves, and stags roared challenge through the glades. Once, far off, they heard a wolf howl. The sun was low when they came to the gate and the saluting guards.

Guy had barely swung down and handed over his mount to the groom when Lord Reynald was upon them.

'Where have you been? How dared you take my son beyond my walls without my leave?'

Guy's eyebrows lifted; he did not care to be rated like a truant urchin before the whole household. 'Roger was obliging enough to show me your demesne, my lord.'

'You take my heir out of my reach – you're practising mischief against him!'

Guy held fast to his temper and to the Slut's collar. 'Where's the mischief in my wishing to improve my acquaintance with my brother and future lord?'

'Do you already look to my death, you unnatural whelp?'

'What's more natural than that a son in course of time should succeed his father?'

Lord Reynald's face darkened to a dusky purple, so that Guy wondered whether he would be smitten down by an apoplexy. 'Yes, you've a talent for back-answers,' he grated. 'Take care it doesn't get your throat slit! But a grown man doesn't take pleasure in a brat's prattle, nor a bastard seek the heir's company except to harm him, so you'll not go with Roger beyond the gate.'

'As you command, my lord,' Guy answered, 'though you're wrong on both counts, and I know where you had those lies.'

'It's not true!' Roger burst out. 'You don't want us to be friends – it's all spite because Guy was kind to me and I like him! I'll always like him!' Before his father, astounded as a stoat attacked by a rabbit, could make a move, he burst into tears and fled for the keep, his breath wheezing to be heard above his sobs.

'By the Horns, now I know your mischief! You'll set my heir against me!'

Guy shook his head. 'In that you need no help from me, my lord.'

Almost, gazing into his face convulsed with rage and longing, he could have found pity for Lord Reynald. The only way to win love was to give it, but what use telling that to a man who did not know what love was, and who strove futilely for possession? He waited a moment for an answer, and then bent his head and turned away.

Wulfrune and Rohese stood together on the edge of the throng, and Guy saw the satisfied smirks on their faces change to chagrin as they set eyes on the Slut pacing beside him. Then she uttered a queer whine, and he turned his head to see a scullion stumping down the keep steps, dragging by the

74

legs the body of a grey-muzzled hound. At Guy's gesture he halted.

'Took wi' some kind o' fit, poor old fellow. All on a twitch, he was, and then he stands up howlin' most woeful, like as his guts was gripin', and drops down dead,' he explained, and shaking his head, tramped off towards the refuse-pit that smouldered malodorously beyond the stables. Feeling more than ever like Judas, Guy watched that summary funeral, and wished he had pitched his evidence straight into the fire. He turned on the two who had intended that end for his Slut.

'I only wish I could have fed it to you!'

Alone in his own room, he flung his arms about his dear bitch and buried his face in her rough coat, the weight of their danger pressing on him for the first time. He would scarcely dare let her out of his sight. Proof against poison she might be, but not against the spear in the dark nor the arrow from ambush. She licked his cheek from ear to temple, whining sympathy, and when he lifted his head grinned and nuzzled his breast. He hugged her, and then got to his feet and opened the chest. From his belongings he extracted her guard-collar, which he had made himself of double bull's hide set with two-inch spikes. He saw another bundle under all else. After supper tonight he must take the Danish sword under his cloak and hide it in the bailey. It had lain ninety years under one forge's thatch; it should be at home under another's.

Chapter 6

On this last day of October in the year of Our Lord 1152 it was delight to be abroad. The air was brisk with a hint of night frost, but the sky was clear blue and the sun gilded the trees; russet oaks, golden beeches, green-gold elms and crimson hawthorns. Drifts of leaves rustled in the track, the bracken had turned brown but still arched high on either hand, birds were busy in the berried thickets and squirrels scolded where the acorns clustered. Once a wildcat, crouched in the path with a pheasant's carcase under its claws, hissed and spat, then bounded away with its meal. The Slut barked after its ringed tail, and nosed the blood-spots and drift of feathers left behind.

'Don't try it,' Guy admonished her as she barked again. 'You'd have your nose clawed off at best.'

She grinned up at him and he smiled, but the smile had vanished before his mount had gone twenty yards. He was more bored and lonely and unhappy than he had ever been in all his life, even in the tedious monastery. He was used to working all his daylight hours at a craft that taxed brain and body; now knightly exercises took up perhaps half the forenoon, and aimless wandering about the countryside to practise horsemanship had already palled. The castle knights refused to admit him to their fellowship; he was an artisan unsuitably aspiring to knighthood, and even Sir James would foregather with Lucifer, an excommunicate mercenary, but not with Lord Reynald's bastard. No one could be happy under Lord Reynald's rule, and the strain of living with his moods was wearing out Guy's natural cheerfulness.

This afternoon his riding was not aimless; Lord Reynald had provided an errand. At the crossways where the track between Warby and Collingford met that to Etherby, the nearest town,

Guy halted and looked about him. Then he dismounted, tethered his horse to a sapling, slipped the bit from his mouth so that he could graze comfortably, and picked himself a handful of hazelnuts. There was a fallen tree, its trunk massed with fungi shaped like great ears. He sat down and cracked his nuts with his knife-hilt. The Slut flopped at his feet and dozed. He finished his nuts and waited, listening to the tearing noises his horse made in the grass-tufts. Other sounds returned as birds and beasts forgot he was there and busied themselves again.

A jay screeched. He knew what that meant now. The horse lifted his head, his ears signalling that something approached along the Etherby road, and the Slut sat erect, her muzzle pointing in the same direction. Guy shifted to face the same way, clearing his sword-hilt, but this was the man he was appointed to meet here. He came openly along the path, a shabby brown fellow of middle height, and halted five paces away as Guy stood up, instantly recognizing the robber captain he had last seen cutting his own follower's throat.

'You're Wulfric, Lord Reynald's foster-brother,' he stated, in the English that would naturally be the man's tongue.

'Aye. And you'll be his bastard.' He surveyed Guy up and down, spat aside, and demanded, 'What stayed me lord from coming hisself?'

'More pressing business.'

He grinned. 'All Hallows' Eve. The whole brood on 'em'll have pressing business for this night. I'd just as soon deal wi' a reasonable man, so let's to it.' He perched on the fallen log.

Guy frowned. He had already picked up something of the knight's touchiness about precedence, and this scoundrel was presumptuous. It was the privilege of the superior in rank to be seated first and to initiate their talk. Instinctively his left hand went to his sword-scabbard to thrust the hilt forward. The outlaw grinned again, with such a likeness to Wulfrune that it set the hair bristling on his neck.

'God's Blood, if I wanted to I'd spill the guts out o' your belly afore you'd got your sword half-drawn.'

'My bitch here would have ripped your throat out first.'

77

Guy laid a hand on the Slut's head; she was up and ready, teeth gleaming.

'Nay, I'm here to do business.'

'I have seen you do murder.'

'Gurth? I beat him to it, and I'm in your debt for making it easy.'

'For you to kill from behind.'

'What sort o' fool 'ud I be to do it from in front? He reckoned he'd be captain, and I hadn't risked turning my back on him for a fortnight. What's fretting you? Wasn't he set on knocking your brains out for your tunic?'

Guy conceded that he was not placed in judgement over an outlaw's discipline by sitting on the log at a prudent distance. Wulfric nodded satisfaction. The Slut subsided, keeping an eye on every move he made.

'What's Lord Reynald want this time?'

'Wine.'

'Wi'out paying for it, o' course?'

'That's for you to manage,' Guy answered distastefully.

'For me to get my neck stretched, you mean. Trick won't work again.' He caught Guy's questioning look. 'Lord Reynald rigged me out in good clothes and sent me into Bristol wi' an escort, claiming I was bailiff to Trevaine. Tried four wine-merchants afore I finds one greedy enough to take the chance, so my face'll be remembered there. Nor I won't try Gloucester neither; they'll ha' heard what happened to the fool. Truth is, there isn't no merchant nowhere as'll venture inside a day's ride o' Warby.'

'And that's the word I take back?'

'Tell him the only way he'll get wine is to send a troop wi' a cart, and to Gloucester, not Bristol, which is nearer anyhow and never mind the higher price further up river, and pay for it in silver.'

Guy had not taken long to discover his sire's reluctance to find cash for anything his household required. 'He'll not fancy that.'

'He can swallow it. I'm not showing my nose in Bristol and getting strung up. Had a bellyful o' his errands. All I got out

78

o' last one was the clothes.' He indicated the brown tunic and hose that had indeed been decent attire once. 'Grouching and grumbling acause there isn't no profit on the roads. Who moves on 'em now but great lords wi' escorts no band dare tackle, and soldiers as is worst thieves of all?'

Guy realized for the first time that highway robbery as an occupation was self-destructive. Merchants, even if they survived, did not return to be robbed a second time, and peasants ten times pillaged were left with nothing but existence.

Wulfric, started in his grievances, was enjoying a listener's attention. 'It was him got me outlawed in the first place. My uncle was smith at Trevaine; I was working peaceable wi' him and my cousin when Lord Reynald, God burn him, raided Thorgastone. He got hisself took, and the ransom cleaned out his treasure-chests which is why he won't lay down the price o' his wine, and when folk remembered I was his foster-brother I had to run. As if that was any blame o' mine!'

'Lord Henry wouldn't think that way.'

'Lord Henry don't think no way.' He spat emphatically. 'The way folks tell, it's a fine free life in the woods. Feasting on King's deer and pheasants. More likely hedgehogs and thrushes, and cursed little meat on either. Argh! Give me a craft in my hands and a roof over my head and food in my belly! Always summer the way they talks, not winter wi' rain and snow and pinched guts – many's the time I'd ha' starved but for my kin.'

'Your sisters?'

He spat with even more emphasis. '*Them?* Pair o' bitches wouldn't step out o' their doors to give me a mouldy crust, and me dying on the threshold. Nor would that old besom as bore us. Nay, it's my Trevaine kin helps me.'

'And Lord Reynald protects you for a share in your plunder.'

'Mighty little plunder these days, but how's an outlaw to live but by thieving? No choice o' mine. D'you reckon as I enjoys skulking by a wayside wi' trees dripping down my neck, to stop one traveller in a month?'

'You could try for burgess freedom,' Guy suggested.

'In *Bristol*?'

'Some far town where no one's likely to know you. London, Norwich, York. A year and a day, and you'd have your freedom.'

'I'm no serf!' His head reared up in affronted pride, and the Slut cocked an ear and blinked at him. 'And what'd I do there?'

'You're a smith, you said. There's always work in towns.'

'I've not so many days left me that I'll live 'em among strangers,' he replied, and Guy did a little belated arithmetic. As Rohese's mother was Wulfrune's youngest child, Wulfric must be several years older than Lord Reynald, in his middle forties, an age few peasants achieved. He did not look it; his hair had kept its colour, his body a trim spareness; he had sound teeth and a hide like leather.

'You've not long to go in the woods,' Guy warned him. 'There'll be strong law in England soon.'

'The Angevin lad?'

'He'll be King. Stephen's spent.'

'Now Lord Reynald sets his hopes on a new war between the Angevin and young Eustace.'

Guy shook his head. 'Except for mercenaries and feuding lords, the country's sick of war. Young Henry's a lion like **his** grandfather, and he'll make one mouthful of Eustace.'

Wulfric grinned. 'And another o' Lord Reynald for backing him? God send I sees him brought down if I hangs next day! I tells you, I've had my bellyful. More'n sixteen years a wolf's head – aye, you may well gawp. Most on us dies first winter. Wet lying as does it. Mark me, if you has to live in woods, stay sober and sleep dry. Bedding down drunk in a heap o' wet leaves'll kill you surer than cold iron. Joint fever, chest cough, bloody water – all hard dying. Shelter and fire and dry your clothes, I tells the fools, comes afore full bellies even, and them as listens lives.'

'I'll bear it in mind,' Guy promised gravely.

'I never thought to live like a wolf neither,' growled the outlaw, regarding him sourly. 'God's Blood, here I've sat grouching to you like a nagging woman, and you pretends to be interested?'

'I am. It's to my advantage to learn all I can.'

'One thing you should ha' learned by now, you're better out o' Warby. Let that old witch get at your pottage and you'll die wi' your guts afire, and what's knighthood worth then?'

Guy set his arm about the Slut. 'She's tried poison on my dog, but –'

Wulfric snorted and stood. 'God's Blood, d'you reckon she'll stop at a dog? She poisoned my father.'

'No!' He stared appalled, and the Slut whined sympathy as his arm tightened.

'Aye. When the nurse-brat were weaned, he wants his woman back, comes to castle and pesters her claiming his rights. So back she goes one night and cooks his supper, the belly-pains takes him and he's dead by morning. I was there and seen it. But what's a six-year brat's word worth, and her the young lord's nurse? So you watch your bite and sup.'

'I do,' Guy answered grimly, and got to his feet.

'If you'll heed sense, you mount your horse and don't stop riding till you're back in Bristol at an honest craft again.' He padded across the clearing and vanished. His brown clothes blended with the brown woods and he was gone, leaving Guy with an itching unease between the shoulders as he turned to his horse.

A dozen paces, and he reined in, his face flaming. He had turned eastward for Etherby, with its bridge of stone and the Roman road running arrow-straight south-west for Gloucester and Bristol. He sat his saddle in the sunlight, his hands folded on the pommel, and fought himself. He wanted to go home. His heart failed him as he contemplated existence with his mad sire, the malevolent witches and bickering knights in that unhappy hold. He took up the reins. Then he thought of his mother's sneers, William's rancour, neighbours' talk. He would have to live out the rest of his days knowing his courage unequal to his ambitions.

'God help me,' Guy said aloud, and the Slut, who had

bounded ahead, came trotting back, tongue lolling and ears pricked, an eager whine in her throat. 'I've wanted knighthood all my life, and here's the only chance I'll ever have to win it. I cannot crawl back to making mail for other men to wear, and admit I've not the guts to earn my spurs!' He turned his horse about and urged him into a gallop faster than was prudent on the rough track.

Chapter 7

Guy was near the border of the royal forest when he at last
turned back, temptation left behind him. He would have to
push his mount to be in Warby before sundown, and briefly
considered his knowledge of the district. The shortest way
back ran through Thorgastone, a Trevaine holding, but he
recklessly told himself that he would encounter no worse
opposition than a few peasants through whose ranks a
mounted man could easily burst.

Plough and pasture were empty, men and beasts returned
to the village, where the smoke of supper-fires spiralled up
from roof-vents. An agitated cluster of folk had gathered in
the street about a couple of riders, and he pushed forward
his sword-hilt. As he cantered nearer, the low sun at his back,
one broke away to accost him, a tall girl in a dark-green
riding-dress astride a bay palfrey. In the crowd a woman
was weeping noisily, and he reined in. The girl's eyes widened
as she recognized him.

"Save you!' She nodded peremptorily at the Slut. 'Has
your bitch a nose?'

'A wolf's,' he answered, responding to her urgency that laid
enmity aside. 'What's amiss?'

'A three-year-old child astray.'

He swung down, and the Slut pushed her nose under his
hand, her lips lifting from her teeth as the crowd pressed
closer. 'Some clothing to give her the scent,' he ordered
sharply, and a girl dived into a cottage. She came running
with a small garment and presented it snivelling, tears streaking her dirty face.

'He's venturesome – I swears I hardly turned me back – '

'Gossiping instead o' minding your brother!' cried the
weeping woman, fetching her a clout that knocked her

spinning. 'We've searched gardens and barns and everywhere – Edmund, Edmund!'

Guy proffered the filthy smock to the Slut, who wrinkled her nose at it, as well she might; he could smell it himself. He dropped it and mounted, and she looked up at him for orders, while the woman sobbed and the peasants muttered. 'Stand away, all of you, and give her room,' he commanded, and as they pressed back, eyeing her doubtfully, he led her towards the cottage and gave the word. 'Seek!'

She nosed about, inside the door and then down the garden, trotting between the cabbage-rows, past the humming hives and the pigsty, and through a gap in the spindly hedge. She turned towards the river, and someone groaned; then she veered slantwise for a corner of woodland that came down to the edge of the plough. Clear of distracting trails, she stretched into a wolf's lope, and Guy urged on his tiring horse to keep up. Crossing the freshly-harrowed field he called out and pointed. Plain in the soft earth were the prints of small bare feet.

The Trevaine girl pounded after, and the groom behind her. The peasants were left behind. Under the trees the light was already failing, the level sunbeams unable to penetrate, and this was open woodland, kept clear of undergrowth by foraging villagers and their swine. It was still easy riding if a man kept an eye lifted for low branches. The Slut ran mute, a dozen yards ahead, working out the trace that meandered in and out between the trees.

The girl ranged up beside Guy. 'We must find him before dark!'

He nodded grimly. Wolves, that had subsisted through the summer on mice and voles and rabbits, were now hunting in family parties, the parents teaching that year's half-grown cubs to pull down deer. Big packs only formed in the worst months of a hard winter; the family packs were not yet famished enough to tackle a man, but they were unlikely to disdain a small child.

The light dimmed fast, and dusk rose from the ground to take all colour out of the woods; only the sky was bright between the half-bare branches. The forest thickened, saplings and undergrowth crowding under the trees to cut off light. They had come well over a mile, and surely three-year-old legs could not have carried the most venturesome of brats much further.

The girl raised her voice. 'Edmund! Edmund! Where are you?'

The Slut barked, and they strained to hear above the rustle of their horses' hooves in the drifted leaves, but no sound answered but the clatter of disturbed pigeons and an owl's hoot. Bats twirled in the pale-green sky.

They all called again and again. The woods muffled sound. Darkness closed down on them. They could hardly see the Slut, still threading out the child's wanderings.

'Lady Helvie, you'd best turn back,' said the groom anxiously. 'No place for you to be, after dark wi' Warby by-blow.'

'Holy Saints, what kind of ravisher d'you take me for?' Guy exclaimed.

'A very desperate one,' the girl answered, chuckling.

'I'll consider you after we've found the brat,' he promised, and heard her laugh. He warmed to her; no one laughed in Warby.

'I still says –' the groom persisted, and then checked. 'What was that?'

The Slut shot from sight, and a moment later Guy too heard a distant whimper. Then the bitch bayed triumph, and mingled with her uproar came a healthy wailing.

'God be praised!' Guy cried, and crashed recklessly through bracken and bushes, following the Slut's barking. He found her under a great oak, standing over the screaming child who was trying to beat her off with fists and feet. She backed away with a final bark as he slid from the saddle, rose on her hind legs and set a forepaw on either shoulder, wiping her tongue over his cheek.

'Good girl! Clever lass!' he praised her, clapping her flanks, and as she dropped to four feet he scooped up the child. 'All's well, Edmund. You're safe now. That's my dog who found you – good dog!' The brat wound his arms about Guy's neck and sobbed against his shoulder, and the Slut's tail threshed the bracken. 'See, there's nothing to fear now. Only my good dog.'

The child slackened his clutch a little, lifted his face and snuffled, 'Dog?'

'She found you. We'll take you home to your mother.'

In the dim light he could just see the howl that swallowed up most of the child's face. 'I want my mammy!'

Guy turned to his horse, which snorted and shied. Lady Helvie and her groom had found them, and were sitting their mounts in silence; the darkness concealed their expressions, and no speech could compete with Edmund's lamentations. Guy caught the reins and hauled down the stallion's head, gripped the urchin in his right arm, found his stirrup and swung astride, settling his burden comfortably against his shoulder. He howled lustily for about twenty paces, hiccoughed a little and fell asleep.

'Thank God!' said Guy devoutly.

The girl laughed. 'Shall I take him?' Her voice was unsteady with relief.

'He'll do well enough as he is. Also he's verminous.'

'And his lice have already accepted your hospitality?'

'With enthusiasm.' He squirmed inside his fine linen shirt, he who had once regarded that state as normal. 'Moreover, while I hold him your groom cannot entertain his suspicions.'

'You underrate Sweyn's suspicions.'

'They must make him a very suitable escort for a young demoiselle.'

'That's precisely why my father appointed him.'

'And he'll not be pleased to learn o' this meeting,' growled Sweyn. They were all speaking English. 'What's this knave doing on Trevaine land – spying?'

'Seeking what I may devour, like Satan,' Guy said flippantly, and was rewarded again with the girl's chuckle.

'When my father found out who you were, I thought he'd have an apoplexy.'

'Since my begetting was my misfortune rather than my

fault, why should I hang for it?'

'You've an argument there.'

'The errand was his, and the hauberk.'

'That added to his rancour.'

Guy laughed, the groom growled, and they pushed on faster, trusting to the horses' senses rather than their own, for now full night had come down. Then they heard a distressful crying in the darkness ahead, and Guy shouted through the woods.

'He's safe! We've found him!'

They pushed out from the last thickets into the tamed glades. The mother stumbled to meet them, sobbing and gasping thanks to God and His Mother and all the Saints. Guy hastened to hand down her son. She clutched him to her breast, and he woke squalling.

'Mother Mary bless you, young master! Praise God — Edmund!'

'Mammy —'

A man reached them and put his arms about both. 'Before God, we're mighty thankful, Master Guy,' he declared, and other voices echoed his thanks as folk gathered about them, a score or more of men, with a few women and a skirmish of older children. Guy flushed.

'My good bitch found him,' he disclaimed. 'But tether the imp to a doorpost until he learns sense.'

The crowd parted to let the horses through; behind them the mother was mingling endearments with scolding.

'First she'll kiss his face flat, and then smack his bottom flatter,' said Guy. On his last word came the unmistakeable crack of a palm on bare flesh, and a howl. The girl laughed.

'How did you know?'

'I have a mother. Lady Helvie, since night has overtaken you so far from home, may I escort you there?'

'I thank you, but I'll remain until morning.'

'Here, my lady?'

'I too have a mother, Master Guy, and she lives in Thorgastone. Sweyn, you may return with the horses and come back for me tomorrow.'

'But, Lady Helvie – ' he began to object, dancing his mount sideways to keep Guy in view.

'Since you don't need me, my lady,' Guy forestalled him, 'I'll take my leave. God keep you.'

'God go with you, Master Guy.'

Guy watched them go between the lighted cottages, their horses moving delicately among the ruts and churned hoofprints set like stone after a dry week. 'Now who'd have guessed,' he enquired of the surrounding air, 'that the only woman I've met who could match jests with me would be that great surly wench?' Immediately he amended that epithet; this night she had not been surly. She had asked and accepted his aid as frankly as a man, and she had laughed with him.

Guy turned his mount towards the waste, marvelling at that laughter. He had encountered few who could understand his straight-faced humour, and had never thought to meet a woman who could match it. There was no laughter in Warby. Agnes had proved a perfect bedmate, but outside his chamber shunned his company so plainly that his pleasure in her was rapidly failing. She made it insultingly obvious that she lay with him only because Lord Reynald commanded it and she dared not disobey. He pushed aside the reflection that he was to blame for accepting an unwilling girl. She was no innocent, but an expert between the sheets. He watched until Helvie de Trevaine had vanished behind the furthest houses, and thought that he would probably exercise his horse again in the direction of Thorgastone.

On the track's hard surface he at once noticed an irregularity in his horse's hoofbeats. A shoe was loose. He halted, looked back at the cottages straggling along the street, and picked out the forge, set apart from the others to reduce the danger of sparks near thatch. He dismounted and led the stallion towards its open front.

The cottage door opened smartly, and candlelight outlined a man's square-shouldered bulk. 'What's amiss?'

'A loose shoe.'

'Fire's banked for night.'

'You can clinch it on cold.'

'Light's gone. I'll do no more this day.'

'D'you think I'll lame a good horse for your idleness?' Guy flared, moved purposefully into the blackness and clattered among tools on the bench for hammer and pincers. 'Fetch a candle and I'll see to it myself!'

'I'll hold a candle to light you into Hell, and all Warby with you!' growled the smith, starting forward. The Slut was at once in his path, poised to leap, her teeth bared in menace.

'I gather you're not mad, but at feud with Warby,' Guy commented.

'No whelp o' that devil need look for help in Thorgastone!' the smith declared thickly. 'Raped my wife and killed her mother, burned half village – '

'What had I to do with that?'

'Eh – ?'

'And as this night I've done Thorgastone some service, you can at least hold the candle.'

The smith grunted. 'I'll do it to be rid o' you. Call off your bitch. What kind o' man-killer is she for a Christian?'

'A useful one.' He snapped his fingers, and she backed to his side, her attention steady on the smith.

He spat, and bawled to someone in the house behind him to fetch a candle. A lanky stripling with the first down smudging his jaws came out bearing a rushlight, and held it over the box of oddments while his father scrabbled for nails. He found what he needed, clouted the lad for dripping hot tallow on his fingers, and took up the hammer, as Guy had expected. No self-respecting craftsman permitted any stranger to make free with his tools.

Another shadow interrupted the shaft of light from the open door, and Guy glanced up. White hair caught the candleshine, and straggles of white beard; a tall thin figure stooped over a staff, and put out a hand with the unmistakeable groping of the blind.

'Come you inside and bar the door, son,' he croaked urgently. 'This night honest men should be safe at their firesides.'

89

'Presently,' the smith grunted, feeling round the stallion's near fore hoof for missing nails. Guy held the beast's head and stroked his nose, and he stood quiet, nuzzling Guy's breast. 'Hold that light steady, boy!'

'There's evil abroad,' the blind man muttered. 'The Devil rides this night.' The rushlight jumped, sending shadows spinning, and the smith swore. As the little flame steadied again he drove the nail and clinched it.

'Go in, feyther, or you'll take cold,' he said over his shoulder.

'The graves open and the ghosts pass,' the cracked voice went on. 'Don't ye hear 'em go by? Feet in the dark – voices in the night – '

'Holy Saints guard us from all harm!' muttered the smith, crossing himself, and then whacked home and made fast the second nail faster than Guy had ever seen it done by daylight. The boy retreated, but the man, with the peasant's grip on essentials, stood holding out his hand. Guy groped in his purse and grudgingly passed him half a penny, gross overpayment. He had laboured too many years for a pittance ever to acquire a knight's lavishness with unearned silver. The smith snorted contempt, tried the money with his teeth, and as Guy mounted, hurried to the blind man and set an arm about him to urge him indoors.

Guy clopped back along the deserted street and up the track to the waste. His horse was tired, and the moon not yet risen, so he went slowly, trusting to his mount's sight on the rough way rather than his own, and pulled to a walk when the track failed and he had to pick his path among rocks and bushes. The sky was clear, pricked with stars. The air held sufficient hint of frost for him to pull his old cloak across his chest and wish he had a pair of gloves.

This was the Eve of All Hallows, an unchancy night to be abroad. Fears of ghosts and evil demons had less impact in a town, snug among streets and houses with folk all about, than out here under the high stars that ruled men's destiny. Alone in this waste where every thicket and crooked tree might conceal some presence, Guy muttered an *Ave* and a

Paternoster under his breath, commended himself to the Saints, and was glad of the silver talisman that guarded him from harm.

Owls called back and forth, but Guy knew their voices, and even when one sailed soundlessly before him, its round head and broad wings sharp against the stars, he was not startled. There were other noises about him, furtive squeaks, rustling and scurrying, the death-squeals of small creatures seized by stoat or owl, a distant clash of antlers and a stag's roar, the far-off howl of a wolf. The horse plodded on. The Slut, long past her puppy days of forays after every scent, paced alongside.

He was more than half-way back to Warby when a scarlet glow of fire on his right hand jerked his misgivings alert. He remembered the circle of stones that Helvie de Trevaine had called the Devil's Ring. He reined in, turned half-about in the saddle, and watched the glow strengthen and white smoke tower, reflecting the blaze that produced it. Then he turned his horse towards it, up the slope.

Some force fiercer than curiosity urged him forward, to see for himself. Half-way there he tethered his horse to a hawthorn, remembering how Dusty and the packhorse had panicked as they came near it. The Slut stayed beside him. What little wind there was blew the smoke towards him, sparks dancing in its coils. He threaded cautiously between gorse-patches and thorn-scrub, and voices came to him, first a confused murmur and then sudden clamour. A beast bleated. He reached the thorny barrier which shut off all sight of the circle; only the inner faces of the great stones reflected the firelight. He cast about, vainly seeking the gap that eluded him in the dark, squeezed and wriggled past obstacles, any sound he made smothered by the babble of an excited throng, until he stood behind one of the stones and could peer round it. As he did so the crowd fell silent.

On the altar-stone, his coat reddened by the glare, his horns and eyes reflecting it, stood a he-goat, surely the patriarch of the mill flock. He tossed his head uneasily, ears flicking and eyes rolling, and strained against tethers that held his forehooves to the stone. The assembly, thirty or forty men and women, were shuffling into a half-circle about the fire, facing the altar. The flaring light made demons of them, and Guy crossed himself.

Another goat's head appeared beside the stone, horned and bearded, ears drooping stiffly, taller than any goat should be unless it reared upright on its hind legs. Then Guy pulled his cloak across his mouth and bit into the cloth to stifle a cry, for it sprang up on to the stone and stood with a man's body mincing on cloven hooves, swinging a tufted tail. It thumped the rock with a three-pointed spear, and the crowd stooped in obeisance.

The earth and sky reeled round Guy, and he leaned against the stone, his legs shaking under him, pressed the silver talisman against his hammering heart and muttered prayers under his breath, expecting the night to erupt about him with smoke of brimstone and bear all here down to Hell's fire. The Devil in his proper person walked abroad and made himself known to his worshippers, and God's earth would surely never abide his presence. But nothing happened. The Slut pushed against him, warm and alive. She was real, and so was this. His heart quieted, his wits steadied.

A tall crone stood before the stone, her arms uplifted. Guy had to look twice before he recognized Wulfrune. He had never before seen her without her staff and black kerchief, her white hair straggling over her shoulders. Her harsh voice slashed the silence in a chant of which he could scarcely make out a word, an invocation addressed not to any unseen Deity but to the visible Fiend posturing above her. Guy shuddered, and the Slut pressed to his side, an uneasy growl vibrating through her throat. The voice ceased, and the company bayed a response. The Devil lifted the trident and extended it over Wulfrune's head.

'Great Master, grant my desire!' she screeched.

The Devil put down the trident, which clanged on the stone with a noise of veritable metal, so that Guy started. His skin rose in gooseflesh, and it seemed the breath stilled in his lungs. The goat bleated. The Devil straddled it. A knife glanced in the firelight. A hand on a horn jerked back the beast's head, and he leaned to cut its throat. As the goat collapsed under him in a gush of blood he waved the knife and uttered an exultant laugh, a laugh Guy knew. He stared, paralysed. The bloody-handed thing on the stone was not the Devil from Hell but a mortal man, Lord Reynald of Warby.

Revulsion seized him, and he bent his head against the stone, his eyes screwed shut. His belly heaved with nausea, and only the stone held him on his feet. The Slut growled softly as the reek of blood reached her, and instinct, not reason, put out a hand to hold her. He lifted his head, accepting the fact all his human nature fought to deny. He was spawn of that thing on the altar, outraging God and receiving homage from his worshippers. His wits recognized the disguise. The head was a mask contrived from a goat's horns and skin, the sleek body a close-fitting leather suit, the tail a cow's, the hooves wooden shoes with stilted heels. Loathing filled him, and horror that this had sired him.

Wulfrune and another woman busied themselves over the carcase. Guy could not see what they were about, but he could not turn away his eyes nor push from the supporting stone. Presently they stood back, and the old woman, who seemed a kind of priestess in these rites, intoned some formula while men piled more wood on the fire. As it blazed up, several seized the dead goat and cast it on the pyre. A stench of burning hair and hide drifted across the circle to Guy's nostrils.

A great yell followed the offering, and a pipe began to tweetle a tune. The throng strung out into a line that followed the piper, a long brisk man, round and round the fire. Faster and wilder jerked the music, faster and wilder the dance, while Wulfrune screeched encouragement and the horned man leaped down from his stone and pranced about inside the ring, capering around the fire and prodding laggards with his trident. Clothing was tossed aside, the women's hair shook free about their shining shoulders, naked limbs glanced in and out of the firelight and smoke as the dance whirled on and on. The piper's wind ran out, the tune died in a last wail, and the circle broke. Men and women seized each other as they reeled from the dance, sank to the grass and coupled shamelessly as dogs in daylight.

Use came back to Guy's limbs. Somehow he found himself shambling down the slope, the reek of burning flesh in his nostrils. The Slut led him to the horse; on his own he would never have found him. He hauled himself into the saddle and rode away, the stink following him through the night. Behind him the fire sank to red coals, but he never turned his head to see.

Chapter 8

'By the Horns,' stormed Lord Reynald, 'that insolent rogue would not have defied *me*! I should have gone myself.' He regarded Guy sourly, and the young man bowed and stepped back, his report finished. 'What more? . . . So, you forget to mention that you dared turn aside from my errand to search for a peasant brat?'

There must be a witch in Thorgastone to carry tales, Guy deduced. He answered evenly, 'Your errand had already been accomplished, my lord.'

'Your duty is to me, and you don't leave it for a dozen serf-whelps!'

'I don't leave a child to the wolves.'

'What's one brat, and a Trevaine villein's at that? The parents can get themselves another and enjoy it. You weren't here to come with me, and I'd have given you delight your pale Church cannot conceive.'

'My lord, I will not practice your Devil-worship.'

'You're mine to command.'

'My soul is God's and my own.'

'What does your weak God grant you, compared with ours?'

'Ask rather what the Devil grants that's worth burning forever in Hell-fire.'

'Power, you fool! Power of life and death, so all men fear and obey you! Why do you suppose Trevaine dares not move a spear against me? Why did my lady's father grant me her hand? You may take what you will and none dare refuse you, if you are one of us!' Guy's revulsion must have shown for all the effort he made, for he demanded violently, 'Why do you look at me as though I were a viper?'

'Is power worth all men's loathing?'

95

The blow went home; his eyelids flickered and his mouth twitched before he summoned anger to his aid. 'Are you saying that you loathe me?'

'Do you give me reason for anything else?'

'Is this courtesy to your father? And you refuse me obedience yet.'

'And warn you again, my lord. Press this and I leave you.'

He stared hungrily at Guy, his face working; then he reached out a hand to grip his arm. Guy jerked back, his body flinching from this monster whose loins had begotten him. His eyes, shadowed after a sleepless night, narrowed with contempt. Lord Reynald uttered a wordless protest, turned and stalked away.

In the days that followed it seemed that he had taken heed of Guy's warning, for he made no more demands on his son's conscience. Indeed, he seemed determined to try conciliation, for he spared him his normal rancour and offered gifts to placate him; a better saddle, an ivory-hilted dagger, a silver cloak-clasp enamelled with a green dragon. He organized a hunt. Guy enjoyed the wild riding and the savage excitement of a kill, but detested Edric the huntsman, a distant kinsman of Wulfrune and one of the few men in Warby who would hold his own face to face with his master. Hawking was a failure; Guy had never before handled a falcon.

Martinmas came, and killing-time. The beasts that could not be fed through the winter were butchered, leaving only the plough teams and breeding stock to struggle through the harsh months on inadequate supplies of hay. This one time in the year everyone could gorge on fresh meat and inwards. Salt though was scarce, and by spring much of the meat in the brine casks would be rotten. No pedlar with his packhorse had appeared that autumn to be robbed. Guy heard men grumble, and marvelled that these predators could not realize that thievery in the end deprived the robbers.

Martinmas was also a day of reckonings. Peasants came to pay their dues of produce, and soon after dawn they began entering the bailey with measures of grain, driven beasts, hens and geese tied by the legs and protesting to the skies, and baskets of eggs, fruit and greenstuff. Guy was obliged to abandon his usual knightly exercises, and watched curiously while servants set up a table and a couple of stools near the gate. Sir James appeared, his seneschal's wand in his hand, and behind him a servant carrying an armful of parchment rolls. He looked impatiently about him. The servant piled the rolls on the table. The village reeve accosted Sir James; he heard the man out, and then flung down his wand with a dust-raising thwack across the parchments.

'Hell's fire! Of all days to choose! What's to do now –'

A squealing pig dived under the table, curvetted as he staggered and rammed his legs from under him. Sir James sat up with the pig in his lap nose to nose, mingling curses with its shrieks until a peasant hauled it off him by the hind leg. Guy ran to help him up, and he scowled ungratefully at him and Sir Conan.

'Aye, you may grin,' he said. He was as finicky about his person as a cat, and contemplated the muddy prints of trotters blazoned across his breast with dismay. 'It's no joke. Here's all the reckoning on us, and the priest sends word he's sick abed and can't see to it. Where this side of Heaven or Hell am I to find someone to make sense of his Latin scratchings?'

'You need not go so far,' Guy told him, grinning. 'Just here.' He unrolled the nearest parchment and ran his eye down the columns.

Both knights gaped at him. 'You can read Latin?' Sir James demanded incredulously. 'Yes, and write it?'

'There was once a plan to make a monk of me. It miscarried, but I was near four years in a monastery school.'

'You're a gift from Heaven at this moment,' Sir James declared, surveying the turmoil about him. 'Let's make a start.'

'Pens and ink?'

A raid on the fletcher's goosequills provided pens enough to copy a chronicle, and while Guy trimmed a handful with his dagger someone unearthed an inkhorn with a little sludge in the bottom. They took the stools, the reeve acted as sheepdog to round up the villagers and bring them forward in some

97

sort of order, and Guy struggled to decipher the priest's hand-writing and make sense of his system for Latinizing English names. Men and women crowded to goggle as at some portent, a man who was no cleric and yet could read and write. But Lucifer gazed in a white fury of envy, turned and stalked away.

Lord Reynald, predictably, was not pleased. 'Is it not shame enough to bear with a craftsman for a son, without finding that he's half a clerk as well?'

'I can claim benefit of clergy if I take to crime,' Guy answered, smiling. He had of course received the first tonsure on admission to the monastery school, but quit before he was old enough for even minor orders. He weighted down the top of a curling scroll with the inkhorn, checked that last year's entry corresponded with his own and set it down, cursing the muddy fluid that clogged his pen. The only way to live with his sire's notions was to agree with him and go his own way. The work must be done and no other could do it. By all reports it was unlikely that the priest, old and frail, would ever rise from his bed again.

Guy sent out a couple of urchins for the ingredients and that evening, when the evil-tempered head cook was snoring-drunk, he borrowed a saucepan in the kitchen and boiled up oak-galls, hawthorn-bark and wine to make his own ink. Once he had mastered the primitive method of accounting there was nothing difficult about the rolls, and he was fascinated to learn the organization that fed, clothed and housed nearly four-score souls, and provided also for their horses, dogs and hawks.

The seneschal must receive all dues, in cash and in kind, check them against the rolls, allocate them to the proper persons, and account for all disbursements. They sat for a couple of days in the bailey, wrapped in cloaks against the wind, with their feet in muddy grass and their stools sinking under them. Sir James struggled in halting English to extract what was owed to Lord Reynald from reluctant peasants, Guy interpreted, blew on numbed fingers and scrawled on the parchments, and a servant cut tally-sticks.

Forage, iron and leather for harness involved the marshal, in charge of the garrison and all pertaining to the horses, and the more he had to do with Sir Gerard the less Guy liked him. He made it quite plain that a bastard artisan was unworthy of more notice than a knight's boot in his backside, and that Lord Reynald had insulted his officers by introducing one among them. He was convinced that courtesy was only needful towards his equals and superiors, and an inept administrator because he reckoned finance as beneath his attention.

Though Sir James was responsible for receiving supplies and must account for them, Lady Mabel was in charge of their preservation and stowage. They worked in close association, with the familiar ease of friends, to lay in stocks for another year. Guy helped both. She supervised butchers, cooks and scullions who scoured casks, packed them with meat and brine, and trundled them into the keep. Down in the undercroft, by the glimmer of tallow dips, Guy made jottings with charcoal on a piece of board as she and Sir James reckoned up their stores. Salt, dried and smoked provisions; ripened cheeses, crocks of butter, lard and honey; grain and malt, peas and beans in the huge wooden bins; barrelled ale, verjuice and the last wine, all were noted, and then in the hall he must set his smudges in order and transcribe them to the rolls.

The winter corn was sown, and woodcutting teams set the forest ringing with axe and saw. The piled ox-carts trundled in, and the stacked cords filled the fuel-sheds. The servants' brats had for days been peeling rushes; now the castle reeked with boiling tallow as candle-dipping engaged every cauldron that could be spared. Lord Reynald made peevish complaint at the stink, and went hawking with Sir Gerard. Lucifer had taken out his troop at daybreak to sweep the roads towards Etherby, seeking what he might devour.

Pouring rain brought them all back, shivering and cursing. Guy was sitting at one end of a table with the rolls, pens and ink; Lady Mabel and Sir James sorted through bundles of tallies, and at his elbow Lady Cecily, the marshal's wife, moved counters* at his direction on a piece of cloth painted in chess-board squares. Guy watched her carefully; she had no head for calculation and was easily flustered. He had no more than a tepid liking for her, yet she had all the attributes of an ideal wife. She was pretty, modest and submissive, uncritically devoted to husband and son, and savourless as unsalted bread.

'Seven and nine's sixteen, and five twenty-one. No, it goes on the next row, Lady Cecily. Twenty-one and four – '

'What are you whispering in my wife's ear?' Sir Gerard roared so fiercely that she squeaked and shrank aside, catching at the cloth. The counters bounded abroad. The Slut rose from Guy's side, bristling threat.

'Arithmetic,' Guy answered, gathering up counters.

'Sir Gerard,' said Lady Mabel acidly, 'are you declaring that your wife may not assist with the accounting, for fear a man may speak to her?'

'My Lady – '

'You insult me if you imagine I'd countenance the slightest impropriety. And I'll remind you that you interrupt our work.'

He glared at her, but she had given her attention again to the tallies. Lady Cecily, shaking so that she could hardly speak, whispered pitifully, 'Indeed – indeed – there was nothing – ' She picked up a counter, and dropped it in the rushes. He growled something that might or might not have been an apology and squelched away in his sodden boots, thrusting past Sir Conan who was grinning at his discomfiture. The mercenary strolled to the table, the envy he had shown before glinting from his eyes.

'Contemplating adultery? I'd not credited you with so much enterprise,' he mocked Guy. Lady Cecily retreated as from a leper, and he sighed. 'Sweet friend, how could you set up a rival, when you know you have my heart's devotion?'

Tears flooded down her cheeks, and she ran for the stairs.

* The Exchequer derives its name from this device. Before the introduction of Arabic numerals such an aid to calculation was essential.

They heard her stumbling up to the bower, sobbing at every step. Lady Mabel dropped her tally-sticks.

'Sir Conan, pestering an honest wife to provoke her husband into challenging you is a vileness beyond toleration. No one expects honour or decency from a mercenary, but remember at least that you were gently-born.'

It was Lucifer's turn to blanch and then redden. 'You take too much – '

'Your morals do not concern me, but Lady Cecily is under my protection. If you're at odds with Sir Gerard, find another pretext for combat.'

Routed, he stalked after the marshal. Guy looked at his stepmother with respect. 'I'm weary of that routier's insolence,' she stated. 'Cecily can scarcely set foot outside the bower for fear of him. She's too soft to deal with such a man. There are strumpets enough in this hold, but he'll not stoop to *them*.'

Out of delicacy she did not add, what every member of the household knew, that Sir Conan, too fastidious to fornicate with public wenches, took his pleasure in rape. When he led out his troops twice or thrice a week on a foray along the roads, any comely woman they encountered was a prey to be enjoyed, first by their captain and then by all the soldiers in turn.

'We'll hope Sir Gerard kills him,' said Sir James, quite seriously. 'They'll come to it yet.'

'God grant it,' she answered piously, and turned again to the tallies. 'And now we have no one to place the counters.' It was not a difficult task but it did require another pair of hands; Guy could not deal with the rolls and the checked cloth together. At his suggestion they summoned Roger. Gratified, he stood on a stool and was soon more competent at addition than Lady Cecily. Lord Reynald complained that they made his heir into a clerk, and then added that he was fit for nothing else. But two more days saw the work accomplished, and the weather cleared so that Guy could resume his training.

He could now hold his own at swordplay with Sir Conan

on foot; the mercenary had the advantage of experience, but Guy was younger, stronger and faster. He could hit the quintain shield in the centre every time, and tilting at the ring suspended from a bar he carried it away two out of three times. His horsemanship was no longer contemptible, and he could vault fully-armed into his saddle without touching the stirrup. Now Lucifer decreed that they should run a course so that he might experience a real encounter, and spectators gathered. They faced each other across the bailey, shields up and lances couched, and spurred headlong.

Clods flew from the sodden turf as the destriers pounded across it. Lucifer's shield hid all but the top of his helmet and his right eye and cheek. Guy peered round his own shield-edge, his heart thudding at his breast-bone, levelled his lance and gripped fast. A tremendous impact shocked both arms at once. The cantle slammed at the base of his spine, his horse skidded, and the sky cartwheeled over him. He crashed on the flat of his back, the wind jarred out of him, and lay gasping with the yells of Lucifer's mercenaries ringing in his ears. He was still clutching the splintered stump of his lance. A couple of grooms ran to hoist him up, and the knights strolled across.

'You broke your lance fairly,' Sir James told him kindly.

'You still ride like a churl,' declared Lord Reynald. The marshal spat, shook his head and walked away as though no words would serve him. The show was over; destriers were too valuable to be risked wantonly.

Guy grinned ruefully at the mud plastering his mail, and picked a wisp of grass from it. 'I'll never make a tourney champion,' he admitted.

'You'll never need to. You stupid whelp, have you no notion how lucky you are?' The despairing envy in Lord Reynald's face astounded Guy. 'A knight who can read and write Latin is the rarest beast in Christendom! Kings and lords will compete for your services. God's Blood, d'you think if I knew one letter from another I'd be a damned mercenary?'

'I thought nothing of it.'

'As soon as you're knighted,' advised Lucifer with an

earnestness entirely at variance with his usual cynical detach-
ment, 'get out of this devil's den and take service with some
rising lord – the Angevin lad if you believe he'll be King.
You'll end seneschal of a castle, even sheriff of some county
and given an heiress in marriage, if you've talent for administration and common diligence. Tourney champion – most
likely you'll never see a battle.'

He swung about, and Guy stared after his back in double
astonishment, first that within Lucifer were to be found the
remnants of a human being, and secondly that a man whose
livelihood was warfare should speak with such savage yearning
of a career devoted to dull stewardship. Guy had dreamed,
like every aspirant to knighthood, of distinguishing himself in
battle and rising in the world by his prowess. It was difficult
to swallow that the learning he had acquired in the cloister
was a likelier aid to advancement.

The next day the manor-court was held. The priest was still
sick. Guy had escorted Lady Mabel on a visit to his side, and
found him feverish and coughing, but a little improved.
Today he must sit by Lord Reynald's high chair to keep the
rolls. The first matters were tedious enough; allocation of
strips in the barley field before the spring sowing; the making-
up of plough teams, appointment of next year's reeve, hay-
ward and the like. There were the miller's tallies and dues to
check, payments of heriot and marriage-fees, a vacant holding
to be allotted.

Finally they reached the criminal offences. These were
petty enough; one man suspected of theft, Guy was not
surprised to learn, had fled the manor. 'Set him down outlawed, and all his goods confiscated,' Lord Reynald instructed
Guy, and turned on the half-dozen shivering offenders herded
before him by the reeve, whose knees were scarcely steadier.
He was more eager for silver than for blood, and imposed
fines to the limit of the peasants' resources. Two men who
could not pay were ordered fifty lashes each, and Lord Reynald led the company out to the bailey to witness their
administration while Guy remained to set down their crimes.
'Trespass with dog on demesne land to take hare . . . Per-

mitting cow to stray in Lord's cornfield . . .' He wiped his pen, sanded the wet ink, tipped the sand back into the caster, and rolled up the parchment. The screaming had begun in the bailey. He had seen floggings in plenty and thought little enough of them, but he did not want to witness these. He sat on at the table. After dinner he would ride abroad to rid his mouth of the flavour Warby left in it, and resolved to ride towards the ford and return by Thorgastone.

Guy's luck was with him. As he reached the crossroads Helvie de Trevaine and her groom were approaching from her father's hold, and he hoped it seemed entirely natural to halt and wait for them.

'God save you, Lady Helvie. A happy encounter.'

'God save you, Master Guy.' She smiled at him. The groom scowled.

'If you ride to Thorgastone, may I escort you?'

'You may.' He reined his mount round to her right hand, and she appraised him candidly. Since their first encounter he had relinquished his beard, and this, oddly, emphasized his dissimilarity to his sire. From some other forebear he had derived a wide mouth and a chin that was square and slightly cleft. Being as vain as most men, he knew the style became him, and that his shining fall of hair, nearer silver than gold, was the envy of every girl in Warby.

'Lady Helvie, your father won't be pleased,' growled the groom.

'If you must tell him, I'll face his wrath.'

'Lady Helvie –'

'Do you choose my company, Sweyn? And where's the harm?'

Guy recognized his duty. 'My lady, I must not embarrass you with my presence,' he said formally.

'You don't. Ride along. I did not render you adequate thanks for your services that night, Master Guy.'

'It was my pleasure, demoiselle.'

'Even to sharing the brat's lice?'

He grimaced. 'I'll except them. But we found him before

the wolves did, and it's my Slut we owe thanks for that.'

The Slut lifted her head at the sound of her name, and the girl regarded her with interest and respect.

'She looks first cousin to a wolf herself.'

'Her sire was one. Her dam was a mastiff bitch that broke her tether and ran off to the woods in heat, and at first sight of her whelps her master knocked them on the head and threw them into the river. I heard this one crying in the reeds and swam to take her up, and then withstood everyone who tried to make me throw her back.'

'So stiffening your resolution. They should have known better. But it could not have been easy?'

'Oh, I procured a mongrel bitch to suckle her, and she thrived. Time for her schooling was hard to come by, but she has a wolf's wits and learned fast. My brother called her a misbred slut, and the name stuck.'

The girl inspected the bitch more particularly. She had the mastiff's heavy muzzle and broad head, and for the rest was an uncommonly stocky wolf. 'She's – imposing. She could kill a man.'

'She has done.'

'What manner o' brute is that to take among Christians?' Sweyn demanded.

'Why, are they Christians in Warby?' his mistress retorted. Her teeth gleamed white in her brown face. Her laughter warmed Guy.

'He's no business outa Warby!' Sweyn grumbled.

'Have you no respect for your neck, to venture it over my father's boundary?' she mocked Guy.

'No respect for his boundaries, you mean?'

'Take care you're not suspended from a wayside tree to mark them.'

'How dismally practical, one's carcase used as a scarecrow.'

'It would serve, while the winter lasts.'

'If that's what you intend by me, demoiselle, I must decline to ride with you.'

'Now how could Sweyn and I achieve so much?'

Guy knew his duty was to ride away, but he could not,

for courtesy and his manhood's pride. Half amused, half alarmed, and wholly fascinated, he chose imprudence, and raised a hand to his threatened neck. 'Jesting apart, Lady Helvie, why did you permit me to ride with you?'

'I confess to my share of curiosity.'

'Curiosity?'

'All the neighbourhood clacks about you. I've heard – ' she ticked the items off one by one on her fingers – 'that you must be a renegade monk, you are armoured against your father's wrath and Wulfrune's spells, too friendly with your stepmother and at feud with your half-sister. I wished to see more of such a portent.'

'Before someone makes an end of him.'

'Especially I would learn how a renegade monk served a craftsman's apprenticeship.'

'When I was nine my parents offered me to the monastery. After four years the Abbot bade them take me away.'

'I'm surprised he tolerated you so long.'

'Oh, the Abbot was almost as obstinate as I am. It was the novice-master begged him be rid of me while he kept his sanity.'

'A repellent whelp you must have been.'

'I escaped. And don't waste sympathy on the novice-master; the qualification for that office is a strong arm with the birch rather than scholarship or understanding.'

'Little use *they*'d be without the strong arm.'

He laughed. 'I'm prejudiced. Most of the last year I couldn't sit down with any ease. But I won.'

'And then?'

'My father – my mother's husband – took me as his apprentice.'

'Then it was not he who'd be rid of you?'

Her insight startled him, and he made haste to do justice to Kenric. 'He was the best of fathers. Though he got six children of his own after me, he used me always as his eldest son.'

She was perceptive enough to probe no further. 'One side

and the other, you're amply provided with kindred of the half-blood.'

'Rohese I'd happily part with,' he said, grimacing. 'And you, Lady Helvie?'

'You know I've none!' she exclaimed, anger flaring. 'That was the curse your father laid on mine!'

Guy stared at her. 'What curse?'

'In seed and breed and generation, that no son should ever call him father.'

'Lady Helvie, this is the first I've heard of it.'

She considered him, her anger receding, and nodded. 'I suppose it's so old a tale none has thought to tell it you.'

'Amend that neglect, my lady, will you?'

'It happened between kings, when word came that King Henry was dead and before Stephen was crowned, and there was no law in the land.'

Guy understood; a King's peace and a King's law died with him, and until his successor had been crowned and anointed men might do as they dared. 'So Lord Reynald raided Thorgastone?'

'Yes. And killed and tortured and raped and burned. My grandmother was one they murdered. But some escaped, and in his arrogance Lord Reynald took no thought of consequences, for they roused Trevaine. When my father rode to avenge his folk they were beast-drunk and still at their filthy pleasures, no guards set. My father's men hunted and killed them among the blazing houses, and in the morning hanged those still alive from the oak in front of the church. Lord Reynald was taken.'

'Justice and prudence suggest your father would have done well to swing him likewise,' commented Lord Reynald's son.

'One nobly-born knight doesn't so use another, and besides, where's the profit from a dead man? He demanded a ransom enough to beggar Warby for your father's lifetime, and Lord Reynald swore to lay the curse on him if he didn't release him freely. Of course my father put no faith in his threats, and wouldn't forgo a clipped farthing. They say his wife was afraid, and wept and pleaded, but he held out for his price. He has rued it since.'

'The curse was real?' Guy crossed himself, and raised a hand to press the talisman that guarded him against witchcraft. The horses had slowed to a walk.

'She was with child, and near her time. They had been married for years, and this was the first; all their hopes were set on it. It was a hard travail. She was in labour four days, and the boy stillborn. When she was told, Lady Clemence went mad.'

'Holy Saviour!' Appalled, Guy crossed himself again.

'Quite witless, and stayed so to the end of her days. She'd sit and sew baby-linen, and sing to herself, biddable as a little child, but she couldn't abide the sight of a man. If one came near her she'd run screaming, or cower in a corner as though she'd force herself into the stones. My father brought in priests and physicians and wise women, but no one could recover her wits, so in the end he built her a little house at the end of the garden, and she lived there with a couple of serving-maids and my mother to tend her until she died last winter.'

'God rest the poor lady's soul.' At mention of her mother he looked at her with curiosity.

'My mother was a sewing-maid in her service, and loved her lady so that when others flinched or sniggered she stayed to care for her. That made my father notice her, and he found comfort in her; she was no light strumpet. But the curse lay on her too. She bore me within the year, sturdy as you see, but the three boys were blighted from the womb; they sickened, turned yellow and died before their week was out. After them came stillbirths and miscarrying as Lord Reynald and his witch-nurse strengthened their spell.'

'Your father has taken a new wife.'

'Yes, and she's pregnant. He has set his hope on an heir at last, and he's in terror lest the curse should destroy this one too.'

'I understand why he would be happy to hang me.'

'His enemy's tall son for his own dead infants.' She gazed

steadfastly at her horse's ears, and they jogged in silence, their mounts' hooves squelching in mire and dead leaves.

'Failing this child, who is your father's heir, my lady?'

'His brother. He's in Normandy, in the Duke's service.'

Few men would provide more than the barest duty required for a brother's bastard, Guy reflected. He watched her, wondering at his own interest; she was not even pretty. At best she had merely a blunt-featured comeliness, fresh colour still overlaid with summer's tan, and a robust body of small appeal to a man who preferred his women little and dark and dainty. Fellow-feeling for another bastard it might be, but sympathy quickened in him.

'Before your father brought home a new wife he should have found you a husband, Lady Helvie.'

She grimaced. 'May it be long before a knight's fee falls vacant and he can find a knight to match with it.'

Guy stared. 'Don't you wish to marry?'

'Why should I?'

'But – but do not all woman wish – ?'

'To be handed over with a parcel of land to some heavy-fisted lout who fancies the bargain?'

It was a definition of marriage that Guy had never encountered before, and it took him several moments to assimilate it. 'But not all husbands are heavy-fisted louts,' he objected.

'What's the difference between a husband and a raptor, beyond a priest's intervention?'

'A few of us,' he declared, nettled by that wholesale condemnation, 'profess some decency.'

'I've never yet encountered a man I'd willingly be yoked to.'

'But how else can a woman live?'

'She has no other choice but a nunnery.'

'Holy Mother, a rare sort of nun you'd make!'

'No, that's not for me. I'll have to reconcile myself in the end to some brute whose size and strength give him the mastery.'

'But,' Guy expostulated, 'it is ordained in Holy Writ – '

'Our Lord said nothing of it.'

'Saint Paul commanded, "Wives, submit yourselves unto your own husbands." '

'Saint Paul,' she stated unanswerably, 'was a man.'

'The world standing as it does,' he commented, 'you'll have no choice but to conform. You'll have an establishment of your own to govern, and children to rear.'

'And the hope of widowhood to sustain me.'

'You – er – regard that as the happiest state of woman?' he enquired, his voice shaking with suppressed laughter.

'A well-provided widowhood, of course.'

'Has your father any candidate to hand, may I ask?'

'None. And he has promised not to give me against my will.'

'Then you may take heart.'

'I may hope at least not to take a husband who will kick me in the belly when I'm six months gone.'

He stared at her without words.

'Oh, don't pretend ignorance!' she said impatiently. 'You must know it's a favourite way to be rid of an unwanted wife.'

He nodded. 'It's a foul thought, but – yes.'

'Twice I've known it, and no justice done on the man. It's his right to chastise his wife, isn't it? And if he's too enthusiastic, a pity, but there are women in plenty to be had.'

Guy nodded again, and reflected that he would be an unwise husband who set about chastising this bitter girl. 'But why tell this to me, or to any man?'

Her brows lifted in surprise. 'I'm safe enough. There's no chance on this earth that my father would ever make me marry you.'

He gasped as if she had smitten the wind out of him. 'Safe enough – ' His first reaction was anger, and then his odd sense of humour prevailed and he doubled over the pommel in rib-straining mirth.

She scowled at him, reddening. He glanced up in time to see a reluctant smile tug at her mouth's corners, and all at once she grinned. 'I've longed for years to speak my mind to a man.'

'In complete safety,' Guy agreed gravely. He suddenly realized that it was no matter for jest. He had an imagination, however seldom it stirred, and he wondered how it would be to be born a woman, condemned to a lifetime of subservience, the pains and perils of child-bearing, household cares and the bringing up of children. Most women seemed to accept their fate; they married the men their parents chose for them and laboured with them to live. For the girl bound to a brutal husband there was no escape in this world but widowhood, and he wondered uneasily how many obedient wives secretly cherished that hope. A rare girl like this one, of courage and spirit and temper that few husbands would tolerate, had reason to rebel. Then, shockingly, he saw why Helvie was no common girl. Most were trained from infancy into submission. He recalled how rigorously his mother had disciplined every spark of independence out of his lively little sisters. Lord Henry de Trevaine's only child had grown up in a freedom few maids were allowed.

'You don't seem shocked. What are you thinking?' she challenged.

'That your father has wronged you, letting you run free when it is woman's fate to be shackled.'

'I was the son he never had. You reckon I should have been broken to the shackles from the first?'

'Would you not be happier so?'

She looked at him, about her at the woods, and shook her head, drawing a long breath that brought his gaze to her breasts. 'No. I have run free, even if I must be chained.'

'God send you a husband of understanding then, my lady.'

'Is there such a creature?'

The woods were thinning, and Guy recognized landmarks; a crooked oak, a tall ash growing from a tangle of blackthorn. The girl drew rein. 'We part here. And you must not seek me out again.'

Startled, he parried the thrust. 'Demoiselle?'

'Don't pretend. Last time was chance, this was not. I've

no wish to pass your corpse swinging by the way every time I visit my mother.'

'I suppose it might diminish your pleasure,' he agreed lightly, concealing disappointment. 'Perhaps on occasion – '

'No. This once I can perhaps persuade Sweyn to hold his tongue, but not again. Someone will probably tell my father even so; there are always eyes to see what you'd not have known, and tongues to make mischief. I'll not be your death.'

He bent his head. 'I must obey, Lady Helvie.' He closed his hands tightly on the reins, his world bleaker, and blurted, 'I've not offended you by seeking you out?'

'Any woman must be gratified by such a compliment, and I've not had enough to weary of them,' she answered candidly. 'That must be why I was daft enough to invite your company.' Again she gazed ahead in silence, and then demanded, 'Why did you?'

'Because you laughed with me.'

'It's a strong bond, isn't it? You're the first man I've met who shared it. A pity. Ride on, Master Guy, before Thorgastone sees us.'

He gathered his reins, hesitated, and then asked, 'Lady Helvie, is it wise for you to ride this way regularly, and so ill-guarded?'

'Ill-guarded? Sweyn's faithful to the death!'

'He's but one man. If I could intercept you, so could others. This feud – you're Lord Henry's only child, victim or hostage if Lord Reynald takes it into his mind.'

'God's Grace, I'll not forgo visiting my mother!'

'God guard you, Lady Helvie.' He touched his stallion with the spurs, and fled before all sense deserted him.

Beyond sight and earshot Guy slowed. The track required more respect than he was granting it, and to gallop through Thorgastone on a lathered horse would provoke curiosity. He uttered a malediction on fathers and feuds, and then wondered at his disappointment. Helvie de Trevaine's only attraction was that of humour. He concluded that he missed his sisters. Four of them accustomed a man to feminine conversation.

The Slut growled, and out of the undergrowth beside the track darted a brown man of middle height in a shabby tunic, and blocked his way. The Slut barked once; the stallion squealed and shied violently, and Guy cursed.

'Of all the Hell-sent fools – '

'What sort o' fool – d'you reckon you are?' Wulfric's breath jerked as though he had been running, and his scowl was as truculent as his words. 'Waylaying Trevaine's lass – if he catches you he'll – string you up – by your own guts!'

'God's Head – '

'Don't you never tell me as it was chance! Seen you, I done, ride to the crossroads and look for her! If you hasn't got no heed for yourself, can't you take none for the lass?'

'Devil take you, what d'you mean by that?' Guy flared. The Slut snarled and gathered to spring, looking to him for the sign, and he motioned her back.

'She's a rare good lass is Helvie, and you're setting about to ruin her. Hard enough to find a fitten husband for a bastard, and what'll her name be worth once it gets known you're meeting her in woods?'

'What's Lady Helvie to you?'

'My blood-kin – me father's brother's gran'daughter.' He backed a pace. 'You take heed to me. If you brings harm to her, you'll never see what skewers you till it's through your liver!' He lifted a hand to touch the bow-stave thrust under the back of his belt and jutting over his shoulder. Then he leaped aside. The bushes swayed and rustled and then were still.

Guy stared blankly after him for a long moment, so long that the horse snorted and tugged at the bit with a chime of steel. The Slut's eyes asked reason, and she uttered a small whine of sympathy. He started back to life. 'Come, good girl,' he said, and gave the stallion his way. His conscience jabbed; he should not have needed an outlaw's admonitions to take some thought for Helvie's reputation. Better than most men he should have realized how vulnerable to slander her bastardy made her.

He retained sense enough to present an untroubled countenance to Thorgastone, where he was accorded civil greeting by all he encountered. At the forge the blind man was sitting on a bench in the thin sunshine, smoothing down an ash shaft with a sanded rag. He lifted his face to the sound of hooves, and Guy realized with a little shock that he must be Helvie's grandfather. The smith, her uncle, drew a bar of glowing iron from the fire and poised it as though he would have enjoyed ramming it into Guy's face; then he thrust it back among the coals and swore at the lad with the bellows.

The Devil's Ring jabbed its stark stones into the sky, against clouds feathering pink along their edges. Guy crossed himself and muttered a prayer against the power of darkness. The stallion, eager for his stable, pulled at the bit, and Guy gave him his head.

Daylight was flaring out in scarlet and purple when Guy crossed Warby bailey to the keep steps. He passed Lady Mabel and Sir James, standing in earnest talk, and exchanged greetings. On the steps he turned and glanced back. Perhaps because his own mind was occupied by a girl, their amity's significance suddenly jolted through his wits. The most censorious could take no exception to a conversation about barley and firewood for tomorrow's brewing, they used a formal courtesy to each other and stood a couple of paces apart, but Guy's feelings rather than his reason recognized that they were in love.

For a moment he stood watching them, conversing with ease untrammelled by any consciousness of guilt. No reason why they should feel any; he had never seen them so much as touch hands, nor speak to each other except in public where any might overhear them. Servants knew everything about their betters, and there had been not a whisper nor a snigger about their association. They could not have gone so far as actual adultery, which for a lady in his stepmother's position depended on the connivance of her waiting-women, too perilous to be ventured.

Wulfrune's stick tapped the steps above him, and he swung round. He had seen little of her since the Eve of All Hallows; she and Rohese had been spending their days with her daughter Bertha, at some sorcery that required the combined malevolence of all three.

'Ha, I've neglected you lately!' she echoed his own thought, lifting her staff to prod at him. He struck it down forcefully enough to make her stumble, and her eyes gleamed venom and then shifted to the bailey, where Lady Mabel and Sir James had halted their talk to look up. 'So that's where the wind sits!' she grinned. Some reflection of the sunset struck red glints from her teeth and eyes, like Hell's embers glowing. 'So you've an eye to your father's wife, my devout Christian?'

'*What*?' Guy burst out before he could check himself.

'And what d'you offer me to keep my mouth shut?' she jeered.

His hand lifted towards his dagger-shaft, and then clenched into a fist. 'A gentleman doesn't stoop to answer so foul a hag,' he declared contemptuously.

'Gentleman? Lord Below, you'll boast of breeding, bastard?' She stiffened with sudden dignity. 'On the day when King Edward was alive and dead,' she declaimed, the legal formula sounding oddly on her lips, 'my grandsire's father was lord of all the lands from Trevaine to Etherby, and he could recite you his noble forebears for thirty generations. What was the first Norman in Warby but a low-born thief who didn't even bring a name out of his own place – or dared not?'

'I don't doubt that,' Guy answered. 'And that's your licence to work evil?'

'I'm of better blood than you or your father, bastard, and anyone who gives me insolence lives to regret it.' She tapped down the stair. He stood and watched her go, understanding with disgust the corroding bitterness that had driven her to destroy her nurseling, in revenge for a wrong over eighty years old.

Lord Reynald was standing by the high table which the servants were setting for supper, idly casting dice, right hand against left. He looked up from the futile pastime, boredom and gloom in his expression. It lighted a little at sight of Guy. He was perhaps the most wretched person in this hold, feared and hated by all the household and ostracized by his neighbours. Guy thought how little occupation the man had. The seneschal and Lady Mabel ordered the household, while the marshal commanded the garrison and stables and with Sir Conan led the forays. Lord Reynald seldom rode abroad; he had given too many men motive for sinking an arrow between his shoulder-blades. His belly was constantly at war with his meat, so that he lived on the blandest fare, milk, eggs and boiled fowl for the most part. Since the Eve of All Hallows Guy had hardly been able to look upon him without seeing the goat-headed fiend of the Devil's Ring. Now he thought of Wulfrune, and knew a measure of sympathy, wondering whether, bred up in love by his natural parents, Lord Reynald might not have made a decent Christian knight.

'Don't stare like that, boy! D'you play chess?'

'Not well, my lord.'

His harsh laugh barked once. 'Nor do I, so we'll be matched.' He tossed the dice once again, shrugged at their faces, and pouched them. 'Poor sport,' he grunted, and scowled at the sunset dying like a spent fire outside the window. 'But what else is there to do, winter nights?' He joined Guy before the hearth. The Slut backed from him, bristling. No custom had reconciled her to Lord Reynald's presence; all beasts were uneasy in his company. 'Wait for the spring. There'll be red war again, when the Angevin lad bids for his grandfather's crown. Sport and loot, and a bastard's chance to make his name and fortune.'

'Young Henry will be King,' Guy declared.

'That cub? Unseat a King who has kept his backside on the throne near eighteen years? Sons to succeed him too; if Stephen's past it young Eustace will fight. War to wage, after the slack years; loot and ransoms, and vengeance for wrongs!' His lips lifted from his teeth in a feral grin.

'And defeat if you hold by Stephen,' Guy persisted. 'I've spoken with the Angevin, and there's fire in him that will win kingdoms.'

'Can you never agree with me? A son owes a duty of respect.' Guy made no answer, and excitement gripped him again. 'Prove yourself, boy, and when you're blooded I'll knight you.'

'All I seek is the chance, my lord.'

'Only wait until the grass* grows in the spring, and armies will move!' A log crumbled in a shower of sparks, and a fragment rolled across the hearth towards him. He kicked it back into the blaze. 'Knighthood for you, boy, and then who's to say how far you'll rise? And there's more, much more I'll do for you if you'll join me as a true son. Accept initiation into our faith, taste our pleasures and learn our powers, and you can rise to lordship, destroy your enemies, enjoy any woman –' He caught Guy by the arms in a fierce hold, shaking him slightly. The firelight glinted on his eyes and teeth as another fire had lighted the goat's mask, and Guy wrenched away.

'Not for all the kingdoms of this world!' he avowed recklessly, and caught back the Slut as she started forward.

Lord Reynald's face whitened. 'Always, always you refuse me! You'll not so much as let me touch you! You're no true son of mine!' His voice skirled to the rafters. He clawed at Guy, who dodged back, hauling the snarling Slut by her scruff to keep her from his throat. A servant, bearing a couple of stools towards the high table, stood palsied. Lord Reynald snatched one by a leg and swung a blow that would have spattered the man's brains across the rushes, but the fellow flung himself aside. The hall emptied. Lord Reynald, spittle frothing at the corners of his mouth, crashed the stool against the fireplace until he had nothing in his hand but the splintered stump of a leg. His hand caught the stone. The pain checked him; he gazed at the blood oozing from his skinned knuckles and stared about him blank-faced, as though his wits had gone. Guy, backed to the wall with his hand fast in the Slut's collar, dared draw breath.

'Leave him to himself,' ordered Lady Mabel's cool voice, and Guy was glad to go. He glanced back over his shoulder,

* Grass fuelled the horse-based medieval armies as oil does today's.

117

nagged by a fleeting memory, and then a grim smile twitched his mouth one-sided; Lord Reynald behaved for all the world like an unspanked two-year-old in a tantrum. The smile died almost as it appeared. A man past forty, and he lord over other men's lives, who had no more self-command than a brat, was cause for weeping rather than laughter.

Supper was late, and a grisly function when it came, with conversation stifled, servants scurrying like mice, and food either scorched or congealed. Lord Reynald picked at a fowl boiled to rags, and nullified any benefit his deranged digestion might have derived from that savourless fare by tipping down cup after cup of wine. He scowled at his son with darkening animosity, and clouted his lame servant when the last pouring from the jug did not half-fill his cup. The other men copied his example with the wine. Guy too had learned in the last weeks to take pleasure in its taste and to drink heavily, partly by example and partly because enough wine blurred the miseries of existence in Warby.

Striving gallantly for normality, Lady Mabel, as the servants went round with water and towels at the end of the last course, informed Guy that she had at last finished his winter cloak lined with coney fur. 'And I reckon you'll be glad of it next week, when we journey to Hernforth to keep Christmas.'

'What's this, wife? You're favouring this whelp with fine garments?'

'As you bade me,' she answered, her brows delicately lifting.

'Did I bid you sew them with your own hands? What's between the pair of you?' He grabbed her arm viciously. 'My nurse warned me –'

'You know, I know, and she knows she lies,' Guy declared. 'And I marvel that the lord of Warby does not tear the tongue from that harridan's jaws for such an insult to his honour!'

'To *my* honour – ah!' He had perceived the pitfall beneath his feet and floundered to save himself.

Lady Mabel drew her arm from his slackened grasp. 'My women will testify that I have never spoken with your son except in company,' she stated in a voice of crackling ice.

'Whatever your hell-spawned faith allows, ours does not

118

permit incest,' Guy stated, loosing all hold on prudence.

'No woman's safe from that randy lecher,' Wulfrune croaked. 'He's been meeting Trevaine's bastard in the woods.'

'*What?*' exclaimed several voices together.

'This very day!' she crowed. 'Your enemy's daughter! That's why he rides abroad alone!' She cackled triumph as all eyes turned on him, and Guy felt the blood scorch under his skin while his hands clubbed to smite her. Rohese sniggered, and at the other end of the table Agnes let fall her knife and leaned to stare at him.

Lord Reynald threw himself back in his chair, his wild laugh pealing. 'Trevaine's girl! By the Horns, that's rare enterprise! Keep at it, boy! Make her love you, seduce her, get her big-bellied!'

'My lord –'

'The rarest revenge you could give me, his girl bearing my son's bastard. Go to it and rub Henry's nose in dishonour!'

He looked no further than that satisfaction, or was reckless of the vengeance Trevaine would exact for such a wrong. But Guy thought of the tall girl who had laughed with him, and said, 'No!'

Lord Reynald slammed a hand flatly on the table, and his winecup rolled in an arc, spilling purple across the linen. 'You never obey me! Where's your duty to your father?'

Guy drained his own cup, and the candle-flames wavered and duplicated themselves before his eyes. Yet his wits seemed to work with preternatural clarity as he hunted words to protect Helvie de Trevaine and himself. 'Don't want her. Only met her twice – by chance. Who'd choose – hulking shrew – when he's got a pretty little leman like mine?' He heaved upright, taking all by surprise, strode round the table and caught Agnes before she could do more than utter a squeal. He swung her up in his arms, struggling and kicking, saw astonishment turn to laughter in the men's faces, to reproach in his stepmother's, and was off the dais in two strides and bearing her to his chamber. Hoots of applause and encouragement followed him; he shouldered round the curtain to lewd advice, and dumped her on the bed.

She had stopped struggling; in the blackness beyond the lighted hall he heard her giggle. 'Where's modesty?' she demanded, as he suddenly checked, recognizing through anger and wine-fumes the public affront he had put on her, treating her as a harlot. Yet she was not displeased. She reckoned it a compliment that he preferred her to a well-born virgin, and was shedding her usual sulkiness with her garments. He shrugged. After all, she was a whore. He fumbled at the lacing of his tunic and forgot his qualms.

Chapter 9

His conscience and his headache nagged Guy equally in the sober morning. He had used Agnes as though she were some trollop from the stews; whore though she was, she had not deserved public humiliation. More uneasily, he wondered how soon Helvie de Trevaine would learn that he had miscalled her a hulking ugly shrew. In the dawnlight his inspiration seemed a deal less brilliant than through last night's wine-fogs. It was as well that next week the household would move to Hernforth in Hampshire, an estate that had come to Lord Reynald through his mother. A journey and a change of scene would take his mind from the brown girl he must not meet again.

Lucifer, whose weapon-skill seemed unaffected by any quantity of wine, trounced Guy at sword-practice and suggested before an appreciative audience that Agnes was taking too much out of him. Sir Gerard led out half the garrison on a foray towards Etherby; fruitless as these excursions usually proved, men and horses must be exercised. After dinner Guy wandered into the bailey, wondering which well-known way would be least tedious to take, now the track to Thorgastone was denied him. Lucifer's six men were lined up two by two at the gate, the stocky sergeant holding the bridle of his captain's mount. Sir Conan was talking with Lord Reynald by the stables.

To maintain an adequate guard the mercenary and Sir Gerard normally alternated their expeditions, and Guy was mildly surprised at the departure from custom. Lucifer stalked to his horse, his brows set in a frown and the lines from nostril to mouth scored more harshly than usual. He led his troop under the gateway arch. Few people found any pleasure in talk with Lord Reynald. Guy thought no more of it, and idly watched the smith at work for a little while.

Lord Reynald strolled back from the stables. He was smiling, and as he passed Guy the smile widened into a grin of pleased malice that sent alarm clamouring along all his pulses. Guy waited only for him to enter the keep and then strode to the stable, saddled up as fast as his hands could order straps and buckles, and took the drawbridge at a run.

Lucifer was nearly half an hour ahead of him, time and to spare for the outrage he guessed at. Reason might reject it, protesting that even Lord Reynald and the mercenary would recoil from the vengeance that would follow, but surer certainty told him that reason was far from either. Guy followed the hoofprints in the track. They were stamped deeply in the mire that had spattered widely from their haste. Beyond the ford the roads diverged; the routiers had taken the woodland way towards Collingford.

He hesitated and then made his gamble, turning his own mount for Thorgastone. That way, though rougher, was shorter by the best part of a league. He touched his mount with the spurs, and the Slut stretched into a lope. He trotted through the village, mindful of pigs, poultry, brats and grand-mothers, and once in the woods spurred to a gallop. Before he gained the crossroads he heard a triumphant yelp, a shout of alarm and a sudden trampling and squealing of horses.

He eased his horse to a canter, thankful for the sodden leaf-mould that muffled the noise of his approach. He was one against seven, and could afford no foolhardiness. He heard Conan's voice, raised in mockery.

'Well met, mistress!'

'You're out of bounds,' Helvie said, steadily enough.

'Why, mistress, our bounds reach as far as our lances – lance of iron or lance of flesh,' he jeered. The groom yelled an oath, and Guy heard sounds of a scuffle. He rounded the last bend in time to see Helvie spur her palfrey at the line of men as her groom went down. Lucifer urged his stallion at her, seized her and wrenched her from the saddle in a flurry of skirts, flinging her to two of his men who tumbled from their mounts to receive her. As they dragged Helvie clear of the flailing hooves and wrenched her arms back to hold her, Conan slid from his rearing horse and lighted face to face. Guy halted, his heart thumping, while the other routiers dropped from their saddles to join in the sport, letting their horses scatter.

'You're brave with a woman, if your men hold her,' Helvie said contemptuously.

'A wasp under your tongue! But you've a deal to offer, mistress, and we'll enjoy all you have.'

He plucked his sergeant's dagger from its sheath, his own being inaccessible under his hauberk, and as Guy started his horse into motion he set it to her throat and ripped her gown and the smock beneath it to her navel, baring her pink-budded breasts.

Guy gasped, and fell upon the routiers like the wrath of God. He burst through the cluster from behind, bowling men over, and the Slut alongside slashed at the nearest, who rolled screeching, his arms up to protect his throat. Lucifer whirled, his hands still lifted, fury and surprise in his snarl. He dropped the knife and snatched for his sword.

'*Take!*'

The Slut soared in a grey-brown lunge full against his chest, and he crashed backwards, the breath grunting out of him. Guy drove at the two still holding Helvie, mouths ajar and eyes bolting. They loosed her as he reached them, grabbing at weapons. He threw himself from the saddle upon them, a hand at either throat, and crashed their helmets together with a clang. Helvie fell and scrambled clear. He cast them down together and tore his sword from its sheath as he swung round to shield her.

Lucifer lay flat, arms outspread, a paw on either shoulder and the Slut's weight on his belly. He stared past white fangs a couple of inches from his nose, down her steaming gullet, and his face turned grey. Anger and arrogance ran out of him like water from a sieve. He did not stir a muscle. The Slut's ruff was flecked with crimson, and her growl rasped in her throat, changing tone as she breathed in and out. His men, picking up limbs and wits as surprise yielded to comprehension, froze as they were.

'If you move,' Guy warned, 'she'll rip your face off.' Conan would derive spiritual benefit from contemplating her teeth a little longer; he fixed his gaze on the routiers. 'Loose that groom and stand away from him,' he ordered, and as they obeyed him sullen-faced he lifted his free hand to unfasten his cloak-clasp and pass the garment over his shoulder to Helvie. Cold fingers brushed his as she caught it from him, and he could hear her ragged breathing that might yet break to sobs.

Sweyn groaned, half-stunned, his hair matted and his face streaked with blood. He was not irreparably damaged; Guy cast one glance at him and then centred his attention on the routiers. He gestured to them with his sword-point to move back. They might have rushed the blade and overwhelmed him by numbers, but they hesitated, looking for initiative from their prostrate captain to his sergeant. Bertin was clutching his thigh, blood soaking down the leg of his chausses, and reluctantly endorsed Guy's bidding by hobbling back, swearing.

'You young fool,' Conan said hoarsely, 'your father himself commanded this!'

'Prompted by Satan his master. D'you reckon obedience absolves you from guilt?'

'You sanctimonious pup in the manger, you'd your chance to claim her for your own and refused, yet you interfere – '

Guy lifted his sword, and the Slut snarled, her lips curling back from her fangs. Lucifer froze, staring at those ranked points.

'Decency's beyond your comprehension. I'm here to defend this noble lady.'

'Another bastard!' Conan sneered.

'An honest maid.' He gestured again to the troopers. 'Back to your horses, and ride for Warby.'

'What d'you aim to do with our captain?' demanded Bertin truculently.

'As he deserves.'

Bertin, judging those deserts, stared in alarm. 'Captain Conan – '

'Do as he bids you,' the mercenary conceded.

Still they hesitated. Sweyn groaned, heaved over, and hoisted himself painfully, hindquarters first, to all fours and then to his knees. He scrabbled after his dagger and scowled through congealing blood, but when he tried to lurch erect dizziness sent him to his knees again. Guy was able to ignore him and concentrate on the routiers.

'Back to Warby,' he repeated.

They looked glumly from him to Conan, nose to nose with the Slut, and at each other. No alternative offered. Bertin shrugged and limped cursing to the horses. He hoisted himself astride. 'We'll avenge our captain,' he growled, more to assure Conan than in hope of being heeded, and led the withdrawal. Guy waited until the last sound of their going had died among the trees.

'You've won,' Lucifer spat. 'Now call off this bitch of yours.'

Guy shook his head. 'I am considering where my duty lies.'

'Duty?'

'It could only please Heaven to rid the earth of such vermin as you.'

'God's Blood!' He jerked convulsively, and the Slut's teeth clashed so close they grazed his nose. 'You'll answer to your father – '

Guy shook his head over the worthless threat. 'D'you imagine he'll avenge you?' A monstrous temptation assailed him. 'What's to hinder me from killing you here and now for your mail and horse and gear, and riding to Bristol to join the Angevin?' He lifted his sword, and looked along it to Lucifer's frozen face, his lips twisting into a wolfish grin. 'Justice, eh? Isn't that the way you reached knighthood?'

'Near enough,' Conan admitted, the mockery returning to his voice and face. 'Have you guts for it?'

'Give me one reason why I should spare you. You cannot pretend you are fit to live.'

'No!' said Helvie from behind him. 'I'll have no man killed for me.'

125

Guy had kept his back turned to her all the time, from some confused motives of delicacy and consideration, though he had all the time been conscious of her presence, aware of her every movement. He looked round almost unwillingly, afraid to see her diminished by Lucifer's assault. She stood erect, gripping his cloak together under her chin with one hand, its folds covering her to her toes. Her face was white but resolute.

'Your magnanimity is wasted, my lady.'

'A gentleman doesn't stain his sword in such trash.'

'Gentleman!' Conan flared. 'A bastard that still stinks of the blacksmith's forge!'

'You must not stoop to his level, Master Guy.' She did not even look at the routier.

Guy bent his head in formal acquiescence. 'Since the injury was yours, retribution is yours to order. Up, lass!'

The Slut snapped her teeth once more and bounded to his side, her tail waving gently in satisfaction at duty accomplished. Guy slapped her flank and fondled her ears as she pushed her head under his hand. 'Good girl! There's my brave lass!' She grinned and lolled her tongue at Conan, who kept his wary gaze on her as he climbed to his feet. 'Thank the lady for your life, and get out of our sight,' Guy ordered, half-hoping for some gesture of attack that would justify his driving his sword through Lucifer's face. His loathing pricked the mercenary, who turned red and then white, scowling from him to Helvie.

'God's Head, I see why you didn't want the wench! What did you call her – a hulking shrew? You may well prefer your whore Agnes!'

He whirled before Guy could strike, flung himself astride his mount and spurred after his men. Guy started to follow, the sword trembling in his grip, and then checked, turning back to Helvie.

She stood rigid, staring at his face with eyes wide and dark in her pallor, and he reached a hand to her. 'My lady –' She struck it aside, and then crumpled inside his cloak, falling to her knees against the slender trunk of a young ash.

'Don't touch – another *man* – like him – '

Guy hesitated, and then dropped beside her. Her sobs tore at his own vitals. For a moment he flinched from fear of rejection, and then set his arm about her as he would have done to one of his sisters, drawing her against his shoulder to comfort her. This time she did not repulse him. As though recognizing that his hold was no more amorous than a brother's she buried her face in his tunic and wept. Compassion and tenderness engulfed him. He murmured disjointed reassurances against her hair, and she fought to control herself, choking back sobs that died to gasps. Then the Slut growled warning, and his head jerked round.

Sweyn was on his feet, his dagger in his hand and his bloody face murderous. The Slut, between him and her master, was poised to lunge.

'Put that knife up or she'll rip your throat out,' Guy recommended.

The lady lifted her face, caught her breath on a gulp, and gasped, 'No! But for him – '

'But for him you'd never ha' been in no danger!'

'He saved me – Master Guy, how do I thank you?'

'*Thank* him, m'lady, when he's laid his lewd tongue about you at his devil-father's board, an' brung them routiers on you?'

She pulled free, catching the cloak together, and huddled away from Guy, staring into his face. Her mouth quivered, and her eyes filled with tears. 'Why did you say it? Why?' she begged, her voice wavering with hurt and bewilderment.

He regarded her miserably, last night's expediency showing more ugly than ever in her presence, but the truth was owed her. 'Lord Reynald had learned of our encounters. He bade me seduce you and get you with child for vengeance on your father. I refused, and thought to turn aside his malice from us by – by – ' His tongue failed him.

'By calling me a hulking shrew?'

'Yes. I was drunk.'

'And you do not desire me for your leman.'

He gazed into her face, tear-smudged but steadfast again,

and paid the tribute due to her. 'No man could dishonour you by such a thought, my lady. He who wins you to wife will be blessed by God.'

He stood up, bowed formally, and extended his hand to help her rise. Her fingers gripped fiercely; she was still shaking. Tears sparkled in her eyes, and she blinked them away; her lips trembled and then set tightly. Guy paid homage to her courage; most girls would have yielded to screeching hysterics before now. He signed to Sweyn to bring her horse. She adjusted the muffling folds of his cloak to free her hand for the reins, and Guy linked his hands and stooped to put her up. Settled in the saddle, she looked down into his face.

'I owe you – I do thank you – '

'Enough!' He mounted and reined alongside. She glanced over her shoulder at the Collingford track and shivered, drawing closer.

'I shall not leave you until I've delivered you into your mother's care, my lady,' he assured her.

'I can guard me lady!' Sweyn asserted.

'I don't doubt your loyalty, but you're one man, and what's a dagger against mail?'

Sweyn subsided, muttering maledictions. They rode in silence along the track until, almost within sight of Thorgastone, Helvie turned aside into a way so narrow that he had to fall back between her and Sweyn. He knew where he was, in that triangle of woodland that came down to the river on the village outskirts, land too rocky and broken for the plough. Axes had bitten a clearing in its midst, and set down on a level patch at its nearer end was a cottage more substantial than most. It sat on stone footings, its frame rose upright to golden thatch, its whitewash gleamed and its door was of planking, no flimsy hurdle. The garden beds, accommodating themselves to the ground, lay at a dozen levels, and a woman in a blue gown straightened herself from one and came to meet them, swinging a head of cabbage.

'Tether the horses and wait, Sweyn,' Helvie ordered in a strangled voice, slid from the saddle before either man could dismount to aid her and ran. Guy heard her sob. Hens scattered squawking. She reached her mother's arms, and Guy dismounted and turned his back. He looped his reins over a branch and slipped the bit from his horse's mouth to let him champ the dead grass still spiking up under the bushes. He foresaw a lengthy wait, and an unpleasant reckoning at its end; he could not depart until he had answered to Helvie's mother for his dealings with her daughter.

The Slut growled. He swung round to face Sweyn's glare. The groom jerked his hand from his dagger-haft, but the hatred in his gaze bristled the hairs on Guy's nape.

'Don't try it.'

Sweyn spat at his feet and led Helvie's mare a few yards away before tethering her. Guy scowled after him, deliberately unclenching his fists, that itched to pummel the head from the groom's shoulders for the insult. Behind him he could hear Helvie's voice, too low for words to reach him, and her mother's murmured reassurances. After a brief silence came her comment.

'Don't take on so; you've kept your maidenhead. Go make yourself decent; men're men, and the best of 'em easy tempted.'

Something between a sob and a laugh broke from Helvie, and her feet padded away. Guy caressed the Slut's warm head, and as the door thudded braced his shoulders and turned to face her mother.

'Master Guy!'

He walked up the path of flat stones. Helvie took her height and colouring from her father. Her mother was short and fair, with grey eyes and a rosy face faintly laughter-lined about eyes and mouth. She was comely still, but even in girlhood could never have been pretty, so that he wondered that Lord Henry, with his choice of all his wife's serving-wenches, had picked this one to comfort his bed. She stood sturdily, still swinging the cabbage by its stalk, and surveyed him.

'God save you, mistress.'

"Save you. We're in your debt.'

'I am here to give account of my fault –'

'I reckons you was more fool than knave, and you've made amends. Come within.'

129

He made formal salutation as he ducked his head under the lintel. 'God's grace on this house.'

'And on all who enter.'

Helvie, standing by the hearth, looked at him with the first shyness he had seen in her, and he smiled. She had changed her ruined gown for an old one of grey homespun, and memory of what he had seen of her reddened her cheeks. Guy unclasped his sword-belt, wrapped it round the sheathed blade and stood it inside the door, looking about him as his eyes accustomed themselves to the dimmer light within.

Lord Henry had made lavish provision for his discarded leman. A lidded iron pot hung over the central hearth, issuing wisps of steam, and about it ranged lesser pots, pans and skillets, a couple of trivets to set them on, a gridiron and a frying-pan. A chest stood against one wall, with trestles and boards for a table. Above them ran a shelf loaded with cheeses, crocks, baskets and bags. In the peak of the rafters, thin smoke curling about them, hung three hams and two sides of bacon. The far end of the room had a loft of hurdles running across, and in the shadows beneath it loomed a fine bed, doubtless the one Lord Henry had shared with his paramour. Fresh rushes strewed the floor, and everything was scrupulously neat. His mother would have approved of this housekeeping.

She waved him to a stool. 'We owe thanks to God and to you that you were in time. But if Helvie's not safe riding her father's roads – you reckon that routier'll try again?'

Guy shook his head. 'Leave him to me.'

'You'll not challenge him?' Helvie cried in alarm.

Her mother rebuked her with a glance. 'Men's business. Don't meddle.'

Guy repeated, 'Leave him to me, Mistress – ?'

'Elswyth. Aye, he's yours. But where's my manners? Sit you down, Master Guy. You'll take a bite and sup with us? Draw us all some ale, Helvie. And my baking's just about done.'

Helvie moved to a barrel in the corner. Elswyth swept hot embers from a large earthenware bowl inverted on the hearthstone, and disclosed under it half a dozen small loaves that added their mouth-watering fragrance to those of onions, apples and ale. She picked them up in a cloth and juggled them to cool. The Slut sat up and watched her with interest, and she smiled, set down the loaves and fetched a pork shank-bone with a few tags of cooked flesh still adhering to it.

'Here you are, my girl. It'll taste better than that routier.'

The bitch turned to Guy and made no move to touch the bone. He reached for it, and tossed it to the Slut. She swept her tail in acknowledgement and settled to work.

'Aye, you done well to train her so. Does your heart good to see her enjoy it,' Elswyth observed. She had learned the graces in a noble household, and offered water to wash before she split a loaf, dribbled honey from a crock, and set it hot and oozing in Guy's hands. Helvie brought a pitcher of ale and accepted her portion, and they sat opposite each other chewing on the hot crusts and licking up the sticky trickles that escaped over their fingers, while Elswyth shredded cabbage for the pot.

Guy no longer wondered that Henry de Trevaine had chosen her for his leman; her warmth was a benediction. If a man's golden girl ripened into this after twenty years of matrimony, he might reckon himself favoured by God. He grinned at Helvie, sucking the last sweetness from her fingers, and as she leaned to dabble them in the bowl of water he saw how creamy-smooth was the skin of her throat inside the neck of her gown, sliding into the swell of her breasts. He remembered what he should not have seen, and felt the heat of embarrassment rise to his brow as he forced his gaze from them and dipped his own hands in the water.

He accepted a horn of ale and declined more bread and honey. Elswyth chatted about the weather, detailed some of her preparations for Christmas, and complained of a fox that menaced her poultry. The Slut worried her bone. Helvie sat silent most of the time, putting in a word now and then. Guy relaxed in the first homely ease he had known since he entered Warby, content to pass half an hour here before he must return to Lucifer and Lord Reynald.

The Slut pricked her ears and lifted her head from her bone; then she bounded to her feet, bristling alarm. A trampling of hooves sounded nearby, and Guy laid aside his empty horn as feet trod to the door. Guy lifted to his feet, and slipped two fingers inside the Slut's spiked collar as he faced Henry de Trevaine.

Chapter 10

'God's Throat, here's treachery!' Lord Henry declaimed. 'My woman and my daughter entertaining my enemy!'

'I am not your enemy,' Guy told him, 'until you make me that.'

'You're Warby's bastard, and should hang at his boundary.'

'Is my begetting my fault?' The Slut, misliking the angry voices, strained slightly at his hold, an almost soundless growl vibrating through her, but she obeyed. Trevaine men crowded about the doorway behind their lord, Sweyn grinning among them.

'He is a guest in my house,' said Elswyth serenely, 'and you are greatly in his debt for our daughter's sake, my lord.'

'He saved me,' Helvie declared. 'But for him, there'd be no way to free me from dishonour but with your sword's point, my lord.'

Neither of the women seemed particularly perturbed by the prospect of Guy's being hauled out and strung up. Helvie moved forward, and Guy said quickly in English, 'Stay behind me, my lady.'

Lord Henry understood. 'So you can set that brute of yours on me?' he demanded in outrage.

'At need, my lord.'

'Well, you don't need. I won't dishonour your roof, Elswyth – though at that it's my roof. And since he saved you, my girl, I'll have to spare his life.'

'I knew you would, father dear.' She swept past Guy to kiss her sire's cheek.

He scowled ferociously and slapped her bottom. 'No blandishing, wench! I acknowledge the debt.' He turned his scowl on Guy, who recognized what he was dealing with; an amiable man making the noises he reckoned appropriate to his rank and power. The two big men confronted each other in silence for a moment. Then Lord Henry's scowl slipped, and his mouth twitched. He hooked a stool towards him with a foot, and looked dubiously at the Slut. 'You've got that bitch under control? I've seen all I need of her teeth, and have no wish to count them from underneath.'

'It would considerably diminish your dignity, my lord,' Guy agreed.

'Diminish – ah, just so.' He sat down. Guy took his fingers from the Slut's collar and touched her head. She sank to her haunches and grinned at Lord Henry. 'What's her breeding?'

'Half wolf, half mastiff.'

'A fine bitch, and you've schooled her well. I'd fancy a pup from her next litter.' He turned to his followers, scuffling in the doorway. They were a couple of knights and their squires, all in riding-dress and unmailed; apparently Sweyn had encountered his lord riding about his own demesne with no more escort than his consequence required. 'Wait for me on the road,' he ordered. 'I'll not be long.' He waited till they had dispersed; Sweyn lingered to scowl at Guy, and retired disappointed.

Lord Henry surveyed Guy in the unimpeded daylight, frowning like a judge considering sentence. Guy stood erect as was seemly in the presence of rank and years and waited for him to speak first.

'If I didn't owe you my girl's honour I should have hanged you,' he said flatly. 'Now you'll give me your oath never to approach her again.'

'I have already made that promise to my lady,' Guy told him.

'Your folly's to blame for all. If you'd stayed outside my boundaries none of this would have happened.'

'No, my lord.' It was truth, and stabbed more keenly for that.

'You took no thought for her good name.'

'My lord,' he protested, 'I have never touched your daughter, nor spoken a word amiss.'

'The man who marries her will still question your meetings

– if I can find her a husband after she's had her clothes ripped off her by a troop of routiers.'

'The man who marries her should thank God on his knees for his good fortune!'

Henry of Trevaine thrust to his feet, the stool clattering against the hearthstone. 'God's Head, are you daring to suggest – I'd see her dead at my feet before I'd bestow her on *you*!'

Guy caught back the Slut, up and bristling at the threat in his voice. 'My lord, you mistake –'

'D'you imagine I'd accept grandchildren with your father's blood in them? Or disparage my girl by giving her to a journeyman from an armourer's forge, whoever sired him?'

It was one matter to know himself unacceptable, another to have it flung in his face. Guy felt the blood scorch to his hair and then drain away. 'You make yourself very plain, my lord,' he said, bowed and turned to the door.

'You have not given your oath!'

'I have broken it already, when it conflicted with my duty to my lady.' He took up his swordbelt and slung it about him. 'Save for that, you have it.'

Helvie started forward, bright colour in her cheeks, her arms full of his heavy cloak. 'Master Guy, we owe you thanks, not insults! Take your own again, and my heart's gratitude goes with you!'

Guy's own heart leaped as their hands met. 'Demoiselle,' he said with careful formality, 'your service shall always be my pleasure.' He bowed again to Lord Henry, swelling with speechless wrath, and walked quickly down the path to his horse. Lord Henry's companions made way for him as he came into the track; they stared curiously but did not try to halt him.

He had reached the ridge, with the stones of the Devil's Ring lifting out of their thickets nearby, when he suddenly chuckled aloud. The lure of forbidden fruit was powerful enough for Lord Henry's prohibition to ensure that whenever Guy or Helvie thought of the other it would be with marriage in mind. He felt himself redden; he remembered more than

135

he would admit to himself of the loveliness Lucifer's outrage had disclosed.

The moment he entered Warby hall the storm he had anticipated broke over his head. Lord Reynald, conferring with Lucifer, turned on him.

'You dare show your face under my roof again, you treacherous hound? Hell devour you, you've cheated me! You've robbed me of my revenge, my rightful revenge that I've planned and waited for all these years! Disloyal bastard!'

Guy stood like a rock in rain and wind, sluiced and lashed by their fury but unmoved. He gazed into the face so like his own, loathing bitter in his belly; this had begotten him and was forever part of him, blood and bone and brain. He knew himself tainted to the core. All the colour had drained from his face, and he thought he would vomit where he stood. Then anger blazed to save him. He jerked free the clasp of his swordbelt and hurled it, sheathed blade and all, to crash at Lord Reynald's feet. The ivory-hafted dagger spun after it.

Lord Reynald jumped back to save his toes. 'What's this? What d'you – *where are you going?*'

'Back to Bristol and the armourer's shop.'

Guy was half-way to his wall-chamber when a different screech halted him, and he checked to look over his shoulder.

'No! You're mine – my son!'

'I'll not call "Father" a monster who sets routiers to rape a maid.'

'But that's my vengeance – my just and long-desired vengeance!'

'I'll not stomach it.'

'But you said you didn't want the wench – *why?*'

'Do you think an honest man could stand by? She's a virtuous maid – '

'What's a whore's daughter to vaunt her virginity?' Rohese jeered from the dais.

'If we speak of whores, the foulest drab from a waterfront brothel would spit on you,' Guy told her, and stalked towards his chamber. One of Oswin's eyes peered fearfully round the curtain, and vanished at his approach.

136

Feet scuffled the rushes, the Slut snarled, and a hand clawed at his sleeve. 'No, no! You're my son! I'll not let you go!'

'Then you'll have to chain me to your wall,' he declared, checking the Slut by the collar.

Fingers hooked like claws dug into Guy's muscles, and Lord Reynald stared up into his inflexible face, his own writhing with the passions that warred behind it. 'I'll never permit – yes, I'll chain you first! You're my manhood's pride – mine!' He checked, swallowed, and then capitulation tore itself out of him. 'Yes, yes! I'll promise the wench shall be safe, if that's what you desire!'

'Where's your pride if you yield to him?' Rohese screeched. 'If he's yours, prove it! Humble him!'

'Don't meddle, you squalling vixen!' he yelled at her over his shoulder, and then tightened his grip on Guy's arm. 'Why, you fool, d'you think Henry of Trevaine would scruple to serve me the same?'

Henry of Trevaine had shown almost the same readiness to avenge his wrongs on the guiltless, and Guy wondered at the poisoned passion for revenge that seemed so essential a part of knightly honour. If Lord Reynald were prepared to relinquish it, it might even be accounted the first sign of grace, and there was no sinner so far gone that he was beyond Christ's redemption. He wavered, and his sire saw it.

'And how else will you win knighthood?'

He must give up that hope forever, Guy realized, and go back to the life of labour, the years of painful thrift before he could establish himself as a master craftsman in his own household. He was ruined for that life now. Behind his impassive face his mind raced, reckoning all the rest he must lose; achievement in arms, the fascinating intricacies of administration, his vision of advancement; a servant to wait on him and a leman to delight his nights; the bodily comforts of hot baths, good food, clothes and wine, a real bed in his private chamber. Most ignoble but most potent of all, he thought of returning to face his mother and William. He nodded.

Lord Reynald laughed and caught him by the shoulders. 'A bargain!' he crowed. 'You're my son, and no man of mine shall molest your wench.'

'A bargain,' Guy agreed reluctantly. Rohese rushed from the hall spitting venom. Sir Conan, who had listened with a cynical smile, suddenly stooped to pick up the weapons he had hurled down in that futile defiance which now set him flushing, and held them out to oblige him to receive them from hands he despised. He jerked back. This was no part of any bargain. Oswin had ventured all of himself from behind the curtain. Guy beckoned him, and he came unwillingly, glancing from one to another of his betters with the whites of his eyes glinting like those of a balky horse. 'Fetch me them.'

'Why, you insolent whelp – '

'I'll not receive my arms from the hands of a ravisher.'

Conan turned white and threw the weapons at Oswin, who ducked, yelped and gathered them up. 'You'll send a serving-man – '

'He is worthier.'

'God's Head, if you were knighted you'd answer for that sword in hand!'

'Enough!' snapped Lord Reynald. 'Are we to waste the evening arguing?'

At his signal the servants emerged like ants from crevices to set up the tables. He turned away, bidding Guy wash and make ready as though he were a half-grown lout who needed his manners mending. Guy trod to his chamber trying to smother his misgivings. Uneasily he recognized that in surrendering to expediency and his own desires he had breached his integrity. He left out of his reckoning the fact that he had forced Lord Reynald to surrender likewise, and how resentment would fester in one who had never acknowledged any rule but his own will.

As he plunged over-ears in the bowl of water Oswin held for him he did recall the exact words of Lord Reynald's promise, 'no man of mine'. Perhaps he had imagined a flickering glance at Lucifer, no man of his but a hireling.

One gain was his; Rohese refused to share cup and dish

with him again. He half-expected Agnes to become his partner, but instead found at his side Gertrude, an amiable girl with as much conversation as a sheep. Guy at first judged that exchange to be merely a manifestation of his half-sister's malice. Observing her exerting her charm upon a wary Lucifer, he began to wonder at other motives, even as he appreciated the benefit of eating a meal in peace.

For what Guy had in mind to say to Sir Conan he required privacy. He took care to remain fully sober, and when the men dispersed for the night and Lucifer quitted the hall to make his rounds of his men's quarters and stables, his step steady for all the wine he had swallowed, Guy gave him time to perform those duties and then collected his cloak and followed.

He had a fair idea where to seek him. Sir Conan was an unsociable animal. He was on the sentry-walk of the curtain wall, leaning in a crenel to gaze out at the night, an unrewarding pastime as the sky was heavily overcast. A few lights glimmered in the village, and down by the gatehouse the new watch was going on duty by torchlight, disembodied voices and tramping footsteps sounding through the dark and wild shadows swinging across the muddy grass.

Lucifer heard the pad of Guy's soft shoes and the click of the Slut's nails upon the stone and turned instantly, his hand slipping to his dagger-haft. 'And what d'you want with me, whelp?' he demanded. Guy's height and pale hair made him recognizable in the poorest light.

'A word with you, Sir Conan.'

'Say it and be gone.'

'If Lady Helvie comes to harm by you or any man of yours, I'll exact retribution on your body.'

'You witless pup, are you planning to challenge me?'

'No more than the hangman does.'

'Who?'

'In any land where law rules, the raptor's penalty is gelding.'

'God's Death—'

'I should take you from behind or unawares without com-

139

punction, for it's no more than your due.'

Lucifer stiffened, and a random touch of the retreating torchlight made two sparks of hell-fire glint from his eyes. The Slut growled, and he expelled a long breath in a hiss and leaned back against the crenel, forcing a laugh. 'The only way you'd dare try!' he sneered. 'So you do fancy the wench yourself!'

'She is a virtuous lady.'

'You lying hypocrite, you've never uttered a squawk about any other I've had sport with, so why else – '

'This lady I know and respect. For your other victims, I despise you no less.'

'What in Hell's name do you know about it, you sanctimonious pup?'

'Enough, being rape-begotten.'

'I'm damned, am I not? Damned from the day I first hired out my sword? Then by God's Blood I'll earn damnation!'

Guy recoiled half a step from the despair in the man's voice. 'You chose it,' he reminded him in cold distaste.

'And what choice – ? Listen, you! I was the fourth son of a poor Breton knight. When I was fifteen my father died, and my eldest brother gave me an old sword and a worn-out horse and kicked me out. How else could I live – how else? And being damned – ' His voice thickened; he checked, breathing hard, and turned away to look over the valley, his hands gripping the stone. Guy remembered the wine at supper, and suppressed a twinge of sympathy; this was maudlin self-pity speaking.

'No man need be damned who truly repents and puts his sins from him,' he declared sententiously.

'Don't blether your smug pieties at me! You're bound for Hell as surely as I am, by another road.'

'*I?*'

'Are you not selling your soul to wear gilded spurs? This very day you've accepted your father's bribe and condoned his sins. You've let him corrupt you little by little since you entered his household – of your own free will, mind you! And you'd a craft in your hands, an honest living! He'll have you dancing within the Devil's Ring before another year's out.'

'No!' Guy rejected the thought with violence. Lucifer laughed. 'You know – you're one – '

'When I do homage,' Conan told him icily, 'I'll set my hands between my lord's in proper form, not kiss the arse of some mummer in a beast's mask.' He pushed away from the battlements, pride and affront in every line of his body, and then his shoulders sagged a little; there was small chance that any lord would take a mercenary's hands between his own. He turned on Guy so savagely that the Slut snarled and gathered herself. 'You witless dolt, what are a knight's spurs to you? Get back to your forge and your repentance while you have a soul to save!'

'That,' Guy said after a moment's silence, 'I can no longer do.'

'Then go to Hell your way and leave me to go mine.'

He went down the steps in three leaps. The bailey was deserted now; yellow light streaked it from the gatehouse windows, but all else was dark. Horses moved in the stables beneath the rampart. Guy heard a squeal and the crash of hooves on wood as one kicked out. A rat perhaps; there were too many about the forage sheds, and he must set the rat-catcher to work with his ferrets and terrier. But that was on the surface of his mind. He stood where Lucifer had stood, unease weighting his belly, and tried to refute his accusation. He had withstood Lord Reynald, refused initiation in witch-craft. As for bribery, knighthood was his by right of birth, bastard though he was, and he had gone too far towards it ever to turn back to the forge. He stared out over the village, seeing the lights go out one by one as though they were leaving him to darkness. Then raindrops spat into his face and he made for the hall, eager to be done with the day.

Guy was done with the day, but the day was not done with him. He came into his chamber, unclasping his cloak and swinging it from his shoulders. Oswin jumped nervously as he slung it over the perch and the shadows swooped. The candle-light glanced from the whites of his eyes. The Slut growled, and Guy checked.

The bitch was a discriminating guard, and her memory was dependable. She never growled at Oswin, nor at Agnes, who had right of entry here. She was bristling, so the alien scent was one she disliked.

'Seek!'

She nosed at the bed, and Guy ripped it apart, flinging pillows and covers to the floor. Oswin tried to sidle out, but Guy jerked his head, the bitch showed him one glint of fangs and he backed into a corner. Guy glanced thoughtfully at him, but concentrated on his search. He tossed the billowing feather-bed over the footboard, and the Slut snuffed at the loose straw, scrabbled with a paw, and grinned up at him.

He had seen something of the sort before; a bit of bone, a hairy shrivelled fragment of some beast, tied together with a twist of blackened rag. He picked it up reluctantly, and it clung to his fingers, slimy and sticky together and stinking of filth. Twined with the rag were a few blond hairs, his own. He looked from it to his servant. Oswin knew.

'Who put this here?' The man shuddered and shook his head, cringing from the thing in abject fear. 'Wulfrune or Rohese?' Guy pressed him, and as he still made no answer, motioned to the Slut. She took a step nearer, and he shrank away as though he would force himself into the stone.

'L – lady Rohese,' he whispered, and crossed himself.

'You did not think to warn me?' A foolish question; no servant would dare betray Rohese. Guy looked at the bed in whose centre it had been hidden, and made a guess. 'A charm to render me impotent?'

Something showed fleetingly in Oswin's face; it might have been but a flicker of the candlelight, but Guy would have sworn he glimpsed disappointment, chagrin, some hint that the spell's success would have satisfied him. Guy considered him, still dangling the grisly tokens at finger-tips, and then turned to the doorway, lifting his hand to the curtain.

'No, Master Guy!' Oswin gasped. 'Don't you never show *that* outside! They – they'll reckon as I told you – '

'Don't fear, they'll know you better than that,' Guy answered scornfully, and strode to the fire. It had been banked with ashes for the night; he kicked a smouldering log and dropped the charm into the glowing cavern beneath it. Flame spat and smoke spurted; then the fragments blackened into the ash and the log settled upon them. The servants, spreading straw pallets or already curled up in the rushes, were gaping at him. As he turned away he heard the mutter of comment swelling at his back.

Oswin's head jerked back behind the curtain, and he gulped and shifted from foot to foot under his master's scrutiny. 'You've served me unwillingly from the first, though I've never lifted a hand to you. You may quit now. Out!'

'Oh no – M-master Guy – don't turn me off – '

'You'll do better in the stables.'

'Please, Master Guy – I never meant nothing – let me stay!' He crumpled to his knees, scrabbling at Guy's tunic-skirts when he recoiled. 'M' lord 'll flay me – indeed I'll serve you faithful – '

'Get up!' He stood with head hanging, for all the world like a cur whose spirit had been thrashed out of it, peering fearfully under his brows at Guy, who reflected that he had no reason to expect loyalty from an unwilling servant, and one torn between fear of witchcraft and of Lord Reynald. 'Oh, I'll keep you. Now get out of my sight!'

He dived round the curtain and out. Guy scowled after him, and then set about putting his bed to rights. He made much of the Slut, grateful to her nose, and pulled out his mother's talisman to gaze reverently upon the likeness of Mother and Child that had protected him from harm.

He was hauling his shirt over his head when the curtain-rings rattled on the rod, and emerged from it to stare at Agnes. Never yet had she visited him openly; always she waited until the lights were extinguished and the household abed. She stood against the bedpost, huddling her cloak about her though she was fully clothed; he could see the hem of her dress beneath it.

'A rare fool you made me look!' she said waspishly.

'How?'

'Pretending last night I was all you wanted, and today

143

risking your life to keep them routiers off o' the Trevaine girl.'

He regarded her with lifted brows. 'You'd rather I'd let them ravish her?'

'You claimed she's nothing to you,' she answered sullenly.

'So I prove it by loosing those wolves on an honest maid?'

'She's an honest maid, is she? And I'm naught but a whore to warm your bed?'

'God's Grace, girl, are you claiming to be anything else?'

'You made a fool o' me. You pretended you was fond o' me,' she complained, and he perceived that, given free rein, Agnes would be a nagging shrew.

'I am fond of you,' he assured her, partly in pity and partly because she had given him pleasure.

'You've an odd way o' showing it. All these nights I've kept you merry betwixt the sheets, and you've never give me any token.'

'Now when have I been within reach of a silversmith to procure you one?' Guy asked, recognizing here a delicate distinction. To a harlot one paid her agreed fee and had done; on a mistress one bestowed costly gifts.

'There's the token you wear about your neck,' she said, nodding at the silver talisman that gleamed against his bare breast.

'And that you cannot have. It was my mother's farewell gift.'

'It's your shield against witchcraft, isn't it?' she asked, too eagerly.

'I'll not part with it.'

She recognized finality, and her mouth drooped. Yet she could scarcely have set her heart on a paltry trinket glimpsed once by candlelight, so he wondered at her obvious disappointment. A knife-edged draught assailed him from the shuttered window-slit, and he threw off hose and braies and slid under the covers. Agnes gazed at him resentfully. 'Either come to bed or go back to your own,' he suggested, moving to make room. For a moment he thought she would take him at his word and flounce out; then she mastered herself, dropped

144

her cloak over the bedfoot and put out the candle. She slid in beside him, and he reached for her.

Resentment remained in Agnes; taking no pleasure herself, she withheld it from him, and Guy turned from her frustrated. Yet he could not in justice reproach her; he should have the generosity to release her and sleep alone. So he said nothing, but rolled on to his back and feigned sleep to let her depart with her pride.

She remained rigid at his side; once she caught her breath on something like a sob and instantly suppressed it. Always she had gone as he slept, and he made his breathing steady and even. Nothing he could say would help matters now, and he realized that, as its only justification had been shared pleasure, with that lost this must be the end of their association. Only let her go with dignity, and no loosing of anger that must make them both a public jest.

It was long before she moved, and his pretence of sleep was sliding into the reality when cold air probed under the covers as she lifted on an elbow. Then her hand touched him softly, sliding over his shoulder to his neck. The silver medallion shifted on his skin, the thong tugged, and cold steel touched him. His hand lunged up to grab her wrist, and he heaved from the pillows, startling a cry of panic out of her. She strained against his grip, and he tightened his hold. Something dropped from her hand between them, and his free hand reached it first and closed on a small knife. He hurled it across the room and heard it ring on the wall. The Slut was up and growling softly, and Agnes collapsed whimpering in the bed.

'So that,' said Guy in the darkness, 'was why you came to me tonight.' He climbed over her out of the bed. 'Guard!' he bade the Slut, and felt along the wall until he found the knife. It was sharp enough. 'You'd have cut my throat?'

'No – ah no!' She was huddled together in the disordered bedding; he could just discern her shape by the light that crept round the curtain's edges from the hall. 'Not that!'

'You're just a thief?'

'Twasn't stealing!' she protested, recovering anger. 'You

owed it me! After all I've taught – '

'Whatever is owed you, this I'd refused.'

'Oh Master Guy, I've asked nothing before – '

'Don't wheedle! You were set to this by Wulfrune and Rohese, because their spells have failed.'

She uttered an assenting whimper. 'They knowed as you was guarded, Master Guy, when you found the charm.'

He laughed without mirth. 'Fools! My bitch nosed it out. And they worked on Oswin, for none but he has seen my keepsake, and then on you.'

'Oh Master Guy, I dursn't go back to 'em wi'out it!'

'You'll have to. Reckon yourself lucky I'll not tell Lord Reynald you're a thief.'

'Oh Master Guy – ' she wailed in pure terror.

'Out! Henceforward I'll sleep alone.'

She scrambled her garments about her in the dark, sobbing in panic so that he felt unwilling sympathy for her, trapped between two fears. Then she reached for the curtain, and turned for the last word, hissing it like any serpent.

'Sleep alone and dream o' your Trevaine wench, since none of us is good enough for you!'

She vanished, and all sympathy with her.

Chapter 11

From the roof of the keep the bailey must have presented the likeness of an overset anthill. Down in the bustle and scurry, Guy found it a marvel of purposeful activity. It was no simple task to shift the entire household, but it was done half a dozen times a year, and every man knew his part. Food, clothes, bedding, tents, kitchen equipment, forage, spare weapons, plate and money had to be assembled, loaded into wagons or on to packhorses, and organized into a train. For all the scuttling, cursing and bawling of orders that made apparent chaos the work went efficiently, and before noon, after an early dinner, the cavalcade was on the road, leaving a bare garrison and a handful of servants in Warby to guard and scour the hold.

First, and well ahead, rode a couple of archers as scouts; then Lord Reynald and Sir Gerard, with the main body. After them went the women and children, on horseback as the weather was dry, with Sir James and a handful of men-at-arms to guard them. Behind creaked and plodded the carts and sumpter-beasts. Guy had been assigned to Conan with the rearguard. He had expected the mercenary to shun his company, but it seemed he did not care what Guy knew of him, and even condescended to instruct him in the art of ambush.

'Watch your horse and hound, the flight of birds for warnings. The worst danger is in mountain and forest country. Never try to ride down unmounted men in either. They can go where a horse cannot, and spring out behind you to hamstring your mount. Hold your men together and stand fast.'

'Stand fast?'

'Just that. There isn't one knight in a hundred – a thousand – can fight with his wits. Daft, isn't it? The man of highest rank is in command, whether he's green as sour grapes, drunk or witless. So they're trained to handle weapons and horses to perfection and leave their brains behind. Head-down at his enemy like a bull. Think, boy. What would a routier troop attack a company like this for?'

Guy did not have to puzzle over it. 'For loot – the treasure-chests.'

'And the women. So if we are ambushed – it's not likely with so strong a guard, but possible – Lord Reynald and his marshal will doubtless take off at full gallop into the next county in pursuit, but you and I fall back on the baggage train. Understand?'

'You must have managed many an ambush.'

'And never departed empty-handed.' He pushed ahead along the line of packhorses to reach Sir James and the ladies. Guy frowned to see Lady Cecily leave her place to fuss over the children.

Held to the pace of the sumpter-beasts and the unmounted servants, the cavalcade could cover no more than twenty miles in a good day. The weather continued cold but clear, the tracks were passable, and only twice in the first day's journey was there delay when a cart bogged down. Every village was deserted when they entered it, the hovels empty of all worth looting, the harvested grain concealed and the beasts hidden in the woods. All the men rode mailed and helmed, sword at hip and lance in hand. Peaceful times would have allowed Lord Reynald and his knights to ride ahead with hawks and hounds for diversion, instead of being held to the convoy's footpace.

The first night they received reluctant hospitality in a castle near Etherby, whose lord knew Lord Reynald's reputation too well to incur his ill-will. Only armed parties moved on the roads. During the afternoon they encountered a dozen crossbowmen in leather brigandines sewn with iron rings, tramping behind a mounted knight. They licked greedy chops over the guarded treasure-cart, and fairly slavered at sight of good-looking women, but even such wolves knew when the odds were too great. As they marched past Guy the knight's eyes met his in a professional survey, pitiless and inhuman. The mercenary would have cut every throat among them as casually as a butcher kills pigs, had they not been too strong. Conan dropped to the tail of the line beside him, and he and Guy rode turned in their saddles, chins on shoulders, until the last glint of the knight's helmet had dwindled from sight.

Lucifer grinned at Guy's expression of loathing. 'Win your spurs, and that's the trade you'll descend to.'

'I will not.'

'Wake out of your silly dreams, boy! What will sword and spurs win you, a landless bastard? There's no glory in them.'

'There will be law in England, and no place for such as you but a gibbet.'

Conan scowled and cantered along the line to annoy Cecily again. Guy frowned. If she had been the woman to turn aside his plaguing with a laugh, his determined pursuit might have been amusing, but it was causing her acute distress. Lady Mabel and the two girls did their best to protect her. Now, to Guy's surprise, Rohese joined their endeavour. She had accosted Lucifer and engaged him in talk.

Rohese had no altruism in her. At Warby she had stayed close by her grandmother, shunned by all for a witch, and he had never known her seek out a man. 'A proper match,' Guy told himself, and took himself up to the treasure-cart to change the guards so that they might get on with their wooing.

He had barely arranged the relief when Conan joined him, white with wrath. He scowled at Guy so malevolently that he stared. 'What's amiss?'

Conan spat. 'A danger I'd not reckoned on. That misbegotten bitch has need of a husband to cover her shame, and by all Hell's devils, she's picked on *me*!'

'She's short of choice.'

'Choice? That poisonous strumpet? I'd not stoop to fornicate with such!'

'But would it not be to your advantage, to marry your lord's daughter?'

'When I marry I'll take a wife of spotless chastity, not a

loose trollop with some witch-churl's brat in her belly!'

Guy marvelled at the arrogance that could reckon himself acceptable to any chaste woman, but merely enquired, 'I've wondered, but are you sure?'

'That she's with child? Why else should she try her wiles on me? And listen, whelp; I've no intention of being named her seducer and forced to wed her at sword's point, so you're my safeguard. Leave me alone with her again and I'll slit your gullet!'

'Never fear, I'll not miss such rare entertainment.'

An unwilling grin twitched Lucifer's mouth. 'Devil fry you,' he said without heat, and dropped back to berate the stragglers.

If Rohese were indeed pregnant it was too early for any physical evidence to show, and she betrayed no such shame and fear as should torment an unmarried girl in that plight. Apart from her sudden fancy for Conan's company she bore herself as she had always done, as though some perverse demon drove her to be detestable. She cared nothing for others' opinions; Guy believed she did not care for anyone, but lived in a sterile limbo of hate and resentment for all mankind. He did wonder who had dared seduce Lord Reynald's daughter, or found liking enough to lie with her. Then he remembered the Devil's Ring, the wild dancing and reckless coupling, and understood.

Lord Reynald made a wide detour beyond Wallingford, where King Stephen was bringing a new urgency to the siege of this outpost that had defied his sovereignty for thirteen years, under the command of the Empress's most devoted adherent Brian FitzCount. The news was heartening to the King's supporters; the defenders were cut off from supplies and reinforcements and could not hold out much longer. No help could be looked for before the spring, when King Louis of France could be expected to renew the assault on Normandy that had prevented Duke Henry from invading England the previous summer. The Lord Eustace, Stephen's elder son, had joined Louis to harass Normandy; there was small hope that Henry would be able to succour Brian Fitz-

Count, and the fall of Wallingford would be a portent to dishearten his supporters.

'So much for your prophecies that the Angevin lad will be King,' Lord Reynald jeered, recounting the news.

'You have not met him,' Guy replied, unshaken.

'And we're not likely to. But look at Brian FitzCount, and see how high a bastard may rise if he gains the King's favour!'

Guy reflected that Brian was acknowledged son of Count Alan of Brittany, bred up at the court of old King Henry and held in high esteem by that monarch, who had made him Constable of England and married him to an heiress. He intended to rise, but such heights were not for him.

For twenty miles and more about Wallingford the land had been ravaged again and again; they rode all day and never saw thatch on house, beast in field or land under plough. That night they had to camp in the open, the wagons set in a circle about the tents and tethered horses, and the men did not unarm, but mounted guard by turn and dozed uneasily in their mail between reliefs. Wolves howled in the dark; Guy listened with the hair prickling on his neck and an arm about the Slut.

On the sixth day they reached Hernforth. Here in the south, where King Stephen had ruled securely, the war had had little effect, though the decay of commerce and tillage showed to a discerning eye. Hernforth itself was a pleasant manor, with a decent stone hall, swept and scoured in readiness for them, set within a defensive palisade and ringed about with barns, stables, dovecote, kennels, dairy and brewhouse. In such a place a knight might settle very comfortably, managing and improving his estate, selling his woolclip to the Flemish and Italian merchants for small luxuries, taking his part in the activities of hundred and shire courts and breeding up sons and daughters beside a bustling wife.

Again Guy's clerical skills were required; he sat with Lord Reynald, the Hernforth bailiff and the manor priest over rolls and tallies, learning yet more of administration. He was tolerated on hawking parties, though he would never be adept; he joined in hare-coursing and an ineffectual wolf-hunt.

Advent was on them, and the household celebrated a mildly festive Christmas from which Lord Reynald and Rohese held aloof. Guy learned that he never kept Christmas or Easter at Warby, preserving from Christian observance that stronghold of his own dark worship.

There could be few secrets in the crowded manor-house, and all knew that Guy and Agnes no longer lay together, though few cared to comment on it. Lord Reynald however had no use for delicacy.

'What's gone amiss between you and that silly wench?' he demanded.

'We find we do not suit,' Guy told him cautiously.

'You've quarrelled? You're not fool enough to be soft with a whore? If she offends you, take your belt to her.'

Guy shook his head. 'We do not agree, and that's an end of it.'

'Humph. Do you fancy Gertrude instead?'

'I'll lie alone, my lord.'

'Look over the peasant wenches. If there's one takes your eye, you can have her scrubbed – or has Agnes worn out your manhood?'

'No, my lord.'

'You've not set your heart on the Trevaine bastard?'

The heart in question jolted, but Guy managed to smile. 'Is it likely?'

Lord Reynald snorted. 'It's the kind of greensick whimsy afflicts young fools, before they learn one woman's as much a nuisance as any other and it's the dowry makes the bargain.' He frowned at Guy, and then his mouth twitched in his lop-sided smile. 'If you *have* set your heart on her, I'll win the wench for you.'

'*What*? Lord Henry would never – '

'Ah, but we've power, boy, power! Maybe he'd rather see his girl dead at his feet, but what of his right-born heir, eh?'

'You'd take off the curse – ?'

'To win her for you, lad. See what we can do for our own! See the power that can be yours, to take all you desire! Can your pale Christ do half as much? Give yourself to our lord,

taste our pleasures, learn our secrets, gain our powers!' His
fingers dug like talons into Guy's arms. 'You can have the
girl, to wife or for your leman, to do as you chose with
her.'

Guy shivered, jerked free, and steadied his voice with an
effort. 'If I wanted her – and I do not – I'd not take my
heart's longing on such terms!'

'You'll wither under Wulfrune's curses then, for I'll protect
you from her no longer.'

'I will not.'

'But this would be the fairest vengeance of all, to make
him give up his girl to my son!'

'I don't want the girl,' Guy said, his belly curdling with
disgust. He must stick to that lest Lord Reynald set his design
into action, for to his shame and dismay he knew himself
tempted. He turned and strode away from further argument,
remembering a creamy throat and the swell of a round breast,
strong courage and shared laughter. He recalled instead the
goat-mask's blank eyes reflecting the firelight, the blood of
sacrifice and the dance within the standing stones. It moved
him to tramp to the church in the village and spend an hour
on his knees before the Rood, praying confusedly for succour
in following the right way.

The children were running and squealing about the garth
as he came through the gate. Maybe the air of these parts
suited him better, for Roger's affliction troubled him less here,
and there was a trace of colour in his cold cheeks. If Lady
Mabel could succeed in detaching him from Lord Reynald's
household he might win to normal manhood, for the spirit
was in him.

So near to Southampton there was still some foreign trade,
and the bailiff had exchanged the woolclip for salt and imported cloth, with a small store of wine, dried fruits, almonds
and spices to augment the Christmas feasting. Another com-
modity was available, news from Normandy. Little of it had
been cheering to King Stephen's adherents. Louis of France
had indeed allied himself with Duke Henry's rebellious brother
Geoffrey, Stephen's heir Eustace and the Count of Cham-

pagne against the Angevin, but their coalition had achieved little. Geoffrey had submitted after defeat, and Louis had fallen sick and sought a truce over the winter.

'But that won't save Wallingford,' Lord Reynald consoled himself. 'Spring will be too late. The Angevin cub won't dare turn his back on so many enemies even then.'

Before January was a fortnight old he had learned his error. Duke Henry was in England; he had embarked on Twelfth Night despite a winter gale, with thirty-six ships of mercenaries. About three thousand men that meant, experts informed Guy, and that was scarcely enough to relieve Wallingford, if they could reach it before it capitulated, let alone conquer a kingdom. Lord Eustace had returned in haste to fight for the throne he was resolved to inherit. Few men had much good to say of Eustace, a brave but barbarous warrior with nothing else to commend him as a ruler.*

Lord Reynald put forward his return to Warby, where he had too many enemies as neighbours to be easy about its diminished garrison. The weather broke, and they floundered northwards through torrents of icy rain. Guy learned the misery of riding day after day in sodden clothes, even his new cloak soaked through its fur lining, his feet frozen in the stirrups and his hands numb on the reins. His wet hauberk chafed his joints; his helmet streamed water over his face, and his shield dragged like lead at his shoulder.

Each day's journey was halved in distance and doubled in effort. Carts mired past their axles and had to be dragged free by extra horses and straining men, only to sink again in the next pool. The men on foot waded through mud that hung heavy on their sodden clothing, their footwear disintegrating; the horsemen were spattered to their heads; horses sickened and went lame. The women and children were bundled into a couple of horse-litters that at least kept them out of the rain, though the boggy tracks and stumbling horses

* After Eustace's sudden death on August 17th, 1173, Stephen relinquished the struggle, and Henry succeeded him peacefully the following year as Henry II.

made the clumsy things lurch like ships in a rough sea.

An overnight halt at castle or abbey let them dry their clothes and sleep out of the weather, but four nights they had to camp by the wayside in the unceasing rain. The women and children huddled in the litters, whose poles were propped on stones or logs; the servants struggled with soaked canvas, iron-hard ropes and slipping pegs to erect tents before crawling under cart-covers or crouching in miserable little shelters of branches and bracken. Guy admired the cooks with all his heart; dry kindling was carried under cover in the carts, and every night they contrived a roaring fire under some sort of windbreak and served up at least bowls of hot pottage to thaw the chill from their bellies.

Three days from Warby they were toiling through woodland. The rain had ceased, and a watery sun glinted in the puddles and gilded the mud. Relief had slackened vigilance; their hardship eased even slightly, men relaxed and lifted their faces to the sunshine. Lord Reynald and Sir Gerard were riding a little ahead, giving their falcons an airing after almost a week in their travelling cages; Roger and Matilda had their heads outside the curtains of the litter, and even the horses picked up their hooves more briskly. Guy squelched along at the rear of the pack-train on a track churned to the consistency of soup and watched the clouds shred to uncover yet more blue.

The Slut bayed, and all the pack of hunting-dogs took up her cry. Guy yelled alarm and swung his shield from his shoulder to his arm, tightened his knees on his mount's barrel and jerked out his sword. Shadows flitted through the leafless thickets. Something clanged on his helmet, jolting his head back, and as he ducked behind his shield another arrow thumped into the wood. At the head of the line was tumult; yells and curses, Lord Reynald screeching orders, horses neighing, dogs barking. He spurred forward. A tattered shape dodged away. He swung from the track after it, swinging his sword low, conscious of others crashing ahead of him through the trees. An arrow whistled past his head. He hauled his horse about on his haunches as the man he was chasing twisted about a tree-bole and came back at him with a glinting knife.

The Slut left his side, launched at the man's shoulder; she bore down his arm and slashed once, and he sprawled kicking in a scarlet gush. Guy leaned down to strike, righted himself and peered about for another, filled with an eagerness wilder than that of the hunt. Lord Reynald and the vanguard were already out of sight, but he could hear their shouts. A yell burst from his lips, the fury of the chase seized him, and he gathered his horse to join it. Then a child's shriek pierced to his wits, and he remembered his orders and his duty and charged back to the train.

A dozen ragged thieves swarmed about the baggage-carts and litters. The bigger litter was slewed half-over, one horse down in the shafts, and between it and Guy was a snarling scrimmage round the treasure-cart. The driver was laying about him with his whip. Conan, half out of his saddle, was hammering with his sword-pommel at the head of a desperate thief clinging to his shield-rim. Guy hewed down and back-hand, filled with the exultation of battle that left no room for fear. The Slut leaped past him to slash and tear. He smashed at a howling face beside his knee, threw up his shield to deflect a spear, felt a blade skid along the hauberk-rings over his thigh and swung his mount about by the pressure of his knees. His blade jarred on bone, gritted and jerked free. A child shrieked in panic.

'Guy! Guy!'

Half a dozen ruffians were tearing at the litter's leather curtains. One had Lady Mabel half out of it. Guy heard him yelp as she slashed with her dagger. Roger tumbled out and grappled the nearest leg, clawing and biting.

Guy drove in the spurs, calling to the Slut who had Conan's assailant by the arm; the mercenary could take care of himself, and had already heaved back into the saddle to thrust his foe through the throat. The thieves had his stepmother out of the litter and were clutching for Cecily and the scream-ing girls when he stormed down on them from behind, striking as he had learned with all the weight of his arm. The blow

156

slammed his buttocks against the cantle as the nearest head split; he wrenched the blade away and swung it under a howling face that leaped from its neck and bounced into the mud. The Slut was on top of a struggling body. Lady Mabel's captor loosed her and stabbed at Roger, fiercely hanging to his leg. Hand and knife flew separately; his eyes gaped witlessly at his spouting wrist until Guy's edge cleft between them.

The rest turned on him like the wolves they were. He flung up his shield and struck past the spear that drove into it. Cecily screamed her husband's name. The outlaws had hauled her from the second litter, and one heaved her up in his arms to fling her over his shoulder and dive for the thickets. Then Conan was on him, abandoning the treasure, storming over and past Guy's enemies straight at the abductor.

Cecily screamed and fought in frenzy, her legs flailing. Conan did not hesitate, but thrust past her billowing skirts as the ruffian looked round on his death, through the ragged beard under his chin. As he fell, jetting scarlet, Conan grabbed her gown and hoisted her into the shelter of his shield. She fought on, still shrieking; the horse reared, striking out with iron-shod hooves, and the outlaws dodged away.

Guy plunged back to the treasure-cart where there was still work to do. One outlaw was in the cart, the whip-thong round his arm, grappling with the driver; a mercenary was down against the wheel, his comrade bestriding his body as he fought off three or four more. One raised a screech of warning as the stallion hurtled squealing at him, staggered and dropped. The driver toppled over the cart-rail. His assailant stooped to grab up one of the small barrels of silver pennies, and glanced up as Guy wrenched the stallion to a trampling stand alongside.

The desperate face was that of Wulfric, a man he knew and had talked with, no nameless vermin. Some impulse he never understood made Guy turn his descending sword so that the flat, not the edge, took him on the shoulder. The barrel fell and rolled across the floorboards. He flung himself over the cart's tail, between the wheels and out past the draught-horse's hooves. Guy swung round. The rabble was gone. The woods rustled, the thickets shook, an arrow sang past his helmet. The Slut danced back to his side, her tail proudly waving, her ruff bloody. He let the sword droop from his hand, suddenly sick and shaking from his first taste of battle.

Roged clawed out screaming from under the dead outlaw, his hair and face spattered scarlet. His mother caught him to her breast and stared over his head at Guy. Cecily was still shrieking, beating at Conan's mailed chest with her fists as he held her across his saddle-bow. Philip pelted back astride his lathered pony that had bolted at the first onset, and out of the woods Lord Reynald and his knights came threshing.

'Let my mother go, you bloody beast!' Philip screeched, lunging his pony at the mercenary.

Conan's stallion shouldered the boy's mount aside, and he slid her down and set her on her feet. She stumbled wailing to her husband, who stormed at Conan as he pulled his horse up.

'What are you doing with my wife?'

'Saving her from rape.'

'You laid your foul hands on her – '

'Where were you when she needed rescue?'

'You hell-spawned raptor – '

'You sound as though you'd rather a dozen wolves'-heads ravished her than that I should save her! What help or comfort are you to her now? You're not worthy – '

'Gerard – Gerard – '

Belatedly he swung out of the saddle to take Cecily in his arms, clumsily patting and muttering awkward endearments. Conan looked down for an instant, and Guy had one glimpse of despairing fury that set his wits racing in comprehension. Then he turned away, the revelation past. In silence they looked at each other, at the sprawled corpses, the dead horse in the treasure-cart's shafts, at the mercenaries and grooms herding together the strung-out train of sumpter-beasts. The women were out of the litters, some weeping, some gaping huge-eyed at blood and death, Rohese cool and contemptuous with a knife in her hand. Matilda stood silently against Lady

Mabel's skirts as she comforted Roger. His stepmother looked up at Guy.

'I'll never forget,' she promised briefly.

Lord Reynald trampled to them. 'By the Horns, do you make such a work of driving off a parcel of thieves?'

'There were few of us left to do it,' Conan reminded him.

'How many d'you need for such a rabble? Stop that snivelling, you wretched little coward! What sort of heir are you for a man to take pride in?'

'Never doubt Roger's courage!' Guy flared. 'He fought like a wildcat to defend his mother!'

'That puling whelp?' He snorted, and looked over the dead. 'Didn't you take any alive to make an example?'

'This one's breathing, my lord,' offered a mercenary, stooping over one huddled heap and heaving it on to its back. As they gathered about it, the breath gurgled in its throat and stopped.

'Not one alive!' Lord Reynald complained, and kicked the dead man.

'We were too hard-pressed to remember examples, my lord.'

The grooms and servants were righting the overturned litter and seeing to the horses. Lord Reynald went to check the treasure-cart. Conan looked down at blood dripping over his knuckles, pulled back his right sleeve, inspected a bloody gash, fumbled to open a saddlebag and proffered a length of linen.

'Tie it up for me.' Guy glanced at the litters, and he shook his head. 'No, I don't want a lady's tender ministrations. Not the lady I'd get, in any event.' A crooked smile twisted his mouth awry. He pulled down his sleeve over the bandage and regarded Guy with his normal mocking grin. 'You're a self-righteous whelp and your company sets my teeth on edge, but as a pupil you do me credit. You actually remembered what I told you and did it.'

Guy flushed, remembering how he had almost forgotten it and left the women unguarded, and some of Conan's contempt for the witless valour of noble knights lodged in his mind. He joined the men working to get the train set to rights and on the road again.

They could have fared worse. Two grooms, the treasure-cart driver and a routier were wounded, but all were able to resume their duties when bound up. One horse was dead and a litter-horse lamed, so they piled two sumpter-beasts' loads in a cart to free them for the shafts. Nine outlaws were left to lie where they had fallen, ragged bony heaps already flattening into the mud as though returning to the earth from which they came without benefit of interment. This stretch of road would be safer for travellers for months to come. When the cavalcade started again, herded closer and soberly guarded, Guy glanced back and saw only the dead horse bulking dark by the wayside.

'They've gained that much at least,' Conan commented.

'Gained?'

'A week's food.'

'The horse?'

'God's Blood, d'you think they'd have attacked so strong a force unless they'd been starved enough to eat each other?'

Guy contemplated that ugly truth, and shivered. Once the dead men had been peasants, toiling to scratch a living from their fields. Marauders had brought them to this wretched end. Men of spirit turned outlaw, those without it begged bread at monastery gates. He said a prayer for the dead and for all victims of the ceaseless strife, and Conan grinned mockery as he crossed himself. Then another thought came to him.

'How many would you say there were?'

'A score at least.'

'That's more than one band. Two or three maybe, joined to attack us.'

Conan looked curiously at him. 'Now how do you know that?'

'And if they took trouble to bring such force together, it was planned against us, not the first chance-met passers-by.'

Lord Reynald and Sir Gerard came spattering along the line to inspect it, and they all glanced back; above the leafless trees crows and kites were spiralling down to their meal. 'You should have saved a prisoner or two for an example,' he complained again. His face was very pale, twitching nervously, and his mount sidled and fretted under him until he swung it about and trotted back in a hail of flying mud.

'Watch yourself, boy,' Conan said quietly. 'He's smelled blood.'

'What do you mean?'

'He'll go weeks, even months, as you've known him, and you start to reckon he's a man you can deal with like any other. Then he gets blood in his nostrils, and he's a fox loose in a hen-roost killing everything that squawks. You've a habit of defying him to his face. When the fit's on him, be wary.'

Guy frowned. 'Why should *you* trouble to warn me?'

'Devil fry me if I know, whelp. Reluctance to lose a pupil who does me credit before I've completed his education, most likely.'

'Very likely!'

He shrugged. 'As you please. But before you came Rohese was his favourite, and I saw him thrash her half-way to death for less impudence than you use.'

Guy nodded. 'My thanks,' he acknowledged grudgingly, unwilling to owe so little gratitude to the mercenary, and for the remainder of their journey noted Lord Reynald's edged temper and the way even his knights avoided causing him annoyance.

Chapter 12

Existence without wine being too hideous a prospect to contemplate, Lord Reynald was obliged to abandon his principles and send Sir James with a wagon and an escort and a bag of silver pennies to Gloucester to procure it. The thought of actually paying for it preyed upon him so that whenever he sat down to a meal he complained, and his digestion suffered as much as his temper. Griping pains in his belly sent him for two days to his bed and the potions Wulfrune administered. She and Rohese spent much of their time brewing them in a hut in the bailey.

During their absence in the south the old priest had one morning been found dead in his bed by his housekeeper. Guy was sorry; he had liked the old man, though he was too weary and frail to make any stand against those who practised a faith opposed to his. Lord Reynald would make no move to replace him, and it might well be months before the Bishop discovered the need. The witches could rejoice. The peasants must trudge to Thorgastone to hear Mass or receive the Sacraments. Lord Reynald sourly permitted his servants to do the same, but refused to let his family or household knights venture over Trevaine's boundary. Guy chafed under the prohibition. A day was ill-begun unless one attended Mass, and he felt his soul was sliding nearer and nearer to perdition. He had another annoyance; the Slut was on heat, and must be shut away by day in an empty stable, round whose door all the loose dogs in Warby gathered whining and scrabbling. In the normal way he would have chosen the best hound and mated her, but if by any chance he won knighthood and might escape from Warby he could not afford to be handicapped by a bitch heavy in whelp or suckling pups.

The eve of Candlemas came. Guy discovered that it

was a major festival in the witches' calendar. Christians kindled candles in honour of the Light of the World, presented in the Temple and hailed by Simeon. The witches kindled the need-fire without the use of cold iron for the fertility of men and beasts. Lord Reynald, abandoning prudence, gave orders after supper that all fires and lights must be extinguished until the unhallowed flame was brought from the Devil's Ring to light them. No one dared remonstrate. Folk huddled to mutter prayers and charms, and prophesy God's vengeance on Warby for the blasphemy.

Guy stood in the hall as the twilight died, feeling that every separate hair on his flesh prickled upright. The last embers of the hall fire, that had never gone out as long as he had known it, winked dully under a veil of ashes, and a raw chill breathed from the walls. The servants had stacked tables and benches and crept out. Guy's head was swimming slightly. He had drunk deeply, but not deeply enough to drown his misgivings. Once again he had rejected initiation into witchcraft, and Lord Reynald had followed persuasion and promises with threats that set him considering ways of escape. Only the lure of knighthood held him under the same roof.

Wulfrune's staff was tapping down the stair, and he scowled into the ashes. Then a squeal from below jerked his head round. Feet pattered up, stumbling in haste. A cackle from the old woman, another squeal, and Roger dived under the curtain, tripped and caught himself, and hurtled across the room to Guy. He flung his arms round his waist and clung with all his strength.

'I won't! I won't!' he shrieked.

Guy held him and looked over his head at Lord Reynald in pursuit. 'My lord – '

'Give the brat to me.'

'I won't be a witch!'

'You'll do as you are bidden, whelp!' Lord Reynald reached for him, and Guy twisted to interpose a shoulder.

'I won't be given to the Devil! Guy, Guy, don't let him! *No*!' As his father stretched out his hand, he screamed and grappled tighter, winding his legs about Guy's so that he

163

staggered, recovered and swung him away.

'He's my son, and he owes me obedience!'

'Not at his soul's cost, my lord,' Guy answered, all at once cold-sober. He tightened his hold on the frantic child whose breath was whistling inside his puny ribs.

'No! No! I won't burn in Hell-fire!'

'That's a Christian fable. There's nothing to fear, I tell you. You'll see them dance the wheel of fire, and the runners carry the flame, and share the feast. You don't think I'd let harm come to my own?' Lord Reynald cajoled.

'No! No!'

'You're mine to do as I will –'

'He's a baptized Christian child and his soul's not yours to claim,' Guy defied him.

'You're my son too, and I bid you –' He snatched his hand back and recoiled. The Slut snarled once in warning and crouched a little, her hindquarters gathered to leap. 'You monster, will you set that killer on *me*?'

'My lord!' There was a slight scuffle in the doorway, where Wulfrune leaned grinning on her staff, and Lady Mabel sent her staggering. The rushes swirled as she darted between her husband and her child. 'You'll not take my son!'

'I've a father's right –'

'He's my son, and by God and His Mother, if you try to destroy his soul I'll destroy you!'

'You dare –'

'All these years I've honoured my marriage-vows as well as any woman yoked to you might, but if you try to make a witch of Roger I'll get word to my brothers that I'll endure you no longer.'

Guy stared at her. His own loathing was a pale ghost beside Lady Mabel's living hatred. Then he felt Roger's grip tighten, and caught up the child in alarm. All his body was tense as a drawn bow with the effort of breathing, his face blue and the cords in his neck standing out.

'There's no question this night of taking him anywhere,' he pronounced.

'Sweet Saviour, you'll kill your own son yet!' Lady Mabel

cried, reaching to him.

'What's such a puling little milksop worth to a man?' Lord Reynald snorted, and stormed out.

Guy cradled his half-brother in his arms, shaking his head as Lady Mabel would have taken him. 'I'll carry him up for you,' he offered, and trod carefully up the dark stair to the bower, where he helped to strip the child, to massage his chest and prop him up on pillows in his parents' bed. His heart thudded as though it would burst out of his body, his hands were claws on Guy's wrists, and he could not for some time swallow the potion his mother hastened to pour out. She looked across him at Guy, her face haggard.

'I've never known it so bad,' she whispered.

'My lady, it's his fear of Lord Reynald working on his body,' Guy answered softly. 'He's too frail for his mind to contain it.'

'D'you think I don't know – that I haven't seen?' Roger's eyes opened wide, fixed with strain and fear, and she crooned mother-words to soothe him. 'All's well now, my lamb, my little love. Nothing to fear, you're safe with me. Nothing to be afraid of now, my darling.'

Gradually the spasm released him, and he huddled wheezing in the bed, his lungs still creaking with a sound like a kitten's mewing. A faint stir jerked Guy's head round. Just inside the doorway stood Matilda, clutching a bedcover about herself, her face screwed up with distress. Discovered, she hesitated and then pattered close. 'Roger?' she whispered doubtfully. 'He – will he die?'

'Not this time, my heart,' Guy said gently. He saw how her blue toes curled into the wolfskin rug. 'Go back to your bed, child. You're cold.'

She shook her head. 'I'm frightened Everyone's frightened.'

Guy scooped her up into his arms, tucking the bedcover round her as he had once done with small sisters. He glanced at Lady Mabel and moved to the curtained door. All the candles had been doused in obedience to Lord Reynald's decree, and a shutter was open to admit thin moonshine and cold air. The women were not abed; they huddled together in the light, and a fearful whimper rose from them as Guy and Lady Mabel came out. The least alarm would set hysteria running through them like fire through dead grass.

'This won't do,' she muttered, drew a hard breath and stalked among them.

Later it would be the oddest memory of ¸hat night, but at the time it seemed wholly reasonable that he should sit beside his stepmother in the bower with most of the household gathered about them, his sword propped against a chest for a crucifix, and repeat for the scared folk's comfort the Psalms and prayers he had learned in the monastery. The roll of the Latin, God's own language to the ignorant, came between them and their fears. Roger slept in exhaustion; Matilda slept across Guy's knees; Philip slept leaning against his mother, and as dread quieted, others slid to the rushes or stumbled to pallets and slept too. Guy's voice grew hoarse, repetition staled his words, and at last he fell silent.

Lady Mabel rose and picked her way between bodies to look in on her son. Returning, she nodded reassurance to Guy's anxious glance. She wiped her eyes with a corner of her kerchief. He had never known her weep before, and shifted uncomfortably.

'I haven't thanked you,' she murmured. 'You've been true brother to Roger, true son to me.'

She was hardly more than two years his elder, three at most, but he did not smile. 'My lady, I've deep respect for your goodness and courage.'

'Oh, I'm not afraid of him. I never was. That's why he married me.'

'My lady?'

'He was benighted in my father's hold once. It's near Hernforth. He saw I despised him, and that made him set his fancy on me, to compel me to his will. He threatened my father with the curse he'd set on Henry of Trevaine, that his sons would die childless before him, for who'd ally himself with Satan? So he agreed.'

Guy freed his hand to cross himself, and the child shifted and sighed against him. 'And you consented, my lady?'

She shrugged. 'I'd been betrothed to a lad I'd known and loved all my life. He died. Fool that I was, I thought nothing mattered after that, and what choice has a girl but to obey her father? When my three brothers found the knot tied, they'd have killed him had I not withstood them, for I *had* consented. So – ' she gave him a wintry grin – 'they vowed to kill him at my asking, or when they learned of my death. That's my shield.'

'And your own valour.'

'We've lived at armed truce for years. I tried, you know. Maybe there'd have been a chance, but for Wulfrune and Rohese. At times I've even pitied him; he's the most wretched soul in this wretched hold. But I've come to the end.'

'Roger?'

'He'll destroy him, soul and body. Wulfrune is set on another generation of witches ruling here. She hated me from the first. I cheated her over Roger. Her grandchild the miller's daughter was with child at the same time, and I'm sure she meant me to die in childbirth so that slut could suckle my son. But once in Hernforth I claimed I could not endure the journey back, and bore him there and nursed him myself.'

Guy nodded. The ignorant firmly believed that a child sucked in its soul with the milk of mother or nurse, which made her moral character of paramount importance. 'My lady, Wulfrune claims descent from the English lords of these parts, before the first William seized England, and reckons herself rightful heir to all. That's at the root of her malice.'

'I did not know it. And for that she has destroyed my lord, and would destroy Roger? No. I've kept my marriage-vows as best I could, but from now I'll think only of my son.'

'Count me your man in that, my lady.'

She stood up. All about them seemed sprawled in sleep, but doubtless some were feigning, speculating why the lady and her stepson talked so long and earnestly. She gave Guy no more than a nod, and returned to Roger.

Guy had never felt more wakeful. He carried Matilda to her bed and covered her, too deeply asleep now to stir, and then trod up the stairs to the roof. The night tingled with

167

frost, and the moon sailed among stars. The sentinel was leaning over the western battlements, and he started almost out of his skin when Guy appeared silently beside him. He flinched as the Slut sniffed at him.

'M-master Guy!'

'God save you, Jehan.'

'Over yonder, see!' He pointed towards Thorgastone Waste, and Guy saw the glow of a great blaze. Peering, he thought he could distinguish separate sparks whirling in a pattern about it, torches carried by the dancers. It was Candlemas night, he realized, the Feast of Lights, older than the faith he lived by.

He stood a long time, heedless of the chill invading his body, until the ring fragmented, scattering the lights. One came dancing across the dark waste, threading the paths like a fiery moth, followed more slowly by a cluster of three or four. It dipped into the valley, and as it reached the ford Guy could discern the black spider-shape of the man carrying it. He splashed across thigh-deep, all the scuttering ripples flaked with flame, and jogged up the slope, through the village and at last, stumbling with weariness, to the castle gate that swung wide to let him in. He gave one wild cry, swinging the flare about his head, and Guy knew him for Edric the huntsman. Men and women scurried to kindle tapers from his torch. It was nearly spent, and he shouldered through the throng to the keep. Guy did not descend to see him thrust the need-fire into the kindling heaped in the hall hearth to receive it. He got to his bed in haste, to take no part in Lord Reynald's celebrations.

Flat days went by, marked only by small events. Conan's arm healed, so he and Guy practised sword-play again. Rohese sought his company with a stubbornness that took no heed of repulsion. Her waist was still slender, but others who could reckon causes were eyeing it. The miller discovered that his youngest daughter was with child and thrust her from his door, setting tongues clacking. He had accepted her eldest sister's bastard complaisantly enough, but possibly the prospect of another belly to fill was too much for his parsimony.

Sir James returned from Gloucester with wine, salt and news that set Lord Reynald cursing. Duke Henry, with more battle-craft than men of twice his years, had made no attempt to relieve Wallingford, but had struck instead at Malmesbury, Stephen's outpost against Bristol and Gloucester. He had seized the town and invested the castle, so that Stephen had been compelled to raise the siege of Wallingford and march to relieve his own. The two armies had confronted each other across the flood-swollen Avon, icy rain beating in the faces of the King's men, whose hands were so numb that they could scarcely grasp their weapons. Their hearts had been numb too, for they had refused battle. Unable to depend on his barons' allegiance, Stephen had offered a truce. That was as much as Sir James had learned, but he had had to dodge back along by-ways, for the countryside was infested by marauders of both parties.

When all reports had been made, the wine stored in the undercroft and the escort dismissed, a trooper accosted Guy behind the stables.

'What is it?'

'I was to tell you, Master Guy, the week afore Advent your sister Gunhild was safely delivered of a fine son, and they christened him Guy.'

'Thanks be to God! That's fair news. Have you any more of my kin?'

'No, Master Guy. A Bristol merchant told me, and I passed word back as you was in fine fettle and showed the makings of a valiant knight.' He grinned and saluted again to soften the impertinence, and Guy fished a couple of pennies out of his purse and dismissed him.

He continued on his way, wondering how to convey a birth-gift to his namesake, and whether he would ever again set eyes on his family. A longing for the close-knotted kindred and the busy town-world seized him, and he doubted for a moment that knighthood was worth the cost. Then he thrust away homesickness and went to the smithy to bespeak the smith's time after dinner to shoe his destrier.

He was telling the smith what a craftsman thought of his

fumble-fisted, ale-rusted standards when he observed Oswin hovering, with a face of fear and misery that took him instantly to the man.

'What is it?'

'Master Guy, I – word's come me feyther's mortal sick o' lung-fever in Collingford. I – I begs you – gi' me leave – let me go to him this last time. Please, Master Guy – '

'Surely. I'm deeply sorry. Collingford? That's near five leagues, isn't it? Borrow Dusty and my old saddle, or you'll not be there before night.'

Oswin's face of unbelief showed how little hope he had had of permission, and he stammered, 'Oh, Master Guy – I – you – God bless you – I swear I'll serve you true – '

'Be off, and my prayers with you. Tell the gate-guard you are on my errand, and stay while you're needed.'

He mentioned the matter to no one, aware that he would be mocked for softness if it were known. A servant had no right to a family if it interfered with his lord's convenience. But it was no inconvenience for Guy to dress and undress himself, and Oswin's absence went unremarked by his betters. A groom sidled up to tell Guy the next day that the father had died in the night and would be buried next morning. The sons must keep the death-watch, so Guy reckoned he need not look for Oswin much before noon.

After a rainy dawn the sky cleared, and Lord Reynald led the three knights out hawking. He had no marshland for the finest fowling, but partridges or a hare would make a change from the monotony of salt meat. Guy took the Slut for a brief run in the woods and then shut her up again, thankful that their enforced separation would be over in a day or two. He went indoors, collected the senior sergeant of the garrison and set about inspecting all the mail and weapons in the armoury for repairs and alterations.

He heard the hawking party ride back but paid little attention. The sergeant, divided between respect for one who knew as much as Guy did and contempt for the way he had learned, grew the more sulky as his excuses for neglect grew the more threadbare. Guy was going over a hauberk with him link by link when a woman's voice called urgently from outside.

'Master Guy? Where's Master Guy?'

'Here – the armoury!' He started for the door; that was Agnes, and they had scarcely spoken to each other since their quarrel.

She flung across the guardroom and grabbed his sleeve. 'Come – oh come quick, Master Guy!' she gasped, dragging at his arm.

Catching alarm from her, he yielded to her hands. 'What is it?'

'Oswin! If you wants a live servant stop it quick – they'll beat him to death – '

Guy broke from her across the room, took the steps outside in three bounds and raced across the muddy grass. The whistle and thwack of a whip were followed by a scream, and he hurled himself at the throng about the whipping-post. Weight and speed carried him through, and he reached the ring's centre as the trooper with the whip swung it round for another blow. Guy's clenched fist struck his arm down, and he wrenched the whip from his slackened grip and thrust him off with such force that he rolled over in the mud.

Oswin sagged against the post, his head down between his upraised arms. Blood ran down his bare back, but a quick glance told Guy that he had taken no more than a dozen strokes. He turned to confront Lord Reynald, coiling up the lash that left red stains on his fingers.

'What's this you do to my servant, my lord?' he demanded.

'You bastard whelp, you dare interfere yet again?'

'What's his fault?'

'Absent two days without leave, and taking a horse from my stables. Give that whip back to Giles to finish his punishment!'

'You punish my servant without referring to me? I gave him leave.'

'I told him so – I told m'lord, Master Guy!' Oswin sobbed behind him.

'He'd no leave from me, and I command here!'

171

'My lord, if you gave me the man to be my servant, who else should grant it? Any fault is mine.'

'The horse – what of the horse?' Lord Reynald's face was ashen, his hands clenching and unclenching at his sides.

'The horse is mine to lend.' Guy tossed down the whip and jerked his head at the nearest sergeant. 'Take him down.'

The man jumped to obey, and Oswin sank against the post when his wrists were released, sobbing as the movement caught at his raw weals. Giles picked up the whip and proffered it to Lord Reynald, who snatched it and struck him across the face with its coils. He yelped and reeled. Lord Reynald stared at Guy, his hand twitching on the whip as though he would strike him also, and Guy faced him until he suddenly swung on his heel and stalked away. The onlookers slowly dispersed in a gabble of excited talk; the sport was over, and more than they had reckoned on witnessing.

Agnes had stayed, and with her the groom who usually tended Guy's horses. They moved to support Oswin, who was recovering somewhat; he let go of the post and stood up, shivering and hanging his head. Rain spattered at them, and he flinched. Guy looked at him in concern. The man was not robust.

'Get him under cover,' he ordered, nodding at the nearest building, a forage-shed. He left them to it and hurried back to the keep to find Lady Mabel. Anticipating his needs, she was half-way down the hall stairs, her hands full of old linen and a jar of ointment. 'I'll see to him,' he said, took them from her with a word of thanks, and sped back to the forage-shed.

He approached the door along the side of the building. It was a flimsy wattle structure, and much of the clay filling had cracked and fallen away from the withies. The voices came as sharply as if he had been inside it, and checked him in mid-stride.

' – If he hasn't guessed already, he's bound to find out now!' Oswin whimpered.

'What could I do? Who else could ha' stopped it?'

'But he'll know – '

'Never sees nothing, that one, till it's thrust under his nose.'
'We'll have to run – '
'Haven't I said so for near a year now?'
'But if we're took – '
'What if that big blond bastard tells his father you 'n' me 've took up again?'
'He's not that bad – '
'What's he care? "Get him under cover" he says, and then off he goes to his dinner!'

Reflecting ruefully that listeners proverbially heard no good of themselves, Guy took three strides along the wall and turned in at the doorway.

A Basilisk whose gaze turned men to stone could hardly have had greater effect. Oswin was sprawled across a heap of hay. Agnes knelt beside him with a bowl of water and a rag, washing the blood from his back. Her hand was petrified in the act of lifting the wet cloth, and the tinkle of a single drop falling back into the bowl rang sharply in the hush.

Guy looked at the two of them, the embodiment of consternation and guilt, and frowned as he realized how blind he had been. Probably every other person in Warby had known about the lovers, and laughed at him behind his back. Wilfully blind he had been, for he had known from the first that only fear of Lord Reynald had constrained Agnes to share his bed. He was too embarrassed and angry at his own folly to say anything, so he knelt at Oswin's other side and began sorting his pieces of linen.

Oswin twisted round to stare up at him. 'You – you heard – '

'Enough.'

Agnes dropped the rag, and it splashed into the bowl. 'I was his woman long before I had to be yours!' she announced belligerently, catching Oswin's hand. The man was too shocked and sick to have any fight left in him, but she was vixen enough for both.

'No concern of mine,' Guy retorted. 'I've dismissed you from my bed. D'you think I'd ever have taken you to it if I'd known?' Her attitude freed him from any obligation to make the apologies he owed. He turned his attention to Oswin, but she exclaimed and flung her arms over the man's shoulders, fending him off in a protective fury.

'No – you shan't – '

'Don't be a fool. What d'you reckon these are for?'

The weals had almost ceased to bleed, were already drying. He pushed away her hand with the bloody rag. He worked off the stiff piece of bladder fastened over the ointment jar's mouth, and scooped out three fingerfuls of aromatic green grease, wound-herbs pounded to paste and mingled with clarified hog's lard. Oswin flinched from his touch, but Guy smoothed the stuff along each darkening ridge, and he relaxed a little, though his eyes still watched him fearfully over his shoulder. The girl hovered, jealously maternal, holding his hand. Guy spread a piece of linen over his back and bound it into place with what looked like worn-out swaddling-bands. A forge-worker of necessity became adept at tending wounds and burns.

'Could have been worse,' he observed as he tied the last knot, 'but you'll sleep on your belly for a week.' He covered the jar again and gathered up the remaining linen, conscious always of their scared eyes. Neither offered any thanks, and he knew nothing he might say or do would diminish their suspicion and fear. His mouth tightened and his thick brows drew together. He bore them no ill-will, indeed a measure of sympathy. He stood up, towering over them as they crouched at his feet, his size and frown intimidating beyond his intention or desire. Yet he turned at the door to offer encouragement, however futile, because he knew the memory of their faces would be with him long enough.

'Running might be your best course,' he told them, 'but choose your time and chance. Good luck go with you both. You'll need it.'

Away from Agnes's wounding tongue, he found his concern for the misery he had caused her and Oswin pressing harder on his conscience. It nagged him to the dinner table, and to quieten it he poured down the first cupful of wine before he had swallowed more than a couple of mouthfuls of spiced beef. Irritably he wished that Gertrude would choose a dish into which a man might set his teeth, and sent a second cupful to join the first.

'Where's Agnes?' demanded Lord Reynald suddenly, looking along the board.

'Tending her paramour, my lord.'

The bitterness in Guy's voice brought a grin to his sire's face. 'So you know that now?'

'Yes. And you knew it when you gave her to me.'

'All Warby knew it.'

'Then –' He checked himself angrily; to ask the obvious only amused half the folk at the table.

'She's learned to bed at my bidding. You've learned you may fancy a wench but that's no warrant she'll fancy you.'

'And you should learn that taking your pleasure in tormenting others makes all who know you hate you!' Guy blazed.

For an instant something looked at him out of Lord Reynald's eyes that made him think of a beast in a trap; then he grinned again. 'Fear's what counts, whelp. What does hate matter if folk fear to cross you? You've a deal to learn yet.'

'Teach him!' cried Rohese. 'You'll not let such insolence pass?'

'Who bade you give tongue?'

'He hasn't learned yet either to fear or obey you, my lord,' she persisted.

'Nor have you, by the way you dispute with me!' he snarled at her.

She flinched and subsided, flashing a glance of hatred at Guy, who reached for his winecup again, aware that he was resorting more and more readily to that anodyne. A grisly silence gripped them, in which the champing of jaws sounded unnaturally loud, and it lasted until the servants went round with water and towels at the end of the first course.

'What's keeping that wench?' Lord Reynald demanded, looking again at the empty place beside Sir James. 'It's an insult to my board to delay so long.' He jerked his head at his own servant behind his chair. 'You, Hamel, fetch her here!'

'Aye, m'lord.' The man limped out. He was gone a long

175

time; the second course was almost over when he lifted the curtain and came up the hall, and the sight of his face hit Guy like a blow in the belly, muzzy as he was after all he had drunk. The man halted at the dais step, out of reach. 'M'lord, she's gone. Her and Oswin both.'

'Gone? Gone where?'

'Dunno, m'lord. Gate-guard says as Oswin took Master Guy's Dusty down to village to see old Ernulf the cattle-doctor. Horse was lame.'

'And the wench?'

'She went out before him, to burn a candle in the church.'

'They've run! By the Horns, they've run, and stolen the horse to carry them!' Lord Reynald leaped up, jolting the heavy table-board and sending his winecup rolling across it. 'Saddle up! Edric, two couple of your hounds in leash! They've best part of an hour's start!'

Knights, soldiers and grooms clattered down to the bailey. Guy was swept along, his wits fogged but his legs steady enough. He found himself in the saddle alongside Conan, listening to Lord Reynald rating the grey-faced gate-guard, who knew better than to offer a word in self-defence. He wondered how Oswin had provided his excuse, but grooms knew many tricks for temporarily laming a horse; a tail-hair tied about a pastern for one. But the man must be mad; a bare hour's start would never be enough, mounted double with Agnes on poor Dusty, already tired from the morning's journey. Then the wine-fogs parted. Not mad, but desperate; in their fear they had taken his parting words for a threat.

The hunt was organized; the household knights, Conan and his troop, Lord Reynald, and Edric the huntsman loping afoot with the hounds in leash, his cased bow thrust under the back of his belt. Guy had no wish to join them, but go he must; he might be able to mitigate the runaways' punishment when they were taken. So he rocked along with the others down the miry track to the village, the wine mercifully blurring his remorse and his disgust at his companions' eagerness.

A peasant summoned from the fields to Lord Reynald's

stirrup disclosed that Oswin and Agnes had taken the road south-east to Etherby, and they cantered after them. The huntsman paddled ahead, slipping and slithering; the horses sloshed along, the mire sucking at their hooves. The mud was too wet and well-trodden to hold tracks, and when they entered the woods and could no longer leave the way to use the verge, conditions became worse.

'They'll be making for Etherby and the Gloucester road,' pronounced Sir Gerard.

'We'll overtake them before they're half-way,' said Conan. 'But ugh, here's more rain.'

It swept down, beating in their faces, trickling down necks and spines, soaking wool and leather, and the wind that drove it numbed them to the bone.

'No scent for the hounds to follow,' said Sir James. 'And the brutes cannot keep up in this mire.'

They were struggling belly-deep, their fur clogged and heavy, and the huntsman was labouring too. 'Keep them up!' Lord Reynald yelled. 'They'll pull down the game when we sight it!'

His face under the spattered mud was crazed with cruelty, and the same fierce lust marked all the rest of the company pursuing the greatest prey, man himself. Even Sir James, so courteous to his equals, was eager, demonstrating a knight's inability to grant his inferiors full human status. Guy flinched. No hope that any protest he made would be heeded.

They reached the fork where a little-used track angled south-west, and churned past it towards Etherby. The wine was out of Guy's wits now. He was miserably sober, his hands frozen on the reins and his feet in the stirrups. The rain hammered at them, dissolving the road; men, horses and dogs were so drenched in mud they were all of one colour with the track itself, but no one proposed giving up.

A horse whinnied greeting nearby, and they reined in. Round the next bend came Dusty, plodding wearily towards his stable and manger. He greeted them eagerly, with lifted head and quickened pace. The reins were fastened to the pommel, the stirrups looped up so they would not thump against his barrel.

'They've turned him loose and gone on afoot!' exclaimed Sir Gerard.

'Hiding in the woods most likely,' said Sir James. He peered about him, blinking as the rain beat into his face. 'We've lost them.'

'Put the hounds on the trail!' ordered Lord Reynald.

'M'lord,' Edric declared firmly but respectfully, 'in this wet they're useless. The scent's washed out.'

'What do we do then?' Sir Gerard queried. 'Push on to Etherby?'

'They can't lie up for long without fire or shelter,' observed Sir James. 'They'll have to break cover.'

'Neither can we wait in ambush outside Etherby for a week,' Sir Gerard pointed out sourly.

'Let them go!' Guy protested. 'Here's my horse back unharmed, and what are a groom and a wench when all's said?'

'You bleat like a calf!' his sire declared. 'Let them go! Thieves and runaways? We'd not have a servant left unless we made an example of these!'

'It's my horse,' Guy persisted. 'And my servant too. If I'm ready to –'

'By the Horns, they'll not go free to boast they bested me! I'll hang the man by the heels from the battlements and give the slut to the men-at-arms!'

'*Summerford!*' cried Edric, with all the force of an oath.

'What?' several voices exclaimed.

'M'lord, I'll wager my head on it. They knew we'd hunt 'em towards Etherby, so they turns the nag loose on this road and doubles back to Summerford. Aiming to reach the Fosse Way by the old track, see, while we're chasing off this road.'

'Summerford this time of year, after all the rain we've had? Drown themselves most likely,' commented Sir James, turning his horse about after Lord Reynald's.

Back to the fork they squelched, and turned into the track that led south-west. It twisted like a loose string, thickets encroached on it and branches clawed at their heads, but because it was so little used the surface of sodden leaf-mould made easier going and they pushed the horses to a canter. They had not gone far when Edric checked.

'M'lord!' He indicated a crooked hawthorn. A couple of twigs were freshly snapped and dangled loosely, and caught on a spike were some wisps of blue wool. 'Here's where they broke through. That's Agnes's blue gown.'

'So you were right. After them!'

On they went through the rain, under the leafless trees, straggling in single file. Guy, riding behind Lord Reynald, vainly sought for some way of stopping the hunt, some way of sparing the desperate lovers. Desperate they must be to risk the ford in a rainy February; it was reckoned passable only in the driest days of summer, and now the rivers were running bank-full. The miles fell behind them. Now and again Edric found further traces that proved he had been right, footprints in wet earth or shreds of cloth snagged on thorns.

'We're near the ford,' Sir Gerard said.

'We'll hunt them into Hell before we let them escape,' answered his lord.

Almost on his last word a hound bayed, and the others joined in chorus. The men raised a hunting-yell, and above it pealed a woman's scream. They spurred their horses. A moment later they swung round the last bend and saw their quarry before them. Edric loosed the dogs.

The ford was a couple of hundred yards away, and Oswin and Agnes were running for it, weariness overmastered by terror. One white glint of faces, and then they were racing down the last few yards to the water's edge, the woman with her skirts hitched almost to her knees. She stumbled once, and Oswin turned back, caught her by the hand and hauled her after him. He carried a long staff hacked from some wayside tree.

The river swirled and eddied in riffles of yellow foam over the ford's approaches, paved with stone slabs, and whirled leaves and sticks and broken branches on its brown waters. Drawn by the hunt's clamour, men and women came running down from the hamlet of Summerford on the opposite bank. Oswin and Agnes plunged in without hesitation, still hand

179

in hand. The stream took them by the knees and then to the thighs, and they staggered at its force. The next step had them waist-deep. Oswin braced himself with the staff, feeling for safe purchase, and now his arm was about Agnes, hers clinging to his shoulders. The freed hounds reached the edge, and one launched himself. The river rolled him under, and with one distressed yowl he was gone. The other three stayed baying at the edge.

The riders checked beyond them, and Guy stared across the twenty yards of fierce water, his hands clenched so that his nails dug painfully into his palms. Oswin and Agnes were past half-way, fighting for foothold, their combined weights barely enough to brace themselves upon the pole and withstand the river's force. On the opposite bank the peasants yelled encouragement to them, execration at the hunters. A stone hurled past Guy's head, but he hardly heeded it; he was praying with all his heart that the fugitives would win across.

A man came with a coil of rope, knotting it as he ran. Reaching the edge, he swung and threw. Oswin loosed his hold on Agnes and grabbed, missing by a bare hand's breadth; it thwacked into the water and was whisked away. The fellow hauled in and coiled it for another throw, and Oswin managed another two steps. More stones were flying. A dog howled as one struck.

'Your bow! Kill!' shrieked Lord Reynald.

Edric already had his bow uncased, the string out of his wallet. He strung the bow, nocked an arrow, drew and aimed as Oswin seized the rope at the second cast. Guy yelled protest and lunged his horse at him. Across the river three men had tailed on to the rope and were hauling in the lovers like hooked fish, while men and women hurled stones and clods and curses at the hunters. The bowstring twanged dully, wet and lifeless, but at that range deadly. The shaft sank feather-deep between Oswin's shoulders. His hands unclosed from the rope and the river took him, rolling him face-up and then over. The girl clung fast. Guy had one glimpse of her white gulping face, and then they were gone.

'Butchers! Bloody murderers!' a woman screamed across the ford. Lord Reynald made to plunge at them, but while his mount jibbed at the yellow-brown water a stone thumped against his body, another on the horse's neck. It reared, squealing. Two men had produced bows, and missiles hailed at them. The horse would not face the combined menaces, but kicked and backed, scattering the dogs. Lord Reynald, winded and gasping, shook his fist at the peasants and called off his force.

'We'll be back!' he promised. 'We'll see who crows then!' He turned from the peasants screeching insults, and his troop followed into the dripping forest.

Guy was the last to go. He stared down-river as though sight could pierce the muddy water that carried Agnes and Oswin, locked in their last embrace, until they should strand on some sandbank or shingle-bar for strangers to wonder at and bury. He crossed himself. 'Lord Christ, have mercy on their souls,' he said aloud. The lost dog crept whimpering from the thickets, its head hanging and its tail clipped between its legs, and fled before him. It was not until an arrow grazed his side that he roused to peril and turned away, leaving it to his horse to choose the path because his eyes were blind with tears.

Chapter 13

The Slut was fit to be released from the stable; that was the day's one consolation. Guy crouched beside her in the straw, his face buried in her ruff and his arms tight about her body. She licked his face and whined her happiness in rejoining him, her sympathy in his trouble, and at last he climbed heavily to his feet and moved to the laundry for a hot bath, the bitch pressing close.

At supper he ate scarcely a morsel. Food stuck in his gullet. He let it congeal on his trencher and then passed it to the Slut, while he morosely gulped cup after cup of wine. It did not help. His head floated from his shoulders, his limbs drifted beyond his command, and hall, table and faces blurred and doubled, while the talk was a meaningless buzz. Always before his inward sight Agnes and Oswin rolled and sank together in the brown flood. Because of him they had fled, through his cowardice and ineptitude they had died. He would blame himself for their deaths as long as he lived.

The women were supping in the bower. Lady Mabel, after denouncing husband and household for murderous monsters, had swept her tearful attendants from the hall, and her look of grief and anger had stabbed Guy to his soul. Only Rohese remained at the high table, and she would have done better to go. Her presence was an offence against womanhood.

The servants scuttled about their duties in silence. Their patent aversion had dealt another hurt to Guy; they believed the vengeance had been his. The page Philip refilled his cup, tilting the jug awkwardly as he tried to avoid contact. Guy flinched. He fumbled for the cup, and then pushed it away. Another mouthful, and he would vomit. Only his body was drunk, his mind undimmed.

All at once the other men were on their feet. The meal was early over, no lingering over wine. Guy sat on. Someone spoke to him. 'Oh, bring him along,' Lord Reynald said. 'Time the whelp was blooded.' Conan and Sir James, with wary eyes on the Slut, heaved him from the stool by either arm and supported his wavering legs from the hall and down the stairs. In the guardroom they hauled his hauberk over his head, buckled on his sword and slung his shield from his shoulder. He mumbled vague protests, and then had to rouse himself to restrain the Slut. They jeered at him, half-drunk themselves.

In the bailey the horses were ready, and they heaved Guy into his saddle. He was by now horseman enough to remain in it whatever his state, and indeed the high pommel and crupper made it difficult to fall out of it. The rain had blown over, and the day had a couple of hours of grey light left. The cold air cleared some of the fumes from his brain. As Conan mounted alongside he asked, 'Where are we going?'

'Summerford, to teach churls courtesy.'

'Summerford? But – ' Words clotted on his tongue, and he could only shake his head.

'And as it's within the Forest and royal property, a prudent man might wonder what the King will say to it,' Conan commented. Guy mumbled some answer that made no sense to himself, and Lucifer's malicious grin flashed between helmet and mail coif. 'Shall I take your reins and lead you?' he mocked. 'You'll be sorry-sober enough by the time we get there.'

Lord Reynald came up, astride a fretting bay. 'Leave that bitch behind. We'll have no hound giving tongue to betray us!'

'She goesh,' Guy answered thickly, while the Slut bristled. 'Not bark.'

'Then I'll hold you to that. You're responsible for her.' He gave her a look of loathing and moved to the head of the line, with half the garrison behind him. Guy followed in the rear with Conan and his troop, the wine buzzing in his head and boiling in his belly.

Lucifer was an accurate prophet. By sunset Guy's head

183

was pounding in time with his mount's hooves, his entrails churning, his eyes afire and his mouth foul. He realized that they had taken the Collingford road, and they passed the first ford under red-edged clouds, the water almost lipping the horses' girths. The last light was fading when they reached the second ford, which was lower, and turned into a vile track leading south.

'I've never fancied night attacks,' Conan commented, breaking a surly silence. 'Some half-wit always forgets his orders and the whole affair's a tangle in the dark. Never you mount one unless you've scouted your ground well by daylight.'

'A night attack?' Guy asked stupidly.

'This one's ranker folly than most. Mark me, we'll lose men we can't afford to waste, and for what? No loot worth carrying away, some sport with the foresters and their women and a quarrel with the King. You stay by me and use what sense you haven't drowned.'

Only then did Guy realize what they were about, a night attack on a sleeping village, murder and rape to avenge Summerford's daring to intervene between Lord Reynald and his prey. A kind of panic assailed him, and his fogged wits struggled to find some way of preventing it. The forest was too dense to let him break away from the troop. If he tried it, among the black trees with no moon to guide him, he would speedily be lost. He could not thrust past the whole force in that narrow way without revealing his intent and being halted. Cold sweat started over his flesh as understanding of his helplessness came to him.

Miles passed. He tried to overtake the column and Conan, ahead of him, cursed him back. If he tried again it would be obvious what he meant to do. Fully sober now, his thoughts scurrying like rats when the ferret enters their runs, he kept his place in the line that advanced on Summerford.

A taint of woodsmoke drifted to his nostrils. A low-voiced order hissed along the column, which straggled and bumped to a halt amid muttered oaths in the dark. 'Not even a moon!' Conan growled beside Guy. But the woods were thinning here; even with the regulations of Forest Law to protect vert and venison, folk seeking fuel and swine rooting for mast destroyed undergrowth and young saplings. Peering ahead, Guy discerned a glimmer of yellow light.

Lord Reynald was marshalling his attack, sending his men right and left to cut off escape and pin the villagers against the river. Some sort of plan sprang into Guy's head. He pulled his mount too eagerly into the darkness under the trees; blundered into a bramble-patch that tore an outraged squeal from his stallion, and then, hidden from sight of his companions, threw back his head and screamed with all the force in his lungs, pitching his cry as shrill as he could make it that it might be taken for a woman's. A dog began to bark, the Slut thundered answer, more screams lifted, and the hamlet erupted.

After curfew folk would have been surprised abed, but they were an hour early. Doors opened on firelight, dark figures scuttled, and someone yelled, 'The Devil o' Warby! Out!' The attackers shouted and spurred forward, but what should have been a taut crescent with both ends secured on the river was a loose straggle with many gaps, and the furthest riders never closed on the river at all but drove straight for the houses. Guy heard the crash of two falls before he reached the ploughland and dared gallop.

Others were before him, and he plunged among them. The Slut ran with him, baying to set the horses kicking and squealing. In a kind of drunken inspiration he blundered and bumbled, thwarting attacks and impeding blows as fugitives dodged among the houses. Curses hailed at him. Once through the hamlet, less than a dozen cottages, some horsemen chased fleeing figures across the narrow ploughland while others turned back. Many were out of their saddles, shouldering into huts for loot or prey, kicking fire across rush-strewn floors, and already one fool was running and hooting with a blazing brand to thrust under thatch-eaves. Smoke billowed across the clearing.

Guy slid down, staggering as his feet touched earth, and looked about him. Someone had loosed the beasts. Swine bolted shrieking through the turmoil, slashing at impeding legs; an ox bellowed terror in his ear and almost shouldered him from his feet, and hens were flapping and squawking everywhere. Steadying his legs, still unruly from the wine, he stumbled through the smoke. A woman plunged under flaring thatch into a hovel, and he threw up his shield to protect his face from the sparks and followed her. Above a cradle she turned on him with claws and teeth; he fended her off, snatched up the squalling baby and tucked it into his shield-arm, grabbed the woman by the hair and hauled her through the blazing doorway. A spear skidded on the shield; a mailed trooper yelled apology and encouragement before pushing past him into the hut, and Guy dragged his struggling captive clear of the burning cottages, shoved the baby into her arms and thrust her towards the woods.

'Two safe,' he muttered and turned again into the tumult, his unstained sword swinging in his hand. Black smoke shot with sparks swirled everywhere, thick and choking, for the outer layers of thatch were sodden after long rain, and demon-shapes capered in and out of it. Several huts were well alight now, the flames flaring over a semblance of Hell itself.

A hand gripped his arm, and Conan's voice barked in his ear. 'Give me a hand!' The mercenary ducked under blazing thatch, and stumbled over a pair of legs sprawled within the doorway. Coughing, he stooped to seize and heave. Guy bent with him in choking murk, finding a mailed arm. A truss of flaming straw fell between them and across the body, scorching their faces. Shields up, they gripped and staggered back, dragging it between them, and dropped it on the muddy earth. Guy straightened. Conan, on his knees, rolled his man over and beat at the fiery remnants, strangling on his coughs.

A huge bulk came at them through the smother, no ox but the village bull wild with rage and terror. It hooked at Conan, caught him up and hurled him aside, plunged after him to gore and trample. Somehow Guy was between them, battering his shield into the beast's face to turn it. Immense force slammed at him; steaming breath, hot hide, bellowing fury; a horn-tip scored his side. The Slut leaped at the bull's

186

muzzle, and he blared his anguish, flinging up his head to expose his throat to her fangs. Somehow Guy's sword was up and lunging. It jarred on bone, twisted and drove on. The bellow rose to a roar, the sword was wrenched almost from his grip, and the bull plunged away, dragging Guy several paces before he could tug his blade free, the Slut tearing at his throat until he tottered to a halt, snorting blood and foam.

Behind the bull ran a man with a pitchfork. Conan was struggling to his knees; the twin tines flashed red in the fire-light as they drove at him. He got his shield up, but the blow sent him sprawling and the points swung again. Driven by the Saints knew what compulsion of comradeship, Guy leaped, got a leg across his body and beat aside the pitchfork. For a heart's beat he stared into a bearded face convulsed with rage; then the points lunged at his belly. He turned them on his shield and heaved the man off. He stumbled, reeled into a blazing hut, recoiled and went down under the onslaught of several mailed men. Guy stared stupidly at the struggle and wished he had struck home. The Slut left the bull, which was down on his knees; as he looked he uttered a last groan and rolled over. Conan was squirming between his feet. He stepped clear to let him up, and realized that the fighting was over, every hut ablaze, Warby men gathering from the darkness.

Conan's first concern was for his man, hauled from the burning cottage. A cursory inspection sufficed; the scorched body had never stirred since they laid hold of it. 'Choked with smoke, the fool, for loot not worth the seeking,' he muttered, and climbed joint by joint to his feet like an old man. He felt at his side, wincing, and scowled at Guy. 'Wipe your sword!' he snapped. 'What kind of lout leaves his blade foul?'

The only object in sight that would serve that purpose was the dead routier, so Guy, suppressing loathing, stooped and wiped off the blood on the man's tunic. He straightened to find Lord Reynald before him, grinning approval.

'So you're blooded, boy!'

Guy sheathed the blade, fumbling over it, and mumbled something about bull's blood, not man's, that went unheeded.

'How did he serve?' Lord Reynald was asking Conan.

'But for him I'd be dead twice over,' the mercenary said sourly.

'Then the time's come. Kneel, boy.'

In a thick daze Guy sank to his knees on the trampled earth. Conan moved to stand before him. 'With your leave, my lord, it's more fitting that another than his father should dub him,' he observed to Lord Reynald, and swung his sword. Guy felt its light tap on his shoulder, hands urging him to his feet, the ritual buffet that was the last blow any man's hand might deal him unavenged. Words sounded in his ears but made no sense. He was a knight. Shame, humiliation, disappointment scorched his soul. It was no honour, no achievement, to be knighted for an onslaught on surprised peasants armed with pitchforks.

Pitchforks were not entirely despicable weapons; Sir Gerard was limping heavily with a pierced thigh, a spearman bleeding from gashed ribs. Two men had been trapped in a burning hut and the survivor was badly injured; an archer lay among trampled cabbages with his skull smashed in, and a man-at-arms was found on the edge of the ploughland with an arrow through his lungs. Half the company had suffered minor burns and hurts, and Guy understood Conan's dislike for night attacks.

The assault had gained them a few poor household goods, a dead pig and three prisoners, two men and a young woman. Guy looked on them sickly as they were shoved and beaten into their midst, and started forward. Conan's hand jerked him back. 'Don't be a fool,' he muttered in Guy's ear. 'They are nothing to you. My lord won't forgo his sport for anything you can say.'

There was some delay while injuries were bound up and they waited for the wounded man-at-arms to finish strangling in his own blood. Then the troop moved out, the dead slung across saddles, the woman tied on a horse, the two men made fast by the wrists to saddlehorns. All the huts were bright ruins out of which thrust skeletal timbers, and as they rode out from among them arrows followed.

188

As the woods closed about them Conan gave a grunt of disgust. 'Did I not say it was folly? The most unprofitable night's work I've shared for years. Four men dead for a few poor pots and a half-grown pig!'

'The prisoners? What will he do?'

'Whatever the Devil puts in his mind. *Don't interfere*! If you can't stomach it, get drunk – more drunk! – and get out.'

The woman was sobbing hopelessly in the dark, and Guy could not close his ears. He was sober enough now, with a throbbing skull and a queasy belly, but her weeping was harder to endure than those. Then one of the men tripped and was dragged along wailing until he could gain his feet again, while his captors mocked him. Guy lagged more and more, and Conan, riding behind him, made no attempt to hurry him but lagged too.

'You gave the warning,' he said abruptly out of the dark.

Guy started. 'I?' he parried.

'I was close behind you. Oh, no one else has guessed, and I shan't betray you.'

'Forbearing of you,' Guy growled.

The older man was silent while they jogged on for a good half-mile.

'God's Blood!' Conan snarled suddenly. 'Why did it have to be you?'

'What?'

'An unlicked cub – a whelp in my training – and from what? A loose bull and a churl with a pitchfork!'

'You'd rather I'd left you to them?'

'Devil fry you! I don't know why you did it – '

'Nor I.'

'But I had Hell's brimstone in my nose. Yet it galls me to owe my life to an unschooled pup.'

'Reckon it your teaching.'

He started to curse, his horse stumbled, and he caught his breath on a hiss.

'Hurt?'

'A rib cracked, I think. Yes, a vilely unprofitable night.'

They reached the lesser ford and crossed without incident. The woman had stopped crying and sat humped and wretched in the man's saddle that must be galling her unaccustomed flesh raw. Guy pushed forward to reach her, but Conan seized his bridle while the guards hustled the prisoners across and re-formed the line.

'Get it into your solid skull, you cannot do anything. Don't you realize they'd turn on you like a wolf-pack if you spoiled their sport?'

'Then why should you stop me?'

'Because I'm your man.'

Guy gasped, the words hitting him like a blow in the wind. He stared at the dim figure beside him, barely seen in the faint light reflected from the water. The Slut jumped up to his saddle-bow as he had taught her when crossing water too deep for easy passage, and wiped her tongue across his cheek. He put his arm about her. The horse snorted, but he had learned to carry her without further fuss. Slowly Guy assimilated Conan's statement. Across the ford he let the Slut down with the customary slap on her flank.

'*What* did you say?'

'Like it or not, I don't deny a debt. I owe you my life twice over, so it's yours.'

'I don't want your life!'

The mercenary uttered his sardonic chuckle. 'However the yoke frets you, we're bound together, you and I.'

'Bound to a Hell-doomed excommunicate –' Guy choked.

'No doubt we'll roast together.' His voice changed to earnestness. 'You've achieved your desire. You're a knight. Now get out! Ride for Malmesbury and take service with the Angevin lad before the week's out.'

'I aim to,' Guy admitted before he could check himself.

'Put all this behind you, never tell who sired you, and never, never come back!'

'And you?'

'I am bought until Easter.'

Faithfulness to the paymaster was, Guy knew, the only point of honour a mercenary observed. 'And then you'll follow your own advice?'

'You don't imagine I'll stay longer than I'm bound?'

At the deeper ford one of the prisoners attempted to drown himself, and came so near achieving his end that the guards had to throw him face-down across a saddle to drain the water out of him. The rain came hissing back, and they squelched on weary horses through the dark at walking-pace, so that it was well after midnight when they reached Warby gates and saw them swing open to admit the company. Spitting torches danced about them, grooms ran to take the horses, and the captives were hustled off to the guardroom.

Tending of hurts, dry clothes and hot fires were their first needs. Guy emerged from his chamber to find Lord Reynald and his knights assembled on the dais with cups and wine-jug, and the troopers who had ridden with them, divested of mail, drifting in to steam about the hearth while servants scurried with ale and mugs.

'Join us, lad!' called Lord Reynald. 'Fill up, all, and we'll drink to my son newly knighted!'

'Good fortune be yours, Sir Guy!' seconded the seneschal, and Sir Gerard grunted acknowledgement as he sat with his bandaged leg extended stiffly. Conan grinned over his cup with his usual mockery, as though he guessed what a travesty of his dreams Guy found this knighting, without a priest to bless it or a lady to grace it. As he reached the dais Lord Reynald tossed something that glittered. He caught it automatically, pricked his hand and gazed stupidly at a pair of gilt spurs.

'There you are. Never thought when I took them off a dead man's heels that they'd adorn my own son.'

Guy crammed the outward symbols of his new status into his pouch, sick at the sight of them. Even the gilded spurs that he had dreamed of achieving all his life came tainted, stolen from some murdered victim. He dropped on to a stool at the end of the dais and gulped the wine someone thrust into his hand. Hippocras appeared, wine mulled with honey and spices, very comforting to the belly and mazing to the wits. Two cups of it eased reality from him, so that when the curtain-

191

rings clashed and a roar of brutal glee went up he did not at first understand what was happening.

Men dragged the prisoners to the dais steps. The woman screamed and struggled, the man who had tried to drown himself, half-dead already, had to be hauled bodily, but the fellow who had used the pitchfork walked on his two feet, grey-faced but steady. Guy's entrails turned to ice, his heart jolted. He glanced quickly along the table. Sir James's face of stone might hide sympathy, but the rest showed only the same horrible eagerness that filled Lord Reynald. Wulfrune and Rohese had joined the company, gloating like devils from a painted Judgement Day. And while he was swallowing hippocras a brazier had been brought in and kindled; a man was energetically working the bellows to set the charcoal glowing throughout. The weaker man roused to wail for mercy.

'Churls shouldn't interfere in their betters' affairs,' Lord Reynald pronounced.

'We're the King's men, not yourn,' the other man protested hoarsely in rough French.

'The King has more urgent concerns than to trouble over a serf or two. What shall we do with them, for the best sport?'

The woman cried out and laid her hands over her belly. 'But me lord, I'm with child! I'm with child! In the Name o' God's Holy Mother, m' lord – '

'We'll have it out of you,' Lord Reynald answered.

She sank to her knees, folding her arms across her womb. 'No, no, not my baby! Me lord – Alfgar – ' She turned to the man who had used the pitchfork.

'Your husband?' Lord Reynald asked with interest.

'Me brother – oh me lord – '

Guy stood up so abruptly that his stool clattered backward. Men jumped and turned to gape at him as he collected his feet and stepped down from the dais to the woman. 'I'll take the wench,' he declared.

'You'll *what*?' exclaimed Lord Reynald.

'I'm the man lost his girl, remember? She'll do instead.' He stood over her, his wits working with sharp clarity. The woman he could save, and there was one service he might do for one of the men.

'I'll see what an unborn brat's like – '

'Then rip up your own bastard!' Guy retorted, jerking his head at Rohese, who shrieked a foul name at him. 'This wench is mine. Unless any chooses to challenge me for her?' He gazed round the astonished assembly, but no one answered. The Slut's growl rumbled in the hush. Conan's sardonic chuckle was the only other sound until the woman roused from her trance to whimper. Guy turned on the braver man, desperately willing him to respond, to give him the excuse he needed for what came next. His hand was on his dagger-haft, and he glimpsed incredulous comprehension in the man's eyes. 'Think of the honour I'm doing your sister while you provide my lord's entertainment!'

'You hell-spawned bastard!'

Guy lurched at him. He had his reward, the gratitude that filled the man's last instant as he saw the blade and braced himself for the blow, up under the ribs' arch to his heart. His eyes blinked shut and open, his body jerked and then slid through the hands holding him to thud on the rushes. Guy backed to the woman, his streaked steel lifted ready, as the silence of shock was followed by a howl of fury from a score of throats. 'Lord God, take his soul in keeping and grant him salvation,' Guy prayed in his heart as he stood with the Slut poised beside him.

'You drunken fool, you've ruined our sport!' screeched Lord Reynald, leaping up from his chair.

'In-shulted me,' Guy declared thickly, though in fact he was now hideously sober, the wine rising in his throat as his stomach heaved.

'He's cheated us a-purpose!' Wulfrune shrilled.

'Take the woman from him!' yelped Rohese.

The woman, still on her knees, scrambled forward to throw herself wailing upon her brother's body. A trooper, bolder or more drunken than the rest, grabbed at Guy as he stooped to her. The Slut slashed, and he yelped and reeled back with his arm laid open to the bone. Guy hoisted her up bodily and slung her over his shoulder. His dagger still ready, he backed to the wall, the Slut backing alongside with bared teeth, and no one cared to dispute his way.

'She's mine,' he declared. 'I'll gut the man who tries to rob me.' He moved crabwise along the wall to the stairhead, and they let him go, turning to the one prisoner left them. Sick to the soul, Guy had to abandon him, but he could only kill once, and had chosen the strong man fit to endure rather than the weakling who would not last long. The first shrieks pierced his vitals as he shouldered past the curtain and down the stair.

The woman kicked his legs and pounded his back with clenched fists, but he held her fast, tightening his hold about her thighs, and went down the spiral steadying himself with his shoulder against the wall. She was a well-fleshed peasant and muscled with field-work; he would be bruised for a fortnight from her thumping. He heaved her up more securely, crossed the deserted guardroom, struggled one-handed with the bolt and won into the air. It made him reel as the wine took hold, his legs tangled and he almost fell. Recovering, he squelched across the muddy grass to the forage-shed and dumped his prize with a grunt of relief on the loose hay.

She rolled over and struck at him, sobbing. Guy caught at her in the dark and gripped her arms. 'Gently, gently, or you'll miscarry!' he urged.

'Butcher – murderer – oh Mother Mary, you killed Alfgar!'

'What else could I do for him?' She had not understood; she was in no state to understand now, but he had to try. 'I promise not to harm you. I'll get you out of here – '

She was on her knees, rocking back and forth and sobbing. 'Oh Alfgar, Alfgar! God smite you into Hell! Alfgar!' He dropped to one knee beside her, and she shrieked and struck at him. The Slut snarled, and she huddled away from them both, her arms about her belly.

'Listen to me. I shall not touch you – '

She uncoiled herself and sprang for the doorway. Guy caught her back by the skirts of her gown and pushed her down on the hay. 'God's Grace, do you *want* to be ravished by every man in the garrison and ripped up after? I tell you, *I don't want you!'*

She stiffened, and drew breath sharply. He stood up, frowning down at the dim shape of her in the hay. The loveliest, most willing of demoiselles would not have tempted him this night, and the peasant-woman was not only lumpish and coarse but unsavoury. The rank stink of her, dirt and sweat and fear, was in his nostrils, and doubtless she was alive with lice.

'Wait here,' he commanded. 'My bitch will keep watch.' He touched the Slut's head as she followed him to the door. 'Guard!' She sank to her haunches, black menace in the dim light, and the woman whimpered.

He stopped at the horse-trough to wash sticky blood from his hands and dagger. From the hall window-slits above came a scream and a roar of laughter. He ran for the gatehouse, stumbled against its chilly stone and leaned there shaking through every muscle to his bones. Dry sobs wrenched him. The cries hunted him, sinking to whimpers and then rising, piercing his hands when he covered his ears.

He had known a crazy hope that the gate-guards had been swept to the hall with all the rest of the garrison, or become incapably drunk, but the whipping-post was a peril none would risk. Yellow lantern-light slashed the tunnel's darkness, and from the guardroom came a rumble of men's voices and a bray of laughter. He might order them to open the gate, but they would not obey him without referring to Lord Reynald for leave; from dusk to dawn no one might enter or depart without his permission. Dawn would be too late.

'No way out of here,' Conan's quiet voice said in his ear.

Guy whirled, his hand leaping to his dagger. 'What – ?'

Conan jerked his head, and Guy, half-suspicious and half-bewildered, followed him out of earshot of the guardroom. Vague uproar drifted down from the lighted windows of the hall, but he was all at once aware that the screams had ceased.

'Where's the wench?' Guy hesitated, and he added impatiently, 'Devil burn you, I don't want her!'

195

Guy nodded to the Slut in the forage-shed doorway.

'They reckon to let you finish the night with her and then take their sport,' Conan told him, 'being otherwise disappointed. Don't fret yourself over the man. He's dead.' He sounded entirely sober.

'God have mercy on his soul,' Guy prayed, crossing himself. Sudden comprehension jerked the question from him. '*You?*'

'Yes. They'd blinded him. He was screeching and blundering about, and I hamstrung him. But being drunk I bungled it and cut the spurting vein behind his knee. And who more regretful than I?' His voice was emotionless.

'Why?'

'You wanted it.' He turned towards the shed, a featureless shape in the night. 'You're an obstinate self-righteous pup and I'd rather anyone else had come between me and that bull, but you were the one and I owe you the debt.' He started for the shed, and then swung back. 'Moreover, when I'd witnessed the risk you ran snatching two from under the devil's claws, I didn't find it – amusing. So I finished your work. Now we've to get you out of here.'

'Over the wall it will have to be.'

'And no way of getting a horse out. That means you'll have to come back. You can't go to Malmesbury afoot like a beggar and expect the Angevin to accept you.'

'Afoot I'd most likely be dragged back at my lord's saddle-bow.'

'What are we dawdling for? Fetch the wench before anyone takes it into his head to seek you.'

The woman still huddled where Guy had left her. Waiting had given her terror time to grow, and at sight of a second man she shrieked and cowered into the hay. He bent over her, pity mastering exasperation, and took her gently by the arm.

'Don't be afraid. We won't harm you. Come now, we're going to get you out of Warby.'

Sobbing, she tried to pull away. He dragged her to her feet, and she struggled in panic.

'You silly slut!' hissed Conan. 'He's trying to help you! Come!'

But Conan had no word of English, and she fought the harder for the menace in his incomprehensible words. The Slut growled, and with a whimper she suddenly gave way and obeyed Guy's towing hand.

'The garden wall is lowest,' Conan murmured, 'and not overlooked.'

They trotted the length of the bailey. The keep was built on the highest point, and beyond it the ground fell steeply towards the river, which circled round the hill's foot and made a ditch unnecessary at the southern end of the curtain-wall. Between keep and wall, sheltered and sloping south, lay the garden, and they squelched over grass paths faintly visible between beds of dug earth. Conan stumbled over something in the grass under the fruit trees, swore and then stooped.

'Your luck's holding,' he observed, heaving up a ladder some gardener had left lying after he pruned the trees.

Guy remembered his cracked rib and gave him a hand with it up the steps to the rampart-walk. They hoisted it over between two merlons and managed to find firm footing for it on the berm beneath the wall.

'You could set the wench loose here and let her go,' Conan suggested as though he reckoned Guy's obligations ended at that.

Guy shook his head. 'I must see her to safety.' He could not abandon the wretched creature to find her own way to shelter after all that had befallen her. Likely enough she would run screaming into the river, or fall and miscarry by the wayside. She stood hunched against the parapet, sobbing in faint gulps. 'I'll go first,' he said. 'Then you help her over.' The Slut whined. He lifted and slung her over his shoulder, slid backwards through a crenel, found the topmost rung with his foot and decended. He anticipated he would have to carry the woman likewise, but Conan bundled her over and he helped her down. He spared time to hoist the ladder up for the mercenary to return, caught the woman's hand and led her down the hill, the Slut loping ahead.

They slanted along the slope to the thickets and rough ground at its foot, and he led along the river bank, leaving it only to skirt the village and the ploughed fields. 'No use seeking help where Lord Reynald rules,' he told her. 'Your nearest safety is Thorgastone.'

The ford was high, and he had almost to carry her over, the icy water swirling about his thighs and her skirts tangling against his legs. The Slut was carried far downstream, but she joined him grinning and shaking herself. His boots sloshed full of water, and the wind bit through his clothes, but the rain had blown away, and the clouds shredded to let gleams of watery moonlight show them the path.

The woman lagged, weighted down by her wet skirts, exhausted by abuse and fear and grief. Again and again he had to stop to let her rest, falling in the lee of some rock or thicket. She was sunk in apathy, silent as a foundered beast, and he soon gave up trying to comfort or reassure her in the face of her mistrust. Even when he lent her his strength over the roughest ground he could feel her flinch and stiffen, and his shame and remorse grew rather than diminished, like the aid she needed.

The eastern sky was greying as they came down the waste's long slope to Thorgastone, and in the hamlet a cock crowed. Guy led the woman, stumbling with exhaustion, to the edge of the ploughland. Already lights were flickering in window-slits as the briskest villagers stirred from sleep.

'You'll find help there,' he told the woman. He had not asked, and never learned her name. 'God keep you and deliver you safely of a fair babe.' He hesitated, and then tried for the last time to reach her understanding. 'Believe me, it was mercy I gave Alfgar – '

She jerked free. 'Mary Mother curse you into Hell, butcher!' she choked, and blundered away down the track to the houses.

Guy watched her to the first door, the blacksmith's, heard her knocking and saw her taken in. He sighed, and the Slut pressed against him. He smoothed her head. Dawn was grey over the waste behind him, over the dark ploughland, the huddled huts of the hamlet, the naked woods beyond, all drenched and desolate as he was. He should return to Warby;

his head ached, his limbs were weighted with weariness, and his belly heaved queasily. Instead he plodded over the fields, using the baulks dividing the ploughed strips for paths, until he reached the woods and in their concealment worked back to the road.

He should go back to Warby; eat, rest, recover and prepare his escape, but he could not. The memory of that night's horrors drove his failing feet further and further, he neither knew nor cared where. Over and over he beat at his wits for some way he could have prevented all that had resulted from a few hasty words. He had his knighthood, and wished with all his heart that he was back in Bristol working at Kenric's forge in the security of lost innocence. He had done Alfgar the only service possible, but he felt that killing would haunt him for the rest of his days and nights.

Guy slouched slower and yet more slowly under the bare branches that spattered heavy drops as the wind stirred them. The mud and leaf-mould sucked at his soft ankle-boots that had never been intended for such use and were fast disintegrating. Once he surprised a fox stepping delicately along the track; it bounded away with a flick of white-tipped brush. The wet woods stretched before him black as his misery. He had no eyes for the first green cracks in hawthorn-buds, the black elder-shoots brightening to green, the first green spears thrusting to the light in sheltered places. He was tired to his bones, but he tramped on as though he could leave himself behind.

At last he came to a fallen tree sprawled by the way, and all at once knew how weary he was. He sat down to rest. The Slut laid her head on his knee, and he fondled her absently. He shrank from the thought of returning to Lord Reynald's hold, eating his food, sleeping under his roof, accepting his gifts, when he loathed and feared the man who had begotten him, hated the blood that ran in his own veins. Return he must. He buried his face in the Slut's ruff, his arms about her solid body, and she, sensing his distress, licked his face.

A throbbing faster than her heart-beats brought his head up. A horse was approaching at a run. He climbed to his feet

199

slowly as an aged man rigid with rheumatism and looked back the way he had come, his hand automatically lifting to his dagger. The rider came into sight round the bend, and he recognized Helvie, the person he wished most and dreaded most to see.

'Mistress Helvie – '

For a moment he thought that she would ride him down, but she hauled the mare back on her haunches so close that foam spattered his tunic.

'*You!*'

He stared up at her face, her eyes that accused and condemned together, and chilled. His tongue would not frame words. 'M-my lady – '

'Out of the way, monster!'

He stood fast because he could not move. 'Please hear me – '

'What can you say? Oh God in Heaven, I thought you were an honest man – gentle and kind – shouldn't I have known that devil could only get his own likeness? You've proved yourself his true son!'

'You cannot blame me more than I blame myself.'

'God's mercy, wasn't it filthy vengeance enough to drown your leman and her lover, but you had to destroy Summerford for helping them?'

'I tried – I could not prevent – '

'You were there! You shared – how could you? How *could* you? And after – after – to murder – '

'Of that I'm not ashamed. It was the only – '

'Will you say you were drunk, as if that were excuse for anything, even to cutting your mother's throat?'

He put out his hand to her bridle as she gathered the reins. 'Mistress Helvie, I beg – '

'*No!*'

Her whip streaked fire from brow to chin, and he stood dumbly as she danced her mare sideways. 'Mary Mother, how could you?' she cried. 'I liked you – God help me, I was beginning to love you!'

She was gone in a spatter of mud and a flurry of skirts, and Guy stood unmoving as long as he could hear her horse's hooves. Then he sank back on the log again, his arms about the Slut for comfort and his desolation blacker than before. The weal on his cheek stung sharply, and he realized that tears were oozing from under his shut lids. He too, he acknowledged, had begun to love. He sat there until all feeling was numb, and he slid from the tree-trunk to huddle against the Slut's warm body, sleep at last mastering him.

He roused when the bitch shifted under him, growling warning, and lifted his head from her coat. Normally he woke all of a piece, but this time his brain was sodden with sleep, and he blinked stupidly at a face he knew.

'Botched it proper, haven't you?' Wulfric spat. 'Not got the sense you was born wi'!'

Guy sat up slowly, his head spinning, and blinked again. 'What?' he mumbled.

'There I was reckoning as you'd match fine wi' Helvie, both o' you bastards so's you couldn't neither o' you cast it at t'other, and you one as'll make his way once you're quit o' Warby.'

'You're mad,' Guy muttered. 'Her father'd never – '

'You expect he'll live forever? Who's to care for her when he's gone? Likeliest man me and Elswyth seen since she come man-high, and you throws your chance – what possessed you to ride wi' them devils?'

'I couldn't – prevent it,' Guy told him, propping his head on both hands. It felt fit to cleave apart. Wulfric's voice sounded oddly, one moment booming in his ears, the next receding to a whisper.

'Get you back to Warby. What are you loitering for? Helvie's gone to rouse her father to help Summerford, and if they finds you here hanging's the least they'll do.'

Guy struggled to his feet, dizzy and stiff. He coughed, and a sharp pain stabbed through his chest and took his breath. The Slut whined. Hands gripped his arms, and his sight cleared to show Wulfric's face suddenly alive with concern.

'You're sick! God in Heaven, didn't I warn you never to bed down in a heap o' wet leaves, you young fool? Come, move while you can and get to your bed.'

'You'll – help me?'

'Didn't you let me go when any other man would ha' killed me?' He drew Guy's arm over his shoulder and steered him along the path. The Slut bared her teeth in a snarl and then, as her master accepted him, did likewise and trotted along at his other side, nuzzling the hand that no longer responded. Guy's mind achieved a sluggish functioning.

'You attacked – tried to kill – '

'Reckon you're to blame for that!'

'*I*?'

'What you said about burgess freedom stuck in my head, but beggary's worse'n bearing the wolf's head. So I puts it to Godwin and Burnt Siward as one o' them barrels o' silver pennies'd set us all up for life, and they comes in wi' me. Money and naught else, I tells 'em over and over; draw off the knights and at that cart for the silver. But as soon's they seen the women they goes mad.'

'So – you won nothing?' Guy, steadied by the smaller man's shoulder, concentrated his wandering wits to understand.

Wulfric spat. 'Not a penny. Two o' my fools got theirselves killed, and the rest blames *me* and goes off wi' Burnt Siward. No sense. You tell anyone you knowed me?'

'No.' Another spasm of coughing shook him, and he realized in dull dismay that he was very sick.

'Thanks for that. Steady, lad. Easy does it. You're mortal bad – lung fever I reckons.'

Guy obeyed his guidance, plodding along the track with no will of his own. He was vaguely aware that they left the road for some dim trail that brought them round Thorgastone to the waste. The long climb took almost the last strength out of him. He was burning with heat, yet seized at shortening intervals by fits of shivering. His breathing rasped painfully in his chest, and he coughed more and more often. His head was inclined to drift from his shoulders, his limbs did not belong to his body. Half-way down the long slope beyond the Devil's Ring an appalling rigor took him and he collapsed, shivering uncontrollably. When it was over Wulfric hauled him up, scarcely able to put one foot before the other. The outlaw exhorted, encouraged, cursed, at the end almost dragged him; without his aid he would have lain down to die. He supported Guy across the ford, that all but took him from his feet, and steered him to the castle path. Guy, roused by the shock of cold water, understood that he dared venture no further.

'God aid you,' Wulfric growled in valediction, and he mumbled some sort of thanks. The Slut tugged at his tunic, whining distress at his state, and he went like a sleep-walker through the village, where folk gaped and pointed but made no move to help or hinder, up the hill to the castle.

The gate-guard spoke to him, but he heard no word. Somehow his feet carried him up the steps to the keep door. There another rigor halted him, and he leaned against the wall inside, fighting to stay upright. His chest was locked in bands of hot iron that would not let him draw breath, and a fit of agonized coughing racked him. He wiped his hand across his mouth, and saw it streaked with rusty phlegm. The Slut whimpered. Someone grabbed his arms. Conan's face filled his darkening vision. Then the world dissolved, and he pitched into a black void.

Chapter 14

The ceiling had receded. After rousing morning by morning
to whitewashed barrel-vaulting close above his head, Guy
stared bewildered at distant rafters. Neither was it morning;
the light was that of full day. He tried to look about him,
but was too feeble to turn his head, buttressed by the soft
upswell of pillow on either side. It did not matter. He shut
his eyes and slid back into sleep.

Full day was there when he woke again, but whether the
same or another he could not tell. The rafters were still dark
overhead, a dusty spiderweb linking one to the wall. Below
it a hanging covered the whitewashed plaster, linen embroidered with stiff little figures riding stiff little horses after
improbably antlered deer. It was vaguely familiar. He wondered where he was and how he came here, and why he was
so weak that he could scarcely move his hand. He tried to
shift his head. His beard clung and rasped on the linen. At
his other side there was a stir, a soft thump, an eager whine;
a broad grey head, prick-eared and open-mouthed, grinned
at him as the Slut stood reared with her forepaws on the bedcover. A warm tongue wiped his cheek.

'Oh lass – good lass –'

His voice was a faint croak; he tried and failed to bring
up a hand to caress her. Behind her a white kerchief moved,
and he blinked up at Lady Mabel's face and tried to move
his head away from the Slut's enthusiastic tongue.

'All's well, lad.'

'Down, lass – enough – down!' he gasped, and she subsided. His stepmother laughed and pushed past the bitch, and
the Slut, whining joyfully, made way for her. 'My lady –'

'Gently, Guy. You've been very sick, but now you'll mend.'
She touched his cheek with the back of her hand, smiled and

announced, 'The fever's gone.' She turned away, and he managed to move his head enough to watch her. A brazier glowed by a window, and on it sat a pot reeking herbal steam. She filled a wooden cup and advanced to put a horn spoon to his lips. The draught was bitter as wormwood, but the viler the potion the more efficacious its action, and Guy meekly swallowed all. Even so slight an effort exhausted him, so he shut his eyes and drowsed again.

Guy dozed and woke through the rest of the day and the night. Every time he opened his eyes Lady Mabel and the Slut were there, sharing vigil. She saw to his needs, dosed him with her herbal brew or with mulled wine to renew his strength, and discouraged any attempt to talk. Too weak to worry about past or future, he was content to lie in comfort, warm and quiet, and surrender control to his stepmother. He realized that he lay, astonishingly, in the great bed in the bower that was normally shared by Lord Reynald and his lady, and supposed hazily that he had been laid there for peace and privacy.

In the first dawn, sated with sleep, Guy woke and watched the grey light strengthen in the slit of sky he could see through the window, on the plaster, and at last reach the rafters. It drowned the flickering candle-flame, and the figures in the hanging that had jumped and galloped through the night moved no more except as the draught stirred them. Memory returned to torment him, as it had done in fevered dreams he vaguely recalled, along with a nightmare of choking in a darker flood than the river that had borne away Agnes and Oswin.

He stirred, and at the movement the Slut's head appeared. Behind her came Lady Mabel, as trim as though she had just come from her tirewoman's hands instead of having watched all night in her clothes. She administered more of the bitter potion, smiling at his grimace, and considered him.

'Yes, you're mending.'

'How long – ?'

'This is the ninth day.' Startled, he gaped at her. 'You had the lung-fever.'

Few enough recovered from that. 'Then – I came near – '
'For a week we thought you would die.'
He looked quickly at the Slut. 'My bitch – she'll be starving – '
She smiled. 'Because she will take food from no other? Don't fret yourself; the children cheated her. They put food in your hand and gave it to her so.'
'The children – '
'You presented them to her as friends, and she accepts them.'
'Down, good lass. She gave – no trouble?'
'She accepted me, and Conan. He carried you up. I meant to have another bed set up, but she wouldn't let my lord through the door, so we laid you here and he sleeps in your place.'
'God's Grace!' said Guy devoutly.
'Oh, after his first fury he was willing enough. You – we all feared you would die. But you're young and hardy.'
'And well-tended,' he supplemented. Daylight showed her face strained and weary, blue-shadowed about her eyes, and he knew whose devotion had cheated the grave. But others, more innocent, had died. Misery engulfed him. 'Was it worth – so much trouble – to keep breath in my carcase?'
'Yes,' she answered firmly, smiling at him. 'Now you are feeling sorry for yourself.'
He opened his mouth to expostulate, and then recognized how much more reason for self-pity Lord Reynald's wife must have, but he had never known her indulge it. He slackened against his pillow, and shut his eyes. 'I did – so very ill,' he muttered.
'So you said, when you rambled in the fever. But the blame was not yours. What more could you have done?'
'For Agnes and Oswin, very little,' he admitted. Weakness was overwhelming him, every word a separate effort, yet he could not rest until he had told her. 'But I should have ridden – to Summerford – by the shortest way – if I had not been drunk – and afraid for myself.'

'That's your share of blame, then.'

'They died – because I was a coward. And the consequences – could hardly have been worse.'

'You're alive.'

'But –'

'Don't wish otherwise. You have the chance to amend matters.'

'Helvie – Helvie hates and despises me.'

'If she did not hate you now she would not be worth loving.'

He gasped, and then nodded. 'She is – worth loving.'

'And since she was angry enough to strike you, she had thought well of you.'

'Then you think – I may hope –'

'Don't despair. Though I see no future for this love, your father and hers being at feud.' She sighed. 'Yet, even though it be fruitless, I believe love is never wasted. The Lord God knows there's little enough in this world.' She blew up the coals in the brazier and set a pan to heat. 'I've wearied you, but it needed saying.'

'You've – heartened me,' he murmured, watching her stir the pan.

'Sickness makes men humble,' she mocked gently, and came to his side with bowl and spoon. It was milk gruel, sweetened with honey; infants' food, but he was dependent as an infant. Then Lady Mabel left him for a time, and he listened to the castle rousing for the day's work and thought how wise her advice had been. Remorse was one matter, despair another, and a sin.

The curtain-rings rattled softly, and the Slut roused up and thumped her tail. Two pairs of owl-eyes peered at Guy, and then the children came in, Matilda carrying a bowl of water that had slopped its contents liberally down her skirt, and Roger bearing a beef blade-bone with a fair amount of flesh and gristle on it.

'Wuff!' said the Slut in pleased anticipation as they set down these offerings, and looked up at her master with pricked ears and jaws a-grin. He smiled and bade her fall to. Matilda climbed on to the high bed with a scramble and a heave, sprawled upon him and gave him a juicy kiss and a throttling embrace.

'You *are* better?' she asked anxiously.

'They said you'd die,' Roger whispered, climbing up beside her and kissing Guy as though afraid he might fall apart. 'You're not going to die, are you?'

'Not this time,' Guy assured them, wishing he had strength to hug them both.

'We said our prayers for you,' Matilda told him. 'All the time we kept saying them. Lady Mabel said God might heed little children.'

'He did,' Guy told them, warmed by their love.

'Yes, because you didn't die.' She kissed him again, and said severely, 'Your face is bristly.'

'I'm sorry.' Dearly as he loved them, in his weakness he found their company exhausting, though nothing would have induced him to say so. The Slut crunched her bone, and he had an inspiration. 'If my poor bitch – has not left me all these days – will you take her for a run?'

Roger slid from the bed and regarded her dubiously. 'Will she go with us?'

The Slut knew the word 'run' and was already on her feet, looking eagerly at her master; then, when he did not move from the bed, her tail drooped and her head hung in dejection.

'Take your ponies – exercise her well. Go with them, lass.'

The Slut looked piteously at him, and then obeyed Matilda's hand on her collar. Guy turned his head on the pillow and shut his eyes in peace. He could hear the women beyond the curtain, chatting quietly as they put away the bedding for the day and settled to their sewing and spinning, more subdued than most feminine gatherings he had heard. He hoped no one would prevent Matilda's truancy from needlework, and found himself wondering what sort of man would take her to wife in eight or nine years' time, and whether he would appreciate his good fortune as she deserved.

Guy was sliding back into sleep when the curtain-rings

heralded another entry. It was too soon for the children to return, so he supposed Lady Mabel was there again, and did not move as soft shoes padded over the dry rushes. The feet halted at his side, and kicked the Slut's abandoned bone aside with a clatter. Lady Mabel was too neat-footed to do that. He shifted his head and looked up into Lord Reynald's face.

'They said you were mending, but you look only fit to be measured for your winding-sheet,' he observed, surveying him with a perturbed expression.

'Then appearance is against me, my lord,' Guy answered, 'for I'm certainly mending.'

'I'm heart-glad of that,' Lord Reynald declared, with the first semblance of a true smile Guy had seen on his face. Then it clouded to petulance again. 'Your wolf-bitch kept me from your side while you were out of your senses.'

'I apologize for her – and for usurping your bed, my lord.'

'You don't reckon I grudged it you? Or anything else that would help to save my son? But that bitch of yours would not let me pass the door.'

'She meant but to guard me, my lord.'

'Teach her I'm no enemy but your father. And an undutiful son you are, spoiling sport and taking that wench out of my hold. If you didn't want her for yourself why deny her to your comrades?'

'To save her from them.'

'You're a soft fool. You'll have to harden if you're to make a knight.' He leaned against the bedfoot, scowling. 'A dear night's work, that. No loot, no sport, and my marshal dead.'

Guy gasped. 'Sir Gerard – dead?'

'Lockjaw, four days ago. As well you're knighted. You can train up to his duties.'

'But my lord, I – I've no experience – '

'You'll get it this summer. The Angevin is marching north.'

'My lord – '

'Why won't you ever call me "Father"?' he demanded with a spurt of temper.

209

'I – it would not be seemly in a bastard, my lord.'

'Seemly? You're my son, my tall fine first-born, for all that you're an undutiful whelp, and I'd be even prouder to have sired you if you'd only conform to my wishes. And when we thought you'd die – ' He broke off, his face working.

'Your lady's tending saved me,' Guy said, moved despite himself by his sire's undoubted concern.

'Not it! I sacrificed for you, a hen and a cock and a goat. *She* wanted a priest, with his oil and his Latin – what use? But I made the offering, and when I came down from the waste the fever had broken and you were asleep. Isn't that proof enough?'

'What did Wulfrune and Rohese sacrifice for?' Guy asked dryly. 'God answered the prayers of my lady and the children.'

'Who gives something for nothing, least of all a god? Blood for blood, life for life – '

'Our Lord made the sacrifice Himself, once and for all time and all sinners.'

'That's what you believe, is it? And too late to change you.'

'It's the faith I was bred in and the truth I hold by,' Guy told him deliberately.

'It's not you I blame, but those who withheld you from me – my son. I'd have bred you up to that power and pleasure, and you'd have led the worship after me. And instead they made a gutless Christian of you, and cheated me – '

He checked abruptly, and stalked out. Guy found that he was trembling through all his body. Many thoughts jostled for his attention, foremost the realization that Lord Reynald would have let him die without the last rites of the Church. His brain refused to cope with them. He lay in a kind of mindless languor, dreamily regarding the figures in the hanging that stirred in the draught from the window, and listening to the twitter of women's voices in the bower.

Lady Mabel returned with a posset of eggs, milk and hot wine, and took a stool by his bed, busying herself with some sewing. When the children returned, flushed and windblown, with the Slut, she shooed them out. The bitch settled to her bone again with small cracking noises. Grey and white clouds scudded across the blue sky in the window-slit, and a sharp wind whistled round the battlements and set the coals winking in the brazier. Now and then Lady Mabel got up to warm her hands at it. Guy was snug enough, deep in the featherbed with covers piled to his nose, rousing to swallow posset, gruel or broth every hour or so and feeling strength slowly creeping back into his body.

About mid-morning the curtain moved again, and Conan entered. Lady Mabel nodded and began to fold up her work. He strolled to the bed and looked down, his eyebrows lifting.

'No funeral this time? You have disappointed me.'

'You've had one funeral!' snapped Lady Mabel, whose many excellences did not include a sense of humour.

'I'd hoped to be quit of my inconvenient obligations.'

'Is that why you've spent your nights and days helping me tend him?'

Guy smiled. 'So I owe you thanks.'

'Oh, soldiers always tend their comrades. First because there's seldom anyone else to do it, and second because it may well be your own turn after the next skirmish. I see you're mending.'

'I'll be as good as new in a few weeks,' Guy said confidently, and then caught a flicker of contradiction in his stepmother's glance. 'Shall I not?' he challenged her.

'You've had the lung-fever,' she said. 'Not many survive it. You'll have a weakness in your chest for years, the rest of your life maybe, and you must guard against chills, wrap warmly and always change wet clothes, for you'll not live through another attack.'

'You mean I must coddle myself like a weakly infant?' Guy demanded in revulsion.

'You young men!' she cried in sudden passion. 'You treat your bodies as though they were hammered out of the same iron as your weapons! Is it any wonder that, if we come through childbed, we weak women outlive you?'

'My lady –'

'You had no more sense than to go wandering in the wind and rain, in soaked clothes without even a cloak to keep out the weather, no food in your belly but wine enough for six – and then you wonder at what you've brought on yourself?'

'But –'

'*Men!*' she enunciated bitterly, and stalked out with a clash of curtain-rings.

The two regarded each other, neither demonstrating the least inclination to laugh. Conan pulled up the stool. 'She's most likely right. Few of us make old bones.'

Contemplating a lifetime's need to consider his health, Guy grimaced. 'Doddering by a fireside like a grandfather!' he muttered.

'By Easter you'll be ready to ride out,' Conan assured him. 'We'll go together.'

'Together? Your service ends then, but –'

'Had you forgotten I'm your man?' He grinned at Guy's embarrassed scowl. 'You'll not leave me behind. Your father has offered me a year's engagement as his marshal, *and* your sister to wife, a prospect to make any man run fast and far.'

Guy grinned. 'I wonder you're not already on your way.'

'Besides being pledged, I've business to finish.' He got up to refuel the brazier, and seeing that Guy was laboriously attempting to change his position, rolled him on to his side, shook up the pillows and tucked the covers round his neck, competently as any woman putting a child to bed. Guy thanked him, inwardly galled to be dependent on the help of this man he detested.

'How go your ribs?' he remembered to ask.

'Mended.'

'A sorry night's work that proved.'

'A night to rejoice for,' Conan contradicted, his face lighting. 'It rid me of my enemy.'

'Gerard?' Guy stiffened in disgust; he had not liked the marshal himself, but to rejoice so blatantly in any man's horrible death was monstrous. 'And now his wife is unprotected for you to ravish?' At the tone of his voice the Slut, dozing beside him, lifted her head and growled softly.

'This time my intentions are entirely honourable.'

'How should anyone guess that?'

'I hope that she'll go with me after Easter, as my wife.'

Guy gaped at him. 'In God's Name, man – '

'She's free, and my hands are clean of his blood. Why not?'

'In God's Name!' Guy repeated. 'She loved Gerard and loathes you. She's in great grief. Go gently – '

'What else is there for her to do? A woman alone?' He walked across to the window and stood looking out. With misgiving Guy regarded the harsh beauty of the mercenary's profile, sharp against the sunlit whitewash, and noted the confident smile on his mouth. His uneasiness deepened. Conan's pursuit of Lady Cecily had not been pure malice against her husband; he intended marriage, not rape, so some semblance of love animated his carcase.

Conan swung round, his back to the light. 'You are going to say I am not fit to hold her horse's bridle,' he mocked.

'Are you?'

'Probably not.'

'Go gently,' Guy appealed again.

'God's Death, I cannot go at all! Not one chance for a word alone with her can I get!' He began to pace across the floor and back like a caged wolf. Guy watched him in silence for a while, too troubled to be amused, until all at once his eyelids fell and the sleep of weakness overwhelmed him unawares.

He mended steadily. After the first few days of utter weakness he was able to lie propped against pillows, his fur-lined cloak wrapped round his shoulders, and play dice and chess with Conan or occasionally with Lord Reynald. He was the children's captive, and Roger begged to be taught his letters. 'I'll never be of any use as a fighting man,' he pointed out with a realism beyond his years, 'but any lord's a fool who puts himself at his clerk's mercy.' He took to it with single-minded determination, but Matilda, who begged to learn also, equalled him.

By the end of a week Lord Reynald's small tolerance for his own inconvenience was at its end. He would no longer be excluded from his own bed-chamber by a mannerless bitch that dared show him her teeth. Lady Mabel therefore had a bed set up for Guy between the partition and the stair, and he had all the bower's activities to entertain him. He had Lord Reynald's servant shave him, and one glance into the polished silver mirror shocked the breath from him. He had expected to look white and wasted, but not fifteen years older. Nothing of boyhood was left in the face that gazed back at him stripped to the skull, mouth and brows set in harsher lines and eyes sunk deep in shadowed sockets.

February was gone, and March brought longer evenings, brighter sun and winds whooping about the battlements. Guy could totter from bed to stool and sit, bundled in his cloak, looking from a window-slit at fields and woods, distant peasants sowing and harrowing, small boys scaring birds and horsemen going to hunt or hawk. He was wearying of inaction. The children knew their letters and could already spell out simple words with charcoal on boards, his chess had improved until he was almost a match for Lord Reynald, and the Slut had resigned herself to a master who lay day-long in bed and left her exercise to young deputies.

One night a serving-woman was brought to bed, and Guy lay listening to the bustle and the cries, watching the lights and flitting figures and offering his prayers, sharing in the occasion from which his sex was normally excluded, the anxieties of the labour and the joy when a boy was safely delivered. On the third day Lady Mabel, having procured the services of Thorgastone's priest, declared a holiday in the bower for the infant's christening. All trooped out to the village church except the mother and Lady Cecily, who was too deep in mourning to go forth in public.

Guy lay alone, propped against several pillows, dozing or watching the sky. Distant voices and the ring of the smith's hammer floated up from the bailey, but the keep was quiet, all but empty. Lady Cecily rustled over the rushes, her black skirts sweeping them into drifts, her face almost swallowed in a black kerchief. Grief had made her a little white ghost. Twice Guy had tried to utter his condolences, but sympathy dissolved her into tears. Now he greeted her, but she merely inclined her head and moved past him to the stair.

He heard her feet go slipping down half a dozen steps and then check, and a mouse-small squeak of fright.

'Lady Cecily!' said Conan's voice.

'No! No! Go away!'

'I must speak to you –'

'I – I won't! Let me pass!'

'Since I have been waiting a fortnight to get a word with you alone, hear me out, my lady –'

'Alone – Mother Mary protect me!'

Guy heard a slight scuffle, and sat up in bed. The Slut rose to her haunches and looked at him with pricked ears. Conan's voice attempted reassurance.

'My lady, don't be afraid. I swear I mean you no harm. Only hear me –'

A terrified whimper broke from her. Guy threw off the covers and reached for his cloak; this intolerable scene must be interrupted.

'You mean you'll ravish me – now my husband's dead –'

'No, no, on my knightly oath! You're free now – alone – and how can a woman fend for herself without a man? Who's to protect you but me? In all honour, my lady! I'll marry you –'

'Never!' she cried, anger breaking through fear. Guy, huddling the cloak about his shoulders, stumbled to the wall, and with its support made for the stair as she rejected him. '*You* – raptor – I'd die first!'

'My lady, my lady, I love you – all along I have loved you! Marry me, and I swear to honour and cherish you all my days –'

Guy reached the stairhead as Conan made his avowal, and stared down at her, tugging ineffectually against his hold on her wrist, and at the mercenary four steps lower, his upturned face eager and earnest. Neither saw him. Feet pelted up from below. Philip's face appeared round the newel and convulsed with fury.

'Take your hand from my mother!' he screeched, and hurtled at Conan, clawing at his hand and then sinking his teeth into it.

The man fended him away. It was no blow, a mere back-handed flick to ward him off, but Philip was on the inner edge of the step with barely an inch of toehold. He toppled backward down the stair out of Guy's sight, but he heard the crack as the boy struck the wall and saw his legs sprawl upward. Conan was after him on the instant as he slithered, calling his name. He caught him up and turned back with the child in his arms. He checked. Guy heard him gasp, and then he lifted a face yellow-grey as tallow.

'Philip!'

The boy's head jolted over Conan's arm at an impossible angle. His mother descended three steps, slowly raising clawed hands to her face, her eyes dilating. 'You've killed him!' she whispered. *'Philip –'* Then she whirled and scudded up the stair.

Guy glimpsed her demented face, lurched to grab and caught only a fold of woollen cloth that jerked through his fingers. Conan, rousing from a trance, laid down the boy and started after her black skirts disappearing round the newel. The door above flung open, the sentinel shouted alarm, feet scurried. An appalling scream fell from the sky and snapped off at the wall's foot in a thump.

Guy stood paralysed, leaning against the wall, his knees melting with shock. Then he lifted his hand to cross himself. 'God have mercy on her,' he muttered.

Conan stared up where he had last seen her, his hands reached out as though he were suddenly blinded and all colour gone from his face. Then his joints folded; he sank to his knees, whimpering between clenched teeth, and beat his head against the wall. Guy stumbled down to him. The Slut howled once. He laid a hand on the man's shuddering shoulder. His legs gave way, and he sat heavily on the stair above. Conan twisted round, his face distorted and blood streaking down his brow. 'My fault – she killed herself – my lady!' he gasped. Involuntarily Guy set his arm about him. 'Oh God, oh God, I loved her!' He sank forward, his head in Guy's lap, sobs rending him. Guy, wrung with pity, could only hold him, uselessly smoothing the black head on his knees, while below the christening party came crying and questioning into the keep.

Chapter 15

Guy had never seen a man so changed by grief as Conan. Remorse and despair devoured him; he could neither eat nor sleep, and daily lost flesh and colour. Despite the testimony of the one eye-witness, none believed him guiltless of even wishing Philip harm. Lord Reynald was indifferent; all others ostracized him. His own ruffians even, who could stomach most sins, looked askance at the man who had tossed a woman's child down a flight of stairs because she rejected his offer of marriage. Guy, whose own misery had made him sensitive to that of others, was intensely sorry for the mercenary, drifting about the sentry-walks or exhausting himself and his horses in wild rides alone through the greening countryside.

Guy's protestations in Conan's defence brought a coolness between himself and his stepmother, sorrowing and furious for her attendant's end. Overbearing all objections, she had seen her buried in consecrated ground between her husband and son, asserting, as indeed none could refute, that she had been deranged with grief when she cast herself from the battlements. She had always loathed Conan, and dismissed Guy's exoneration of the mercenary so savagely that he abandoned further attempts to convince her. After two days of strain and resentment he discharged himself from the bower and returned to his chamber off the hall.

Conan lent him an arm down the stair and steadied him as far as his bed. The relationship between them had warmed. Guy was the only person who did not shun the mercenary, and Conan lingered in his company as though he found comfort in it. Guy lay flat, breathing hard after the effort, and Conan sat on the bed by his feet, apparently studying the tattered rushes. The Slut gently thumped her tail. Guy reached out to fondle her head, his gaze on the mercenary's profile, almost as gaunt as his own.

Conan had been free of tongue; now he scarcely opened his mouth. He had gone his way contemptuous of his fellows' opinions, and now flinched from their condemnation. He had despised Guy as an artisan thrust upon men of knightly breeding, and he stayed here because no one else would tolerate his presence. Sensing the scrutiny, he glanced up, his light-grey eyes unnaturally bright in their shadowed sockets.

'God help you, man!' Guy burst out, lifting on an elbow. 'It was not your fault!'

'It was.'

'It was an accident—'

'I killed her.' He looked down again at the rushes, scuffling them with one foot. 'If I had not tormented her when she was Gerard's wife, she would have turned to me as her friend, and in the end married me.'

Guy had not reckoned back to first causes, but that undoubted truth struck him dumb. He could only stare at the man who must live with that realization.

'Damnation makes monsters of us,' the lifeless voice broke their silence. 'Hire your sword, and you are doomed to hellfire, so in defiance and revenge you set yourself to earn it. If burn you must, as well burn for every crime man may commit, and vie with your comrades in evil. So you smother your conscience under a weight of sin until it is dead, and you're another routier who would slit his mother's throat for a silver penny.'

Guy wondered sharply whether he would have done better, kicked out of his home at fifteen with an old sword and a worn-out horse for his only patrimony. He had never thought to feel so much sympathy for this damned soul, and though he wondered how bitterly Conan would hate him for hearing his self-betrayal when he regained command of his silence, his need was to ease his burden by confession.

'She was my enemy's wife, another woman I wanted to lay, to drag into the muck with me—oh God! I made her afraid of me—mocked and tormented her—my perverse pleasure—' He caught his breath on something like a sob. Guy

219

sat up and put out a hand, and Conan clutched it so that
his bones ground together. 'Then she was free, and not any
woman but the one – and now she's dead I know she was the
only woman – no other ever – my love.'

'God comfort you,' Guy said helplessly.

'How? I'm damned.'

'Pray for Christ's mercy, Sir Conan. No man is past redemption who repents.'

'Is that what they taught you in the monastery?'

'Yes. And it's a priest you need.'

'What should any priest do but consign me to perdition
before he's heard the half?' Conan demanded, heaved himself
from the bed and plunged past the curtain.

Guy's strength came steadily back to him, but not as fast
as he desired. Impatiently he measured the milestones; the
day he could dress unassisted; the hours he could spend on
a stool beside the fire, or on sunny days in a bright window-
splay, wrapped against the outer air; meal-times when he
could walk to the table and set his teeth into solid fare.

A mild afternoon in late March tempted him to his first
excursion outdoors, and he sat on a mounting-block by the
gate, his cloak pulled closely about him, watching all that
went on in the bailey and lifting his face to the sun while
he gathered breath and strength to return. Lord Reynald
and Sir James, drawn forth by the fine weather, had taken
the hounds out upon a report of a pair of wolves prowling
about the lambing-fold. Conan had led his troop on a foray
towards Etherby. He did not neglect his duty to his men, but
their growls had come to Guy's hearing; not only did he no
longer indulge in rape himself but he would not permit any
man of his to molest a woman.

Guy stretched out his legs. The bailey's mud was drying,
and fresh grass springing in the less trampled places. Sparrows
hopped and chirped. The Slut regarded them tolerantly,
stretched nose on paws at his side, and blinked lazily when
they fluttered within inches of her muzzle. Doves strutted
and crooned along the battlements. Some servants' children

were playing tag about the stables. Hooves thumped on wood, and a stallion bugled. Hens were scratching on the midden. By this hour the day's work was over for all but the kitchen servants with supper to prepare, and hardly an adult moved in the bailey. From the guardroom came a muted rumble of voices.

The sentinel on the gatehouse roof called a warning, and with a scrape and clatter the guard turned out. Beyond the gate Guy heard dogs barking, trampling hooves and jingling harness. The hunters were returning. For strangers the watchman would have sounded his horn. Guy sat where he was, listening to the windlass creak and the chains rattle as the drawbridge was lowered. The planks reverberated, roused grooms came running from stables and huts, dog-boys from the kennels and scullions from the kitchen. The pack streamed in, vociferous at homecoming, Edric the huntsman stalking in their midst with spear and whip.

Wulfrune and Rohese had emerged also from their brewhouse to greet Lord Reynald, the foremost rider through the gateway. Behind him on a dispirited nag came the last man Guy had ever expected to see in Warby. He sprang up, his face lighting, and in joyous surprise greeted him by the last name that should have passed his lips.

'Father!'

Kenric swung stiffly down, transfigured by thankfulness. 'God be praised!' he cried, and ran to seize him in a bear's embrace. 'Guy, dear lad!' They hugged each other, and then Kenric caught him by the shoulders and held him off to inspect him. 'We had word you were dying,' he said. 'I had not hoped – but God is good.' He released Guy, and the Slut, greeting an old friend, reared up to set her paws on his shoulders and lick his cheek. He slapped her flank and laughed. 'Hey, old lass!' His voice shook slightly.

'Who is this man,' Lord Reynald demanded, 'that you call by the name which should be mine?'

The hairs tingled erect along Guy's spine. He looked up into a mask of menace. 'My lord, my mother's husband.'

'You call *him* "Father"?'

'He has been that from my birth.'

'What's he here for? To claim you?'

'My lord,' said Kenric, his brow creasing in puzzlement, 'we heard our lad was sick to death. His mother has been ailing all winter, fretting for him. To ease her grief I must come, if I were too late to do more than pray by his grave.' He turned to smile at Guy. 'I'm heart-glad that's not needful, and I can take back joyful word of you.'

'He's not your lad!' exclaimed Lord Reynald. 'He's mine!'

'Aye, and withheld from you,' Wulfrune croaked with malice.

'And it's plain which father he prefers,' Rohese added.

'You robbed me!' Lord Reynald cried, looking from Guy to Kenric. 'It's you he loves! My son!' He abruptly swung his leg over the saddle and dropped to the ground. The Slut growled, and Guy slipped his fingers under her collar to restrain her. Edric moved up behind his lord, his eyes watchful, his favourite black hound at his heels. 'Even that ugly bitch of yours snarls at me and licks his face!'

'She has known him from a pup, my lord.'

'He stole my son –'

'In law a bastard is his mother's alone –'

'Stole my son, and bred him up an artisan to shame me and my blood!'

'My lord,' Kenric protested reasonably, 'you begot his body, and at the last he has followed that blood in him. But to me he is my first-born, the son of my heart.'

'Your heart? By the Horns, I'm minded to cut the heart out of you!'

Guy stepped between them and held his voice level with an effort, as he made his appeal to the last shred of reason behind that livid face. 'My lord and father, remember, I chose to be your son. Yet I owe a duty to the man who bred me up. Let him return safely to my mother, and you will have my undying gratitude and service.'

For a breath's space he thought he had won. He dared not

look at Kenric, who had realized his peril and stood as if
carved from wood, but fixed his gaze on his sire's indecisive
face. Then Wulfrune snickered.

'Let him go, when he kept your whelp for his own? Where's
vengeance? Where's manhood?'

'A cheap price he offers, and for love of that peasant, not
you!' Rohese jeered.

Lord Reynald's face whitened, and his lips lifted in a
snarl. In desperation Guy loosed the Slut. 'Take!'

She launched herself. Edric leaped between her and his
lord, his spear driving. It crunched through her ribs from side
to side, and before he could brace its butt against earth her
weight bore him down, her teeth slashed short his screech,
and they rolled over together in a scarlet welter. His legs
kicked twice, like a frog's, and were still. The Slut turned
her gaze to Guy, and her tail twitched; then her eyes filmed,
her head sank, she shuddered and was gone.

Stunned with horror, Guy wasted precious moments staring;
then he uttered a hoarse yell and flung himself before Kenric
to shield him. Lord Reynald shrieked an order, there was a
rush of feet, hands grappled him and dragged him aside,
resisting all the way. Horses squealed and reared, alarmed by
the scent of blood. Excited dogs surged barking about them,
and Edric's black hound came nosing to his side, lifted his
head and howled desolately.

'My lord – ' Kenric gasped, confronting madness and a
knife.

'Son of your heart, is he?'

The knife went in and up, under the ribs' arch. Kenric
stared astonished. His head jerked back, his knees buckled,
and he dropped, dead before he hit the ground. Lord Reynald went down with him. On his knees he slashed and groped
and wrenched, then straightened and hurled a dripping red
lump to the pack. One leaped to snatch it, snapped and
gulped. The rest surged about him in a snarling worry, and
the fight raged across the bailey towards the kennels.

A hideous trance held everyone moveless and speechless.

223

But for the hounds' uproar there was silence under the sky. Guy stared at Kenric's body. The surprise had already gone from his face as it settled into the familiar emptiness of death. The black hound howled again, the cry piercing to the void of his belly, and but for the hold on his arms he would have collapsed where he stood.

Sir James, the hue of tallow, lifted a hand to cross himself. The spell broke. A kennel-boy dropped senseless upon his face among the dogs, a groom broke away to vomit. Wulfrune cackled.

Lord Reynald, red to the elbows, the skirt of his tunic dripping, stood back, white as curd. He looked from Guy to the bodies, and then kicked the mourning dog so that it fled to the kennels yelping. When he spoke a line of froth gathered between his lips and teeth.

'You loosed your bitch on *me*! You'd spill your father's blood!'

Strength came back to Guy. He braced himself to stand steady in the men's hold, and spoke for all to hear.

'You begot my body, but *this* was my father, whom I loved and honoured! Now make an end, for it shames me to live with your blood in me!'

'Spill it from him!' Rohese shrieked.

Lord Reynald lifted the knife, and then threw it down. 'You're my son! Mine! Spill what's mine?' He slapped her from him with his bloody hand so that she staggered and fell, and then snatched up the whip he had dropped. 'It's a father's right to chastise his own!' He gestured to the whipping-post.

The men-at-arms dragged Guy to it, fighting all the way, the one thought in his mind to break free and drive his own dagger into his sire's guts. It took half a dozen of them to pin him down while they dragged tunic and shirt over his head, and to force him against the post, haul his arms up and fasten the shackles.

He stopped struggling as the iron clamped down, and braced himself against the smooth-worn wood. His wits still

spun in unbelief that this was really happening as he pressed
his head against the post and clenched his teeth. The wind
struck coldly across his bare shoulders, and he could not
prevent his muscles from shivering as weakness asserted itself
again.

'No! No! *No*!'

With the screech a small body hurtled across the grass.
Guy twisted his neck and opened his eyes in time to see
Roger's head take Lord Reynald in the belly with the impact
of a mangonel missile as his hands clawed for the whip. He
yelled and folded forward, flinging one aimless blow that sent
the boy spinning into the circle of spectators, and fell to his
knees, hugging his middle with both arms.

Lady Mabel flung round between him and Guy with a
sweep of skirts. 'Will you murder both your sons, monster?'

He groaned lamentably, his face distorted with agony. 'Oh
– oh – the whelp – unnatural – oh – ' He rocked back and
forth, retched and turned green. 'Murderous – the rat's killed
– argh!' He vomited, collapsed sideways, and lay with his
knees drawn up, clutching his belly and whimpering.

Wulfrune and Rohese rushed to him. The girl knelt and
tried to raise him, but he groaned protest.

'Hell's curse on the little parricide!' Wulfrune snarled.

Another voice shouted from the gate, and Conan's stallion
trampled through the circle, scattering men and women
before his hooves. The mercenary took one comprehensive
glance about him and wasted no time asking questions.

'You and you, carry your lord in to his bed. Stop screeching
and go tend him, you hag – out of my sight!' His savage
gesture sent the women scuttling after the servants, who lifted
Lord Reynald and staggered off with him to the keep. He
dropped from the saddle beside the whipping-post, wrenched
the bar from the shackles and flung an arm about Guy as
he reeled free, steadying him while he shuddered with shock
and reaction. 'Who was he?' he asked with a jerk of his head.

'My father – '

The grip tightened, and Guy felt him draw in a hard

breath. He lifted his face, surprised by the tear-tracks drying chill on his cheeks, and braced himself. Conan released him, caught up Lord Reynald's whip and turned on the crowd, swinging it back so that the lash snaked behind him for a slash.

'God's Blood, have none of you work to do, goggling here frog-eyed? *Go!*'

They fled. Guy's knees melted beneath him. He sank down against the post and bowed his head between them, while above him Conan raged at Sir James.

'What were you about? You stood with no more wits nor guts than a wooden image and never tried to stop him?'

'It's no duty of mine to interfere with anything my lord – '

'Here's foul murder – '

'God's Head, *you* to squawk at murder? And what was he but a low-born craftsman when all's said?'

'And his son?'

'A lord has a right to do as he wills with his own.'

'To flog a knight like a thieving serf? An insult to all knighthood!'

'That oaf a knight, still sweating from the forge? It was no concern of mine. I repeat, my lord had the right – '

'Afraid to open your mouth, you lily-livered rat!'

'God's Head, you'll meet me – '

'I'll happily put steel through your belly when I've nothing more urgent to do!'

Skirts brushed Guy's shoulder, and small cold hands seized his arm. He lifted his head, and automatically reached to enfold Roger, sobbing and wheezing together. He looked up. Lady Mabel stood over him, regarding Sir James as though she had never seen him before.

'Enough! Is this a time for challenges?'

'This excommunicate routier miscalled – '

'Enough, I say!'

Roger clung to Guy's shoulders. 'He didn't do it – you're not hurt – I did stop him – '

'I owe you my life, little brother,' Guy said. His voice

would scarcely obey him. The child shivered and sobbed, pressing closer, his tears wet against Guy's skin.

'Oh, oh, oh, what will he do to us now?'

'At this moment I've no doubt he's in his bed clutching at his belly,' said Lady Mabel bracingly. 'He'll not harm either of you.'

Guy lifted his head to meet her gaze. 'Would you – ?'

'Leave all here to me, my lady,' said Conan.

She hesitated. Guy started to struggle up, hampered by Roger's grappling hold, and the routier bent to lift him off. The child shrank from him and clutched tighter. Lady Mabel moved impulsively to come between them, and Conan straightened.

'You did well, boy. You're twice the man already that this dumb stockfish could be. Now stand on your own two feet like the valiant brat you are.'

He gaped up, rigid in Guy's arms, his breath wheezing. Then he stood erect beside his mother, who nodded the first approval she had ever bestowed on the mercenary. Guy heaved to his feet and gestured to the keep. She went briskly across the grass, and Sir James roused himself to escort her.

'Made a leak in that bladder of self-righteousness,' Conan observed. 'Here, don't stand half-stripped in this wind or you'll be sick again.'

Guy had not realized how chilled he had become; he was so clumsy that Conan had to help him. But when Roger passed him his belt with knife and purse he came to life and clawed out the gilded spurs to hurl them upon the dunghill. Conan caught his wrist and forced his arm down.

'That's folly! They are your tokens of knighthood!'

'*Knighthood!*'

'For good or ill it's yours. How can dumb metal offend? Live so that you do them honour, Sir Guy!'

Guy stared resentfully into his eyes, and then bent his head. Conan was right. He braced himself, and moved to Kenric's body. Faint surprise remained in his open eyes and dropped jaw. His blood had sunk into the earth and congealed stickily on his clothes. Guy knelt and pressed his lids shut, crossed himself and muttered a prayer. Feeling was numb in him. This was not Kenric, this chilling clay. Kenric was gone before God, Who would surely have mercy. He tried to straighten the heavy body, but that was beyond his strength. He stood up, moving like an old man.

Conan's voice roughened awkwardly at its novel task of comforting sorrow. 'You'll blame yourself, lad, but he was old, and it was a quick end, easier than any mortal illness.'

'That doesn't absolve me.'

'It's worth remembering.' His own men were waiting; at his signal two of them came forward to take the dead armourer up between them and carry him to the nearest shed. Another heaved the Slut clear of Edric's corpse. At that Guy started forward, fell to his knees and lifted her, cradling her broad head against his chest and burying his face in her harsh fur. She had no soul he could pray for, her love and loyalty and courage were gone into air and darkness, and tears brimmed hot in his eyes as grief and pain tore him.

Presently he mastered himself and stumbled to his feet. His skull seemed stuffed with wool, but he looked at the shed where Kenric had been bestowed and croaked, 'My father –'

'My fellows will prepare him for decent burial and take him to the church.' He steered Guy by the arm to the mounting-block. 'Sit down. You're still unfit.'

'My Slut – not the dunghill –'

Conan raised his voice. 'Gautier, Ivo, take a spade and bury the bitch outside the walls.'

'Bury the *bitch*, cap'n?'

'Doesn't she deserve a grave, dying for her master? Under the ash-tree by the track, to keep her memory before men.'

'What about this rogue she killed, cap'n?'

'You may fling *him* on the dunghill for all I care.'

'We'll observe the decencies,' said Lady Mabel behind him. 'Gertrude is bringing two shrouds. Sir James, have them taken into the church, and tomorrow the priest can be summoned from Thorgastone.'

'I shall see to it, my lady.'

'Lord Reynald, my lady?' Conan asked.

'Lying in his bed bewailing his belly-ache and his unnatural sons,' she answered, her bitterness manifested by her saying as much to the detested mercenary. 'Wulfrune has given him a potion to make him sleep.'

'God send she poisons him,' the routier growled.

'What will he do – oh what will he do when he wakes?' Roger whispered.

'That need not trouble us,' Guy declared. 'None of us will be here to find out.'

They gaped at him, and glanced about lest any had overheard. 'You mean we – we go?' she whispered.

'What better chance will ever offer, with him laid aside and Conan in command of the guard? After supper – '

'Supper? Are we to sit down and eat as though none of this has happened?'

'How will fasting help? When he's asleep, collect money, jewels, a change of clothes, a warm cloak. Bring the children and any of your women who will come, and we'll be away.'

'It's madness!' Sir James protested. 'My lord's wife, and his son – '

'Do you pretend we've any duty to that monster? To go free – ' She caught her breath, and her eyes widened with hope. Then dejection quenched it. 'Do you reckon I haven't thought of it a hundred – a thousand times? What's one night's start, when he'll have the whole garrison after us by morning? Where can we go for safety?'

'To Trevaine.'

'*Trevaine*? Henry of Trevaine – he'd hang Roger from his battlements for revenge!'

'Tell him a fairer revenge would be to escort you to Bristol and put you aboard a ship for Southampton. He's not an unreasonable man. He'll threaten and bluster at first, but face him boldly and he'll agree to it.'

Her eyes steady on his, she said, 'I'll do it. I'll take any risk to get Roger out of his hold.'

'Yes, yes!' Roger whispered.

'Go to supper and behave as usual.'

'As usual, Our Lady help me! And you?'

'Would any expect me to enter again under his roof?' he asked in revulsion, his face twisting as he struggled for self-command.

'The Devil knows what *he* expects, but he's preoccupied with his belly and by now filled with Wulfrune's potions. And here's a scullion sweating from the kitchen to learn whether we sup.'

She turned to meet the man, who cast shifty glances from Guy to the stained grass as he gabbled his message. Then she touched Guy's shoulder and moved away, Roger beside her and Sir James trailing after.

Conan put a hand under Guy's arm. 'You're not fit to ride half a mile.'

'What choice have I?'

'None. So rest until it's time.' He steered Guy to the forage-shed, and he stretched out on the heap of musty hay in the corner, where grooms and scullions laid their wenches, with a grunt of relief. Conan went out, and Guy fought a foolish urge to call him back. He had never felt so desolate. He stared at the dustmotes wavering in the shafts of sunlight that slanted through the warped frames. Kenric was dead, Emma widowed, the children fatherless, and if Guy had not been mastered by pride and ambition his stepfather could have lived out his days in honour and died in his bed with his family about him and a priest to pass him from life with the last rites of the Church. And all for the Dead Sea fruit of knighthood, that had turned to ashes on his lips. Guy turned his face into the hay's prickles and felt tears ooze from under his closed lids.

The door opened at the thrust of Conan's foot. He carried a steaming bowl, a hunk of bread and a cup. Guy sat up with a grunt. The scent of stewed fish made his belly heave, and he shook his head. 'Folly to starve,' Conan warned. 'You'll not go far with nothing in you.' He had said as much himself to Lady Mabel, so after a moment's hesitation he accepted the cup and sipped slowly. The hot spiced wine, sweetened with honey, glowed in his stomach and spread warmth through his body. It quelled his queasiness, and he knew he must swallow something.

'If only I'd been back in time!' Conan growled, more to himself than to Guy.

'Why, what could you have done?'

'Held him off at sword-point – or run him through.'

'I thought you were pledged until Easter?'

'I owe *him* no debt. The other way; he's not paid me since Michaelmas. Justification to any routier. Here.' He set the bowl and bread in Guy's hands. It was Lenten fare, stewed fish in savoury broth. After the first dubious moment Guy found that it would stay with him.

'If you are to get away tonight I've arrangements to make. My own men on gate-guard for one.' The door closed behind him. Guy ate perhaps half the food before its congealing clamminess defeated him, finished the wine and lay back, pulling his fur-lined cloak about him. He huddled into the comfort of it and listened to sounds of activity in the bailey. For a time he contemplated a bleak and prospectless future, and then weakness had its way with him. Against all expectation he slept.

Guy roused in darkness to a trampling and a squeal or two in the stables, and climbed to his feet, catching at the wall for support. A group of people were standing in the bailey, lighted by a torch on the gatehouse wall. Horses were being led out. He crossed to the stables, moving more easily as the stiffness worked out of his limbs, and encountered Conan by the doorway.

'I'll saddle up for you.'

'My own Dusty, and my old saddle. I'll go as I came, owing nothing.'

The children came running. Roger gripped his arm in silence and pressed close. Matilda caught his hand and bounced up and down. 'I mustn't make a noise,' she whispered. 'We're running away in the dark.'

'Yes, it's a brave adventure,' Guy murmured.

'My father says it's crazy, but Lady Mabel said she wouldn't stay another hour and she wouldn't leave me –'

'Hush, Matilda.' He held them both, feeling already the pang of parting; after tonight it was unlikely that he would ever see either again. He counted over the company; Lady Mabel, Gertrude, two of the sewing-women, and Sir James glinting in mail and helmet.

It was not difficult to understand Sir James. For years he had lived in as much security as any man might know in Lord Reynald's service, accepting the atrocities he witnessed as no responsibility of his, aided by the common inability of the gently-born to grant that their inferiors possessed any human rights. Now he was uprooted, in rebellion against his lord, his future in doubt. And of course he cast the blame for his adversity on Guy.

As quietly as might be they got to horse. Lady Mabel came to take Matilda up in front of her. Conan led two mounts from the stable. Guy started to expostulate. 'There's no need for you – '

'Don't be a fool. If you should fall out of the saddle d'you expect that wooden image to stop to pick you up?'

'The keys?' Lady Mabel asked.

'I command the guard this night,' he reminded them. 'The keys went to my lord, but the gate's not locked.'

Guy managed to mount with the help of the block, and the high pommel and cantle held a man so that once in the saddle it was difficult to fall, but he wondered how far he could ride, remembering that this afternoon, that seemed an age ago, had seen his first venture out of doors since his illness. Then he was following Conan's back under the gate-arch. There was no sound nor sight of the guards, only a line of light under the guardroom door. The gate stood wide, the drawbridge down. Once over Conan reined aside to let the little troop pass out, and as soon as the last hooves clopped from the planks the windlass creaked and the bridge began to rise.

'Your men?'

'Oh, I'm going back. I'm pledged until Easter.'

'But you – when he finds out – '

'I'm not sick and unarmed, to be sent to the whipping-post.'

They followed the others in silence, stirrup to stirrup, down the track to the village. Under the ash beside the track a rectangular mound showed darkly. Guy turned his gaze from it and swallowed hard, blinking mist from his eyes. Dogs barked in the village, and no doubt eyes enough watched through window-slits, but no one challenged them. The ford was thigh-deep to a man, and they walked the horses slowly through it to avoid splashing and reached the far bank dry.

Dusty kept turning his head and checking as if seeking something at his side, and with a lurch of his heart Guy realized that he was looking for the Slut, who had run with him so many years. He dug his heels into the gelding's ribs to overtake Lady Mabel and Sir James at the head of the troop.

'Which way?' she asked.

'The Collingford road's the better, by Thorgastone shorter.'

'I'll not take the children within sight of the Devil's Ring.'

'Then our ways part here, my lady.'

'You don't go with us to Trevaine?'

'I could not ride four leagues. Also I gave Lord Henry my word I'd not approach his daughter again.'

'But you – where will you find shelter? Still weak as you are – '

'Don't trouble for me. There's a roof in Thorgastone I can claim.'

'Then this – this is farewell?'

'God guard and keep you, my lady, now and always. Commend me to Lord Henry, and convey my duty to Lady Helvie,' he said, and lifted her hand to his lips, taking refuge in formality.

Matilda wailed, 'You're not coming with us, Guy?' Roger pulled his pony close. He stooped to two throttling embraces, two wet kisses, and was tempted to stay with them at least a little longer. But parting was inevitable. He had given his word, and he knew himself incapable of the journey; the five miles to Thorgastone would tax him harshly enough.

'When I'm a man, and Lord of Warby, w-will you come back to me, Guy?'

'If I may, little brother.'

'I wish you'd stay *now*! P-please, Guy –' Matilda wept.

'Dear child, I cannot. Farewell, and God keep you always.'

'Guy, being come to Bristol, I'll seek out your mother,' Lady Mabel promised.

He remembered Emma's last words to him. His knighthood had proved costly indeed, and Kenric had paid the price. 'My lady, I have – I have no words to thank you. Tell her I shall come as soon as I may.'

'Go with God, Guy.'

Sir James, waiting with impatience plain in every restless movement, took her bridle. 'Enough! We waste time here,' he declared, and without a word of farewell led off. The woods swallowed them, and the last Guy heard of their going was Matilda's weeping.

He turned Dusty's head for the track over the waste. He had his knighthood, and the price had been everything else he valued in life. Each time Dusty turned his foolish head to look for the Slut the pang stabbed him. Kenric lay in the church for strangers to bury, and he might not even do the son's office of casting earth into his grave. Emma would curse him, Helvie had turned from him, he would never see the children again. His thighs had no power in them, and his muscles protested that he was less than a fortnight out of a sick-bed.

'So we don't go to the lady who slashed your face?'

'Her mother.'

'Will she help you?'

'I – I hope so.'

'She will, if I have to force her door.'

They halted on the crest to breathe their horses. By then Guy was riding on stubborn endurance. Conan edged his horse closer and put a hand on his shoulder. 'We could rest a while, but starting again –'

'Once out of the saddle I'd never get back. We'll go on.'

Whenever the track permitted it Conan rode alongside, steadying him with a hand on his arm, and later an arm about his waist. But for his aid Guy knew that he would have fallen from the horse somewhere on the waste and lain until cold and exhaustion made an end. He ached as though he had been pounded in a mortar, his head swam dizzily, he had long since relinquished all control over Dusty and bowed over the saddlehorn, holding to it with both hands. They came down at last to the pasture, and he lifted his head to find his bearings in the moonlight. The village lay before them, no glimmer of light showing; curfew hour was long past.

'Go round – by the fields,' he gasped. 'The other side – that woodland on the left of the road.' It was the way he had taken that other night over a month ago, after he had escorted the woman from Summerford to safety.

They plodded on. Then Dusty, with no guiding hand on the reins, stumbled over a stone. Guy fell forward, and sank over the horse's neck until his face was in the rough mane. Conan exclaimed and checked his slide with a grip on his arm, pulling him upright, but Guy was spent. He had not lost consciousness, but no strength was left in him. He felt arms about him, hauling him from Dusty's back, and found himself half-sitting, half-lying across Conan's saddlebow in the hold of one hard arm while he compelled the reluctant stallion to accept the unaccustomed burden.

'Hold on, lad. Not far now.'

Guy subsided against his shoulder, aware of the warmth of his body and the steady thudding of the man's heart. No obligation, no mere goodwill, could explain the mercenary's kindness, that Guy had never dreamed was in him. He muttered, 'Whatever you owed me – it's more than paid.'

'You fool, what I owe you is beyond measure or counting,' Conan said roughly. 'And I don't mean my life.'

Guy gave up trying to reckon what he did mean. They circled the village without rousing even a dog in Thorgastone, and came back to the track. After one false cast they found the path through the trees, and at last reached the cottage in its garden-patch and trod up to its door. The shod hooves clinked on the stones. Conan hesitated a moment, faced with the difficulty of dismounting; Guy was now beyond helping at all. Then he set all his weight in the near stirrup, swung his right leg over the horse's rump, slid down and heaved Guy over his shoulder as he descended.

'Who's there?' a woman's voice, sharp with alarm, demanded from behind the door.

Conan steadied himself, shifted his grip, and hoisted Guy up in his arms with a grunt of effort.

'Who is it?' the voice insisted. Dim scuffling sounded within the cottage.

'Guy of Warby,' the mercenary answered.

'That's not his voice!' another voice that Guy knew exclaimed. 'Let him speak for himself or be gone!'

'Helvie – ' Guy croaked.

The door opened a crack, and the moonlight touched a cold glint from a spear-blade's edge in the gap. 'There's an arrow nocked!' Helvie's voice warned, and then she caught her breath in a gasp.

Conan moved closer. 'Lady, he's sick and far spent. If you will not take him in, there's nothing for him but to die in the woods this night.'

The door swung back. 'Bring him in,' Elswyth commanded, and set aside the spear. Helvie, a blacker shadow in the dark, retreated before them. Conan halted in the doorway, moonlight behind him and blackness before, until a red ember glowed, grew and brightened to a blaze as Elswyth stirred up the fire, banked with ash to smoulder all night. Then he came forward into the light.

'You!' Helvie raised the bow, and the arrowhead winked red as if it had already found blood.

'Helvie – no – ' Guy whispered, turning his face to her as the firelight spun about him and his wits reeled into blackness. 'Helvie – '

'Does it matter what I am?' Conan growled, shouldering past Elswyth to kneel in the rushes by the hearth with Guy in his arms. 'You are his only refuge. He loves you. Will you turn him away because I have brought him to you?'

Helvie stood a heart's beat in the red glow, her hair streaming over her unlaced gown, her hands steady on the half-drawn bow and the arrow on the string. 'No,' she answered simply, tossed the weapon aside and dropped to her knees. 'Give him to me.' She reached out her hands. Guy sighed and sank into darkness before they touched him.

Chapter 16

Woodsmoke, the scent of drying linen, and a whiff of simmering pottage reached Guy first; then a murmur of women's voices, a pot's purring, and a thrush's jubilant whistle. He stirred in a warmth of woollen blanket, and opened his eyes on fireglow, sunlight slanting through a roof-vent and an open door, films of blue smoke eddying up, and the backs of two women sitting on stools at the doorway, one sewing and one spinning. Dreamily he watched the needle glint in and out, the fingers tease and twirl the wool, the spindle sink to the floor as the thread lengthened and was wound up afresh.

He looked on love and warmth and beauty as he had done all his life, the cuckoo-child with no right and no abiding-place. He had no share in this peace. He watched Helvie's deft hands draw and twist, wind and hitch, the spindle falling over and over in the rhythm he had known all his days. Just so his mother and sisters had sat, endlessly turning fleece to yarn for the looms to work as women had done since Eve fled the garden, endlessly sewing garments to clothe husbands and children. Thought of his mother made him bite at his lips.

Elswyth got up, crossed to the fire and bent to whisk the ashes and stir the pot. Guy let his lids fall and feigned sleep, postponing confrontation, the questioning, explaining and apology. The rushes whispered. She was approaching. Shame scorched him. He opened his eyes and looked up into her face.

She smiled, and smoothed his hair. 'You're safe, lad, with friends.'

Helvie let distaff and spindle clatter and came running, her eyes anxiously searching his face. 'Guy –'

'Helvie,' he croaked. His throat was dry, and his voice did not seem to belong to him. He rolled on to his back.

'A bowl of pottage for you,' Elswyth suggested briskly, and Helvie went to fetch it. Guy heaved up on one elbow. Every muscle in his body twanged protest like a mis-struck lutestring. He shoved himself to a sitting position, the blankets sliding down to his waist, and Elswyth flung his cloak over his shoulders and tucked it round him as though he were an infant.

'You took me in,' he said, reaching a hand to her. 'I – I cannot thank – '

'What else should we have done? Cast you out? Sup your pottage and don't be foolish.'

Feeling indeed like an admonished urchin, Guy took the bowl with a word of thanks, spoke a brief grace and dipped the spoon. It was meatless for Lent, pulses and roots made savoury with herbs, hot and comforting. The first mouthful woke hunger, and nothing was said until he had finished and handed back the bowl. It was high morning by the sun; last night's collapse of exhaustion had passed into sleep. He looked from Elswyth, sitting on the edge of the bed and smiling at him, to Helvie standing by looking troubled and doubtful.

'You haven't asked any questions.'

'No need. Your friend told us all.'

Some sort of spasm twisted Helvie's mouth. Loathing and anger looked for an instant from her eyes. Guy turned to her. 'What's amiss, my lady?'

'How could you?' she demanded in revulsion. 'That man – how could you make a friend of such a monster?'

'I didn't,' he answered mildly. 'He befriended me.'

'He told me – it was *he* told me – that you loved me! You – you discussed me – '

'No, my lady. He guessed.' Some of the anger left her face, but not the regret. 'I'm sorry. You should not have learned that from any lips but mine. None the less, it is true.'

'I – I had dreamed – had hoped – ' He could scarcely catch her whisper, and she bowed her head to hide the flush that rose to her hair. 'And then – to hear that foul beast – '

'My lady, he has been most truly my friend. But for his help I should have fallen and died, last night on the waste.'

239

'No doubt he saw advantage in it!'

'He carried me here to you.'

'That murderous raptor!'

'Can you not find a little charity for him, Lady Helvie? He is even more wretched than I.'

'Charity? How can you ask it? A ravisher, a child-murderer –'

'No. The boy's death was accident. I saw.'

'You defend him?'

'He loved the mother, and she killed herself. Now he's in hell. I owe him too much to turn my back on his need.'

'*Need?*'

'He has no one else in all the world.' And that, of course, was the riddle's answer.

'We're quarrelling,' said Helvie on a note of bewilderment, tears gemming her lashes. 'We're quarrelling over that monster who tried to rape me.'

'He would not harm you or any woman now.'

Elswyth, who had been sitting with the empty bowl in her hands, said unexpectedly, 'He left you a message. He said, "Tell the lad I shall come for him at Easter." '

The bond still held. Helvie, watching his face, asked bitterly, 'You'll go with *him*?'

'Lady Helvie,' he implored, 'try to understand, if you can't forgive –'

'Do I mean nothing to you?'

'You know you hold my heart. But is it proof of love to spit on friendship?'

Helvie turned from him, gulping on a sob. He reached out his hand, but she blundered across the cottage and out of the door.

Horrified and ashamed, Guy swung his legs round and grabbed at the covers to cast them back. Elswyth shoved him sprawling against the pillow.

'Let her go.'

'But Helvie – I cannot –'

'Will you chase her naked?' He subsided, his flush scorching, and she grinned. 'You obstinate whelp, I never guessed you had that much gall in you.' She slapped him lightly on the shoulder.

'I've hurt Helvie – she'll not forgive – '

'Hold to it, and she'll respect you for it. Too mettlesome for her own good, but she'll see sense when she cools.'

He looked doubtfully at her, shaken by the quarrel, and acknowledged the truth; to make his peace with Helvie at this moment he must disown Conan. 'What can I do?' he muttered aloud.

'What's right and not what's soft. The husband should be master.'

'Husband?'

'Your aims are honest, aren't they?'

'Marriage – Lord Henry wouldn't call that honest. But it's impossible.'

'Let be. You lie back now. Rest and eat to put some cover on them great bones.' She went to the fire to set on more wood and stir the pot.

Guy lay still a little while, frowning in abstraction as he fought his urgent desire to find Helvie and promise whatever she asked to comfort her. Then he sat up purposefully. 'I'll have my clothes.'

'Still damp. They were bloody, and we washed them.' She turned his tunic, lying on the rushes. 'You'll not chance your death wearing wet clothes, sick as you've been, so you stay where you are.' Guy grinned reluctantly. Her admonishments and her kindness took him back to his childhood, reducing him and Helvie to a pair of squabbling brats. He subsided into the tangle of blankets, troubled to imagine his hardy Helvie weeping in the woods.

'I was too hard,' he muttered, more to himself than to Elswyth.

'You stand fast. It's for her to come to you. Give way now and she'll rule you all your lives, and a shrew's a misery to herself and everyone about her.'

'You talk as though we were betrothed!' Guy expostulated. 'Her father would never permit – his enemy's cast-off bastard, without land or prospects.'

Elswyth came to sit again on the edge of the bed. 'I worry over her,' she confided. 'Me lord's only child, and given her way too much, but a bastard all the same. Past seventeen now. And what every woman wants for her girl is a good husband. Gentry matches for land and gear and joining high kin, but us as has none weds for liking. You'd gentle her steady and loving, not break her like a balky horse.'

'You honour me,' Guy said wryly. 'But her marriage is in her father's gift.'

'If you *must* have his consent,' she agreed, and returned to her fire. He stared after her with mouth ajar, trying to assimilate the implications of that remark while he watched Elswyth mix barley-meal with water, pat it into flat cakes, brush the embers back from the hearth-stone and invert a large pot over her baking. She heaped the hot ashes over the pot and tidied the hearth.

Helvie came in. Her eyelids were reddened, but she had washed her face, the tendrils of hair about her brow and cheek were dark and damp. She came to the bedfoot, and her voice was hard with the effort she made to control it. 'I ask your pardon. I have no right to question your friendships.'

'No one has a greater right, my lady.'

'I d-do not question it –'

'It's a debt, the greatest of all. My life.'

'I – then I suppose I should be *grateful!*' She spat the last word.

'Lady Helvie, my heart, is there so much kindness in this world that we can throw any in the giver's face?'

She gulped and turned away, dragging her stool to the fire on a pretence of tending the cookery. Guy knew that she had not reconciled herself and probably never would, and did not know how to heal her hurt. It was another problem to go over and over as he waited to recover his strength. He could not repudiate Conan. If he turned his back on the man he would, Guy was sure, kill himself in utter despair.

In the silence a blackbird called alarm, and they heard a staff tapping along the stones of the path. Guy looked about him for his belt and dagger, knowing he had no time to reach them, but Helvie, scrambling up, shoved him flat, jerked the blankets above his head and dragged them straight. As darkness closed over him, he glimpsed Elswyth whisking up his drying clothes to bundle away. Helvie's weight sank into the feather-bed beside him.

"Save you, father!' Elswyth called tranquilly. 'Come you in and set. I'm just baking.'

'God save all here,' croaked a voice Guy had heard before. He dared draw breath; this was the blacksmith's blind father, her father too. Straining to hear through the muffling woollen, he recognized the scrape of the staff and the scuffle of feet in the rushes. Helvie rose from his side.

'Here's your stool, grandfather. A horn of ale now?'

'Aye, aye, gran'daughter . . . Ah-h, that's a right good brewing. I'd not say nay to another, nor a bite o' new bread neither. Still got teeth enough to chew a crust, m'girl; not down to spoon-meat yet.' He cackled. Guy delicately drew down a corner of the bedclothes to uncover one eye. The old man's wild hair made a flame-reddened nimbus about his head as he leaned to the fire, extending veined and knobby hands to its glow. Elswyth heaped fresh embers over the pot.

''Twon't be long,' she said brightly. 'All well at the forge?'

'Aye –' His head jerked up, turned to one side and the other, not to see but to listen. Guy held his breath, his body rigid. 'Who's here wi' you?'

'Father –'

'There's a man here where no man should be!' He grabbed his staff and creaked upright, his blind face turned to the bed. 'A man in your house – I can feel and smell him! Ha' you turned whore like your mother, girl?' He towered under the smoky rafters like Elias condemning sin.

'No!'

Guy pushed back the blankets, and Elswyth frantically gestured to him to be silent. The blind man sniffed, his nostrils working; Elswyth crouched on her knees beside the fire, and Helvie stood like stone with the alehorn in her hand. The fragrance of baking bread was filling the hut.

'Ha, it's Warby's bastard you've took in, when he fled from

243

his father. Fools that you were, if you're not whores. There'll no good come of it.'

'Father – '

'What good's Warby ever done to us and ourn?' He reached his staff before him, feeling for obstacles, and stumped unerringly to the door. 'Ill done to meddle. Put the devil's get from under your roof afore he brings harm to it. No luck ever came to honest folk wi' a Warby.' His staff tapped away down the path.

Guy sat up and reached for his cloak, wondering how the blind man had recognized his presence; maybe by sensing another rhythm of breathing, or smelling him as a dog would. 'He'll talk?' he asked.

'M'brother's wife'll have it all over the village by nightfall.'

'Then I cannot remain here.'

'Why not?'

'You and Helvie – if Lord Reynald comes to take me, or Lord Henry. I must go.'

'How? And where?'

He had no answer, but looked from one to the other, remembering how Conan had had to carry him here last night. There was no other roof that might shelter him within twenty miles, and he had proved unfit to ride five. It was barely April, and the air still held the bite of frost; he knew he would scarcely survive a night in the open. 'But if I bring harm upon you – '

'No one's likely to run tattling. They've goodwill towards you in the village.'

'Will you tell me there's no witch in it, owing allegiance to Lord Reynald? And this house stands alone.'

'Leave off fretting. Another day or two o' rest and feeding'll set you up.' She spread his clothes again by the fire and held his tunic to its heat. Steam curled over the cloth and wisped away. 'And don't you trouble over Lord Henry. He'll ha' guessed you're here, and he's not on the doorstep to drag you out.'

Helvie swept the ashes from the pot, tipped it back and took up the hot bread in a cloth with the ease of habit. She must be living here with her mother; she had made no move to return to Trevaine.

'I had not expected to find you here, Lady Helvie,' he said a little stiffly, 'and had no intention of breaking my promise not to approach you again. Have you left your father's hold?'

'For a time. It's his wife.' She turned to face him, absently juggling a cake of bread in the cloth. 'She's past living with these last weeks. Her time's near, and she's carrying badly, and she finds my presence an offence. My father daren't cross her for his heir's sake. She quarrels with everyone, and she has sent two of her demoiselles home in disgrace – the two most useful ones of course.'

'And you?'

'We've always been at odds, but I don't trust the midwife and said so. I was a fool. If I'd praised her to heaven she'd have taken against her.'

'Isn't she competent?'

'At her duties, I reckon so. But she's moved into the castle for the last weeks, and she's working on Alice's suspicions and turning her against everyone, to increase her own influence and consequence I suppose. As for the wench she's brought in for a wetnurse, she sits about idle eyeing the men, and guzzling like a sow in farrow – sly trollop.'

'You're well out of that household.'

'It's not been home to me since my father married her.' Helvie smiled at her mother in a content that proved her happier living as a peasant in this cottage filled with warmth and love, rather than as her father's daughter in Trevaine castle. He watched her move about her tasks, shredding cabbage for the pot, carrying the outer leaves to the pig in her sty across the garden, sweeping the hearth and turning his clothes before the fire. Watching her eased his misery.

The bread was cool enough to eat, and the women served dinner; bread and cheese, bowls of pottage, wrinkled winter apples and ale. When they had eaten Elswyth pronounced his clothes fit to wear, and Guy thankfully left the bed. He was stiff and saddle-galled, but he threw his cloak over his

245

shoulders and made for the door. He stood in the spring sunlight, looking about him at the garden, the winter roots almost done and sprouting green, the empty beds dug and raked, the apple-trees budding pink and the pear frothing white. Four straw hives were humming alive. A winter-gaunt cow and Helvie's palfrey shared a patch of grass beyond them. He drew a long breath.

'Where's Dusty – my horse?'

'I hid him in the woods,' Helvie told him, pointing.

'I'll see all's well with him.' A knight looked to his mount before himself, and if Dusty were as poor an apology for a charger as an armourer's journeyman for a knight, Guy knew his duty.

'Go gently, lad. You're unfit – '

'It's a bare fortnight to Easter,' Guy pointed out. 'I must make myself fit.' He moved away across the garden.

Dusty was glad to see him, and Guy made much of him, shifted his tether to fresh grazing, and then tried his legs by walking down the path to the Trevaine track. He had to rest before he could return, and twice on the way back, but urgency pressed him; he must compel his strength to its limits day by day to force its return. His legs were trembling under him when he came to the cottage door, and Elswyth took one look at him and jerked her head at the bed, where he was indeed glad to stretch his length.

'You've done too much!' Helvie expostulated.

'You're not a hen, my girl,' said her mother. 'Don't cluck.'

Guy was surprised into laughing. Helvie looked mutinous and then grinned. 'My chick's a great gosling.' She took up her spinning.

Guy watched, and dozed. He dreamed of Warby bailey, and started awake with a cry to find Helvie stooping over him. 'My father – '

She put her hand on his, the first time she had touched him since their dispute, and he gripped her fingers. 'Would he wish you to grieve so?'

'No. But the grief's no less. And my mother – how shall I tell my mother it was my fault he died?'

246

'Won't it console her that you live?'

'*I?*' His surprise betrayed him; comprehension drove the colour from her face.

'Guy – no – '

'It – she's not to blame. Only to her – to her I'm the raptor's get. To him I was his first-born son.'

Her hand closed tighter. 'Oh my dear – you loved him.'

'And it was my fault – '

'Here's folly,' Elswyth's voice declared. "Twasn't your hand used the knife. How could it be your fault?'

He sat up, thrusting his fingers through his hair in a distracted gesture. 'It would never have happened if I'd resisted temptation – his offer of knighthood.'

Elswyth snorted. 'If men could foresee the furthest end o' their deeds, none of 'em'd do nothing but squat on their tailbones and howl. Take it back to its beginning, and it was him raped your mother to beget you.'

'Yet the blame – '

'Look, lad. It's right you should grieve. It's right you should look to your faults. But I reckon any priest'd call it vanity to take blame for *his* sins. You're not that important.'

He gazed at her plump back as she stooped to lay on fresh logs, and her common-sense shifted some of the burden of his guilt. He swung his feet to the floor and looked up at Helvie.

'And what of my word to your father, my lady?' he asked grimly.

'Now who had a better right to take you in?'

'That was in ignorance of your presence, but I've since spoken words I'd no right to utter.' He frowned at the floor, remembering that he was nothing, possessed nothing. 'I forgot – '

She stood a moment, and then leaned to trace with one finger the faint mark she had left down his cheek. He tingled at her touch. 'Forgive me that, Sir Guy. Later, I thought. There was no other boon you could give that poor captive.'

'A quick end. But I never blamed you, my lady.'

'Your habit, helping fools to your own cost.' Her hand slid up his bristled cheek to his hair, and so startled him from

247

his self-command that he caught it to his lips, heedless of the reverence owed her position, the obstacles between them, the watchful mother. Her fingers were roughened by riding and household tasks, and they trembled and then gripped fast. He gazed into her eyes, and her lashes fluttered and fell. A flush ran up her smooth throat, over her face to her brow, and her breasts rose in quickened breathing. His own heart thudded. She pulled free as if to flee, and then took his face between her palms, stooped and kissed him on the mouth. Then she ran to the doorway and caught up her spinning, her back to Guy and her fingers bungling the thread.

Stunned and marvelling, he was unable to move or speak. Elswyth placidly stirred the pot. Guy stared at Helvie's bent head, more embarrassed than she was. A noble virgin moved in man's presence with downcast gaze. No lewd word should reach her ear; she must be approached with reverence, her purity unassailed by any hint of carnal lust. So he had imagined, but his vision of bloodless virtue had been destroyed by Helvie's kiss. It had been wonder and delight, but he knew her wholly innocent, and could not look her in the face lest she read the entirely carnal thoughts the contact had fired in him.

The thread snapped in her fingers, and she uttered a smothered ejaculation. The spindle bounced and rolled in an arc across the floor. They both moved for it, each glancing sidelong at the other. Guy saw Helvie's mouth set in sullen lines that he realized all at once indicated hurt. He reached out a hand to her and she recoiled, her eyes brimming and her lips quivering.

'My lady, what's amiss?'

Elswyth gave them one look, picked up a wooden bucket and closed the door behind her.

'I – I've given offence,' she muttered, gripping her hands together against her breast. 'But I never meant to – to disgust you by – by playing the wanton. Sir Guy, by God's holy Mother I swear I've never kissed any other man but my father!'

'My dear lady – '

'You were so unhappy – I forgot all shame – '

'It was the loveliest thing ever happened to me, my lady, and took my foolish wits away.'

'Then – ' she choked, moved blindly to him and burst into tears upon his shoulder. Guy forgot all scruples, closed his arms about her, leaned his cheek against her warm hair and waited out the storm, shaken himself by feeling he had never guessed was in him. He slid one hand up to her nape and stroked her neck and hair. His heart hammered at his ribs, and hers beat against him; her sobs pressed her breasts to his. He kissed her hair, brought his hand under her chin and gently turned her face from the damp patch on his tunic.

She looked up. 'I love you,' she gulped.

He bent his head. The first kiss fell awry and was salt with tears, and then his mouth found hers, her hands came up behind his neck, and they clung fast until for bodily weakness he must draw back, jerking breath into his lungs.

'My heart – my own lady – my dear love – '

She steadied him, and there was no shame in leaning on her generous strength. Helvie was wife and helpmate, no man's plaything. Where she loved she would give all she was. Guy held her by the shoulders, gazing as though he had never seen beauty before; for him it was forever eyes between green and brown, tawny hair springing from a broad brow and mouth wide for laughter. Her hands clasped his arms, and as she blinked the tears from her lashes her lips quivered into a smile.

'Helvie, you are all my joy on this earth, my heart's love.'

'And you are mine.'

A bucket clanked outside, and the latch rattled warning for them to draw apart. Elswyth surveyed them benignly, and Guy was guiltily aware that they looked like a pair of peasants surprised embracing on a haystack. Girls of Helvie's quality were not tousled by reckless hands; they came untouched to their spouses between the sheets of their marriage-beds. His conscience prodded him; he had made his avowal, and his promise to Lord Henry was past repair. Elswyth made no rebuke, but set about serving supper.

Helvie sat beside Guy on the bed with her own bread and pottage. They plied horn spoons in silence, oddly shy yet with each other. Guy was conscious of every move she made, of the long swell of her thigh, the lift and play of hand and arm, the line of down-bent brow, cheekbone and jaw and the wrench of strong teeth as she worried the tough crust.

'I have never learned to please men,' she murmured to the spoon. 'But – but I will try.'

'Don't. You please me as you are.'

'Shameless enough to – to kiss unasked?'

'You don't fear I'd think any ill of your lovely honesty, my heart?'

'I don't fear you in any way,' she assured him, lifting her face to smile at him. 'I – I could never love where I couldn't trust.'

'May I always deserve it,' he murmured.

Elswyth, who had paid no apparent heed to their whispering, rose to proffer a bowl of apples and hazelnuts, and by reminding them of her presence thrust convention between them. Her shrewd gaze pierced the mists that requited love had wrapped about Guy's wits.

'I know your intentions are honest, for you've told me them,' she said. 'But don't go too fast. She is still her father's daughter.'

'There is nothing under heaven I desire more than to marry Helvie,' Guy declared, but did not add that he saw no honest way under heaven of achieving that. He looked on reality, and that was so harsh that Helvie paused with a bitten apple half-way to her mouth to stare at his haggard face, and then laid her hand on his. He said nothing, merely gripped her fingers, and presently reached for an apple himself.

Later Guy slept, badly and under protest, on a pallet on the floor, and rose more resolute to enforce recovery on his convalescent body. If he walked as far as his legs would bear him, he must compel them to return. There was no pleasure in budding woods, opening flowers or birdsong. He grieved for Kenric, but could thrust that to the back of his mind; he missed the Slut with every step he took.

He was hunched on a fallen tree beside the track, gazing without seeing at celandines golden about his feet, when a shadow moved upon them. He glanced up, his hand leaping to his dagger and then falling empty. Wulfric was standing with his thumbs hooked into his belt, grimly regarding him.

'Proper bad luck you're having, eh? How you faring?'

'Well enough. You followed me?'

'Keeping an eye on you.' He sat on the other end of the log.

'You –' Guy checked himself. 'I was glad enough of you last time we met,' he conceded. 'Any news from Warby?'

'Fair chucked a rock into the hornet's nest, you done, setting Lady Mabel to run wi' the brat. Lord Henry took 'em in, sweet enough to drip honey, and they're on the way to Bristol already. Me lord o' Hell's near splitting wi' rage and the garrison out hunting you.'

'Does he know who helped me away?'

'The routier? Faced him down in his own bailey, and claimed he'd paid his debt, and if me lord pressed it further they'd see whose guts got spilt first. Neither's dead, so they never got past words, and five men's five men when war's to hand.'

'War?'

'Malmesbury Castle's gone over to the Angevin instead o' being pulled down like they agreed. And there's a whisper Lord Robert o' Leicester's making peace wi' the Duke.'

Guy stiffened. Lord Robert had always been Stephen's most prominent and faithful supporter; his defection would be a portent to shake allegiances. 'If that's true,' he pronounced, 'he's recognizing young Henry's right to succeed Stephen. The King's past fifty and spent with trouble. His army refused battle at Malmesbury. Wulfric, it's more likely to mean peace than war.'

'Lord Reynald's counting on war. And he's plotting some harm to Helvie's father.' He plainly reckoned that kinship gave him the right to use her name untitled, and the presumption jarred on Guy, who had barely achieved that right himself. 'And if I knowed what, d'you reckon I'd conceal it?'

he protested to the implied question. 'It's witchcraft; the stink of it's in my nose, and the old besom don't croak joy but for evil in hand. And me lord's offering twenty marks for word o' where to find you.'

Guy pushed to his feet. 'A temptation,' he said.

Wulfric spat. 'Judas silver. What's your intent, once you've mended yourself?'

'I'm for Bristol and Duke Henry, peace and strong law in England.'

'Aye, no place for you here. I'll keep my eyes open for you.'

'What's your interest in this coil?' Guy asked him bluntly.

'Elswyth. Never been no other woman for me, all my life.'

'*Elswyth*? But – '

'No way we could marry. We're too close kin, our fathers brothers. So she took service in Trevaine and caught Lord Henry's fancy. Helvie's hers.'

Guy understood, so well that he could find no words. They walked back in silence to the path, where they parted.

'If you needs me, send to the forge. I'll be inside reach. God keep you,' Wulfric said, and vanished into the budding undergrowth.

Guy repeated his news to the women over dinner. 'So you're laying your wager on Duke Henry?' Elswyth asked thoughtfully.

'I did that when I spoke with him in – in my father's workshop. Sir Conan and I are pledged to ride to Bristol after Easter, when his service is up.'

Helvie's face darkened. 'That – ' She bit off expostulation, and after a moment asked as temperately as she could, 'Must you, Guy? Must you?'

'I've no choice. And I'm promised. He was my good friend, Helvie, when I needed one most.'

'I can't forget – '

'He has changed. He is truly repentant, and in bitter grief.'

She bent her head. Elswyth, bustling about the hearth, said unexpectedly, 'Will you deny there's virtue in repentance?'

'Oh – oh no. How dare I?' Visibly she struggled with her

252

grudge, and then turned to Guy, leaning from her stool to take his hands. 'He saved you. He brought you to me, and for that I must forgive him and be grateful.'

Guy slid from his own stool to kneel beside her. 'My generous lass!'

'I will try to – to conform to your desires in all things – '

'Little as that has been your custom? I'll not strain conformity too harshly, Helvie.' He sobered, gazing into her anxious eyes. 'We are truly pledged to each other, lady of my heart.' He tugged at the thong round his neck, hauling it over his head. The medallion glinted on his palm. 'Wear this as token, Helvie. I've nothing else for a betrothal gift.'

'It's your shield against witchcraft, isn't it? Oh Guy – '

'I had rather it shielded you. It was my mother's gift.' He dropped it over her head, drew her plaits through the loop and slid it into the valley between her breasts. She laid her hand over it, and then clutched at him.

'Take me with you, Guy! Don't leave me behind! We can be married by the first priest we meet. In Mary Mother's name, don't leave me!'

Guy's heart jarred against his ribs. 'Helvie, my heart, how can I?'

She stared at him, her face whitening. 'Don't – Guy, don't you wish – ?'

'Haven't I shown you there is nothing in this world I desire more?' he said violently, and reached out to her. She came into his arms, clinging fiercely, pressing to him so that all his body thrilled to the contact. 'Oh Helvie, my heart, my own love!' Her head was on his shoulder, his cheek against her springing hair, his hand cupped a warm breast.

'Why, why?' she whispered.

'Listen, Helvie. You don't know what you ask. I will not marry you until I can give you the honour I owe you.'

'But I don't care for that, only for you! I can be poor as a peasant – I can cook and wash and sew for you – '

'Helvie, I'm a knight who cannot furnish his helm. I have nothing but the clothes I wear and a poor nag.'

'Do you think that matters to me?'

253

'I shall have to serve Sir Conan as his squire, or even as a common soldier if he requires it, until I have equipped myself and won a place in the world fit for you. I cannot take a wife among routiers. Dear girl, you must not ask it. The only women in an army's tail are whores, Helvie, any man's women. Do you understand why it's not possible?'

She moved against him, her hands sliding up to clasp his neck. 'Yes. Yes. I'd only make it harder. You would have to defend me, fight for me.'

'You will be in my heart and mind every day. For you I'll accomplish it. We are pledged. If you can withstand your father and wait for me, Helvie, I swear to come for you as soon as God permits.'

'Wait? For you I'd wait forever. I'll be faithful, Guy.'

'As soon as I have honourably won horse and mail, helm and sword —' A shock like a blow halted him, and he tightened his hold on Helvie until she gasped. An abyss of horror opened under him.

'What is it, Guy? Oh, what is it?'

'I *have* a sword,' he told her, his voice cracking. 'It is hidden in Warby, waiting for me to return for it.'

Chapter 17

Holy Week was with them. Elswyth and Helvie had borne grey-tufted willow branches back from church on Palm Sunday. Guy had not accompanied them. Though everyone in the village must know his whereabouts, he reckoned it imprudent to flaunt his presence in their house. He was recovered enough to help the women about their tasks, despite their protests that a knight should not demean himself to hew wood and draw water, and to spend more and more time walking and riding in the woods, alone and lonely. No four feet padded beside him, no broad head thrust under his head for a caress, no warm body pressed close when he stopped to rest. The Slut's death had torn a void in his life that nothing could fill, and he knew that as soon as the chance offered he would tether a mastiff bitch on heat in the woods for a wolf to cover, though he would never have another to equal her.

Henry de Trevaine had not approached the cottage, though he must know Guy was there with his daughter and her mother, and Guy wondered and worried about his reaction when he learned that Helvie was pledged to his enemy's son. For himself he did not care, but Guy feared how his wrath might fall on Helvie, and lay awake at nights racking his wits for some means by which he might honourably wed her and take her with him.

Guy had no word from Conan either. He had not expected any; only a fool would entrust so treasonous a secret to an underling, or send a routier to a lonely cottage inhabited by two women and an unfit man. Yet in moments of depression Guy would wonder whether Conan would abide by their compact, or whether his reformation would prove too hard to sustain. He grew more anxious as Easter approached.

Likely enough Lord Reynald would try to prevent his desertion, and Guy imagined Conan trying to fight his way out of Warby and cut down in the gateway, his one friend lost to him and with him his own future.

His strength was slower in returning than he had expected. He still tired easily, and had not regained much of his lost weight. Yet he was impatient to be gone, to redeem the shame of his knighting by honourable service, to seek a place in the world he could share with Helvie. To live in the same cottage with her was at once delight and torment. Daily the strain of unfulfilled desire grew harder to bear. Honour forbade that he should lie with her before marriage, and marriage was the most distant of prospects.

Elswyth watched shrewdly, saw to it that they were seldom alone together, and spoke once to the point. 'You'll do for Helvie, because you sets her afore yourself. I don't hold wi' snatching.'

'I've learned it's a mistake,' he answered, thinking painfully of Agnes. Loving Helvie had taught him how deeply he had wronged the girl who had died for his errors.

The Monday closed in clear sunlight, and as day faded they sat round the fire, the women spinning. Guy, setting new teeth in a wooden rake, was idly reckoning how much more efficient an iron one would be if peasants could only afford smith's work for their tools, when shod hooves came clopping along the path through the woods. Three heads jerked round. Guy lifted to his feet and moved to the door, poising the rake for an under-arm swing at a man's face.

The hooves halted. Feet trod up the path. A hand first tapped and then pushed the unbarred door, which swung back. A tall shape stood darkly against the afterglow, and the firelight danced in red sparks on mail and helmet. 'God save all within,' Henry de Trevaine saluted them formally.

'And all who enter. Come you in, my lord.'

Guy grounded the rake and waited with his hands on the shaft. Lord Henry, punctilious in the courtesies, removed his helmet and thrust back the padded coif beneath, unbuckled his swordbelt and set the weapon against the doorpost. He nodded to Elswyth, kissed Helvie on the brow, and surveyed Guy over her head.

'Put that rake down. God's Head, d'you think I didn't know you were here?'

Guy flushed and set it in its place. 'Your pardon, my lord. I did not know who approached.'

'And I'll acquit you of breaking your word to me, since you didn't know Helvie was here.' He accepted the stool Elswyth offered and extended his spurred boots to the fire. 'Couldn't make the ride to Trevaine, eh? I had it all from your stepmother.'

'She and my brother are safe, my lord?'

'My marshal set out with them to Bristol the next day, with orders to see them on the first ship to Southampton. Should be in Bristol by now.'

Guy sighed in relief. 'My lord, I am more grateful than I can say.'

Lord Henry smiled somewhat grimly. 'The devil's own gall you had, sending them to me. How did you know I'd not clap them into prison for hostages or ransom?'

'Because you did not hang me at your boundary, my lord,' Guy answered with a grin. 'A sweeter vengeance to set them on their way, beyond Lord Reynald's reach?'

'I don't war on women and brats. A sickly one that, but valiant.' He became aware that he had not granted his hearers leave to sit, and gestured impatiently. There were only three stools, so Guy subsided on to the rushes, where he was subjected to close scrutiny by eyes like Helvie's. 'You look like death warmed up yourself, but you've had over a week to mend, and I reckoned I'd ride over.'

'You've not come alone, my lord?'

'Left my escort on the road. Don't cluck, woman. Surely I can ride where I please inside my own demesne? And I want no witnesses to tattle afterwards. I've a proposal to put to you, young man.'

'My lord?' A pulse began to throb in Guy's throat.

'Come with me to Trevaine, and I'll furnish you with horse, mail, sword and gear and set you on the way to Bristol, for

257

your sworn oath to give up all thought of my daughter.'

Guy rose to his feet to give answer. 'You are too late, my lord.'

Lord Henry's stool went clattering. 'Too late? What's that mean?'

'Helvie and I are pledged to each other.'

He turned on his daughter, his face engorged. 'Has he had your maidenhead?'

'No, my lord. He has never attempted it.'

'My lady's honour is mine. I shall not touch her until we are wedded.'

'And I will marry no other man,' Helvie stated with a flat certainty that forbade contradiction.

Lord Henry looked from one to the other, the anger dying in his face. 'So it's worse than I thought,' he pronounced heavily.

'Worse?' Elswyth caught him up.

'Any lout can fill a wench's belly with his bastard. It's the man who fills her heart and mind she holds to – aye, even if you kill him at her feet.'

'You'll not –' Helvie's hand lifted to her throat.

Her sire shot her an irritated glance. 'I'm not such a fool. I don't want you to hate me forever. But I'll not consent. I've nothing against you in person, understand? Daresay you'll go far. But I'll not have your father's blood mingle with mine in my grandsons.'

'I cannot blame you for that,' Guy answered. 'If I could spill it from my own veins –'

He checked and flung up his head at a confused trampling in the woods. The door crashed open, and Wulfric fell inside, gasping so that he could scarcely jerk out warning. 'Warby – on you – run!'

Guy grabbed Helvie and thrust her towards the door as the noise of horsemen crashing through thickets resolved itself into a clatter of hooves on stone. Lord Henry was in the doorway before him, settling his helmet on his head and swinging his swordbelt about him; as he stepped into the space, dark against the firelight, an arrow streaked at him, missed his head so narrowly that he ducked, and thudded into the far wall. He loosed an oath, jumped back and slammed the door on a glimpse of mailed men running across the garden.

'Too late!' gasped Wulfric, leaning against the wall to catch his breath.

Helvie broke from Guy's hold to seize and string her bow. Elswyth already had her spear in hand. Guy looked about him for a weapon. The best that presented itself was a spade, its pointed head shod with iron. A clamour of yells and jeers and threats swelled about the cottage, and axes and swords began beating at the door. He leaped at the bed, tumbled blankets and pillows aside, and heaved frantically at a footpost. Wulfric joined him. Lord Henry abandoned his heroic stand before the door, whose planking was already splintered into jagged shapes of darkness. They tugged the bed forward between them in uneven jerks.

The door gave way with a squeal of tortured wood. Helvie shot instantly into the gap, and a man yelped. Guy let go the bedpost, caught up a blanket from under his feet, and stooped to the fire beside him. He grabbed the bubbling pot from the tripod, swung it up with the blanket to shield his hands and hurled the seething pottage upon the scrimmage thrusting through the doorway. Men recoiled screeching, clawing at scalded faces and searing garments. The pot clattered across the floor, the women joined their strength to the effort and the up-ended bed crashed against the doorframe, filling half the wall on either side. They wedged it with the chest and stood looking at each other.

'How by all Hell's craft – ?' growled Lord Henry.

'Fire-arrows – signal,' Wulfric croaked. 'I was on waste – saw first from Trevaine – then Devil's Ring. Ran – all way – but they'd horses – overtook – '

'We were the bait in the trap,' Guy said grimly, realizing why Lord Reynald had made no move to re-take him. He could have captured his son whenever he chose; he had waited for the greater quarry to walk into his snare, and now the noose was drawn close.

'Henry de Trevaine!' shouted the voice he knew, high and wild with a triumph that lifted every hair in Guy's skin. 'Come out to my vengeance! Come out with your woman and your bastard and mine!'

'God damn you to everlasting Hell-fire!' Lord Henry bellowed, swinging back his sword as though he saw his enemy within reach.

'We're lost,' Wulfric said hopelessly, straightening from the wall and moving towards the women. 'Stay close by me. It will be quick, I promise.' He drew his knife. 'Ah, Elswyth, Elswyth!'

Guy's eyes went to and fro, his wits scurried like a trapped rodent as he sought a way out of the snare. 'Don't be a fool, man!' he snarled. 'We're not yet – '

'Henry de Trevaine! Come out before we fire the house! Come out or roast!'

Outside was a confusion of footsteps and voices. The axes had ceased beating at the barricaded door. Guy peered through one of the window-slits under the thatch, well back from a chance thrust, and saw dark figures moving under the moon. Flint chinked on steel, again and again, and then a small flame spurted low on the ground, outlining black legs and leaning bodies. Cold sweat ran along his spine. He looked about him urgently, at the doorway blocked by the bed, the one room, the narrow windows that offered no way out to any body larger than a small child's. The noose was tight. He looked into Helvie's face, colourless but steadfast, and she gazed gravely back and moved a little towards him, mutely asking that he should deal her the death-blow.

Lord Henry stood irresolute, his sword-point grounded; with no foe to smite he had no idea what to do. Wulfric waited between the two women, knife ready, and though Guy had called him a fool for resorting too speedily to that expedient, he knew well it might yet be needful. He crushed down rising panic. Outside a howl of glee greeted a kindled blaze, weapons poked and tore at the thatch over the door, and the first ominous crackling sounded. Trickles of smoke began to ooze under the rafters.

'There's the byre!' Elswyth said suddenly. 'We could break through!'

The byre was under the same roof, but its door was at the further end. Lord Henry leaped at the partition and hacked with his sword at the clay-covered withies. The cow within, that had been lowing uneasily since the attack began, bellowed in fear.

'They've thought o' that!' said Wulfric, but none the less he joined his efforts to Lord Henry's. Clay fragments scattered. Men yelled to each other; they were covering the byre door ready for a sally. The thatch was well alight now, roaring high, and shreds of flaming straw sprinkled down, setting the rushes afire. Elswyth and Helvie leaped at them with broom and rake to clear the floor. The smoke coiled in the rafters, catching Guy's throat and eyes, and as the partition gave way Lord Reynald could be heard shouting orders above the cow's bawling.

Lord Henry turned from the gap. 'There's nothing for it but to kill our women and die fighting,' he said heavily.

'*No!*' Guy said violently, and rags of a desperate plan fluttered into his mind. 'Loose the cow and drive her out! I'll break a way through the wall!' he gasped, and poised his spade.

With his weight behind the blade the wattle and daub filling made little resistance. He chopped at the fill between the studs, aimed and purposeful blows that broke out the spiles, and again above the groundsill to take out the whole panel. It bowed and fell inwards.

Wulfric, snatching at the plan in his mind, scrambled through into the byre, where the cow bellowed and plunged, frantic with fear, and hens flapped and squawked insanely under the flaring thatch. He loosed the beast and flung wide the door. A horse would have balked, but she stampeded through to freedom, and men skipped aside from her horns and hooves. The hens erupted in a storm of feathers.

'You first, my lord, to defend the women,' Guy commanded quietly under the tumult, and Lord Henry stooped to crawl through. Elswyth and Helvie scrambled after, tearing

261

their skirts past projecting snags. Wulfric, having shown himself in the byre doorway, slammed the plank door in the attackers' faces and dived out, and Guy followed last of all, flinging himself under a rain of sparks and rolling clear with the spade still clutched in his hand. The others were already running, Helvie hanging back a little for him to emerge.

A man shouted and came at him, spear poised. He threw himself forward under it and on to his feet, swinging the spade horizontally at shoulder-height. It crunched full across the man's extended throat and threw him against the burning wall where the crackling thatch showered sparks and embers. Guy snatched up the spear as it dropped and fled across the irregular garden, moonshine and firelight combining to guide his feet. An arrow whistled past and screeched on stone, curses and hunting-yells and a scurry of feet followed, and he heard the howl and clatter of a heavy fall through the outcry of demented hens and the cow's diminished bellows as she crashed away through the woods. Then blackness engulfed him, branches whipped at his head, and a hard hand gripped his arm and drew him on under the trees, away from the clearing and the ineffectual pursuit.

Guy caught his breath and drew his sleeve across his face. Singed hair broke away as he touched it, and smarting spots told him where sparks had touched his skin. Others moved in the darkness; as his eyes adjusted to it he saw they were all safely away, and gasped in thankfulness. Helvie moved mutely to his side. Heedless of her sire's presence, he kissed her and set an arm about her, drawing her close. He turned to look back. The cottage was all ablaze, the roof already consumed to the rafters that thrust blackened ribs among the flames. Elswyth made some sound of protest, and Lord Henry put his mailed arm round her shoulders.

'I'll build it for you again, Elswyth, and better than before!'

The red glare probed after them through the half-leaved trees. Wulfric tugged again at Guy's arm. The enemy trampled and shouted on the woods' edge, but without enthusiasm, and somewhere Lord Reynald was shrilling orders and oaths.

'Let's go,' growled Wulfric.

'My horse –' Lord Henry objected.

'They've took him, and Helvie's palfrey too.'

'We'll not get far without horses, nor will I leave mine in their vile hands,' proclaimed the knight who would call for his mount to traverse a hundred yards.

'There's my Dusty,' Guy said, and indeed they were near the spot where he was tethered; he could hear him kicking and whinnying. 'I'll get him.'

Dusty, alarmed by the uproar, the scent of smoke and the glare of fire, whickered pleasure, tugging at the rope. Guy calmed him and led him back, and found Lord Henry unreconciled to his own loss.

'What manner of beast's that for a knight to ride? I'll have my own, not crawl home afoot while Warby boasts of having unhorsed me! One quick charge –'

He lifted his sword and started forward. Guy and Wulfric converged to block his way, knowing he would thrust them aside.

'Father, no! There are too many –'

Guy put by the sword with his spear. 'Let us try, my lord, while you guard the women.' He saw him swell, his mouth open to blast him for presumption, and added hastily, 'Your mail takes the light to betray you.' He thrust Dusty's bridle into his left hand.

'Guy –'

'Wait here.' He kissed her quickly and followed Wulfric between the trees without staying for argument. They dodged from trunk to trunk, skirted bramble-patches and hawthorn-thickets, flitted across gaps of pulsing light. The cottage flamed from end to end, its walls crumbling to bright ruin, an acrid stink of burned bacon charging its smoke. Lord Reynald was sitting his fidgety horse in the glare, screeching to his men to search out the fugitives, outlined against the blaze that edged his mail with sparkles of red light.

Wulfric jerked a thumb at the ten or twelve horses milling restively at the garden's edge, herded by a couple of men on foot who were hard-worked to control them. 'See? Get us all

263

killed, that fool will, if we don't watch out. There's Helvie's mare.'

Guy considered. The horse-holders, each struggling with several bridles, could be felled easily enough, whereupon the brutes would infallibly bolt headlong. The palfrey and Lord Henry's mount were fast tethered. But now the other men were gathering from the useless search despite Lord Reynald's curses, already making for their mounts, and by the noises amid the trees several horsemen were advancing along the path.

'Only get ourselves chopped down,' Wulfric muttered.

A yell pealed across the garden. 'Trevaine! Trevaine!' A tight group of three riders erupted from the dark, charging straight across the clearing at Lord Reynald, lifted swords catching the light. Lord Henry's voice shouted back, 'Trevaine!' Guy saw him burst from the woods to join his escort, drawn to their lord's rescue by the fire-glare and tumult, and uttered a fervent curse.

'Come!'

He leaped at the nearer horse-holder, and rammed his spear-point between crunching rib-bones. The fellow grunted and folded forward, loosing the bridles he held. Horses milled and reared about him, a hoof grazed his arm, his ears filled with squeals of fear and anger. Then they broke away, into the scrimmage by the blaze as the light drew them. Wulfric's man uttered a half-yell that broke to a gurgle, staggered and dropped. Guy threw down the spear to tug desperately at looped reins in the dark, and snapped off the branch to free them. Wulfric cursed beside him as Lord Henry's stallion plunged and kicked to join the others; then they were both running across the garden, each dragging a reluctant horse.

The loose horses had broken up the fight; it surged and milled in the blaze that lighted tossing manes and rolling eyes, burnished metal and yelling faces. Guy glimpsed Helvie, perched astride his Dusty and following her father, who had caught one of the runaways by the bridle and was already heaving himself into the saddle. Other men were catching mounts, joining in the struggle. Lord Reynald was battling like a cornered weasel with a Trevaine squire. It was past time to be gone.

'Trevaine!' bellowed Lord Henry. 'To me, Trevaine!'

'This way!' Guy shouted. 'Helvie! *Helvie*! Back to the woods!'

She veered aside for him, and he hauled her palfrey to a halt for her. Something whistled and thwacked into flesh beside him, and the stallion ran free. Wulfric was on his knees among the cabbage-plants, an arrow's flights between his shoulders; as Guy turned he vomited black blood and fell on his face.

'Guy – oh quickly – '

One of the squires had cut his way out of the worry; the other two were down. Lord Henry was fighting the strange stallion, an arrow standing in his sword-arm; at twenty yards' range no mail was proof against a shaft. He recognized impossible odds. 'Helvie! Elswyth! Run for it!' he shouted, backing his horse to cover as the squire joined him. Elswyth came running from under the trees, skirts kilted, and he leaned to hoist her to his crupper. The archer, one still point in the shifting turmoil, drew and loosed again, and the sky-tearing scream of a wounded horse filled Guy's brain. Dusty reared and collapsed.

Guy ran. Helvie had thrown herself clear and was rolling beyond the threshing hooves. As he reached her she struggled up. The palfrey squealed terror at the smell of blood, but Guy had the bridle and dragged her head down, hauled Helvie to him by the arm and heaved her bodily into the saddle. She righted herself and found the stirrups. He thrust the reins into her hands.

'Guy – up behind – '

'Ride!'

He struck the mare's haunch with the edge of his hand, and she bolted straight into the woods. Lord Henry raised a yell and plunged after her, the squire at his back and his own loose stallion running with them. Helvie's despairing cry rang in Guy's ears as enemies drove at him.

He had to spring back or be trampled. The stallion reared

black against the firelight, shod hooves glinting, and his furious squeal flecked foam across Guy's face. He caught his heel against an upthrust of stone and sprawled backwards on soft earth. They were all about him, yelling threats and curses, abandoning nobler quarry to escape unpursued as they thumped from their saddles and wrenched him to his knees with his arms twisted behind him.

All his strength ran out of Guy like wine from a staved cask, and but for the hands holding him he would have fallen on his face. Numbness paralysed body and wits. It was no matter what happened to him. Helvie was safe and he was spent. Then the men fell silent, and there was no sound but the dying crackle of the fire, the snorts and jingles of restive horses, and the distant crashing of Lord Henry's retreat. Lord Reynald, standing over him, spoke flatly.

'I begot you for my own ruin.'

Guy managed to lift his head, his neck-muscles straining. 'That's God's justice, seeing how – '

'You Hell-sent bastard, you've robbed me of the vengeance I've planned and waited for – my own son !'

'I've disowned you.'

'My son. All I've done for you, all I've given you, thrown in my teeth !' His voice cracked on something like a sob. He lifted both hands to his face, and his voice came muffled and shaking from behind them. 'Gone over to my enemies, my first-born son !'

'I am not your son.'

'Mine, mine, no other's !' he cried lamentably, and then his voice hardened. 'Fetch the renegade along !'

Someone produced thongs, and they tied Guy's wrists, fingers fumbling in the dark. He was past resisting; the strength that had been granted him through battle and peril was all used. They had to haul him bodily to his feet, and boost him into a saddle with heaves and oaths. They secured his wrists to the pommel, someone took the reins, wounded and dead were slung over horses and they trampled out of the woods, skirted the village cowering silent behind unlighted windows and headed for the waste. As they went,

Elswyth's cock crowed behind them, and bird after bird answered along the valley, crying hope and a kind of triumph. The troop was descending from the waste before Guy roused from his stupor of exhaustion. He lifted his head, straightened his bowed shoulders and looked about him. The sergeant in charge of his reins likewise assumed an alert bearing, turning a blistered and scowling face on him. There was little regard wasted between Guy and Lord Reynald's men-at-arms; better men found better service. He observed with some satisfaction five dead men tied over saddles and as many wounded. His own capture was small profit to set against the losses, however Lord Reynald balanced his tallies. His garrison was depleted near inadequacy.

Guy had noted from the first that neither Conan nor any of his mercenaries was present, and wondered whether his service had now expired, or whether he had been left in Warby as untrustworthy for this venture. Through his fear ran a small thread of hope that the routier might be his friend still. It failed and sank as the castle loomed before them, its black shape pierced here and there by windowfuls of dull light. The drawbridge descended as they approached, and creaked up as the last horse clopped off its planks. The gate thudded, and the blow's finality slammed through Guy's brain and body. There was no escape now, nothing left but endurance of whatever punishment Lord Reynald ordained. He gripped fast the consolation that he had saved Helvie.

Torches flared about him. Guy braced himself to betray none of his dread and horror, holding his face impassive. He was shivering in any case; passing the ford had soaked his hose and tunic-hem, and the chilly wind froze the sodden cloth on his limbs. He took one quick glance at the crowding faces as the troop dismounted. The light fell on Conan, who turned indifferent eyes to his. Not by an eyelid's flicker did he reveal any sympathy, and Guy realized that he must not expect it of him. The mercenary might well reckon it expedient to side with his paymaster. He felt the colour drain out of his face, and sick fear gripped him. Then one certainty returned to hold by; Kenric's sword was here in Warby, and

267

it was his fate to take it into his hands again.

The thongs were loosed from the saddlehorn, and rough hands dragged him down. He staggered, his legs pithless, and braced his feet apart to stand fast on them. A torchlit ring of faces surrounded him, no trace of kindliness among them. Lord Reynald contemplated him, more sombre than furious. He had been drunk, with hate and lust for vengeance as much as wine, and now was sobering, near maudlin.

'My son,' he said heavily. 'My tall fair first-born. I'd have given you whatever your heart desired if you'd been a true son to me.'

All hushed, holding their breath, remembering as Guy did their last confrontation in this bailey. This mood of grief rather than fury frightened them with its strangeness. Guy's whole being shuddered from the creature who had begotten him.

'What's to be done with a son who betrays his father? Who robs him of his lawful heir and leaves him desolate?' Lord Reynald mourned.

'Flay him!' squalled Rohese, thrusting through the crowd that flinched away from her skirts. 'Tear his eyes out – cut him in pieces living!'

Someone gasped, several crossed themselves, one muttered, 'Mary Mother protect us!' and a woman exclaimed, 'He's her brother!'

'Here's sisterly affection!' Guy mocked, his skin rough with gooseflesh.

'Make him an example to terrify your enemies!'

As usual, whatever she advocated to Guy's harm Lord Reynald instantly rejected. 'That's for me to order!'

Conan's voice came calm and faintly amused. 'I thought you wanted a son?'

'What's that?'

'Her way you'd have only a dead carcase.'

'He is my son. The only son I have left, since he incited my treacherous wife to rob me of my heir.'

'I've disowned you,' Guy reminded him.

'Did he not say you'd have to chain him to your wall to keep him against his will?'

'Ha! Out of his own mouth! You remember well. Take him down to the cell.'

'Better yet, my lord, humble him until he is ready to give you a son's duty. Chain him in your kitchen to turn the spit.'

'Humility – that's a lesson he needs teaching.'

'Don't heed him! He's trying to save the traitor from your justice!' Rohese shrilled. 'Remember he helped him to escape before!'

Lord Reynald turned with ready suspicion. Conan shrugged. 'I've discharged what I owed, life for life. Who pays a debt twice?'

He stepped back, out of the torchlight. Again silence gripped them while Lord Reynald pondered life and death. At last he nodded. 'Bring him to the kitchen. Rouse up the smith, and the cook.'

It was reprieve, of a sort; the worst of shames to a knight, but life. Guy had not guessed how paralysing a hold fear had on him until it was loosed, and his body would scarcely obey him as they hustled him across the bailey to the kitchen close under the keep.

Heat gushed out as they opened the hurdle door, and a stink chiefly compounded of burnt tallow, rancid fat, decomposing offal and unwashed humanity hit Guy like a blow. The fire was banked with ash to keep it safe for the night. Someone kicked it to life, and a scullion who knew his way about the darkness found a couple of candles and lighted them. They flared wildly to illumine avid faces, and he set them on wall-prickets.

The smith appeared, jangling with iron, and then Egbert the cook, most likely roused from some slut's straw and doing up his garments as he came. All watched while the smith produced six feet of heavy chain with an ankle-ring attached, selected one of the main timbers that upheld the kitchen wall and whacked a stout staple deep into it to secure its free end. The guards pushed Guy within reach and held him while the smith closed the ring about his left ankle and made it fast with a padlock that would have secured a bull. The key clicked. He handed it to Lord Reynald with a clumsy

269

bow. A knife released Guy's wrists.

'Egbert, here's your new turnspit. Teach him his duties. He is yours to discipline as you choose.' Lord Reynald tossed the key, red-gleaming in the fireglow, from hand to hand.

'Mine, m'lord?'

'He is to learn humility, obedience, submission – virtues you're well qualified to teach.'

Egbert scratched his mat-head in some perplexity. 'Oh, aye, m'lord. Kitchen work. That tunic's a sight too good to get mucked up turning spit, m'lord.'

'It would fit you, I believe.'

The cook's heavy face lighted. Guy stared from one to the other, choking on fury and dismay as he recognized the depths of his abasement, and at Lord Reynald's signal someone jerked the chain and brought him to his knees in the filthy rushes. They pinned him down and dragged his tunic over his head and arms. In shirt and chausses he lurched to his feet, standing like a baited bear, to be brought to his knees again by the chain. This time he remained there.

'Yours to discipline, as you do your other scullions,' Lord Reynald said gently.

Grinning comprehension, Egbert unbuckled his belt. Guy threw up his arms to guard his head and clenched his teeth.

Chapter 18

Humility was a lesson in many parts, all bitter. Guy learned to submit to blows, kicks and abuse, keep his mouth shut and go on working. He learned that impotent rage is the most destructive of all emotions. He learned to retreat within the fastnesses of patience and endurance, to suffer oppression with the dumb stubbornness of a misused ox. A true knight would have died, he knew, rather than accept such abasement; Guy set himself to live through it, holding to the one dignity left him, silence.

Lord Reynald came to the kitchen doorway the morning after his capture. 'Any tamer for a night's reflection? Ah, but I value you! I've just dismissed a messenger from Henry de Trevaine, offering to ransom you. There's a jest! Can he not depend on me to deal with you as a father should? . . . Smitten dumb? . . . You ruined one plan, but you'll see me triumph yet!'

He came daily to cajole, promise and threaten until, maddened by Guy's refusing to answer, he would turn maudlin or fall into screeching rage. He was nearly always drunk, doubled up with belly-ache every evening, his sanity visibly disintegrating. Rohese and Wulfrune would come to taunt Guy, but the entertainment palled for lack of response. Conan never showed his face at all.

In the few days without a mistress's relentless supervision, the kitchen conditions had degenerated into squalor. Egbert was drunk as often as he could achieve it. His notion of discipline was to lay about him indiscriminately with the huge wooden spoon that was his symbol of office, but no one scoured the utensils, swept the floor, cleared away decaying remnants or emptied the reeking bucket that served the prisoner's bodily needs.

Guy turned the spits, filthier than ever the forge had made him. Yet his strength came slowly back to him. The labour had never been beyond his physical capacity; spit-turning was boy's work. He was never fed, but it was difficult to starve a kitchen-worker who could snatch and gulp, particularly when the scullions conspired to toss him food behind Egbert's back. He had never abused them when the power was his, and was repaid with surreptitious kindness.

News filtered to the kitchen. Henry FitzEmpress was leading his army north and east through the Midlands, castles and towns falling to him like ripe fruit from a shaken bough. For two days of alarm Warby prepared for assault, but he passed over twenty miles away. Stephen was falling. Lord Reynald railed wildly at his Master who cheated his faithful servants, more wildly yet at news from Hernforth. Lady Mabel had reached her brothers, and as first-fruits of vengeance all Lord Reynald's lands in Hampshire had fallen to them. Guy thanked God; she and the children were safe. Lord Reynald's time was running out; at any time it might please the Devil to summon him to Hell. Yet all his friends were powerless, and he had no help in Warby. Then, on the fifth day, he laid hand on hope.

He knelt on it, dodging a blow from Egbert's spoon; some sharply-angled object embedded in the floor's dirt. Later he found and worked it out, a finger's length of broken whetstone that he clutched to him in unbelief.

He had examined the chain and fetter over and over, with a trained iron-worker's knowledge. Staple and chain would have held a baited bear, but the fetter was a clumsy job probably turned out by the castle smith. It closed with a hasp and staple secured by the padlock, and was hinged at the back on a rivet passing through three loops turned over in the iron. He fingered the rivet, the weakest part. It would take days, but with persistence he might wear away the rivet-head and pluck it from the hinge like a pin.

He chose the lower head, more difficult of access but out of sight, and ground away at it whenever he was alone. With all sweet April out of doors the kitchen was deserted after

272

meals had been served, and he was alone for several hours each day. He desisted at night lest the persistent scratching carry too far in the quiet. He fretted at the iron until his finger-tips rubbed raw, the stone ground down, and the rivet-head wore away, disguising the bright metal with spittle and dirt between stints.

During the last week in April, word flew; Lady Alice of Trevaine had borne a sturdy son. The curse was broken, but Lord Reynald's reaction set men muttering; he had received the news with glee. Next day Guy learned that she had died a few hours after the birth. He remembered the silly girl, spiteful with jealousy, and said a prayer for her soul's salvation. The rivet-head was worn to less than a finger-nail's thickness; tomorrow he would be loose.

That day was harder to get through than all its predecessors. Egbert, suffering from last night's ale, made sure his underlings suffered more. Guy, harried and abused, was aware of unusual activity; men drilling, horses moving in and out of the stables, the smithy clanging. Supper was eaten an hour earlier than usual, and while the servants were clearing away, a large force, most of the garrison by the sound, marched out. Lord Reynald's new scheme was moving to fulfilment, and the unknown threat to Helvie and her father had Guy in a fret of impatience to be free. He had lost track of the date; it was an overheard grumble that no one was permitted to leave the castle, on this one night of the year when all went abroad to fetch home the May, that informed him this was May Eve, the fairies' night, the greatest celebration of the witches' year. He remembered the Eve of All Hallows, the lights of Candlemas, and rasped savagely at the rivet. A wafer of iron still held fast when the horn blew.

Guy heard the drawbridge rattle, hooves clatter over the planks, a scurrying of grooms to take charge of returning mounts. Lord Reynald's exultant laughter was followed by a silence that brought a prickle of gooseflesh over his skin. Many feet were tramping towards the kitchen where he sat alone, and he stood up and moved to the chain's limit to see the crowd advancing. A very young baby wailed thinly. A blonde girl he did not know, her dress marked over her breasts with two patches of leaked milk, carried it at Lord Reynald's heels, holding the tiny swaddled body aloft like a trophy won in battle. He knew at once that the infant was Trevaine's heir, and froze. Behind her two troopers held another woman by the arms, forcing her along. The company halted, the girl moved aside. Guy stared into Helvie's face.

In anguished silence they looked at each other. One of Helvie's plaits streamed loose, her gown was ripped open at the neck. Her eyes, dark in the terrified pallor of her face, dilated with deeper distress at sight of him, bearded and filthy in ragged shirt and chausses.

Lord Reynald crowed with glee. 'Ah, you're well met, well met! Yes, and you'll see a change in each other!'

The wet-nurse giggled, glancing from one to the other in bright malice. No one else seemed amused. Helvie straightened against the grip on her arms, and Guy knew a savage pride in her. She did not weep or whine for mercy.

'My son, my traitor son who fancied my enemy's bastard and denied me. Here she is! But I don't forget I am your father. You can have her. Do you hear me, my son? You can still have her!'

He laughed again, and a man behind him crossed himself, his lips moving. The baby wailed afresh. Guy stood dumb and paralysed, his gaze never shifting from Helvie's face.

'Will that tame you, my fine tall first-born? Acknowledge me, obey me, accept my faith and my power, and learn how loving a father I'll prove. I'll give her to you as virgin as we took her, for your own.' Guy made neither move nor answer, and he stamped a foot. 'Do you hear me, or are you smitten witless? Refuse, and I'll strip her in this bailey and let every man in the garrison enjoy her – yes, and the grooms and scullions also, while you look on!'

Locked fast in nightmare, Guy still made no response. Helvie could go no paler, but for a moment it seemed horror melted the bones in her body, for the men shifted their grip to prop her on her feet. The blonde girl giggled again and bounced the baby casually. He howled. For some reason that steadied Helvie; she stiffened and glanced quickly at him with anger and yearning.

'Suckle that brat and quiet him!' Lord Reynald commanded. He turned to Guy. 'Consider it until morning, and choose aright! By morning Trevaine will be dead, his lands mine, my vengeance accomplished! 'Choose aright!' He jerked his head at Helvie's guards. 'Bestow her safely, and if any man lays a hand on her before I give leave I'll geld him. She's my son's bride. Now hasten! We've no time to waste this night.'

Helvie looked back once with desperate eyes, and Guy watched her hustled up the keep steps and through the door. He watched Lord Reynald stride towards the gate, followed by the wet-nurse bearing the heir of Trevaine. The troopers came scurrying down the stair, as if thankful to be rid of that duty. He stood like stone until they had all ridden out once more, and then turned back into the dark kitchen, dropped heavily upon the rushes, and laid his head upon his updrawn knees. He drew a shuddering breath.

'Lord God, now I know why you brought me to this trial,' he murmured aloud. 'Now grant me Your aid this night to thwart the Devil.'

Reckless of noise now he rubbed the stone to and fro, while the sun slid down the sky and sank beyond the wall. As the first stars pricked the blue the rivet rattled loose. He tested it with his thumbnail, easing it up a quarter-inch and letting it drop back. He could slip his fetter when he chose. The bailey was still filled with light like a cup held up to the sky, and people lingered in the open air. Children dodged and squealed in and out of the buildings. Slowly the twilight deepened, voices ceased, silence came down with night.

Full dark had come, and the bailey was quiet, when Guy released himself. He stood erect and stretched, his hair brushing the rafters, looking across the kitchen to the chopping-block where careless hands had left a cleaver lying. He had had his mind on it since supper; he would not go out weaponless.

He halted in the doorway to look about him, straining to

listen, and then flitted through moonlight to the forge. He leaned the cleaver handily against the wall and reached to the rafters in the darkest corner, pawing into the sooty thatch for Kenric's sword. He had just laid hold on its woollen wrappings when he heard movement and low voices. He stood motionless, his heart thumping, and reminded himself that there was no reason for anyone to enter here. But feet were approaching, brisk and purposeful, and round the corner of the forge came a tall shape helmed and mailed. Discovery was inevitable; Guy's shirt caught the light. He dropped the bundled sword and swooped for the cleaver. The man checked, black and featureless with the moon behind him, and snatched at his own hilt. The blade glinted.

'Who – out of there!' came Conan's voice. He peered over his levelled blade and Guy swung back the cleaver. *'Guy!'* He thrust the sword back into its scabbard and sprang to catch him in a fierce hug. 'Guy, lad!'

The cleaver clattered down. There was no doubting his delight, and Guy's arms went round him in spontaneous response. He received a disagreeable impression that he embraced a mailed skeleton; under the hauberk there seemed nothing but bones. Conan loosed him and caught him by the arms, but Guy pulled back to tear the wrappings from his sword and clasp the belt about his waist.

'You're loose! I came for tools to free you, but you've freed yourself. Good lad!' He reached for his hilt. 'Come – what's that you have? A sword?' Guy drew it, and the blade glittered silver. 'God's Blood, how'd you come by *that*?'

'My father's gift – my true father.'

'Your girl's in the keep.' He whistled softly, and three shadows detached themselves from building shadows and became armed men. Conan beckoned, and led at a run, jerking out explana..ions. 'First chance I've had – thought it would never come – my own men on guard. The devil's run mad – not a dozen men left in the hold – '

They took the keep steps three at a time. A taper flickered as the guardroom door flung back. Three men started up from pallets. Conan plunged past their startled faces for the

276

stairs, and before they could disentangle themselves from their blankets or lay hands on weapons his routiers were on them, stabbing expertly. Guy heard one strangled cry as he dived past the curtain.

Round and down into blackness; one of the men scrambling after had caught up the taper, which sent their shadows reeling wildly over the grey stone curving at their right hands. At the bottom they fell against a heavy door bound and studded with wrought iron, the door of the undercroft.

'Light here!' Conan ordered, and the tallow dip leaned over them, dripping hot fat on his hands as he sorted over a bunch of keys.

'This one.' Guy knew it from his previous experience among the stores. 'And here!' From a ledge by the door he took down a torch and held it to the taper, and as it flared thrust it into the second trooper's hand. The third had remained above to secure the stairhead.

The door groaned open, and they trod into odorous darkness, the light wavering on stacked barrels and sacks, woolbales and cornbins. The air was dry and cool. Guy bore left, threading between obstacles to the cells in the corner, the torchbearer extending the flare to shine over his shoulder. They stopped before another door. This was bolted, top and bottom, with a small barred slot for surveillance. 'Helvie!' he called, as he wrenched back the upper bolt, and heard an incredulous cry. 'Helvie, it's Guy!' He heaved the door back on stinking blackness, and the torchlight touched her face. 'Helvie!'

She hurled herself into his arms, her own clutching fast, dry sobs shaking her. Her head burrowed into his shoulder, and she gasped his name over and over, clinging as though she would become part of him. He gripped her to him, kissed her hair and ear, and swung her away from the black den of her prison.

'Steady, steady, my heart – I have you now, Helvie – '

'Be quick!' Conan interrupted. 'You've a lifetime to embrace if we survive, but no time to waste now. Move!' He sank talons in Guy's shoulder that jerked him to reality.

277

'Helvie, he's right. Come!'

'Yes, yes –' She loosed him, gulped a great breath, and lifted her white face and wide eyes to the torchlight. He caught her arm and hurried her to the stair. 'Guy, the baby – my little brother –'

'I guessed it – the wet-nurse's brat for a changeling.'

'That devil – the witches – they'll sacrifice him tonight to the Devil –'

'May Eve!' It broke from him like an oath, and he hauled her after him up the stair with barely time to catch her skirts from under her feet. The door thudded, the trooper followed with the torch, and the third man stood aside for them at the stairhead with his sword swinging ready. Conan's voice rasped.

'Out and saddle up! A horse for the lady!'

Helvie passed the dead men with scarcely a glance as they sped across the guardroom. They tumbled down the moonlit stair and ran to the gate, the torchbearer at their heels, while the other two routiers slanted across the bailey to the stables. The porter popped his head out of his lodge. His eyes and mouth gaped wide, but before he could yell the torchbearer thrust him through the throat. The man wrenched back his spear, set the torch in the iron holder on the gatehouse wall and glanced interrogatively at his captain. Conan nodded. He plunged into the guardroom. Guy heard a muffled cry, a crash as a bench went over and a brief scrambling.

'The sergeant was not my man,' Conan explained.

Guy shuddered a little, and Helvie made a small sound of protest, pressing close to his side. He set his left arm about her and held her fast.

'Lady, my task this night is to bring Guy and you out of Warby with your lives,' Conan told her. He stood sword in hand against the wall, watching the bailey. Shadows emerged from the guardroom and stooped to the windlass. The portcullis began to grind up, the drawbridge down. 'The man on the roof is not mine, nor the two on the walls. Forgive me, Guy, for leaving you so long in that foul den. I was watched nearly as closely as you. I had to wait. You understood when I gave you the word? One chance only. It had to be sure.'

'You don't imagine I blame you?'

'You knew I'd never abandon you, lad.' He dropped his left hand on Guy's shoulder. 'All I owe you can never be paid. I knew you'd remember.'

'Of course I knew it,' Guy lied. In the face of that fierce confidence he could never admit to the truth.

The last man emerged from the guardroom and stood by the portcullis release. Three more trotted across the bailey leading horses enough for the company. Conan signalled impatiently. A voice shouted a question from the wall-walk, but by then they were swinging into their saddles. Guy linked his hands to toss Helvie up, and they rode two by two out of the gate and over the drawbridge. The voice yelled alarm, and feet thudded along the walk. As they urged their horses into a run down the track a screech followed, and then the horn bellowing to rouse all Warby.

'They can blow their teeth out,' said Conan contemptuously. 'They are barely enough to man the gate.' He leaned to address Helvie across Guy. 'Lord Reynald's taken your father's heir, lady?'

'Yes – yes.' Speech suddenly tumbled from her. 'I was riding home from visiting Thorgastone. I saw that wench making for the waste, and I *knew* – I can't tell how – the way she was carrying the baby perhaps. I never trusted her. I knew it wasn't hers but my brother, it was her changeling in his cradle. So I sent my groom to tell my father, and rode after her – I never thought past that. But Lord Reynald and his men were waiting to meet her, and I rode into their arms.' She shuddered violently. 'They'll kill him, Guy. They'll kill him, offer baby Hervey to the Devil in sacrifice. Guy, Guy, you'll stop them, you'll save him?'

'If I can.'

'A *changeling*? How's that to profit Warby?' exclaimed Conan.

'Wulfrune,' Guy pronounced, all the monstrous pattern suddenly laid clear before him. 'She told me once, when I enraged her, that on the day when King Edward was alive and dead, her grandsire's father was lord of all the lands between Trevaine and Etherby. She has set her will and her witchcraft to bring one of her blood to rule again.'

'Wulfrune – that foul crone? Then that nurse-wench must be the miller's daughter he threw out of doors!'

'So that she could be brought to Trevaine. She has worked for this over forty years. This is the third – no, the fourth try.'

'How d'you reckon – the *fourth*?'

'If you are to substitute a changeling for the true-born heir, you must meet three conditions,' Guy said soberly over the trampling of hooves, the creak and jingle of harness. 'The midwife must be party to the plan, the mother must die –' He checked as they shattered the ford to moonlit spray – 'and the children must be of the same sex.'

'Yes, yes, but what –'

'This is the first time all three have been met?' Helvie was the quicker to take his meaning.

'I think she first conceived the plan when she was chosen to suckle Lord Reynald. Midwives are often witches; they know the charms and the simples, and Wulfrune commands them. So his mother died, but Wulfrune's child was a girl. Her ambition possessed her the stronger for being thwarted; she waited for another chance and meantime corrupted her nurseling. Rohese is seventeen –'

'My father's first child would have been that age!'

'But was stillborn, and the mother lived witless. Then her eldest granddaughter bore a son at the same time Lady Mabel bore Roger, but she cheated them – she told me this herself – by contriving to remain at Hernforth for his birth. This time it's the miller's younger daughter provides the changeling. Brought into your household, you told me, by the midwife.'

'Mother of God, so Alice brought in her own death!'

'And to make doubly sure Rohese is pregnant too, but that's been mis-timed.'

'But how can she hope to trick – there's my father, and Alice's women –'

'Which of them knows one baby from the other?'

'Lord Henry's not intended to learn,' Conan said. 'There's an ambush laid on Thorgastone Waste for him this night, when he rides to rescue his girl and the brat. I arranged it myself. Lord Reynald bade me leave my men to guard Warby and command his knaves, telling off one of them to cut my throat should I fail him. Then he left for his devil's celebration, I deployed his fellows on either side of the way, told each party I'd wait with the other, did a little throat-cutting on my own account and slipped away to get you out of the kitchen.'

'Where's your ambush?'

'Just beneath the Devil's Ring, where the way's roughest and the rocks and thickets crowd on both sides.'

'That's – that's two miles more!' Helvie cried. 'My father – and the baby – oh Mary Mother of God – '

She urged her horse forward, almost into the troopers riding ahead, and he balked, half-reared, whinnied and sidled. Guy reached to take her reins.

'What good will it do to lame your horse? You can't gallop on this track,' Conan rasped.

'My father – my little brother – '

'You'll not help them by breaking your neck.'

She caught her breath in a gulping sob. 'Guy – '

'We are in God's hands,' he said steadily. 'May He grant that we are in time.' He thought of the tiny swaddled body he had seen brandished as a trophy, and of the he-goat he had seen sacrificed, and had to restrain himself from pressing his own mount; they were already riding much faster than was safe at night on so vile a track.

'You intend to save them?' Conan enquired.

'What else can I do?'

'Where you go I follow.'

There had been muttering among the routiers at their backs. Suddenly the stocky sergeant spoke out. 'Captain Conan!'

'Yes?'

'Your pardon, Captain, but are you aiming to fight against

m'lord o' Warby?'

'I am. Have you any objection, Bertin?'

'Indeed and isn't he paying us?'

'Since he has not paid us a penny since Christmas I reckon we are free to quit his service. Do you wish to continue in it?'

'*Me*, Captain? Brings me up in gooseflesh to look at him, nor I don't hold with witches and sacrificing babies. But who's paying us?'

'This once, Bertin, we fight without pay, unless you count the benefit to your damned soul.'

'Captain Conan,' Bertin gasped, insubordinate with alarm, 'are you turning *religious*?'

For the first time since Guy had known him, Conan laughed with genuine mirth. 'After this foray I'll take the cowl,' he declared, and the sergeant guffawed with relief and said something in Breton that brought laughter from the rest of the troop. They fell back a little, chuckling as they embroidered the jest.

'But in God's Name, why?' Guy burst out. 'It's against all your advantage, and Trevaine is nothing to you.'

'You ɛre. I'm your man. I was damned and in Hell, and you reached your hand to me. And didn't I see you throw away all advantage, almost your life, for an old done man doomed whatever you did? It came to me that if you could save your soul at such cost, I too could crawl out of Hell at your heels.'

Guy was overwhelmed beyond answering. It was for a priest to save souls, not a sinner as fallible as himself. He crossed himself. '*In nomine Patris, Filii et Spiritus Sancti*,' he murmured. 'May God's Grace uphold us this night against the Devil's power.'

Helvie was repeating prayers under her breath. Guy could discern glistening streaks of moonlight down her cheeks. They were mounting the ridge, what track there was twisting between ragged boulders and bloom-spangled thickets. Through the aroma of sweating horseflesh and the stink of his own foul clothing the fragrance of budding hawthorn and flowering gorse reached Guy's nostrils, and he breathed deeply of sweetness. It was an outrage against all God's world that this May Eve was the witches' night, that there was a changeling in Trevaine's cradle, Lord Henry was riding into an ambush, that Lady Alice had died and her heir was to be offered to the Devil to accomplish the evil Wulfrune had plotted for forty years and more. Only he and Helvie, Conan and his five routiers stood between her and that achievement.

From a lesser ridge they looked over the waste, grey dappled with darkness under the soaring moon, near full. Rock faces glimmered ghostlike, angled against their own black shadows, the crouching bushes were curdled with white bloom, and thin clouds drifted across the stars. One of the leading routiers exclaimed and lifted an arm. On the further ridge dark blocks nicked the skyline, and a thread of white smoke, flushed red at its base, climbed thickening and coiling into the night.

Helvie cried out. 'We're too late! Guy, Guy –'

'Take heart!' he said quickly, urging his horse down the slope. 'That's new-lighted!'

Haste overcame reason. Conan gave an order, the two men in the lead crowded aside, and he, Guy and Helvie headed the line, lifting into a run. Threading between obstacles, slashed by branches, holding their horses on a strong rein they went, and up the further slope to the ridge without concealment. The smoke towered, flame reflecting on its lower coils and sparks dancing away, and Helvie was gasping prayers. Fury mounted in Guy like the mounting blaze, a driving urgency to reach the Devil's Ring before the offering was accomplished.

'Pull out of the line before we reach the ambush,' he ordered Helvie, 'and get to your father as soon as may be !'

Conan checked on the ridge to point. A little below them something moved, a face's pallor with the glint of a helmet atop turned in their direction. A spear lifted in salute. And pricking up the slope from Thorgastone came a moving blackness of horses and men, twinkling with metal under the moon.

'Look at the fools, riding into ambush without even a scout

ahead! God's Blood, you could fit Lord Henry's wits into a nutshell without extracting the nut!'

Guy paused only to make out the nearest of the Warby men, crouching behind bushes and rocks, and then his fury broke. Kenric's sword came sweetly into his hand with a chime of steel. He tightened his knees, rammed spurless heels into his mount's barrel, and hurtled down the path. A wild yell pealed from his throat. Conan echoed it, and the routiers crashed bellowing behind.

The foremost man, already on his feet to welcome friends, yowled dismay at betrayal. Concealment disgorged screeching, scrambling figures. Panicked by treachery, they revealed themselves when their safest course was to lie hidden. They impeded Guy's way to the Devil's Ring. He thundered upon them, pale hair and face and shirt taking the moonlight and sword swinging low, leaping to the work it had not known through all the years of disuse. It jarred on bone, wrenched free; a yelling face fell away, and blood spattered warmly. More faces were about him, mailed shapes scurrying for cover or standing desperately. An arrow sang past his ear, a spear tore his shirt, his horse squealed at a grazing blow, but he burst through the ambush, and as Lord Reynald's men rallied he was beyond them, leaving a savage worry locked behind him. He heard distant yells from the approaching force as he set his face for the stone circle and the fire and the witches' rite.

The horse stumbled and crashed headlong. Catapulted over his head, Guy plunged into gorse, rolled, wrenched clear without heeding the spines, and ran uphill, his sword still balanced in his grip. The fire was flaring. He heard voices raised in incantation, Wulfrune's cracked screech, and flung himself at the barrier of bushes. Blind chance or God's own guidance brought him to the break, and before him a stone loomed black against the blaze. He dodged round it, his heart slamming and his breath jerking, and checked an instant to see where he stood.

The witches were just ringing the fire and the altar-stone, the last few shuffling into position; twice as many, Guy estimated, as he had seen on the night of All Hallows. They fell utterly silent. The din of joined battle came up the hill, the crashing of someone below fighting through the thickets, and above it the baby's wailing. There was a different quality about the hush tonight, a tenseness of horror and dread and revulsion. An infant was not a he-goat

The masked fiend sprang up on to the altar-stone and brandished his trident. Wulfrune held up the naked baby, feebly squirming in the firelight, and the throng, though no one moved, seemed to draw together as though a tightened cord gripped the circle. Guy moved cautiously forward through the trailing brambles as she made her invocation, and laid the child on the stone. The Devil set down his trident, and all the company held its breath.

'God aid us!' Guy yelled, and drove at the ring. He slammed into warm flesh that went down before him, trod over something that quailed and heaved aside under his foot, struck back-handed with his swordhilt into a bearded face and swerved round the fire, that lighted his blond head like a nimbus. Wulfrune screeched and flung herself in his way, arms outspread and white hair streaming. His shoulder and elbow beat into bones and musty woollens, and she spun away as he scooped up the baby from under the knife and sprang upon the altar-stone.

'*You!*'

Lord Reynald recoiled, the mask-eyes glinting red. The Danish sword swung up, but some fundamental instinct stayed Guy's arm. The man who had begotten him tottered on his stilted heels as he ducked, then dropped to one knee and caught up the trident. The three bright points lunged. Guy twisted aside, and it grazed his hip, tugging him off-balance as it ripped his chausses. He almost reeled over the edge of the stone, and as he staggered Lord Reynald thrust again. Guy dodged under it, hampered by the baby, and stabbed desperately. His point pierced, jarred and drove on to grit deep into bone.

The trident clattered across the stone. Lord Reynald flung up his arms, and from the unmoved beast-mask issued a

285

human cry of pain and fear and desolation. Then he crumpled, his weight tearing from the blade, and fell backward from the altar-stone, twisting as he dropped, to lie on his face beside it. The goat-head shifted, the man's hands scrabbled, and then were still.

Guy stood a moment, sick with horror and a queer regret for the kinship that should have been, the blood-fatherhood begun in rape and ended in parricide. A woman screamed and went on screaming mindlessly. She was Rohese. He lifted his hand, and the blade lifted too, its brightness glimmering through dull streaks. The witch-horde confronted him, palsied by calamity; staring eyes and gaping mouths turned on him. Their God Incarnate was dead, and they were poised either to rip his killer to rags in vengeance or to flee in panic from the wrath of Heaven that had felled him.

Rohese had thrown herself on her knees beside her sire and was tearing her hair and clothing as she shrieked, her face lifted to the moon. Wulfrune was struggling to rise, gathering strength to summon revenge. Guy tucked the baby under his arm, his left hand supporting the small head, and he wailed steadily. The ring swayed towards him in menace, and he braced himself for the rush, swinging back the sword. Then a familiar yell lifted behind him, and round the altar-stone Conan stormed, the firelight reddening his mail and helmet. Wulfrune, on her knees, clawed at his legs. He staggered and kicked out, taking her under the jaw. Bone snapped with a sharp crack, and she sprawled without a sound.

Rohese leaped up and away, still screaming. The circle broke like a string of beads; men and women plunged among the stones and into the thickets. The scrambling and crashing of their passage faded. Guy descended from the stone, and stood over the dead man with the beast's head. The mask had twisted awry in the fall, and one horn and a blank eye caught the light. In revulsion he dropped the stained sword across the body. Conan's mailed arm came round his shoulders.

'You had no choice,' he said roughly. 'Don't mourn. This

286

world's the cleaner for his leaving it. And that's no way to use a fine sword.' He took it up, tried it lovingly for balance, and then stooped to wipe the blade on Wulfrune's skirts. He thrust it back into the sheath. 'It has served justice, lad.' He stirred the heap of black woollens with his foot. 'Yes, I killed her, without intent. But that was justice too.'

Guy sat down on the altar-stone because his legs would no longer uphold him. The baby cried, flailing the air with feeble fists. He was hungry and cold, and one of those ills it was within Guy's power to remedy. He laid the child across his knees and hauled his dirty, lousy shirt over his head for want of anything better. He swaddled Lord Henry's heir and held him in his arm, innocent new life in exchange for the one he had taken.

Then Helvie was with him, fighting through briar and bramble with skirts hitched calf-high into her belt for the climb, torn and scratched and her hair falling loose over her shoulders. She sped across the turf and flung herself into his hold laughing and crying together. 'Guy, you're safe – not hurt – you did it! You've saved Hervey! Praise God – oh, Guy!'

He gripped her to him with the one arm he could spare and kissed her thankfully. 'Helvie, my heart's love, it's done.'

Others were toiling up the ridge towards the fire and the lighted stones, their progress marked by curses and a crashing of bushes and the ring of horseshoes on rock. The fighting was ended. Lord Henry battled through the thickets, hewing his path with his sword and beating through by bull-force and impervious mail. He stood gaping a moment in the blaze. Guy sighed. Now his exertions were over his strength was spent. Weariness weighted his limbs, and the last thing he desired was to dispute over Helvie with her father. He heaved to his feet, the baby quiet now in the crook of his left arm and the other about Helvie.

'Helvie!' Lord Henry croaked, and lumbered forward. 'Helvie – safe – and my son?'

'Safe too, father! Guy killed that devil and rescued him!'

'My son!' He plunged past the fire and grappled Helvie

to him. 'You're not harmed? Both of you – praise God!' He gulped, and gingerly touched the bundle in Guy's hold. 'You're sure?'

'I was in time.'

'He saved me too, father, maidenhead and life.'

Henry de Trevaine loosed her and turned to Guy. 'It's a great debt I owe you,' he said with dignity. 'All that's dear to me. And you killed your own father to save my son.'

'That's no grief,' Guy answered harshly.

'You owe him your own life too,' Conan stated from behind him. 'He broke the ambush you were charging into head-down.'

'I acknowledge the debt,' he rebuked the mercenary, 'and I'll discharge it in full.'

'His needs now,' Helvie declared practically, 'are a bath and a barber and a bed.'

'We'll not find them in this foul place.' He looked about him, shivered and crossed himself. 'God's Life, why do we linger here? Tomorrow I'll bring up my men to this accursed ring and purge it with fire and water until every one of these stones is powder blowing on the wind.'

'And Lord Reynald?' Conan asked.

They all turned to look on the dead man, and started to see his head and feet bare, shining pale in the moonlight that was conquering the fire's dying glare. While they talked, some bold disciple of his had made away with the goat-mask and the cloven clogs. The trident too was gone, taken, Guy knew, for Lord Reynald's successor in the ritual. They stood gazing down at him, somehow shrunken now that he was emptied of malice and power, no more than a small dead man in a close-fitting costume of dark leather.

'What's to be done?' asked Conan again. 'Call in the sheriff and make a public scandal?'

'He would have murdered my son. Reason enough to take possession of Warby.'

'Are you as greedy a thief as he was?' Guy exclaimed, pricked from his trance of weariness. 'Warby is Roger's now, and I'll defend my brother's right to inherit!'

'How will you stop me?' Lord Henry growled.

'I hold your heir,' Guy reminded him, his lips suddenly twitching one-sided into a small grim smile. Once assured his son was safe, the noble lord had never dreamed of demeaning his manhood by taking the baby into his own arms.

'And I'm with him,' Conan said. 'But is this a scandal to be published abroad?'

Lord Henry thumbed his chin. 'Scandal – yes. There's my daughter's good name to be considered. Best hushed up. Dishonours all gentle blood, a nobly-born knight taking to these foul practices. Bury him privately and keep silence, I say.'

'And Roger succeeds him as is his right,' Guy insisted.

'Have your way,' Lord Henry said impatiently, and began to move from the circle. Guy tightened his hold on Helvie and followed. She made a gesture towards the baby, offering to take him, but he was soundly asleep and Guy shook his head. Lord Henry turned to him.

'As for you, young man, there's some will say you should hang as a parricide –'

'*Father!*'

'So the sooner we get you out of this district the safer you'll be. I'll take you to Bristol myself and sponsor you to the service of the Duke of Normandy, who will be King.'

Guy looked at him, his heaviness lifting, and then remembered. 'It's what I'd choose before all other service, my lord. But if your offer depends on my renouncing Helvie, I must refuse. And I cannot furnish my helm.'

'You can,' Conan contradicted. 'You have my arms and horses, and my last three men if they'll follow you.'

'*Conan?*'

The mercenary nodded. 'I'll go with you as far as Bristol, and ask the nearest monastery to admit me as a lay-brother.'

They were all startled dumb. It was Helvie who uttered the first shocked murmur of protest, 'Oh no!'

'To pass my days in penance and prayer for my lady's soul and my own. It will not be for long, I think.'

'Conan –' Guy said again, and then checked, remembering the mailed skeleton he had embraced that night, and all that had brought them to this moment. 'I'll grieve,' he said steadily, 'but I'll not attempt to dissuade you. And I'll do honour to your gift.'

'More than I ever did. You have a better sword to leave your heir, but keep mine to give your second son when you knight him.'

'Your sword, and your name.'

'Memorial enough.'

Other men had straggled into the Devil's Ring, entering it between curiosity and flinching and remaining to gape. Lord Henry ordered the nearest to take up the dead and bear them down to the horses. They obeyed unwillingly. He turned grimly to Guy.

'What sort of ingrate d'you take me for?' he demanded belligerently. 'Who said anything about renouncing Helvie? If ever a man earned a wench's hand you have done, and the fattest dowry I can assemble to clinch the bargain. All we need is a priest and a marriage-feast, and we'll go see to it.'

Guy hugged Helvie and suddenly laughed, light-headed with joy and thankfulness. 'My chief need just now is a shirt,' he said.

'Oh, I'll provide that too,' declared Lord Henry with an abrupt guffaw. He slapped Guy on the shoulder. 'Fetch Helvie and that brat along, son, and we'll all go home.'